ONE THOUSAND CHESTNUT TREES

A Novel of Korea

MIRA STOUT

Praise for
One Thousand Chestnut Trees

"This marvelous—and very moving—book tells its Korean story stylishly and with great skill."

—William Trevor

"Thoughtful, beguiling, and tinged with romantic regrets."

—*Marie Claire*

"[*One Thousand Chestnut Trees*] may be one of the finest, most sensitively wrought renderings of the Korean War that I've encountered in nearly three decades of reading about it. . . . It's remarkable that Mira Stout, a writer obviously too young to have experienced the Korean War, so effectively evokes its terrifying details. . . . This [is a] gifted storyteller."

—*The Washington Post*

"Moving and tremendously exciting reading. Stout's descriptions bring Korea's stately cultured civilization and heavenly landscape into sharp focus like a jewel-colored miniature."

—*The Independent on Sunday* (London)

"Stout handles the sweeping scope of her debut novel—the story of a young Korean American woman who journeys to Korea to discover her family's complex history—with great skill."

—*Ms.*

"Stout's work will make a welcome addition to larger fiction and Asian American fiction collections."

—*Library Journal*

"Valuable . . . The reader truly comes away with a fuller picture not only of what turmoil Koreans have experienced this century but also of what defines Koreanness."

—*Chicago Tribune*

ONE
THOUSAND
CHESTNUT
TREES

A NOVEL OF KOREA

MIRA STOUT

RIVERHEAD
BOOKS

New York

RIVERHEAD BOOKS
Published by The Berkley Publishing Group
A division of Penguin Putnam Inc.
375 Hudson Street
New York, New York 10014

First Riverhead hardcover edition: May 1998
First Riverhead trade paperback edition: May 1999
Riverhead trade paperback ISBN: 1-57322-738-2

The Penguin Putnam Inc. World Wide Web site address is
http://www.penguinputnam.com

The Library of Congress has catalogued the Riverhead hardcover edition as follows:

Stout, Mira.
One thousand chestnut trees : a novel of Korea / Mira Stout.
        p.   cm.
        ISBN 1-57322-073-6
        1. Korea—Fiction.   I. Title.
PS3569.T6595064   1998   97-37521 CIP
        813'.54—dc21

Printed in the United States of America

10   9   8   7   6   5   4   3   2   1

ACKNOWLEDGMENTS

Above all, I am indebted to Koh Chaewoon, my mother, for her generous and vital contributions of time and memory, without whom this novel could not have been realized.

I also wish to thank my uncle, Koh Kwang-chun, and Miss Chang Kyongsil for their kind help.

With special gratitude and love to the memory of Kate Vandegrift (1928–1983) and her son Dominic (1964–1993).

MIRA STOUT
London
1997

For
MY MOTHER AND FATHER,
AND
THE KOH FAMILY

CONTENTS

ONE
THOUSAND
CHESTNUT
TREES

PART ONE

DAUGHTER

CHAPTER ONE

A Memory

It was winter in Vermont. Beyond my window, the pines would have bristled sparsely against the hushed white snow. The gray, swelling sky would have been as vast and lonely as a northern sea. But I can't recall Hong-do's arrival. His presence was ghostly then, so tentative that he scarcely left an imprint. Yet now, years later, when I remember that emptiness, Hong-do's face follows.

My uncle from Seoul came to stay with us when I was just fourteen, my first year of boarding school. His jet eyes, wide-boned pallor, and shock hair gave him an outward boldness, but he was actually quite shy. Although I'd met my mother's Korean friends, Hong-do was different, more foreign somehow; pungent and unfiltered.

Even gestures required translating; Hong-do's sneeze was a violent "YA-shee" rather than a tame "Ker-CHOO." And when he was in a hurry, he walked in Korean too, lightly trotting, arms stationary and body canted forward. He rather stuck out in our redneck town.

My mother must have looked equally Oriental, but I noticed less—she was a mother, already a separate species. Besides, they didn't look alike. My uncle's face was paler, and round like a moon,

There was something remote and masked about him, as if he were stranded in his skin.

Despite our kinship, I felt little for my new relation then. Though he was young enough to be a brother (I hadn't any siblings), no reassuring sympathy for him welled up, and to my alarm, no rescuing tug of filial loyalty helped me to pretend otherwise. Hong-do was a spaceling to me. The rapid, guttural language of clucking, hacking noises that he and my mother spoke sounded ugly and comical to my teenage ears, separating us like barbed wire.

As a child, I had refused to learn Korean. I'd even blocked out most of my mother's worn stories of Seoul, which were as unreal as fairy tales, but with tragic endings. The gilded family sagas ended in divided lands, ruined gold mines, betrayals and torture at the hands of Japanese invaders, even *before* the beginning of the catastrophic Korean War.

Hong-do had been born after my mother's departure for America, so she was meeting him for the first time too. My mother had returned home just once in thirty years, so the narrative store could not be replenished. By default, the whole of Korea had shrunk to meaning little to me but my mother's iron discipline, and eating dried squid after school instead of luscious Marshmallow Fluff.

Until now, I had known my uncle only from photographs in our album. In an old sepia-tinted family portrait, Hong-do was a small, doll-like boy in a sailor suit, shyly holding my grandmother's hand. (She died before we could meet.) The family looked grave and distinguished; tall men in wirerimmed spectacles, stiff collars and boutonnières, and women, fragile, but assured, wrapped in stiff silk *han-boks*, seated in a shadowy, peony-filled garden. My mother's chubby-faced younger sister, Myung-hi, hair severely bobbed, stood protectively next to Hong-do.

I daydreamed secretly about them, especially about my great-uncle, Yong-lae, the wastrel poet, so vain that he would only be seen in public astride a white horse—which sometimes returned empty-saddled, its master having passed out in a ditch. In a later black-and-white image, dog-eared from handling, Hong-do was grown up, dressed in military uniform, leaning against a wooden footbridge before a pagoda, smiling confidently at the camera—roguishly handsome. I had looked forward to meeting *him*.

But this full-color, three-dimensional stranger seemed jarringly unrelated to those glamorous photographs. For a start, he was here in our kitchen rather than safely *there*. He reminded me a bit of a prisoner then, hiding out in our isolated house in his geeky ironed denims, gazing out the window as if contemplating an escape. But he had nowhere to go.

During his visit, my mother became more enlivened and fluent than I had ever seen before. They would stay up late together drinking ginseng tea and talking excitedly. Sometimes they spoke with a raw, almost animal pain that frightened me. Gradually, the sound became less exclusive, and flowed generously, like water released from a dam. This awesome current bypassed me and my Boston Irish father (who also spoke no Korean), but neither of us remarked upon it. I was content to pretend that they were discussing dull matters like jobs in Boston, where Hong-do was to attend university in the autumn. Korea was so much static to be tuned out of my consciousness.

During those winter evenings, my father and I tactfully watched ice hockey on television, but neither of us could really concentrate. Although we were silent, I was acutely aware of Hong-do's presence. I would sneak glances at him from the sofa as if he were a surprise package that had been delivered which I hoped someone else would open. While I had decided he was to be a marginal figure in my life, I kept a self-interested eye on him anyway during those first cold nights. I sensed, with some dread, that he contained secrets I might someday need to know.

One morning after Hong-do had just arrived, we drove out

through the snowbanked woods for an educational breakfast at the Timberline Restaurant on Route 9, renowned for its sixteen varieties of pancakes, and its tourist-pulling "Famous 100-Mile View" over Massachusetts.

Lavender-haired waitresses in white uniforms and orthopedic shoes delivered the orgiastic fare with medical briskness; steaming cranberry and banana-dot pancakes, French toast piled with blue-berries, waffles shining with melted butter and hot maple syrup, spice-scented sausage patties, link sausages, mouthwatering bacon, Canadian bacon, steak and eggs, eggs any style, oatmeal, home fries, toast and English muffins. MaryLou—as her name tag announced— refilled your coffee cup instantly, and offered free second and third helpings like someone arriving to plow your driveway.

That sunny morning, the dining room was crowded with skiers, bunched around the colonial wagon-wheel tables in pneumatic Technicolor overalls. They roared with pre-sport gusto, clanking their cutlery uninhibitedly, as if their appetites might extend to the creamy blue mountains which beckoned beyond the plate-glass win-dows like a majestic frozen dessert.

At first my uncle looked overwhelmed, but soon glanced about delightedly, taking tiny, experimental sips from the coffee cup he held ceremoniously in both palms. People stared baldly at us, jaws momen-tarily disengaged. Orientals were rarely seen then in the Vermont hills. We ignored their dismay—led by my mother's well-practiced example—but I felt scalding embarrassment. Although we'd begun by speaking in English, my mother and Hong-do soon broke into vol-uble Korean as if my father and I were not there.

At last our breakfast arrived. Still feeling unwell after his long journey, my uncle faced a modest fried egg and toast. He hesitated a moment, but with a final scowl of concentration seized the sides of the egg white with his fingers, and crammed the whole object in his mouth in one piece. Head bowed and cheeks bulging, he chewed the egg penitently, as if ridding his plate of an obstacle. My father and I froze in surprise. Never having seen an egg dispatched in this way, I began to laugh, but my mother's eyes stopped me like a pair of bullets.

The next week my mother urged Hong-do to look for a job in Starksboro—the nearest big town—in order to improve his English and relieve cabin fever. As his classes were not to begin for several months, he acquiesced, but found nothing. I suspect he was secretly relieved.

In the mornings after a bit of coaching, my mother and I would drop him off in the icy parking lot off Main Street, the *Starksboro Reformer* help-wanted ads folded neatly inside his glove. Yet by noon Hong-do would be waiting for us dejectedly at the counter of Dunkin' Donuts, attracting hostile stares from beery lumberjacks grimly chewing their jelly doughnuts, puddles forming on the pink linoleum beneath their snowmobile boots. After a week, his only offer had been a part-time window-washing shift in the sub-zero February winds. Dad said they must have thought he was an Eskimo.

Struggle was foreign to my uncle. He was the pampered youngest son of an old, noble family, accustomed to a big house in town with servants, and estates in the country. My mother even claimed that Hong-do was renowned in Seoul as a "happy-go-lucky playboy," inconceivable though it was to me, as I examined him critically through a gap in the car's headrest. Here, he was assumed to be a refugee.

I saw Hong-do again at Easter. At home, snow still scabbed the fields, but the ground had thawed, and squelched underfoot. Wild gusts of fresh, sweet wind roared through the bare treetops. Unpacking my duffel bag, I resolved to be a bit kinder to my uncle, providing it was not too painful.

But I had forgotten little things about him—like the way he chewed spearmint gum with smacking gusto, and sang corny songs in the car. And his sense of humor! I rarely saw him laughing, but when he did, it was a razor-edged alto giggle. Then, at moments of unanimous family mirth he would be isolated in a deaf silence. He thought most American food was disgusting, and I never saw him reading a newspaper or book in English.

My uncle was like unconvertible currency; he refused to be tendered or melted down. There was no Western equivalent of his value. Sometimes I suspected he was simply saving himself so that he would not have to change again when he returned home.

Yet in my absence there were surprising developments. One afternoon as I studied for exams, I looked out at the faithful view of sloping, scrubby fields, towering pines, and immense sky, and noticed something peculiar about the row of younger trees opposite. Their lower branches had been brutally pruned to resemble topiary, but their trunks looked disastrously bald, like shorn poodle shanks. When I protested to my mother she smiled, and insisted that they now looked more like Korean bonsai; an observation gratingly inaccurate, to my affronted sensibilities.

Hong-do soon appeared back from Starksboro with a red-and-white-striped parcel from Sam's Army-Navy Store, and went off to his room. As I was reading, something caught my eye out of the window; there was my uncle, zipped into a new tracksuit, vigorously touching his toes in the fresh air. I smiled patronizingly at his strict precision, exercising in the waist-high weeds as if in an indoor gym.

Then he stopped, approached a pine-bonsai, and playfully shook its slender trunk. After an interval of staring, bull-like, at the tree, he suddenly charged at it, yelling murderously, and began raining deft side kicks and karate chops upon the little tree.

I rose from my chair. Had he gone mad? I heard my father's chair scraping in his studio, and ran off to confer with him. He had left his easel, and stood at the window watching Hong-do. Without speaking, we observed him warily circling the tree like a shadow boxer, delivering the odd kickchop. Dad finally rapped on the windowpane, and my uncle twisted around, confused and red-faced with exertion and waved at us enthusiastically. We laughed and waved back, marveling. From then on, my uncle performed his tae kwon do exercises on the lawn without further interruptions.

After this, the atmosphere was lighter between us. Tae kwon do tree attacks seemed to relax Hong-do, he smiled more readily, and began to look quite as handsome as his photographs. This unexpected glimpse of him lent a wider circumference to my mean perception of his character.

Still, an unnavigable distance separated us. I regarded him more as an exotic zoo tiger than as my only living uncle. It was safe to observe him through bars, to admire him wryly from the window, but I couldn't begin to relinquish those barriers. The schoolyard bullies who had kicked me behind the apple trees with their pointy-toed cowboy boots might come running back through the years to punish me again for having oriental blood.

Hong-do's foreignness might be contagious; I could be ostracized not only for harboring an alien, but for becoming more of one myself. With my layers of sportswear and Celtic freckles I could pass for Caucasian, but my uncle's incriminating features might give me away. It would be wiser to stay clear of him until my immunity was established. My secret Korean half was exiled to a remote inner gulag that even I was unable to find.

In the evenings, reading after supper, I sometimes caught Hong-do staring unhappily out of the window into the dark woods beyond his own cantilevered reflection. Only then did I regret not being a confidante. With the dumb instinct of a golden retriever, I itched to go out into the darkness and bring him back inside again, but just on the point of speaking to him, decided I was too small and unqualified for such a rescue. It was beyond me.

It was easier to pretend that he was not quite human. I don't remember asking him much about our relations in Seoul, or why he had come to the West when life seemed to be so pleasing there. What was he thinking of when he was so quiet at the dinner table? What did he miss about Korea? Would he have liked to learn to ski? I allowed his elementary English to deter me from asking.

But my uncle, for his part, was maddeningly opaque. His eyes were so black that I couldn't see his pupils. It was *me* that I saw squinting back irritably from those distant planets. His silences alone were new desert continents, exposing me as a mere water-dependent speck.

Yet Hong-do could be alarmingly vocal. Sometimes he would pluck away at Beatles chords on my old, badly tuned guitar, yodeling "Yesterday" plaintively from his room. To my distress, he and my mother also sang rapturous Korean songs together in the study, in a twangy, throbbing Oriental vibrato which sounded surreal and faintly sinister in the puritan Vermont woods. I was glad we had no neighbors.

Why did they *wail* like that?

"Because we express *han*," said Hong-do good-naturedly.

And what on earth was *han*?

There was a long pause.

"*Han* is sorrow and yearning and resentment; it lasts centuries, and never goes away. It is at the core of us," said my mother.

But what were the words?

Another pause.

"*Han* is so deep, that it comes before language."

I rolled my eyes at my father, hoping to enlist his support, but he looked away. Then I went to my room, and drowned out the *han* with the more familiar ululations of Neil Young.

I remember one final episode that Easter holiday. As I was studying one afternoon at my usual place by the window, Hong-do slipped into the kitchen to toast some seaweed. After offering me a warm, sulfurous black square—which I ate, grudgingly—he went outdoors to join my mother in the garden.

Then I heard a yell, and saw Hong-do push my mother aside, his eyes locked to the ground. Running out to see what was wrong, I found Hong-do down on all fours, stabbing spasmodically at the earth with a trowel. Now quite inured to his unpredictable ways, I asked casually what he was doing.

"A grass snake," said my mother.

"But they're harmless," I said, popping my eyes.

"Maybe, but to him, serpents are a symbol of evil, and should be destroyed."

My uncle had lost sight of the snake, and was shouting at my mother in Korean.

"What's he saying now?" I piped.

"He can't believe that we allow snakes to pollute our land," she said neutrally, as if unsure of where she herself stood on the matter. Still muttering, Hong-do was crouched in a combat stance in the dead asparagus patch, gingerly parting weeds with his trowel. I wished him luck insincerely, and went back indoors. Minutes later, my parents left on an errand.

Hong-do came indoors, and began rummaging angrily through drawers and cupboards. Next, he changed into his new Wrangler jeans, my father's too-big rubber boots and wood-chopping gloves. He'd even produced a fireman-style slicker from somewhere, cuffs rolled neatly. Then he left without a word, carrying a long, fat stick he'd found beneath the porch.

"Unbelievable," I muttered, looking around reflexively to see if anyone could confirm what I was seeing. Being alone, I shook my head and returned to the reassuring mental hygiene of my algebra book. But now and then I looked up at the field expectantly.

My mother and father returned from town with the groceries, and asked after Hong-do, smiling when they heard about his hunting preparations. We watched a muted sunset, and took tea and Chinese steam buns in the sitting room, half listening to the news on the radio. I felt too ruffled by my uncle's eccentric behavior to concentrate.

Just then the front door opened, and Hong-do stamped in, displaying a small green snake by its tail as if it were a ten-foot swordfish. Dutifully, my parents admired his catch while I trained a skeptical eye on the pitiful reptile. Then, however, I caught a glimpse of my uncle's expression, which shamed me. The pride brimming in his eyes was remarkable and disconcerting. His pride was so intense that I almost found myself wishing I could see the snake as he saw it. I stared at it hard, hoping for something magic to happen, but nothing did. My doubt remained and divided us.

Hong-do soon went back outdoors to dispose of his quarry. I watched from the window as he scaled the stone wall and stood there, surveying the darkening woods below. He whipped the snake around his head like a lasso, and cast it high into the air with a defiant shout.

For many years I carried that image with me; Hong-do, snake slayer of Vermont, arm raised against the sky like a warrior throwing his sword into the spokes of the universe, hoping to arrest its wheels upon his victory. At least, that was what I wanted to see.

Now I recall it differently. The sun had set, and my uncle was mostly in shadow. After he'd flung away the snake he looked so small, and vulnerable, and alone out on the ledge that I could hardly bear to look at him.

Hong-do spent the following few years at university in Boston, one of ten thousand anonymous freshmen. News of Hong-do often came to me months after events had passed, subtly filtered by my mother's own approval or disappointment, and slightly distorted by translation into English. Trying to follow uncle's progress in Boston was like monitoring conditions on Jupiter through an unreliable satellite link. He was an abstract fuzz, composed of long shadows and receding footprints. Only his most dramatic actions survived the relay.

To my uncle's surprise, he was not quite the star he had been in Seoul, though he had plenty of friends. My mother, able to make oracular judgments from several hundred miles away, pronounced him bright, but lackadaisical. He was lackadaisical, perhaps, but hardly lazy. Hong-do took a night job as a taxi driver, though he barely knew the streets beyond Copley Square. He was almost immediately robbed and beaten at gunpoint by two thugs on a midnight fare to Roxbury.

Next, he took on odd shifts as a waiter in Chinatown. He felt safer there. Although he studied business administration by day, on his free nights he gambled away his earnings and made extravagant barroom loans to acquaintances much larger than himself.

My uncle then had a pretty Irish girlfriend called Mary. He was crazy for her.

"The Irish and the Koreans are so alike; so sentimental," he told my mother over the phone. One day, Mary told him he was a worthless male chauvinist pig, and left him forever. Then he met a rich Korean girl, and drove all the way to California in his cab to escape her. Six months later they were married.

Hong-do set up a small shipping business in New York, and moved to a model home in Fort Lee, New Jersey, with his wife and two babies. He wore a gold Rolex watch, and drank impressive amounts of whiskey with his golf cronies—all Korean. During my uncle's Fort Lee tenure, we saw very little of him. He didn't much care for the Vermont wilds, but preferred neon nightlife and the siren call of near-fatal business schemes. Yet unexpectedly, when I moved to New York myself after university, I began to see Hong-do quite regularly.

We would always meet in a Korean restaurant off Fifth Avenue and Thirty-fourth Street. Young Bin Kwan was his favorite. He was often outrageously late, but I didn't mind. The mean-faced maître d' would bring me a dish of exquisite grilled dumplings and *boricha* (barley tea), and like a character from a spy thriller, I would bask there in the suspect glamour of floor-to-ceiling fish-tanks and Las Vegas chandeliers. Anticipation of the ritual feast ahead and the fascinating denouements of my uncle's family tales put me in a buoyant mood.

When Hong-do finally arrived, he transformed into the playboy, clapping imperiously for more Korean beer and kimchi and barking commands at the twirling, traditionally robed waitresses with breathtaking, but goodnatured arrogance. They served him adoringly, fleetly replacing empty celadon dishes with fresh *bulgoki*, and bearing smoking iron cauldrons of demonically spicy *mae-un-tang*. My uncle grinned, slurped and chewed with the confident abandon of the Oriental business magnate.

Once, as I watched him stuff a rolled lettuce parcel into his mouth in one bite, distending his cheeks like a chipmunk's, I suddenly recalled the fried egg incident at the Timberline all those years ago, and understood it.

"It's the custom," he explained, motioning for me to do the same, "it is better manners; it doesn't fall apart." When I'd packed the *bulgoki* into my straining jaws we both laughed achingly, my eyes swam with tears, and the juices exploded in my mouth and ran down my chin.

Hong-do showed me how to hold my teacup deferentially in both hands, like a proper Korean lady, and taught me heatedly about Korean history and Confucian philosophy. Railing about the ignorance of the West, he would glare at me unforgivingly as if I were no longer his niece, or even anyone he knew, but a symbol of the entire "West" and its calumny.

Back out on the street I felt chastened, subtly changed by our dinner. The chili of the kimchi and the fire of my uncle's beliefs began to penetrate the cool skin of my habitual indifference. But I was daunted by what I began to discover. Identity, nationality comprised manifold layers, and I was only just exploring the crude outer surfaces, straining to detect the character of the invisible blood beneath.

One night, after several beers, Hong-do became pleasantly sentimental, and drew the yin-yang circle of the *Tae-gŭkki*—the Korean flag—for me on the tablecloth with his chopstick, explaining its symbolism of integrated opposites. Then, smiling cruelly, he drew a diagram of himself and me, comparing our closeness to two independent circles, overlapping only slightly at the farthest parameters.

I was stung. I wanted to protest that he was being harsh, and that there was more between us; but I could not. Perhaps it was true that only this segment of tablecloth had joined us; perhaps we had never before succeeded in meeting. But if we were not as intimate as some relations, we had come a long, painful way to our present distance. I clung to this small achievement.

Over melon and toothpicks Hong-do listened rapt, but uncomprehending, to my hopes and woes, then smacked my shoulder encouragingly when I'd finished. Perhaps he couldn't follow the language or my way of seeing things, but somehow it didn't matter. The smack made me laugh, deflating my worries.

Then my uncle paid the stiff bill grandly, and drove me home to unfashionable West One Hundredth Street in his plush blue Chevrolet Royale, with the amazing shock absorbers. During that nocturnal ride I felt a rare, childish joy, as if no danger or sadness could reach me within that safety of newfound blood kinship, padded vinyl, and electronic locks.

It was not to last.

A couple of months later Hong-do's trusted business partner vanished in the middle of the night with all the firm's assets. The investigators could not trace him. Ruined, Hong-do sold his house and moved his family back to Seoul for good.

On our final evening together before my uncle's departure, I glanced over at him in the driver's seat on the way home. Neon lights from the Broadway marquees washed over his tired face. He ignored the crowds and the limousines, and focused blankly on the red traffic light ahead. A ghostly feeling emanated from him. I recognized it from years ago when he first came; as if his body had landed but his spirit had remained behind in Korea. There was now a similar emptiness about him, as if his soul were in transit, and had already begun the long journey home.

I wondered if Hong-do had really dreamed of success in America, and if it grieved him to see it eluding him now. Perhaps he was glad to leave; I still had not learned how to read his face. There were many things I did not know about him, and it seemed now that I might never know them. It was too late to ask those questions.

The chance had arrived that winter, ten years ago, when he had come to stay, and I had not taken it. I had been neither kind nor unkind to my uncle, but had saved up knowing him for a future time, when it would be easier. I thought he would always be there to discover, like a locked family treasure chest, too substantial to be moved. I would surely inherit it one day, and be given the key. A sick, black feeling welled up in me, and I realized then that the key had been inside me all along, and I hadn't known it was there.

The streets flowed quickly past the window, bringing our farewell closer. Through my uncle, Korea had grown nearly real to me. But I suspected that when he left, the floating embryo of coded dynasties, diagrams, religious precepts and war dates might perish. Korea would exist only in the unfinished, idealized monument my mother's memory had carved, in the rare, transient taste of kimchi and in random visits to greengrocer immigrants, whose faces, behind the bountiful rows of fruit, were closed with forgetting.

I didn't see it then, but my uncle was a drawbridge to the destroyed homeland my mother had left. Through him I visited the mansion with the green gates where my mother was born, the Northern estates, and my greatgrandfather's temple on Mount Sorak surrounded by one thousand chestnut trees he had planted for longevity.

Although the Japanese had burned down these Northern estates, and the lands were now divided on the thirty-eighth parallel, I felt I had walked through these places, and breathed them. All of this still lived inside of him, intact, and beyond reach. The drawbridge was now closing.

I forget what we said when we parted. The glare of oncoming headlights numbed me. The car door slammed, a reflection of the street facade obscured his face, and he was gone.

Later, I stood in my apartment and looked down on the myriad changing signals and dim taillights below that formed an endless, sweeping canon of arrivals and departures. With pain, I imagined Hong-do at the window of his airplane back to Seoul, contemplating the same city.

What would he be thinking of as the brute streets of New York contracted into cool, glittering grids? What would he recall of his years with us? Eating fried egg with his fingers, an afternoon's serpent hunting? He'd probably want to forget all that. Perhaps a dinner at Young Bin Kwan.

These incidents were meager, but I hoped he would remember them. I wanted to be there in the background, and to appear across the table from him, years later. But I couldn't break into his memories. Too much flesh, and glass, and time sealed them. I had to be content just to picture him thinking, suspended somewhere over the Pacific.

I remember being seven years old and the smell of apples. A boy was twisting my arm behind my back just for fun.

"Say uncle!" the boy taunted. A crowd gathered. For some reason, "uncle" was the word bullies used then to torture you. I wouldn't say it. He twisted my arm harder and harder until my shoulder was shooting with pain, and my face was red and sweating.

"Uncle! Uncle!" I cried in furious shame.

CHAPTER TWO

Cardboard Boxes

After my uncle's return to Seoul, life in Manhattan resumed its former shape as if he had not been there at all. Buses and taxis plowed up and down Broadway, the phone rang, mail arrived. Pedestrians poured over crosswalks like columns of ants. The physical vacuum my uncle left was refilled instantly. The hard pavements sealed over my few, precious memories of him with the finality of quicksand.

When I tried to picture Hong-do's life in Seoul, I could not. Its city smells, noises, and moods were inconceivable to me. Besides, it was too draining to imagine a world beyond New York. It was like living on the floor of an enclosed glass tank with unscalable walls. Only occasional, chastising glimpses of clear blue sky, in the gaps between buildings, reminded me of a remote natural order greater than Manhattan, quite beyond reach.

When I sat down to think of things to tell my uncle—in the letter that I never wrote him—I began to notice how marginal my life was. Days were measured out in so many tea bags, bus transfers, tuna sandwiches, cash withdrawals, and hangovers.

I attempted to keep alive a connection to Hong-do through the occasional trip to Thirty-fourth Street for a Korean meal with friends, but this rather indirect approach failed, and without him the experience felt somewhat hollow. As predicted, my flimsy template of Korean awareness dissolved quickly, and attentions were soon fully reabsorbed in the lowly struggle for financial survival which had occupied my life before Hong-do's departure. In my efforts to become a painter—and live in Manhattan—my life had become an undignified scramble for dry ground. I spent much of my time collecting cardboard boxes to move house with. Reasons for moving were various and unexciting: rent hikes, lease violations, buildings going co-op, and roommates like Ted, at West One Hundredth Street.

Ted was perhaps no better or worse than you'd expect from a New York roommate. Ted had a honking Connecticut voice, and was a former Fly Club treasurer at Harvard, possessing the strange ability to bounce checks selectively: rent and utilities checks failing to clear, while extravagant entertainment and wardrobe bills found deep, instant funds. Ted stole your spaghetti sauce and lowered the tone of the bathroom with his depressing liters of bargain shampoo and generic deodorant. Pip, Alice and I were obliged to take numerous phone messages for Ted from the Hair Club for Men (where, at only twenty-four, he elected to go for weekly hair implants) and then struggle to pretend that we didn't notice anything strange about the sudden presence of oddly tinted brown hairs which appeared on his pate on alternate Thursdays. Unfortunately for us, this did not prevent him from attracting a girlfriend called Pierce, a law student with an aggressive laugh, who left items of clothing draped on the living-room furniture to signal her presence like a cat spraying its turf. But Ted's most challenging habit was his nude sleepwalking. Fully clothed, Ted was irritating enough, but Ted entering my room late at night, buck naked, and climbing into my bed was pretty much the last straw. He would also make regular late-night sojourns into the kitchen when we were talking, and urinate into the refrigerator.

It was unfortunate that Ted's name was on the lease. Although the unsolved murders of three young women on the rooftop of the building next door cast an eerie menace over the block, and the peeling mustard-colored paint and tumbleweed dustballs in the corridor were slightly dispiriting, the apartment's high ceilings, parquet floors, and wrought-iron balconies lent my existence a spurious graciousness that I appreciated very much at the time.

Sight unseen, I moved into my next place on a searing August afternoon during a sanitation workers' strike, my belongings fitting into just two checker-cab trips. It was a sixth-floor walk-up on MacDougal Street, illegally sublet from a friend's vacationing boyfriend. The strike was a bad omen: an almighty stench of food, cooked and rotting, hit me like a damp wall upon quitting the taxi; great banks of black plastic garbage bags were shored up generously on both sides of the street, shimmering in the heat. Up and down the block, an espresso bar, shishkebab house, hot dog-calzone-and-pizza stand, veggie-burger cart, sushi vendor and falafel emporium made MacDougal Street a sort of United Nations of fast food, whose dependence on the city's sanitation workers was total.

I shared this apartment with Mona, a timid garment-district secretary from Belchertown, Massachusetts, her two neurotic long-haired cats, Mick and Mike, and a medical student, Ethan, who proudly told me on our first meeting that his father was the actor in the famous double-edged razor television commercials during the seventies.

The apartment's subtly crippled appearance was owed to Delia's vacationing boyfriend being something of an amateur carpenter. Interior walls were makeshift partitions he had enterprisingly nailed together late at night, apparently under the influence of hard drugs. The sturdiness of his carpentry was such that the cats could—and did—enter my bedroom by hurling themselves against the closed door at a gallop, whereupon they would lie down and moult on my pillow.

As it was summer, one didn't mind that the frightening-looking gas stove was broken, but the bathroom arrangements were more testing. There was nothing as definite as a door to this bathroom; merely a friendly, cathairy, Indian bedspread thumbtacked to the doorframe, adding a certain anxiety to one's activities therein. The superintendent had pledged to fix the plumbing, but in the meantime, toilet flushing involved two trips to the kitchen tap with a bucket. Turning on the shower required the assistance of a pair of pliers. Once activated successfully, the exuberant shower spray kept Mick and Mike's kitty-litter tray in a continuous state of deliquescence.

When I think of MacDougal Street, I remember the inescapable melancholy of three ill-suited people sharing a small space, and the overwhelming smell of falafel. The airduct of the Middle Eastern restaurant downstairs expelled its kitchen fumes directly outside my bedroom window, which in August had to be permanently thrown open. I awoke in the mornings lightly coated in a dew of congealed falafel exhalation and cat hair, provoking frequent bad-tempered battles with the shower pliers.

That August it was too hot to paint in the studio, so sweltering free weekends were spent at friends' summer places on Fisher's Island and in Bridgehampton, or eating cherry Italian ices near the spray of the fountain in Washington Square Park, avoiding my roommates. I spent many evenings at Laura's, seated directly in the path of her electric fan, drinking cold beer and listening to the sound of other people's stereos drifting in the stale night air.

I was grateful to my friend Delia for helping me out with a quick sublet, but having exhausted the charms of MacDougal Street, it was now time to move on. Laura, possessing a compassionate nature, agreed to split the rent with me, temporarily, on her studio apartment on Twenty-third Street and Eighth Avenue.

Our narrow, sooty tenement was positioned sensitively between a transvestite brothel and a funeral parlor. Laura had a bed in the living room, while I slept on a glorified shelf above a wardrobe, accessible by ladder. Being New York, it wasn't even cheap. I also had to pay rent on a shared painting studio in the meat-packing district above the Hellfire Club, which I used on weekends and odd evenings. To keep up these two shelters, I held a full-time job uptown, with an antiquarian bookseller.

In the mornings at nine-fifteen I took the crowded subway uptown to Fifty-ninth and Lexington, stopped in at Frankie's for my Styrofoamed coffee and salt bagel with cream cheese, and entered a modest doormanned building with my grease-spotted paper bag.

Through the bronze elevator doors awaited Oliver's morocco-lined apartment, alias Cadogan Books, steaming with the force of three leather-preserving humidifiers. I let myself in with a key, and generally found Oliver, ruddy-faced, in a dark suit, tie, and half-lenses, sitting at the kitchen table sourly consuming a bowl of Frosted Flakes. He would be depressed about the uselessness of his life, occasioned by having spent another evening escorting a Mayflower matron to a dull gala at the Met.

Being a handsome, albeit impecunious Englishman of leisure, Oliver Flood was popular with various Pamelas, Aprils and Brookes. Although he felt himself well above being a walker, he was quite unable to refuse invitations, however repulsive he found them. Newly divorced, he was flattered by any reasonable attention, and admitted to being rather lonely.

After our usual morning banter, I would sit down at an elegant mahogany desk and attend first to the opening of Oliver's mail, which he could not countenance without a human shock absorber. Sometimes plastic charge cards arrived snipped in two. Oliver confronted the arrival of credit card statements with the ritual of cowering in the kitchen doorway, half-lenses glinting, grunting softly, like an anxious primate. When the bill was very high, he hopped painfully from foot to foot, as if standing on hot coals.

Then began the grinding, circumlocutory task of updating the Cadogan Books mailing list and card catalog. With a sense of hopelessness, I typed and retyped on index cards the names of cautious collectors, secondhand bookshop owners, and changing department heads of a number of universities and their often peevish and grand librarians (to whom I had already written) to try to sell off some rare volume, but Oliver's books were usually too rare or too common to tempt the holders of these immensely fatbudgeted university funds. Meanwhile, Cadogan Books limped along, each day a little closer to bankruptcy.

Occasionally someone—Mrs. Doris L. Vinehopper, for example, of 21 Mashpee Drive, Winnetka, Illinois 60093—would mail-order two 1930s editions of Omar Khayyám's *Rubáiyát*, and the fulfillment of Mrs. Vinehopper's desire would occupy the rest of the morning, dragged out with the aid of two further cups of coffee.

The ritual of preparing the books for their journey to 21 Mashpee Drive lent a sense of purpose to my otherwise aimless days at Cadogan Books, and kept the mind from wandering to the unpleasant reality that one was not doing any painting at all. The sheer beauty of the books made me lethargic—their gilded embossing, the satin feel of the calf book covers, and their pages' mysterious, mushroomy smell.

But there was no slacking at Cadogan Books. Despite his considerable personal scattiness, Oliver was a stickler for book-wrapping formalities, hawkishly observing my erasure of extraneous pencil marks and smudges, the strategic insertion of a Cadogan Books compliments slip and invoice, cutting and snug taping of an underwear layer of sheet newsprint, followed by a vest of corrugated cardboard—X-Acto-knifed to precise cover dimensions—folded and taped to the tightest possible fit, and topped with a final overcoat of brown parcel paper, string reinforcement and sticky label: the book-wrapping equivalent of Jermyn Street winter tailoring.

Oliver himself went to the post office to mail the books, this being one of the more glamorous of the day's activities, and a rare chance for people to know that he was wearing a suit. But oddly, if there was an auction to attend at Swann's or Sotheby's—dizzyingly social events for us—Oliver would insist that I do the bidding. At first it seemed that he was being generous, varying tasks to minimize staff boredom, but it became apparent, from arch comments he made about rival dealers Ephraim Pastov and John Speed, that he found the openly mercantile aspect of his profession a bit grubby.

While Oliver cut an enviable dash in the post office line, selling books was one of his weaker points. His afternoons were generally spent attending art exhibitions, visiting the dry cleaners, lunching with potential clients, and sometimes listening to Puccini and Verdi, jotting down notes in an important hand for pedantic musical studies that he had been fine-tuning for years. Where such a desultory approach might be expected to yield limited results, Oliver was so annoyingly well connected and clever that the books, however ordinary, and however long they might take to write, would be published by a decent house in England for quite a high fee, with no apparent negotiations undertaken.

One January morning after the arrival of a particularly emasculating credit card demand, Oliver took in the bad news with uncharacteristic silence. He eyed a priceless book of eighteenth-century botanical illustrations with stupendous color plates.

"Susan Yankowitz-Miller," he said, melodramatically announcing his intended sales target.

"Do you have to?"

He raised an eyebrow.

"I suppose so," I said, glancing up from a new VISA statement. Perversely, Oliver appeared to hire his assistants for their flightiness and insubordination rather than their competence. My predecessor had been a London brewery heiress who dripped mayonnaise and nail polish onto the book covers, and conducted her intimidating social life on the phone in a particularly loud voice when introverted clients came to call.

Oliver went into the kitchen, and after the usual noise of cascading dirty crockery that accompanied most kitchen visits, emerged with a half-empty bottle of vodka, settled into a cracked brown leather armchair near the telephone, and crossed his legs.

"What are you doing? It's only ten-thirty."

Ignoring this obvious remark, he struggled to remove the cap. "She's terribly pretty, you know, half his age," he said, taking a tense swig from the bottle.

"Who?"

"Susan Yankowitz-Miller. Airline hostess emeritus; richest wife of the year. Said she might be interested in the book."

"Since when are you and Susan Miller having chats?"

"*Yankowitz*-Miller. She insists. Saw her at Nonie Warburton's ghastly bridge evening . . . If she *does* bite, that would be a ready eight thousand in the coffers. You've got to ring her up for me now."

I protested.

"You can. I pay you . . ." Oliver handed me the bottle with a bland expression. I took an experimental pull. He passed me the number.

"Meelair residence," said a distant Hispanic voice.

"Hello, this is Mr. Flood's secretary calling for Mrs. Miller."

"Mrs. Meelair ees not home."

"May I please speak with her secretary?"

"Chust a moment."

Oliver mouthed something. I waved him away.

"Avedon Buckley speaking, Mrs. Yankowitz-Miller's personal assistant, may I help you?" said a lockjawed, blaring female, as if guarding access to one of the more important Pentagon generals. A protracted and farcical exchange of rude evasions (secretary) and slimy begging (me) ensued, and at last the mighty Mrs. Yankowitz-Miller consented to come to the phone, despite having no recollection of having been interested in buying a "book"—a word she pronounced with genuine surprise. Oliver, primed by the Smirnoff, sat on the edge of his chair, knees pressed together in a supplicatory pose, and injected into his voice an oily *bonhomie* for which he later loathed himself, and which instantly secured him an afternoon's audience.

After a bloody three-week telephone campaign fought between Cadogan Books and Mrs. Yankowitz-Miller's manicurist, masseuse, hairdresser, chiropodist, colonic irrigator, fitness trainer, voice coach, personal shopper, florist, caterers, flamenco teacher, and the Save Tibet Foundation, Mrs. Yankowitz-Miller duly bought the priceless book, and instructed Rodrigo, her decorator, to cut out the plates to hang in the baby's bathroom. She also bought twenty-five yards of tooled leather books of no interest whatever to plump out her husband's library. Cadogan Books was temporarily reprieved.

We celebrated by going to the movies at noon the following day to see *Aliens*, and Oliver took me out for a late lunch at the Plaza afterward. His jutting chin, diplomat-gray hair and dapper suit found an approving audience among the waiters and divorcees, who craned their necks with interest as he entered the room. The attention agreed with him, and he even bothered to pull in his stomach self-consciously as he got up to make a telephone call. As he turned, the vents of his suit seemed to flap deliberately, revealing a scarlet silk lining that flashed like mating plumage.

Oliver ordered an expensive bottle of Mercurey to impress the impudent *sommelier*, who had sized us up as illicit lovers, and although he was fairly merry at first, by the time coffee had arrived he was in quite a fragile state.

"I'm thinking of packing it in, you know. . . . Do you think I should pack it in? I've already had to sell some furniture."

I was a bit shocked. "I don't know . . . Maybe we should both pack it in," I said half-joking, emboldened by the wine and false security of multiple waiters. "Of course I'm grateful you gave me the job, Oliver, but it's a bit tricky getting my own stuff done working for you full-time."

Oliver eyed me critically, annoyed at my candor; he disliked being reminded that I had aspirations beyond Cadogan Books.

"Come on, Ol. Maybe it's not as bad as it seems. What about going back to England?"

"Clapped-out place. Truth is, I can't. Too many enemies. Customs & Excise, solicitors, creditors, cheated colleagues, ex-wife nonsense . . ."

"Where would you go? Would you stay here? You can't. You'd turn into an old soak who dines off old ladies," I slurred. He looked up sharply.

"Well, it's settled then. I'm going. To Brazil . . . Why not Brazil?"

"A bit melodramatic, isn't it? That's where war criminals go. Besides, it's so far away."

Oliver looked far away already, quite alone with his misfortunes. Betrayed by his wife, business crashing, on the run from some past stain that made him jumpy and sour. But it wasn't any good telling *me* these things, I was on the brink of telling him, I was just as derailed as he was.

"The climate's good in Brazil," he said pathetically.

Sitting there looking out on Central Park amid thick napery and gilt, it was hard to feel too sorry for Oliver. He looked so sturdy; a mature oak of a man, enjoying the deepest possible roots, but these he had severed long ago. Like most New Yorkers, he was a socio-geographic amputee, a handsome trunk, cut off at the knees.

I was saddened and mildly alarmed by this display of middle-aged vulnerability. But before I could offer any modest kindness, a wave of jadedness drowned the tender sprout of compassion. *This is New York, pal*, said the preemptive voice, *Get a grip*. Unnerved by his lost expression, I faltered, then remembered that people here came and went with every toilet flush. Oliver was a bubble on the effluvient foam of the East River; a wad of chewing gum on the city's stiletto. You had to get used to people leaving New York. You reeled in the severed ties of friendship quickly. You learned to let go in advance.

Numbness set in as I realized that I was jobless. We parted in the freezing rain on the wide, optimistic steps of the Plaza. Oliver and his troubles were dwarfed standing there beneath the bright waving flags of Canada, America, France, and Guam. He forced a smile, and hunched his shoulders in farewell.

I would miss Oliver very much, despite his manifold obnoxiousness. In my heart's psychiatric wing, he was almost like family. As with my uncle's demise, there would be no mayoral committee, no special envoy at the airport thanking him for his brave effort, nothing to soften his humiliation. Just a thirty-five-dollar cab ride.

It was odd thinking of my uncle and Oliver together. They met only once; not surprising, given that Hong-do and I met only occasionally, but the two men were so different that they refused to share the same memory.

The one time Hong-do came to Cadogan Books was a tense occasion. Opening the door to Oliver's apartment, I kissed my uncle's cheek awkwardly, truly happy to see him. But a chilling moment followed, when I saw him through Oliver Flood's eyes. After a perfunctory stab of courtesy, Oliver seemed only to notice my uncle's awkward business English, slightly inferior suit and rather dodgy shoes. These preliminary findings appeared to relieve him of further interest. It was also apparent from Hong-do's sharp-eyed silence that he thought Oliver an arrogant, trivial man.

Seeing these two worlds standing side by side in the same room, yet failing to meet in any way, was painful. I was torn; insulted by Oliver's flippant welcome to Hong-do, yet ashamed to be able to understand Oliver and his limitations better than I could follow my own uncle's thoughts.

During those years in New York, Hong-do had remained in his own Korean enclave, and I stayed in my Western one. It was as if we had been moored in the same harbor on separate submarines. Although I invited him aboard my vessel, he never stayed long; he seemed to know about the leaks. I should have done better, made the necessary repairs to accommodate him.

I reflected on these failures walking down Fifth Avenue, past the unappetizing, superfluous luxuries behind shatterproof glass. I searched the faces streaming toward me with detached curiosity, with painter's eye, but was soon numbed by the insistent drumming of impressions on the retinae. Infinitesimal variations on one *eyes-nose-mouth* theme, so many individual snowflake faces in the blizzard of urban rush-hour humanity. A face missing one quality was superseded by a face possessing that quality, and missing another. One race complemented another race. Perhaps the incomplete, jigsaw faces all added up to one consummate face, reflecting God's obscured likeness.

It was getting dark. I ate a warm pretzel more for recreation than hunger, looked at my watch, and decided to go into St. Thomas's for evensong. Its choir was justly famous. Despite being Catholic, I preferred the intimacy of this Anglican church to the cavernous nave of St. Patrick's Cathedral down the street, with its dwarfing gothic stalagmites. I entered the dim church and slid into a pew at the back, like a stray. A row of fur coats and blond heads swiveled around in impious curiosity. Through the tracery of the altar screen and the rose window, the night glowed a rich cobalt blue.

The service had begun, and my eardrums were bathed in silky, sweet, golden music. The boys' voices were arrows of piercing sound, bright as stars; still, chill, and distant. Aimed at the heavens, the notes were like austere fireworks, going so high and no further, bursting and falling gracefully, no less beautiful for their vain striving. I felt both pain and relief at the sound, as my selfish, jagged yearnings bled into insignificance. The voices sliced through my pretense at being happy, exposed my false footing. The discomfort was oddly strengthening. Often I sat here, coated with a light scum of petty dishonesties and rank thoughts, and by the end of the service would feel quite clean; spirits rinsed by the acid purity of the music, anxieties temporarily assuaged by the healing words of the prayers.

"O God . . . give unto thy servant that peace which the world cannot give . . . Lighten our darkness, we beseech thee, O Lord; and by thy great mercy defend us from all perils and dangers of this night; for the love of thy only Son, our Savior, Jesus Christ, Amen."

Then I would slink out again into the lucre-grimed circus of Fifth Avenue, where the invisible particles of acquisition and struggle accumulated again within like a layer of plaque.

Now I sat still after the fur coats and cashmeres had filed out solemnly, and stayed behind to think. I had not taken communion, partly for tribal reasons. I would feel a fraud not being Anglican. Who were my "people"? Did one need a people? An artist was meant to be a pioneer, a pilgrim, yet a submerged need to belong surfaced at odd moments. The Catholic church was a spiritual family, but somehow the bond was obscure, impersonal, like St. Patrick's itself. One longed for a more acute, flesh-and-blood connection, smaller than God, and more enduring, more forgiving than a lover. A chill of doubt and wonder enclosed me in the church. Rueful thoughts came of my own small family, scattered by discord and continental drift. I had no siblings or living relatives at all on my father's side. I thought of my uncle Hong-do, and a tiny spark of warmth lightened the void. Clashes with my mother had prevented me from exploring the Korean side of my family. I wondered if it might be possible to try now, or if it was already too late. Had I the maturity to attempt such a radical reversal of the entrenched ostrich position that I'd assumed toward her culture?

Wriggling, I tried to calculate what it would cost to embrace the Orient. It could be restrictive. One might even lose one's former identity. Besides, would one be acceptable to *them*, as a half-Westerner? A quasi-Oriental face would only go so far to reassure them. Inner qualities would be needed to bridge the gap. Did these qualities already exist in me, or could they be developed as one went along?

Strangely, Korea was the last destination I thought of traveling to. It was a world I accepted as being permanently and impossibly remote. In my warped thinking, I vaguely imagined it to be full of Korean mothers who would give me a hard time. Perhaps I wasn't strong enough to face the sad endings of the fairy-tale past related to me as a child. Yet the prospect held out an undeniable sense of promise. Maybe it was the key to some locked door which needed opening. Although one shrank from becoming a racebore, for the first time it seemed that there might be a middle way between exaggerating its importance and denying it altogether. Perhaps it would be possible to *go* to Korea.

Full of nascent intentions, I took the express train downtown, somewhat sedated by evensong and the good wine from lunch. But after a few minutes under the cauterizing lights of the jolting carriage and the barbed stare of a drunk vagrant, my nerves were soon fraying again. Korea was pulled from my thoughts like an expensive scarf caught in the subway turnstile.

I slightly dreaded arriving at the Twenty-third Street exit. Wesley, the one-legged black Vietnam veteran on crutches, might be there at the top of the stairs, bellowing "Marry me!" to all the young women walking past. Much as I had a soft spot for Wesley, I couldn't face him tonight, and to my relief he was not there. Back out on the street, the air had grown colder and the wind had picked up. I checked the train entrance reflexively to make sure that I was not being followed by the drunk from the subway car, nodded a greeting to Jésus at the Ti Amo Cigar Stand on the corner, and let myself into the dark apartment building, the sleet cutting into my cheek like a spray of crushed glass.

The apartment was empty. Laura was out at an uptown gallery opening with her married lover. Not hungry, I went into the bathroom to brush my teeth. As I switched on the light the waterbugs startled me—and I them. Fat as dates, the bugs scrambled sluggishly out of the bathtub and filed into the large gaps in the tile-caulking that the landlord had promised to see to months ago.

I went to bed early, ascending the ladder to my carpeted shelf to read by the clip-on lamp. One could just about sit up without scraping one's head. Without pleasure I drank the large glass of whiskey I'd poured myself, feeling a sense of disgusted relief as the alcohol burned and seeped its way toxically around my bloodstream. In the semi-dark I drifted off—the marquee lights of the Chelsea Cinema stayed on all night, bathing the curtainless apartment in ice-blue illumination. Since my small epiphany about Korea, I felt quite restless, unable to block out the usual nocturnal serenade. Traffic noise roared down Twenty-third street. I was roused by the shout of a wino, the sound of a taxi honking. Around four A.M., someone's newly discovered favorite song boomeranged around the building's airshaft. The loud noise had a pointless, sad defiance to it, like a prisoner shaking the bars of his cell. It repeated three times more and abruptly stopped. Just before dawn, I slept.

CHAPTER THREE

Five Martinis

At six o'clock the next morning I was awakened, as usual, by the hydraulic twangs of the industrial elevators delivering shipments to the storage basement below the funeral parlor. Feeling jetlagged from sleep interruption, I dozed on until nearly nine. Standing in the narrow, gloomy kitchen waiting for the kettle to boil, I remembered that Oliver had given me a month's notice. Familiar financial fear started to spread through my lungs like camphor.

Obviously, rents and utilities had to be paid; food, drink, and art supplies had to be bankrolled, and a surreally large college loan needed repaying. I had difficulty swallowing my toast. I took a scorching swig of coffee and glanced around the apartment. Laura had not come home last night. The apartment looked dusty and neglected in daylight. It *was* dusty and neglected.

That afternoon Laura rang me at Cadogan Books and asked me to meet her for a drink at The Algonquin. Harry, my beau, also called, back from his business trip to Philadelphia. He would join us there later. Laura and I met at six-thirty, and sat on a sofa trying to look nonchalant. I hadn't seen her in a couple of days. She looked tired.

"It's my birthday," she said, brushing a lock of wavy blond hair out of her martini glass. I had forgotten her birthday. So had Philip, the married lover.

"About Philip," she said, "I think I'm in trouble."

"Not pregnant."

"No. In love," she said.

"It's not an affliction, you know."

"But it wasn't supposed to happen. I was supposed to just like his company. Appreciate the square meals. Now I really *mind*; I mind that he's married; I mind that I mind. And of course . . ." she trailed off, "It's tacky, I know . . ."

"Maybe you could bail out now, before you get hurt any more."

"Easier said than done, old thing."

"Yeah, I know. But you've got to think about the big picture. Meals come and go."

Laura looked upset.

"Well, I've lost my job; Oliver's going out of business."

Laura raised an eyebrow. A balding waiter politely brought us our second round of martinis and another dish of greasy mixed nuts.

I had known Laura since university. Since before she had become an unknown actress. She hadn't met anyone nice since her junior year, when she'd gone out with Charlie Downs. It was widely assumed that they would get married. Charlie surprised everyone by getting engaged to the eighteen-year-old daughter of the senator for whom he'd worked in Washington.

Across the room I noticed a couple of preppy-looking boys, probably around our age. One of them was long and droopy, and the other had curly hair and wore a cream-colored Irish fisherman's sweater draped around his neck. Unexpectedly, the droopy one made his way over to our sofa.

"Would you ladies condescend to have a drink with us?"

"*Suave*," Laura said, smirking, "I guess I wouldn't mind another."

I shot her a questioning look. One worried almost equally about Laura's man judgment as about her drinking judgment. She tended neither to eat enough to avoid instant drunkenness, nor to get enough decent male attention to repulse dodgy advances. However, a diversion from the adultery question was welcome. Noting his friend's success, the boy in the fisherman's sweater rose from his corner and sauntered over to our table.

"Hi there. Wen Stanley. Tommy introduced himself? Tom Morgan. Morgan-Stanley, I know, I know . . . Mind if we sit down?" he asked.

"What kind of a name is 'Wen'?" said Laura.

"Short for Wendell," said Wen, visibly warming to his subject. He and Tommy smiled conspiratorially. "Waiter! Another round, please. Put these on my tab, will you?" said Wen, untying his sweater sleeves.

I don't remember a great deal of the ensuing conversation, nor was any of it surprising. Condensed version: them; Groton, Middlebury, Manufacturer's Hanover training program, Fisher's Island. Laura knew Tommy Morgan's sister from St. Pauls. Wen knew a few people from Brown, including my old boyfriend, Fred, and a slew of friends of my friends' cousins. Wen lived on the Upper East Side in his maiden aunt's apartment. Would we like to go up there for a nightcap?

Laura said she'd like to, and excused herself to go to the ladies' room. I sat there between the boys, smashed. We had eaten some nuts and pretzels. I counted having drunk five martinis. (A first.)

Just then Harry entered the hotel and looked around inquisitively. He spotted me sandwiched between two strange men, and his face hardened a fraction. I had forgotten that Harry was coming.

"How was Philadelphia?"

"Fine," he said, scrutinizing me. "Harry Palmer. Pleased to meet you," he said, shaking hands insincerely with Morgan-Stanley. He fired me another look and settled heavily into Laura's seat. The boys exchanged men-of-the-world glances.

"Not Palmer, of Palmer's Peanut Butter, I trust?" said Tommy, in an inspired gambit.

" 'Fraid so," said Harry, looking about distractedly.

"Weh-hey! Palmer's Peanut Butter! The King of Peanut Butters. That makes you—what—King Peanut?" said Wen.

Harry flinched. "My father's the boss."

"So what do you do, crack the shells?" Tommy drained his martini glass languidly.

Harry ignored him.

"So you must be an incredibly rich guy. Plus all the peanut butter you could ever desire."

"I'm flattered at your interest in the family business. Why, what does your father do?"

"Here are the drinks. Cheers, Mr. Peanut!" Wen raised his glass. Harry's jaw tightened again, and he looked at me with distaste.

"I'd better go see what's happened to Laura," I excused myself. As I walked to the ladies' room the force of the martinis asserted itself in a blaze of dizziness and acidic hunger. Legs, which felt like they belonged to someone else, carried me to the little wood-paneled bar with the grouchy bartender. Ignoring his eyeballing intimidation tactics, I crammed a handful of mini-pretzels from the napkined bowl into my mouth and walked away, crunching, pleased to be able to negotiate the crowded reception area without mishap. I found Laura behind a locked cubicle in the ladies' room.

"Are you all right, Laur?" I got down on all fours onto the spotless black-and-white checkerboard floor and looked under the door.

"Absolutely not," came a weak voice above her familiar feet, "I've been sick."

Worried that I might get sick as well, I started to do some light jumping jacks and toe-touching calisthenics, hoping that violent blood circulation might speed the alcohol-processing, and chatted with some difficulty to Laura as I performed them.

The sound of Laura retching ripped through the echoey sanctum. It was so hushed in the Algonquin that one could imagine being ejected for making audible bodily function noises. A middle-aged woman in a fur coat entered and looked horrified, catching me mid—jumping jack, and experiencing Laura's vomiting noises as they peaked acoustically. She left in an outraged huff, trailing the scent of ancient Blue Grass.

"I don't want to rush you, but are you OK yet?" I asked under the door.

"Getting there."

"You can't really want to go uptown with these clowns. I mean, it's not as if we *know* them or anything. And Harry certainly won't want to go."

"What is there to *know*, for Christ's sake? Where's your spirit of adventure? It's my birthday after all . . . Won't you at least go along with me *on my birthday*?" she wheedled from under the door.

"Excuse me for pointing this out, but look where 'spirit of adventure' has gotten you so far, Laur—the tiles."

"Oh, come on. Forget Harry. You don't like him anyway."

"Thanks, Laur. I'll see you back out there. And hurry up, will you? Do you need anything?"

"Nah. Be out in a minute."

Twenty minutes later, the five of us were in a taxi headed uptown. Tommy tried to charge the bill to his father's reciprocal Harvard Club account, but the waiter refused. Harry, looking blacker and blacker, ended up paying the tab. The air was somewhat tense.

Although Morgan-Stanley were a bit of a joke, Harry's martyred patience and plodding reliability were not especially endearing that evening. There in the taxi I was chilled by the thought that I didn't actually care much what he thought or felt. Though we had been seeing each other for only a month, he was becoming quite proprietorial. Our watery liaison boiled down to a flirty evening shouting over the Palladium's sound system, a couple of unrelaxed beers at Fanelli's, a harrowing weekend at his parents', and an intensely interrogatory dinner at Mortimer's.

There had been a curious lack of urgency about our attraction. Harry's advances, like his opinions, were politic, and had remained delayed on the ground for a disarmingly long time, like the takeoff of a well-maintenanced jumbo aircraft. Although he was kind and well meaning, I had been attracted to a friend's racy description of what he had been like during college. As time went on, I wondered if perhaps the friend had been thinking of someone else.

Squashed up against Harry as the taxi gunned up Park Avenue, mildly sickened, I wondered about romantic Love. The rare, invisible currency running through people's lives, whose presence tripled your blood count in the night. People pretended it didn't matter if you had it or not, but it did. Maverick and precious, it was a wild thread stitching together unlikely people, strengthening them, suturing their wounds, weaving surprising designs in the chaos. Whatever it was, Harry and I had not been selected for its grace.

I recalled that weekend, being brought home speculatively, and prematurely, to his family's gray-shingled mansion in Sands Point, to see how I went with the decor, and the weft and weave of other family members. Harry's other blond brothers, Mark, Randy, and Junior, were all lined up at the enormous mirror-polished dining table with their blond-highlighted, Nautilized wives. It was like being cast in an East Coast setting of a Tennessee Williams play. Mr. Walter Palmer, rheumy-eyed, ruddy-faced manufacturing magnate and patriarch, sat at the head of the table sallying and interrogating his slightly cowed sons with brittle humor. Mrs. Betty Palmer, with spun-sugar hairdo and kind, suffering expression, made conversation with Junior's new wife, Donna, about an upcoming cancer benefit at the Pierre.

Harry smiled a little too encouragingly at me over his cut-crystal wine goblet. That I was an apprentice artist had been bad enough, but when Mr. Palmer asked what my father did for a living, he took the news that my father was an artist too as if it were a personal insult. He couldn't quite place me socially, which irritated him; artist father— could be some communism there—the slightly Oriental eyes, the prep-school and Ivy League background, it didn't tally squarely on the balance sheet. Mrs. Palmer was just asking where my mother was from when Mr. Palmer launched into a well-rehearsed anecdote about how Mr. Palmer senior had worked his way up and across from air-conditioning units to the dizzying heights of the peanut butter world. We laughed tactfully, and filed into the equestrian-print-lined, chintzy study for coffee and Mrs. Palmer's special-recipe peanut brownies à la mode, as prepared by Dolores, the Filipina cook. I smiled inanely, and sat down on a needlepoint cushion that read Nouveau Riche is Better Than No Riche At All.

Why had I gone? What was I now doing in a taxi with him and these other strangers? I didn't really know. Muddling along, trying anything once. Lost. That most people I knew appeared to be equally lost blurred this fact, and removed the stigma.

During the cab ride Wen accidentally dropped his fisherman's sweater out of the open window. The taxi driver refused to stop for it. Back out on the pavement Laura, now sober, paid for the cab as the rest of us were having considerable trouble finding correct change. Harry's pale blue eyes looked more puzzled and washed out than usual, and he said that he was going to walk home. I told him I would be keeping an eye on Laura. As I said this, it occurred to me that I might not be seeing Harry again. I felt a needling regret as I remembered that Harry was quite nice really. I wished him well, and selfishly disliked losing an admirer. Harry walked away, head down and hands jammed in his coat pockets, and disappeared into a gap of dark pavement between the streetlights.

Wen, Tommy, Laura and I crushed into the carved wooden elevator under the disapproving stare of the doorman, and entered Wen's aunt's apartment with a respectful silence as we took in the regulation Upper East Side brocades, severe Chippendale and grandiose blackamoor figures flanking the doorway to the dining room.

Tommy, the polite one, decanted generous glasses of Aunt Stanley's vintage Armagnac. A lock of Laura's hair caught fire as he lit her cigarette. It wasn't serious, but she was a bit shaken. We ate some Baskin Robbins Rocky Road ice cream and leftover microwaved macaroni, in that order. After a couple of Armagnacs and some frugal lines of cocaine from a little waxed envelope in his wallet, Wen emerged from a bedroom without any trousers on, and sat down wittily on the ottoman at Laura's feet in his socks and protruding boxer shorts.

This seemed like a good moment to leave. Wen, still trouserless, and Tommy escorted us downstairs in the elevator, and Laura—nursing her singed lock of hair—and I got into a cab and went home. We never saw them again.

As I lay on my mattress trying to get to sleep that night, my head throbbed. I was terribly thirsty, but refused to get a glass of water, having just drunk an unbelievable amount of water only moments before. I was too lazy to get up again, and could not guarantee a successful reprise of going up and down the ladder. It seemed unfair to have contracted a hangover while still technically drunk.

The garbled mess of the day circulated through my head like hard lumps of batter through an eggbeater, gradually growing smaller. Each diminishing thought was accompanied by increasing feelings of disgust, and surprising sadness. Oliver's impending departure and Harry's retreat formed one lump of ambivalent, unmelting loss. Laura's troubled, sleeping presence nearby did not lessen the loneliness which seemed to have welled up from beneath the darkened furniture and flooded the room.

Was anybody else's life so disjointed? If so, didn't they worry about it? Perhaps this was just the normal texture of postgraduate life in New York at the end of a fractured, narcissistic decade. Even couched in the sedative language of *Newsweek*, the condition hurt. The disjointed bits had spikes, and the missing piece, whatever it was, had left behind a canyon of emptiness around which I had organized my life quite well.

At first I thought the missing thing might be Love, but wasn't sure. Was Love so big?

Perhaps the force itself was still mighty, but its public image had been diminished by the same hype as less important things; it had been used to sell economy cars, diet soft drinks, untrue songs, banal movies, and anti-wrinkle creams. Although cheapened, private Love still exacted the same high price.

Dull thoughts followed, so boring that they slipped from beneath me, half-formed. I found myself thinking again of Korea.

The roar of traffic held me in a web of continuous noise. The light of the cinema marquee across the street flooded beneath my closed lids and strained my eyes, despite their being closed. Thoughts racing, I longed for rest, for peace.

Often, when my mind tired of its ineffectual wonderings, I would think of cool, green leaves and imagine fresh, verdant smells. Fanned, rustling leaves enfolded me. The woods were so deep I couldn't tell if it was night or day. I lay my head on some moss, and to the sound of rushing leaves, eventually I fell asleep.

CHAPTER FOUR

History

Cardboard boxes and canvases slid across the back of the rented station wagon as the car's wide hips swung around the corners of Route 9. Driving up the Interstate earlier, my spirits felt progressively lighter the farther from New York I sped; Bridgeport, New Haven, Hartford, Holyoke, Northampton, Greenfield, and finally Exit 3 to Starksboro. The names of the towns on these green-and-white signs were tattooed in my memory; their familiar singsong syllables, like nursery rhymes, prompting the mixed emotions of childhood, with its maddening dreads and comforts. The landscape growing steeper and wilder, I floored the accelerator up the final hill, impatient to arrive.

The next morning, sitting at the dining-room window, I gazed out at the high clouds and pine branches tossing in the March wind, drinking coffee from my preferred blue-willow cup and saucer. I smiled at the sight of my mother, weeding as usual, at the edge of the window frame. She would never run out of weeds in Vermont. For years, she had tried to grow tiger lilies, her favorites, by the front steps, but they always died. Resigned to the cantankerousness of the Vermont soil, my mother discovered an unusual answer. She made a garden out of the weeds themselves, cultivating the prettiest, and uprooting the nastier-looking ones. Growing up, I had found this practice—as well as making monster bonsai out of Scots pines—rather embarrassing, but now thought it quite inventive. Looking at the Scots pine–bonsai next to her, now much taller, I thought of Hong-do.

After quite a lot of thinking and worrying, I had moved out of New York and bought a one-way ticket to Seoul. It sounded a bit melodramatic, but the open-ended ticket had more to do with ignorance of how long the trip would take than with a desire to stay forever. It almost felt as if I were going to Korea against my will. Although no one was forcing me to go, thoughts of going to Seoul kept returning insistently during quiet moments, creating a pressure impossible to ignore.

Despite being unhappy about giving up my studio, it felt likely that if I didn't go now, I might easily resist it later. The paintings I'd been working on were terrible anyway—a series of self-conscious fauve fire-escapes. They were leading nowhere at all, and a break could only help. The exact purpose of this trip was fuzzy, but its vagueness seemed appropriate. While it had seemed so small at the time, my uncle's visit had opened up something unaccountably big. Clearly, going to Korea would be the most direct way of finding out what the nature of this something might be. Hong-do sent a brief note welcoming my visit.

My mother had been very surprised when told of my plan over the phone, but also seemed pleased. Being reserved, it was sometimes quite difficult to tell when she approved of things. I'd decided to try and learn some Korean, but unfortunately, my mother would be away on a recital tour for most of that short interval, so I was unable to learn from, and practice on, her. Instead, I brought with me a Linguaphone Korean language course purchased in the city: one of those instruct-yourself kits, complete with cassettes and a couple of bewildering booklets designed to simplify and decode the cryptic Hangul characters.

Nearly blue with frustration, I sat in my old bedroom with the headphones on and tried again and again to halt the tape in the spot where the frail thread of comprehensible sound became a locomotive of complete gibberish. I studied the Korean alphabet chart and tried to think in ideograms rather than in individual letters. The concentration required was strenuous in the extreme; like trying to cut something by first melting down a knife, recasting it into a pair of scissors and waiting for the metal to cool each time you needed to cut with it, the scissors turning back into a knife as soon as the immediate task was complete.

"Annyong haseyo. Annyong-i kyeseyo . . ." I repeated over and over. Hangul required six syllables simply to say "good-bye." King Sejong, inventor of the Korean language, promised that it would take only a day or two for his subjects to learn it, but he must have been flattering his countrymen. The difficulty of following Hangul on the earphones was hallucinatory. As the grammatical and conceptual differences between English and Hangul widened further, my metaphorical scissors shrank. It was like trying to penetrate a concrete wall with a safety pin. It filled me with indignation and disbelief. For the first time, I began to get a measure of the formidable barrier my mother had overcome.

Those few weeks were spent painting during the day, cooking for my father, and leafing through Western books about Korea in the evenings. Besides needing to know some facts, I craved a tangible definition of Koreanness. The books' indexes yielded such dry characteristics as (a) the sanctity of hierarchical Confucian family and social relationships, (b) ancestor worship, (c) advanced scholarship and artistic achievement; (d) self-reliance; (e) self-sacrifice; (f) pacifism; (g) harmony with nature. Although not unhelpful, the words failed to construct a convincing picture. It was like trying to understand the soul of a missing person from police forensic reports and identikit features.

Reading the encyclopaedia, I grew embarrassed by my ignorance. Even the most pedestrian of facts had passed me by.

I learned that Korea— "the Hermit Kingdom"—was one of the oldest, most insular nations on earth, autonomous, racially, linguistically and culturally distinct for 5,000 years. Legend held that Koreans were descended from a semi-divine bear king, Tan-gun, in 2333 B.C. Science dated Korea's origins to the Paleolithic Age, identifying Koreans, rather unpoetically, I thought, as Tungusic Mongoloids, a Mongolian subspecies taller and fairer than other Asiatic races, though not through Caucasian influence, and unrelated to the Ainu-descended Japanese.

I studied these bald, creaky facts as if for an exam, stopping frequently to make cups of tea. It was not that the exercise was exactly boring, but it was painful, like doing years of ignored accounts. I grilled my father for any intelligence he might be hiding, but his knowledge was fairly sketchy, too. He had left art school to serve as a draftsman in the Navy in World War II, but hadn't left Maryland. They heard little on the boats; minimalist wire reports, crude newsreel propaganda, leaflets—that was all. My mother had told him odd family stories over the years, but they were mostly the same ones I had heard. Teeth gritted, I persevered with the history books.

Korea had been the last Far Eastern country to open her gates to the West in the nineteenth century, and only then under severe foreign trading pressure. Its xenophobia developed over the centuries by devastating foreign invasions, multiple regicides, organized mass rape, mass torturings, massacres and cultural repression. These and other deeds of shocking opportunism had been performed enthusiastically by the Japanese, with occasional cameos by Mongols and Manchus. During periods of peace, Korea had been a vital cultural channel between Japan and China, bringing Buddhism, art forms, and technologies to developing Japan, some two thousand years younger than Korea.

When Christianity was brought to Korea in the eighteenth century by the French, it was a catastrophe. Unprecedented division and slaughter ensued, creating the chaos that neighboring Russia, China, and above all Imperial Japan, were to exploit to their advantage in the nineteenth century.

Japan ordered the assassination of the Korean Queen Min in 1895, and had annexed the country by 1910, turning it, like Manchuria, into a puppet state, brutally suppressing its language and culture for nearly four decades. When the deposed and humiliated King Kojong refused to grant further concessions, Japan allegedly ordered *his* fatal poisoning in 1919, provoking the pacifist March 1 Independence Uprising, in which the Japanese massacred thousands of unarmed Koreans.

During World War II, Japan forced two hundred thousand Korean women into sexual slavery for the Japanese Army along with thousands of Dutch, Malaysians, and Chinese women; they reduced millions of educated Koreans into menial laborers, confiscated wealth and property, and imprisoned or executed all dissidents. Only Japan's defeat in World War II briefly restored Korea's freedom.

Then came more familiar tragedies: 1945: Korea partitioned without its people's consent on the 38th Parallel—an arbitrary north-south division designated by Russia and the Allies at Yalta to facilitate the withdrawal of Japanese troops; north under Communist aegis; south capitalist. Five years later came the Korean War: one of the most savage in recorded history. Seventy-four thousand UN fatalities, thirty-five thousand American fatalities, and a staggering three million Korean dead. It accorded no glorious victory, only a bitter thirty-five year cease-fire. UN Forces under American command managed

to protect the south from Communist takeover, but had virtually decimated the country through bombing.

As a direct result of the three-year war, Korea was left geograph-
ically and ideologically divided against the wishes of its own people,
impoverished, and razed to the ground.

Freakish result of the war: thirty-five years later South Korea had
become one of the richest capitalist economies in the world, while the
communist North stood isolated, starving, and virtually brainwashed
under the bizarre leadership of Kim Il Sung, the planet's last Stalinist
dictator.

After reading this catalog of woe, I was almost winded by the
scale of it.

I remembered a conversation my mother and I had once had about
the war.

"It was our fault," she said ruefully, "for not developing an effec-
tive army when we could see the Japanese arming themselves to the
teeth. We were arrogant, not wanting to adopt Western industrialism
and militarism. We believed that we could stick our heads in the sand
while other countries joined the race. We were romantic, unrealis-
tic . . . All we wanted to do was to read our books, farm the land, and
watch the sunset," she said.

"We were not interested enough in worldly power. And we were
punished for it. So *now* we are interested in money and troops.
Probably too interested."

I was more upset about her tolerant attitude toward the Japanese
invasions than I was about watching sunsets.

"You don't understand," she said.

"Well, tell me!"

"Don't raise your voice. You still twine. You're too old to twine."

"WHINE, not twine."

"Don't talk back like that . . ."

"Oh, *please* go on."

"Well, you must *know* this. . . . For centuries Korea always regarded Japan as an . . . unruly younger brother, to be tolerated, in the Confucian way, rather than to be treated as an enemy. Aggression against a neighbor was considered shameful to Koreans . . . modesty and pacifism are important national ideals. We would do anything to avoid a conflict with our brothers; Japan knew this very well, and simply chose to take advantage of it," she said.

I kept silent, well out of my depth.

"Don't think that the West was ignorant of what Japan was up to," my mother went on, "On the contrary! Until Pearl Harbor, the United States and Great Britain actually encouraged Japan's expansionist policy as a check against Communist Russia! When Syngman Rhee—the Korean President—appealed to the League of Nations in the thirties to put a stop to the Japanese, did the West help us? Absolutely not. They appeased the Japanese," she said with a sudden burst of animation. "We always felt that the West was more of an enemy than the Japanese, who were at least fellow Orientals."

"But it wasn't the *West* who kept invading Korea; it was Japan. Don't you resent what the Japanese did at all?" I asked, incredulous.

She looked at me in surprise, and spoke slowly again, weighing her words.

"Calm down. . . . Well, as a nation Japan was always . . . competitive and a bit immature, big-headed. Blinded by visions of power and empire. Their sense of humanity got lost . . . Japan was not alone in this way of thinking, you know. Think of revolutionary Russia, of Nazi Germany, of China and Tibet, there are too many to single out."

"But, Ma, they were uniquely cruel to Koreans! Inhuman. Surely you don't defend them."

"They are still our brothers. Human. All human beings are capable of evil, especially in times of war. Human nature is weak," she said.

I was faintly scandalized by her forgiveness of a people who had systematically raped her country, stamped out her language—even forced her to change her name to Japanese. To top it off, they claimed creepy racial superiority, and denied the Nanking Massacre and the existence of the "Comfort Women" until confronted with the disgust of other nations. Yet my mother had never spoken maliciously of the Japanese, not in my presence, at least, and she refused to speak ill of them now. Although her patently worthy Christian stance was admirable, I was irked that my mother had never shown anger about it, and refused to acknowledge the damage to her country, even when the Japanese would express no remorse or make formal reparations for their war crimes. If she had ever felt strong emotions, she never admitted them.

"War is war," she said simply. "Bad things happen."

But I began to wonder. I wondered at my mother's silence all these years. It was full of unanswered questions. Apart from this single conversation, she had barely mentioned the events I was now reading about. Had they seemed irrelevant to her new life, been a source of discomfort? Perhaps she had been sparing herself the hurt of my habitual indifference. It was true, I had shut out her stories as a child.

My mother and father had talked of going to Korea one day, but my mother quietly resisted it. Dad and I didn't question her decision to stay away from Korea. Perhaps she dreaded the immense changes she might discover, both in herself and in the war-battered country she had fled. She had returned only once since then, after her parents' deaths. She had not seen them again, or been able to say good-bye before they died. This was so sad to me that I'd never dared ask her about it.

I had often wondered why she was so self-contained in her feelings. Reading about the country's traumas now, I began to understand her a little more. It was only in her playing that my mother expressed deep emotion. Through the violin she could enjoy a safe, dignified release, externalized, separate from herself. Music seemed to liberate and to structure her feelings. Perhaps she feared that if she ever started grieving her losses, she might be unable to stop. Maybe time and distance had frozen them, as a kindness, deep inside her.

I looked out the dining-room window, quite exhausted from reading. The horizon returned my stare with peaceful blankness. There was no doubting that New England, with its stone walls, woods, and red barns, was an utterly different world. The Yankee landscape had its own past to digest. Murdered colonial settlers lay beneath the foundations of the ruined mill behind our house. The summer camp nearby, Camp Winnepesaukee, had a quaint Native American name, but no Native Americans remained in the county. Ghosts of unknown soldiers, Ethan Allen's Green Mountain boys, were said to haunt the overgrown woods nearby. A Mississippi-born Vietnam veteran turned motel-owner had shot himself in the head on our road in 1974. I felt little connection to any of it.

America had been fortunate to avoid wars at home this century; its recent history seemed to contain mostly the weird, scattershot tragedies of unlucky motorists and airline passengers, assassins, terrorists, and lone maniacs. Apart from conveniently invisible Vietnam veterans, America's sufferings were unusually noisy and individualistic, celebrated in internationally televised courtroom battles and sumptuous spreads of marital woe in *People* magazine and the *National Enquirer*.

Korea's annexation, wars, and partitioning had been blows to the roots of its nationhood, withstood in a global silence. Its obscurity, aristocratic disdain for trade and militarism, and deliberate aloofness from the West ensured that no one cared about its traumas. Korea was too old and complicated to be understood by a world that worshiped youth and Caucasian notions of glamour. What did it matter if Korea had been the artistic, intellectual, and spiritual center of the Orient in the eleventh century, advancing painting, ceramics, medicine, Buddhism, and cartography, producing books in movable type in 1234—two centuries before the Gutenberg Bible—or that pilgrims, monks, poets, scholars, courtiers, painters, goldsmiths, and ceramicists had come to learn at her feet. Again, in eighteenth-century Choson, Korea's level of civilization was unsurpassed in the Far East. But twentieth-century Korea was war-scarred and rebuilt; its back still turned somewhat defensively against the encroaching West, whose condescension Korea felt keenly.

When my mother returned from her concert tour a few days later, violin case in one hand, suitcase in the other, I welcomed her differently. Maybe I imagined it, but her face looked more complete to me, and slightly harder, too.

As she walked up the flagstone path and handed her suitcase to my father, it occurred to me for the first time that she must have been carrying cases when she first arrived in America. There had been a moment just as specific as this one. Had she walked down a gangplank? What would she have brought with her? Had anything survived from those days? I tried to imagine her as she was then, but could only picture her in a snapshot from the late fifties, when she was a music student in New York. How different she looked then, her face round and babyish, hair bobbed and permed; barely recognizable. She had long ago lost the open vulnerability of that sheltered girl from Seoul. I remembered a photograph of her even further back, in the forties, before leaving Korea. She was standing on the wide bank of the River Han in a brown overcoat, a tiny figure against a vast blue sky. It was taken at such a distance that you could barely make out her face. Over time the colors have bleached out, the image gradually dis-appearing in its frame.

Looking at my parents' backs as they climbed the front steps, I realized how incomplete my knowledge was of them both. Perhaps I would always see them through the keyhole of childhood, reduced and truncated by my own self-interest, their limbs moving predictably in and out of the light; Mother's hand stirring a soup pot, tuning her violin, Dad's shoulders hunched over a canvas, shoveling snow, studying the sports results in the newspaper. The keyhole was dark during years of absence; boarding school, summers, and university. Periodically I sought clues in the enigmatic black-and-white tableau of their wedding photograph—the disapproved-of wedding that nei-ther set of parents had attended on racial objections—but their young, exultant faces revealed nothing but youth and exultation, their mobile eyes frozen in the recording of the moment.

There was a landlocked familiarity about my parents; I had been content to stick to the limited territory I knew, to ignore their pasts, and avoid the entire ocean of their inner lives. Perhaps this was how it was meant to be between parents and children, our lives unequal par-allel lines, never meeting. But it no longer felt quite right.

That night my mother regained control of the kitchen with an assured clatter, and as usual, prepared us a fine quasi-Eastern, quasi-Western supper; homemade *mandu-guk* (dumpling soup) with Chinese leaf, and Irish beef stew—kimchi optional—accompanied by rice *and* potatoes. Despite decades of inculcation, Dad still preferred potatoes to rice, and my mother rice to potatoes. I ate both.

I told my mother about the books I'd read. She listened carefully and said little. She carried on eating quietly. She gave me a penetrating, measured look, neither warm nor hostile, which said, "We'll see how long this interest lasts."

After supper when my father went upstairs to watch the news, my mother made some ginseng tea and we sat down together a bit edgily, as always. Like many daughters and mothers, we had had fearsome disagreements over the years, but ours were magnified by a cultural gulf.

My mother had been a distant and rather puzzling figure, as unpredictable and all-powerful as the weather. Often abroad on concert tours, her absences and bad moods affected me like rain. Early on, I had been raised mostly by nannies. Feeling excluded by my father and me, my mother would be perfectionistic when she returned home, and I shrank from the force of her criticisms. Yet when she was happy, it was as if the sun had broken through at last, transforming everything, bestowing a warmth—that only she could bring—to cold corners of my being. Her kindness was never cloying or phony, but vital.

We disagreed over petty things—her convent strictness over manners, clothes, curfews, and boy-girl etiquette—but more fundamentally, we did not speak the same language. I could not understand her mother tongue. Even when she spoke in English, the meaning of her words was pure Korean. I did not understand what she meant by "respect": to me, it meant politeness; to her it meant *filial piety*—children *revering* their parents. How did one revere? I thought it unfair to be expected to behave in ways I had never seen practiced. America did not tend to produce reverent teenagers; why should I be the first?

Yet inadvertently—and sometimes knowingly—my behavior hurt her deeply. *She* had worshiped her own mother, yielding at times I would not even consider, while I was fresh and moody, continuously breaking the code of obedience upon which her very childhood, and generations of Confucian childhoods, had been unquestioningly founded.

But compared to my boarding-school friends, I was fairly virtuous. Like a good Korean child, I was flirtatious but chaste, worked hard at school, was competent at sports and the arts, skeptical but conscientious. Got into trouble only once: suspended for smoking a cigarette in the girls' lavatory. My mother's rage was frightening: when I got home, she locked me out of the house until dark. To her, I was a barbarian, needing urgent curbing.

Although we got along in a crippled sort of way, with the advent of teenage hormones, communication became untenable. Trivially, I scorned the square clothes she bought me and told her so, while she would upset me by dismissing F. Scott Fitzgerald and Sylvia Plath as a colossal waste of time. She disapproved of my acting in school plays.

"Vulgar," she pronounced.

More distressing, when I tried to confide tremulous worries to my mother, she would respond with an authoritarian maxim or reproval which I would angrily reject, thinking that she didn't care. Tears were ignored, along with achievements.

"Mothers are not friends, they are mothers," she would say in defense of her sternness. We would make up, and row again. The turmoil was painful for us both. It was like having a diseased tooth; a dormant infection that flared up regularly, only worse. Beneath the irritable surface symptoms lay profound guilt and despair, a sense that I should have prevented it somehow, should have been stronger. It provided the first disturbing and confounding proof that two people could be biologically close, and yet be as strangers. My father and I got along easily, which may have aggravated things. But for all that, I loved my mother fiercely. Although I could not express it to her, I found her strength and principles quite awesome. I longed to please her above anyone else.

Sitting at the dining-room table, acute frustrations between us had relaxed with time.

"Get a pen," my mother instructed gently. Then she got out a battered old address book and opened it. The writing was mostly in Korean. Thanks to the Linguaphone booklet, I recognized the odd vowel. The pages were yellowed and flaking at the edges. She squinted at the page, and smiled with rare spontaneity. It reminded me of the way she had looked ten years before, when I spied on her speaking Korean with Hong-do.

"You must go and see my cousin and his family; he was once my tutor. This is his name and address. And of course, your aunt, Myung-hi, and our eldest brother, your uncle Jin-ho, if he is still alive."

This last comment chilled me. Didn't she know if her brother was still alive? Why didn't she know?

"It's complicated. I can't really say," she said. "My older brother has not been well, and since my parents' death, I lost touch with other relatives."

I was shocked by her refusal to talk about it, or even to think about it. This mention of my other uncle brought a heavy sadness to my mother's face that I did not understand then, but later would.

She moved on to discussing another relation. I listened, bemused, and grew cautiously excited about these names and places. It was like mapping the first inches of the unknown iceberg of my mother's past.

Although she was silent, one could sense the importance she attached to bequeathing these family details. After twenty-seven years I was still not wholly ready to receive these names, delivered in her difficult handwriting, in Korean. But somehow, a lazy willingness *to try* had come, and just outweighed the reluctance.

Between sips of tea my mother mentioned that So-and-so was now president of a hospital in Seoul, and that Such-and-such was a prominent banker, that X was a drunk and a womanizer. Because I had not yet met them, characters became jumbled, and I forgot which of them to avoid and which to pursue. But my appetite to find them began to sharpen.

"I wish I were going with you," said my mother, to my surprise. "But I can't go now. There is too much to do. Another day maybe we can go," she said, as if not entirely convinced that she could.

I kissed her good night. She moved her face away slightly, as usual. Sometimes I had been a bit hurt by this aversion, but my uncle had told me that in Korea, grown-up relations did not express their affection in the casually physical Western manner.

"Good night," she said, and turned to mount the stairs.

One day toward the end of March, my mother and father drove me to the airport. My journey was to be especially long; I was flying first to London to see an old art professor, on a cheap fare, naturally, and the trip would take a further eighteen hours from London; a punishing London-Paris-Anchorage-Seoul route.

Inwardly, I said good-bye to the pines, and to the long pebbly curve of our drive that was carved by repetition into my bones. The northern sky boiled purple over the roof of the car. The maple trees on the dirt road were in bud, their red-tipped branches forming an untidy ceremonial arch under which we drove until we reached Route 9. I turned and looked back through the mud-splattered rear window. The receding tunnel of maple trees was telescoping smaller and tighter, like a closing lens.

This departure felt different from the rest. How many times had I left home, for many purposes, usually doing so with an ungrateful sense of relief? Like most adolescents, I'd wanted to teethe on a bigger world.

These woods, these fields, were kindly guardians I had outgrown; I had become blind to their possibilities. I had never felt a sense of belonging to this landscape; not like our tractor-driving, dyed-in-the-wool Yankee neighbor, Addison White, and the generations of Whites before him, or like Judith, the ex–New York sophisticate in the hilltop farmhouse who proudly wore her handwoven shawl, whatever the occasion, the way a grateful immigrant might fly a flag over the front door.

Somehow, this didn't feel like home. Throughout my life I longed to recognize a picture of home. My heart was an empty frame, waiting. There was nothing wrong with the view out of the dining-room window, but it didn't fit the frame. It was both too vast and too small. Yet I was grateful to these trees and ditches; for their mute acceptance of their limited role, for being there, unchanged, whenever I came back. I was grateful to the backs of my parents' heads in the car for the same reason, although I never said so.

A clear purpose began to form as I sat in the car. With the family names as foundation stones, I might begin to build a sort of makeshift bridge from West to East, between my mother and myself. It was over-optimistic, even a grandiose idea. The bridge would have to be much stronger than both of us to succeed. The help of something far greater was needed; perhaps God, upon whom I depended with shallow irregularity. Despite the unlikelihood of achieving this ambition, a constructive impulse in this direction was a welcome surprise. I felt tentative hope. Then a heavier thought nearly eclipsed it. This journey would take me far away from where I had been before, and deliver me somewhere I might not want to go. It was likely to take a long time. Worst of all, I might have to change.

At Logan Airport my parents and I entered the international departures terminal. Dad heaved my heavy suitcase onto the luggage belt at the ticket counter, and my mother fussed, telling me as she always did that I was carrying too much.

"Don't take so much next time. You *always* carry too much. Next time . . ."

"Ma . . ."

"It's true, you always . . ."

"I know, I should travel more lightly."

I rolled my eyes at Dad, who smiled. I embraced him good-bye, and he clasped me awkwardly, his cheek rough, big shoulders hunching down to reach me, his usual silence containing patient affection. His clothes smelled of turpentine. My mother looked very serious and her eyes, level with mine, were liquid with tears.

"What can I tell you? . . . Be good. Don't impose on anyone . . . Make sure to say hello to everyone. I . . . Too bad I can't go with you . . . Write."

I threw my arms around her small, slightly rigid frame, and squeezed her tightly until she softened. I felt a single sob escape her body. My past petty hatreds melted into intense regret and crooked love for her.

"I'll be back, don't worry. I'll tell you everything . . . I want to find the temple on Mount Sorak. And the chestnut trees. I'm going to find them."

I don't know what made me mention the temple or the trees. It just came out. I swung a satchel over my shoulder and headed for passport control. I looked back, and my mother and father waved, their gestures small and uncertain. My mother looked forlorn. Suddenly she waved again, this time bigger. She waved again and again.

PART TWO

MOTHER

CHAPTER FIVE

Et in Arcadia Ego

Korea

Kangwon Province

1936

I looked up at the sky. It was all of heaven to me, and the world. Korea *was* the world; wide and clear and blue. And it jiggled. I was sitting in the basket of my father's bicycle, with my head tipped back, laughing. The rays of the sun pierced through my eyes, blinding me pleasantly.

The pebbles on the dirt track made the handlebars judder. My father was not looking at the sky, nor was he laughing. He looked very serious, concentrating on the road ahead. I tilted my head from side to side in the basket, to make him smile.

We were on our way to the marketplace in Yangyang, a few miles away from home. I loved this ritual. For a few hours, it was just my father and me. No interference from my naughty brother or crying baby sister, *and* he bought me rice toffee. Usually it was the eldest boy who had the honor of escorting a father to market, but Jin-ho made my father so cross that I, being next eldest, and nearly six years old, inherited the fun.

I wish I could tell my daughter the way it was then. But where would I begin? Seeing her to the airport, all that I left behind comes flooding back as we drive back through this northern landscape, a landscape that I now accept as having little to do with me. I am a small leaf, blown here by history.

Riding in the big basket of my father's bicycle, everything was golden. It was spring. Sun glistened upon the pine needles, it danced in the poets' stream in the village, and it warmed the barley grasses of the fields on our family estate. The breeze washed the scent of jasmine and acacia past my eager nostrils. Exploded cherry blossom hung like pink popcorn in the boughs of trees along the road winding down to Yangyang. There was a slight mist in the valley, and the light was soft, a softness that would be gone by June.

In the noisy marketplace we parked the bicycle outside the sweet shop, and father bought the toffee for us children. I got to carry the little paper packet, and was also entitled to pick out a sweet or two as we promenaded around the market.

The square in Yangyang was like a circus to me. Awnings, tents, carts overflowing with goods, and well-groomed livestock crowded the center. Villagers jostled each other, and picked their way between tables and groundcloths loaded with bountiful baskets of grain, displays of glistening fish and shellfish, dried cuttlefish and octopus, seaweed, heaped kimchi, pine nuts and chestnuts, fruit, vegetables, rice cakes, and dainties. Stalls offered bolts of rainbow-colored silks, fine handwoven linen and cheap cotton muslin, native canoe-shaped rubber slippers, metal chopsticks, brass, porcelain, and celadon bowls, books, lacquer trays and chests, mother-of-pearl inlaid boxes, ink and inkstones, rice paper, linen, calligraphy brushes, ivory and tortoiseshell combs. Familiar vendors crowed and yelled their bargain prices, competing with lowing cows and squawking fowl.

I stared boldly at the other children strapped to their mothers' backs or holding their grandmothers' hands. They looked much more babyish than I; I was allowed to roam freely by my father's side, making what I believed to be adult conversation.

We bumped into Baby Uncle near the well in the square. His name was Gong-lae, but I called him Baby Uncle, as he was the youngest of the Min brothers. Bending down, Uncle pinched my cheek and stole a piece of toffee in one motion. Then my father told me to wait for him by the willow tree while he and Baby Uncle went into a small office to deliver some papers to a colleague. Uncle bought me a rice cake. I sat down near an old grandmother and inspected the cake, which I dismantled and ate kernel by kernel to make it last as long as possible, and surveyed the crowd, quite giddy with happiness.

My father eventually came out of the little building, and furtively tucked an envelope into his breast pocket. He looked a little happier than before, and swung my hand in his as we walked back down the street to the bicycle. With Father's help, I squashed back into the basket, legs dangling out, and we pushed off heavily onto the dusty track, wobbling off for a few yards as we headed back home.

I did not realize then how terrible those spring days were for my father. That day, as every day since June 1910, we were living under a military dictatorship. Japan, fresh from their victory over Russia, had begun colonizing Korea. Our Emperor Kojong was reduced to the status of king. The same blue sky that entranced me was oppressive to Father. For him, nothing would be right and good until Korea was free.

Here, at market, Father, *Aboji*, perceived a very different scene from the one I did. Yangyang had once been fairly rich. Now it was poorer and shabbier. On this eastern coast, there were bounteous fishing and farming, but the best catch and produce were now skimmed off and profits channeled to the occupying Japanese government in Seoul.

Our clan, the Min, were the chief landowners of Kangwon Province, our estates straddling what is now both North and South

Korea. We had been rulers here for centuries. Over the course of my father's childhood he had seen our ancestors' ancient hereditary and honorary titles stripped from us, and for a pittance, we had been forced to sell major land holdings to the Japanese. We were one of the last *yangban* families to remain in the province. Father felt that we could not leave, so deep were our roots here. Less fortunate landowners and the middle classes suffered the seizure of their land without payment, and those who opposed this were shot by the Japanese. Many had fled to Manchuria and Siberia to avoid impoverishment and Japanese persecution. Only bankrupt commoners and former serfs stayed on.

The market square was nearly deserted compared to its former self, the grass near the well was overgrown and ragged, even the poets' stream was now a muddy trickle, drying up in its bed. Japanese officials disguised as Korean peasants roamed the streets of Yangyang for signs of local underground activism, but fooled no one with their blatantly Japanese features, squatter physiques, and pidgin Hangul. But the authorities were correct to be worried about the underground resistance movement. My father and Baby Uncle had that morning been attending an independence meeting in the ironmonger's storeroom. Both of them had already been sent to prison once for their efforts.

Yet naturally I knew nothing then of my father's political secrets. The grown-up world was a remote kingdom in the eyes of Korean children. One trusted, accepted, and obeyed the word of parents and elders. This was Confucian law.

As the rise of a steep hill loomed before us on the bicycle, I saw that familiar stretch of the road which led to the green gates of our estate, a view that was the most beautiful I have known. The wing-tipped lilt of the tiled roof-gates made my heart swoop upward, for within the walls of the estate lay what I can only call happiness. Years later, the silhouette of those gates is still scarred in my memory with the burning iron of loss.

At this point in the road I descended from the bicycle, and walked with my father the rest of the way, shaded by an avenue of ginkgo trees. Soon the gravel drive forked, and we took the right, turning to our farmhouse on the crest of a hill, while the road continued to the left, leading eventually to the grand main house, a mansion, where my eldest uncle, Yong-lae, lived with his family, along with Baby Uncle, who was still a bachelor.

My grandfather, Lord Min, was now dead. I remember him only slightly, but those impressions cast a giant shadow. He was a splendid, rather mythical figure in his red silk court robes, carried aloft by serfs in his sedan chair. At home, he had been no less awe-inspiring in his high black horsehair hat, with his long white beard and gray silk robes. He moved slowly and walked with a silver-topped cane, a gift from the king.

Grandfather had been the last of the *jinsas* in the family. *Jinsa* was a *yangban* imperial scholar's title, now obsolete, bestowed on him by the late King Kojong. Grandfather had been a courtier to the king in Seoul, and was also a distant cousin of the queen. But Lord Min— Gong-ju was his first name—was too ambitious for the king's liking. My grandfather's private armies exceeded the royal quota, and with some relish, the king exiled him to his northern estate until his death.

At the time of his marriage, my grandfather had a vivid dream of three birds flying. His wife later gave birth to three sons: Yong-lae (Dragon arriving), Bong-lae—my father (Phoenix arriving), and Gong-lae (Peacock arriving). That he should have had so poetic a premonition was said to be typical of him. He also fathered two daughters, but being female, my aunts had merited no such privileged iconography in my grandfather's dreams.

People spoke of Grandfather as if he were a god, and we all were happy enough to go along with the indulgent descriptions. Min Gong-ju was princely, witty, a brilliant scholar of Chinese classics from the age of seven, a formidable poet and horseman, never seen merely riding on his white horse across the fields, always *galloping*. He was considered a good and merciful feudal lord. As a youth, he had been strikingly handsome: fair and rosy, with liquid hazel eyes and shiny amber-black hair. Noble Manchurian blood accounted for the European features of some of the Min clan. I remember his uproarious laugh, quite terrifying, coming from beneath his towering, solemn scholar's hat.

But at the end of his life, Grandfather was rarely even seen in public, much less laughing. When he went to the village he wore a Western Homburg low over his eyes so that no one would recognize him, so humiliated was he by the effects of the Japanese occupation, and our family's disgrace.

It was Grandfather's generation that had witnessed the fall of Korea: he had been alive when the rebel army was defeated by the Japanese, and had witnessed the dissolution of the entire Korean Armed Forces by the occupying militia. He had been at court in Seoul when a group of government ministers had committed mass suicide in protest of annexation; he had even seen the expression upon the king's face when the Japanese declaration was presented to him.

My grandfather stood by politely as Japanese police ransacked his personal library, confiscating heirloom history books and irreplaceable hand-calligraphed works of Korean poetry and ancient literature that had been declared subversive. Grandfather was made to watch as armed police burned his dearest books in a public bonfire, their wisdom vanishing in a column of destructive black smoke.

The takeover was a nightmarish echo of the Hideyoshi invasions of the sixteenth century, when Japan had systematically devastated Korea. Arson had been perpetrated on such a scale that virtually no building in Korea not constructed of masonry survived that invasion: even Kyongbok Palace, the royal residence, was burned to the ground, and later had to be rebuilt. All government buildings and royal libraries holding irreplaceable Yi Dynasty records were burned. Thousands of farmers and civilians had been slaughtered and their property destroyed by Japanese troops. The noses of twenty thousand Koreans had been sliced off their faces. Artisans, doctors, and print- ers had been captured and kidnapped, taken prisoner to Japan for their technological and medical expertise. Although despised and mal- treated by the Japanese, they were never allowed to return home to Korea.

Now the descendants of those Japanese invaders were back in Seoul repeating their public book-burnings—eradicating virtually all of the country's new historical and political texts, schoolbooks, and works of nationalist literature—and replacing them with their own accounts of Korean history. The Japanese literally rewrote our his- tory, redrafting political events to diminish and excuse their atrocities, and teaching this sanitized version of history to Korean and Japanese schoolchildren. Lord Min was furious to learn that those children whose parents could not afford private education were deliberately being kept illiterate by the Japanese government, who had closed down over two-thirds of the schools to this end. Knowing scholarship to be the cornerstone of Korean society, Grandfather said the Japanese could not have chosen a more cynical form of cultural stran- gulation. Cruder totalitarianism came in the banning of Korean news- papers and of public gatherings, and the changing of street signs from Hangul to Japanese.

Our family could not understand how it had been allowed to hap- pen. The West made no moves to intervene. The League of Nations did not respond to our pleas. Forty years earlier the West had been vir- tually silent when Queen Min had been murdered in her own palace by a mob of Japanese assassins, who had hacked her body to pieces with machetes and burned her still-living remains with kerosene in the Royal Gardens. Had the Japanese even attempted such an act on a

European monarch, would Japan not have provoked a war, or at the very least been ostracized with sanctions by the world powers? The West's appeasement had outraged my grandfather.

Millennia of civilization were being systematically destroyed by a Japan drunk on the liquor of new military and industrial power. The last vestiges of the Korean aristocracy were abrogated. Our country was finished, as far as Grandfather could see.

Grandfather had often said that the *yangban* class had brought the 1894 reforms upon themselves through gross abuse. Corrupt aristocrats used their rank as an excuse to do nothing all day but gossip, smoke pipes, play chess, and practice archery. These reprobates still insisted that commoners dismount when meeting them on the road and when passing before a *yangban* house. For centuries *yangbans* had had the right to ignore tradesmen's bills, to exact loans from farmers and neighbors, demand free labor from peasants and unlimited use of their cattle and horses, the right to free food and lodging at the homes of magistrates, and amnesty from the law except in rare cases of treason. Such blatant injustice was wrong and deserved to be abolished along with slavery, thought Grandfather, but he also felt strongly that the class structure ensured civilization, and with reforms, should remain intact.

Lord Min did not like to understand the success of the Japanese; Japan was amoral, and yet it flourished. Right and wrong were reversed. How could the world be blind to their perfidy? He had said that the Japanese were accepted by the West as civilized beings only because they adopted European haircuts. He was partly serious. Even in such an outwardly trivial matter as hairdressing, he saw the contrasting character of Korea and Japan. Where the Japanese had passively accepted a daft government edict for all men to cut their hair short in the European fashion, in Korea, when the Japanese consul, Inoue, decreed a similar order for Korean men to cut off their topknots, it caused a national furor, and Korean ministers resigned their posts in protest. Although the king himself, out of diplomacy, finally adopted the edict, those Koreans in the country who cut their hair were beaten up in broad daylight by topknotted dissidents.

For Grandfather, who had been raised to pity the barbarian ways of the Japanese rather than to condemn them, being forced to bow to them in his waning years became an intolerable degradation. He grew ill, aging quickly.

Near the end of his life, Min Gong-ju, now a commoner, returned with a Buddhist monk to the land he once owned in the stupendous Sorak Mountains, confiscated by the Japanese. Grandfather became obsessed with erecting a family temple on the highest peak, in defiance of the loss of centuries of stewardship.

He ordered the temple to be built in the grounds of a hermitage to symbolize the lonely and vain path of enlightenment, and to represent inviolate Korean sovereignty. The Min name was to be carved upon the temple pillars. Min Gong-ju ordered one thousand chestnut trees to be planted around the temple for longevity, their eventual lushness and strength were to screen it from enemy detection. The temple was constructed in secret by several of his former serfs, who risked their lives to do so. Soon after its completion, my grandfather died. He never saw the temple.

Since Lord Min's death, the muscular gables of our ancestral house had lost their air of potency and assurance. The calm and old-fashioned grace within its rooms had also vanished with my grandmother's spirit. She had died six months after her husband. But the heaviness in the household had set in a few years before, with the unhappy behavior of Yong-lae, the eldest Min son, now in his thirties.

Yong-lae, it was said, had inherited his father's good looks, intelligence, and fondness for riding a white horse, but entirely lacked his backbone. Where Lord Min had reveled in the responsibility and dignity of his station, dutifully officiating at dull civic and royal ceremonies wherever he was needed, and lending his attention to humble and humdrum estate maintenance, Yong-lae wrote the occasional poem and spent the greater part of his time visiting his tailor in Seoul.

One year, Yong-lae secretly ordered seventy splendid coats to be made for himself. This was a great mystery to us, because we never particularly noticed his new clothes. When the bill arrived, my grandfather was enraged. He confined Yong-lae to the estate grounds for two months, and ordered a servant to burn all of his son's trousers but one scruffy pair, which he was ordered to wear with his new coats.

But this ploy backfired. Yong-lae's sartorial appetite remained undiminished. Once the dramatic value of grandfather's action had faded, Yong-lae genuinely needed new trousers. But a weakness for fine clothing was the lesser of his peccadilloes.

"Going to his tailor in Seoul" soon became a euphemism for drinking binges, which began tamely enough, but worsened. Predictably, not even Yong-lae's marriage to a lovely and sympathetic young woman of a neighboring clan could keep him away from the bars and taverns of Seoul.

Yong-lae's drunkenness shamed the family. It was an awful cliché, my grandfather complained to him, for an eldest son to be so irresponsible. But Yong-lae did not smile and promise to reform, as he might have done before. It was now as if his father were discussing someone else, whom he only vaguely remembered.

Grandfather, already shattered by the invasion, could not fully fathom that his right-hand son, traditionally relied upon for support and leadership in parents' old age, was a sick human being, as useless as a broken leg. Toward the end of Grandfather's life, the look of disbelief frozen in his eyes was terrible to see. The burden of assuaging Yong-lae's failure fell to my father, Bong-lae, the second son.

Father was silent now as he pushed his bicycle. Although the big house would always be splendid, a symbol of better times, the farther we withdrew from the grand main house, the happier I felt. The hill rose up a gentle slope to our farm, and soon we were home.

How can I describe it? It was nothing special. And yet to me, it was a paradise. Just a traditional Korean farmhouse of wood and white clay, with a winged gray tiled roof set comfortably in a crab apple orchard, watched over by jagged blue mountains. Unlike the big house, we did not have a colony of live-in servants, just a housekeeper, and a tenant farmer and his small family in a nearby cottage to perform heavy chores, tend the livestock and vegetable garden, and help with the prodigious work of preparing food for winter.

Above all, home was *green*. The green of new rice grasses. The green of ripening fruit. The green of a bride's gown. Out of my bedroom window, wide verdant fields, thick copses, bamboo groves, and gracious trees stretched outward, uninterrupted on all sides. The teasing mists of the East Sea added enigma to the solidity of the land.

My mother, wearing a pale blue linen *han-bok* with white ribbons, descended the step to greet us. My little sister, who was two, followed her out of doors and fastened herself onto my father's leg. He picked her up and gave her a piece of toffee.

I took off my shoes, entered the house, and, thirsty from the journey, went straight into the kitchen to get a drink of water from the well. The enormous kitchen was very much the center of the house, quite literally the hearth of our home.

It was a two-story annex where grain and dry goods were stored above, with an outdoor wing for the chickens and pigs, and below, the furnace and ovens generated our *ondol* heating—the Korean system of flue pipes that carry heat beneath the oiled, sepia-papered floors of every room so that they are warm to sit and sleep upon. Here, behind a large embroidered silk screen, we also bathed, drawing our water from the indoor well, which was kept covered with a huge carved wooden lid.

It was the smell of that dark timbered kitchen that I remember still; a sweet and earthy scent of hay and fermenting soybeans. More than any other, this was the smell of my childhood. It also held the transient odors of delicious soups simmering in great iron cauldrons and succulent *bulgoki* grilling, but the scent of spicy hay was the irreplaceable constant, lingering in the eaves, and deep in my memory.

My mother supervised the making of our own soy sauce, *duenjang* and *kochujang* sauces in the grindstones, the slicing of radish and cucumber for pickles, and, of course, the hand manufacture of several varieties of hot kimchi, which were kept in enormous stone urns on the *jang* terrace in the garden. It was a year-round activity to keep the food stores filled.

My brother, sister, and I played boisterous games of hide-and-seek in the storage loft beneath the mighty oak beams, trying not to upset colorful baskets, jars, and sacks of provisions. Jin-ho—showing off that he could read and I couldn't—called it Ali Baba's treasure cave, for it held everything we could imagine.

There were baskets of garlic and ginger, brass bowls of whole green chilies, dried red chili flakes, cold iron cauldrons of soybeans for sprouts and curd, huge sacks of rice, barley, maize, flour, potatoes, sweet potatoes, ceramic jars of dried chestnuts, ginseng root, green and preserved persimmons and crystallized ginger, dried plums, dried mushrooms, anchovies, and stacks of kite-shaped dried cuttlefish—a local specialty. Serried rows of stone flagons stood by the staircase; honey, sesame, and fish oil, homemade rice wine and *soju*, a fiery and disgusting grown-up drink which Jin-ho had been recently sick on.

I drank the cold spring water and went out to climb the crab apple tree. I amused myself for some time by sitting on the highest bough, pelting my little sister with apple blossoms. At first she loved it, tipping up her face to welcome the petals, but then decided it was all too much, and began to scream.

My mother opened the kitchen door and struck the brass gong. Forgetting our petal fight, Myung-hi and I raced inside for a simple lunch. Afterward we had our usual nap. I fell asleep dreaming blissfully of rice cakes and bicycles.

By suppertime it was cool outside. My mother closed the papered screen door overlooking the flower garden and lit the dining-room lanterns. We all sat around the low mahogany table keenly looking forward to eating. Jin-ho's hands, for once, passed inspection, so there was no delay.

My mother ladled out the *mandu-guk*—dumpling soup—and then we had rice, hot kimchi, steamed bracken stalks with sesame oil, dressed cucumber, radish, spinach and beansprouts, toasted seaweed, and marinated grilled chicken slices dipped in spicy bean sauce and wrapped in fresh lettuce leaves, followed by juicy scarlet strawberries. Our meals were very simple, but delicious, with everything fresh from our farm.

Toward the end of supper, there was a sound outside the door; someone clearing her throat. We all looked up in surprise, and my father got up to slide back the screen. There, accompanied by a maidservant, was Yong-lae's wife, in tears, black hair loose and flowing. She apologized for interrupting, but said she must speak with us.

Jin-ho and I glanced at each other, electrified with excitement.

"Of course, of course," said my father, standing up. My mother also rose, gently touching her sister-in-law's forearm, and stood before her, shielding her from our inquisitive eyes.

"Children, go into the library and play, take Myung-hi, and make sure she doesn't disturb any of your father's things," instructed my mother.

Jin-ho and I bowed obediently, but pouted in our mother's direction to express our maximum disappointment at this cruel exclusion. I dragged Myung-hi by the arm into the study, leaving the door pointedly open. Jinho and I immediately slithered out and regrouped by the dining-room door, which was slightly ajar. Myung-hi sat on her fat bottom in the corridor looking at us quizzically.

Jin-ho stuck his ear to the crack in the door. I shoved him aside to make room for myself, and with a sly tilt to my head, caught a narrow slice of Yong-lae's wife's face, twisted in distress. We only rarely saw her. She was very pretty, despite her tears and streaming hair, and wore a sumptuous midnight blue silk gown edged in white satin. She was unbearably glamorous.

". . . and the groom found him in a ditch, he had been robbed. His pockets were reversed and empty, the horse was nowhere to be seen. Unconscious. The groom had to fetch help from the farmer, and take him on his own horse. . . . He was in Seoul for three days . . . and there is no more money. Our children are always asking me where he is. What can I do? How shall I manage? . . . My own family will not give me any money; they know he will just squander it. They say he is making a fool of me," said Ok-ja, sobbing into her fine handkerchief.

My mother tried to calm her with soft words, but one could see that the situation was worse than she knew how to cope with. She looked at my father for prompting. My father was silent, his face drawn with worry.

"Somehow we will help you. Please continue to be brave. For your children, too. We will do what we can. I will speak with him, but you must be prepared for him to carry on. You know how he is. But you were right to come to me," said Father. My mother handed her a beaker of ginseng tea.

Jin-ho and I looked at each other with coy satisfaction at the quality of entertainment being offered. Then Jin-ho sneezed. My mother rushed to the door hissing admonitions, grabbed our elbows, swooped up Myung-hi, and propelled us into our rooms.

"Children. You are wrong to listen at doors. Very naughty. You mustn't repeat to *anyone* what you have heard, and you must learn to obey your father and me. Where do you learn such habits? This is grown-up business, and that is that. You will soon be old enough to have your own worries, so be glad not knowing."

"But I'm not tired, Mother, and it's so *interesting*," said Jin-ho, smiling his most charming smile. A lock of shiny hair caught in his long, blinking eyelashes. You couldn't help adoring him. Mother told him to go to bed anyway, and not to be fresh, but her anger had disappeared.

"I'm not tired, either," I echoed.

"Oh, yes you are. You went all the way to market today. And you mustn't argue, Myung-ja! Your father is not happy with the way you imitate your brother's bad habits. By the way, get up early tomorrow, Jin-ho. We are going to your grandparents' for the day. No reading all night in bed. No singing and dancing on the mattress, either. Up early, Jin-ho, remember."

Jin-ho shrugged his shoulders and trudged off to bed without saying good night to anyone. It was true that he'd been more disobedient than usual of late. Mother stroked my cheek absently, and tucked me in after putting Myung-hi to bed. Myung-hi cried again to remind everyone that she still had a point of view, even lying down. I went to sleep looking forward to tomorrow, and wondering about our aunt in the beautiful gown. What would Father be able to do for them? Would Uncle go to jail for being such a bad husband?

It was a beautiful, mild morning. Jin-ho and I were terribly excited about going to our grandparents', not only because of the novelty of their seaside household, which was filled with cousins and other exotica, but because the visit would involve a ride in the estate's glamorous black Packard, which my father would be borrowing for the day. Grandfather Min was the first in the province to have bought a motorcar.

"Eat more!" instructed my mother, urging me to finish the rice in my bowl.

"But I'm not hungry!"

"You will be—when we're halfway there. Have more kimchi."

I frowned and forced myself to finish breakfast. Jin-ho was already in the car, sitting behind the steering wheel on my father's lap. Even on my father's lap, he could not see much over the wheel, so gigantic was the car's chassis. Jin-ho was not at all mechanically adept, but liked the flattering image of himself as a motor-racing driver.

Once we were out on the dirt road I pretended to be a princess, making a state visit. The landscape floated by in a dream. I waved to the cherry blossoms, pretending they were loving subjects, and bowed my head modestly to the ginkgo tree courtiers and bracken ladies-in-waiting. Sadly, we were going only six miles.

We drove very slowly up a winding hill encircled by tall pines and zigzagged blue peaks, and there, on a breathtaking clifftop, lay my mother's family estate. Jin-ho and I cheered with excitement, and Myung-hi imitated us, her joy causing a strand of saliva to hang from her chin.

Father drove around to the stables at the back of the house, and parked next to one of the traps. We burst out of the car, and patted the warm muzzles of the horses. The air smelt delicious; sharp and briny from the sea, and fragrant with acacia-blossom. My mother gave Jin-ho a basket of honeyed rice cakes to offer to our grandmother. As we approached the stone steps, Jin-ho pinched off a corner from one of the cakes and ate it with provocative gusto. Father frowned, and meant it.

The house was far less grand than our grandfather Min's, which had many wings for servants, tutors, guests, and visiting family, courtyards, pavilions, a temple, outbuildings and stables, and serfs' cottages in separate enclosures. Although simple, our grandfather Kang's home had the most unforgettable garden and position looking out to sea.

The Kangs were landowning gentry. Unlike Grandfather Min, Grandfather Kang had no burdensome title, and had never been obliged to perform the grinding administrative duties incumbent on men of the Mins' rank. Kang's sunny, youthful demeanor reflected the fact that he spent most of his time engaged in his greatest pleasures: gardening, fishing, and eating.

When we arrived, plump, balding Grandfather Kang was out on one of the terraces in his elegant gray linen *jugori* and white *paji* trousers fingering the leaf of an azalea bush with rapt consideration. He smiled and waved us down to show us a new addition to his exotic specimens.

Being on a hilltop, his was a many-tiered garden, bordered with stones and flowering pine bushes, *che-song-wha*. Bright colors vibrated against their deep green setting. Grandfather grew prodigious quantities of pink, white, and red peonies, camellias, azaleas, rhododendrons, lilacs, wild beach roses, calla lilies, tiger lilies, white, gold, and purple irises. The acacia and wisteria were so heady that the smell made me drunk. There were also the mysterious yellow moonflowers that blossomed only at night. During summer visits my brother, cousins, and I told ghost stories at night behind the luminous moonflowers, hiding our faces behind the blossoms, and screaming in the bushes until we were dragged inside to our beds.

Like most Koreans, Grandfather had a deep love of trees. He had a mulberry grove in which he cultivated silkworms for his tenant farmers to produce silk. He also grew orchards of plum, apple, peach, cherry, pear, and nectarine trees. He had almond and walnut trees, persimmon trees, dates, bamboo, and trellised grapevines, all of which Grandfather complained withstood more hardship from the greedy hands of us children than from birds or insects. In the autumn it was one of my favorite things to come with my mother and gather fallen chestnuts from beneath the chestnut trees, whose last dying leaves fanned out brilliant orange against the deep blue sky. I loved the earthy smell of the rotting leaves underfoot, and the delight of finding the shining, heavy brown orbs hiding in the damp grass and papery foliage, fishing them out, and plunking them into Grandmother's old straw basket.

Being one of Grandfather Kang's favorites, I was given the privilege of tending a small row of tiger lilies. These precious lilies I weeded and watered with ostentatious ruthlessness to prove that Grandfather's trust was not misplaced. Thus began my lifelong love of gardening.

Soon my grandmother, two aunts, and various moppet-headed cousins came out of the house to greet us, amid shouts and laughter. Grandmother, in a cream silk *han-bok*, was small and deceptively frail looking, her hair in a tight black bun. Actually, my honored grandmother was incredibly tough, with a grip like an iron clamp. My aunts, Chosan and Chungsun—thus called by the children because they lived in the nearby towns of Chosan and Chungsun—were dressed more simply in pastel pink and blue linen with white edging.

The elder, Chosan-*daek*, was fat and newly a Christian, while Chungsun-*daek* was skinny and underconfident. The beauty of the family, Aunt Pusan, lived a long way away, in the southernmost port of the country, but we were very excited that she was here now, resting indoors from the long railway journey.

Pusan-*daek* was my favourite aunt, not only because of her easy manner and porcelain beauty, but because she was thrillingly clever and lively. She was also generous; whenever I saw her she let me try on her many pairs of high-heeled shoes and laughed with delight as I clumped around the room in them, turning clumsily to show off the different pumps to their best advantage. I was slightly silly about her shoes, but she never behaved as if I were a nuisance. Although she was as busy as any of my other aunts on her visits, Aunt Pusan always made time to brush my hair tenderly before I went to sleep. This small gesture warmed me to the tips of my toes, and I went to sleep feeling that my head had just been touched by the hands of a fairy princess.

Aunt Pusan had had many proposals of marriage, and ended up marrying the richest and handsomest of the lot. Yet I overheard Grandmother telling my mother that Pusan-*daek*'s nouveau riche husband had turned out to be too much of a peacock to notice his wife's qualities. Although, as an uncle, he was senior to me, I thought him a very stupid man indeed.

After the luncheon feast, which my aunts had spent three days preparing, my brother, two boy cousins, Jae-sung and Jae-dal—sons of fat Aunt Chosan—and I announced our intention of going down to the sea, a fifteen minute walk away. However, before going off, Jin-ho and I sneaked away to Aunt Pusan's quarters to catch a glimpse of her, as we had been denied that opportunity during lunch, when Grandmother Kang declared her still too tired to make an appearance.

One of the best things about our grandparents' rambling, busy household was that we could be naughty for much longer before being discovered. We stood very quietly in the cedar-scented corridor outside Pusan-*daek*'s room. A muffled but distinct whimpering sound could be heard. Fortunately for us, the door was open a crack, irresistibly inviting us to look through it.

I gasped and covered my mouth. Jin-ho was shocked, too. There, sitting in the corner leaning her head against the wall, was Aunt Pusan, wearing a frightening white canvas coat with her arms wrapped round her body so that she couldn't move.

Jin-ho and I looked at each other in horror. Neither of us had ever seen a straitjacket. What had happened? Why was she strapped into this diabolical contraption? Her face was downcast, but even so, you could tell that she was utterly altered; her spirit strangled. She was pale, like a crushed moth.

Tearfully, I ran to my mother, leaving Jin-ho dumbstruck at this extraordinary sight. Mother was in the sunny mulberry grove with Aunt Chosan. They were talking animatedly about the plight of Uncle Yong-lae. I told mother what we'd seen. First she was angry that I had been spying again, but seeing how upset I was, she softened.

"You are too young to understand, but your aunt is not well. She is so sick that she tries to harm herself." I looked at my mother blankly. She sighed.

"Sometimes, my daughter, after a woman has a baby, she becomes very sad like this. So she must rest in this ugly coat, away from other people who would tire her."

Aunt Chosan nodded her double chins.

"But she can't move, Mother!"

"I know. . . . Now that's enough, Myung-ja. You are too young to understand such things. Go and play. Do as you are told," she said, looking unhappy.

"But it must make her worse to be alone in that scary thing!"

"Myung-ja! Do you criticize your grandmother's wisdom?"

I could not reply.

"Now, you are not to mention this again. Not to your cousins, not to Father, or Jin-ho. This is ladies' business. You must promise to be silent now that I have explained this private matter. This is not for small children's bigmouthed gossiping."

I promised, and dragged my feet back to the house. Jin-ho was sitting quietly outside Pusan-*daek*'s door like a faithful dog. Our aunt was now sleeping sideways on the silk mat, her face still pale, but tranquil. Naturally, I told Jin-ho immediately what Mother had said. We drew away sadly from Pusan-*daek*'s door, but I soon perked up a little, remembering that we were going down to the sea.

Jae-dal and Jae-sung had lost patience, and were already on their way down the meadow. To catch up, Jin-ho and I started leaping over the spring grasses like crickets. Around the next bend I could see and hear the ocean. My heart thumped in excitement. There it was! Still distant, but roaring, and jade green, its whitecapped waves veiled by a gray mist.

There was something grave and cruel about the sea near Nagsan cliff. It was so remote that you could imagine anything happening and no one knowing about it. No ships could be seen, just miles and miles of dark, racing ocean. I could not conceive of a world existing beyond the waves of Nagsan. This was the only sea, the only Kingdom; I could imagine nothing but death beyond the low black horizon. This harshness was strangely comforting.

The air grew damper and saltier against my face. Jin-ho was ahead of me, his small black head bobbing in the livid green grass.

"Wait for me!" I cried, a bit frightened, tripping over the uneven terrain, my arms windmilling in the air. Jin-ho couldn't hear me. Now he was somersaulting down the hill, whooping and laughing his lungs out, the wind whipping away any sound from our lips.

The roar of the sea grew louder still. I shivered, a little afraid. My cousins had taught me to swim last summer by throwing me in the sea, pulling me out only when I was on the point of drowning. To their disgust, I cried inconsolably and trailed up the hill alone behind them, following from a distance on the rough path that Jae-dal had beaten down in the high grass. I was still scared of the ocean, a year later.

The hill gradually declined into spongy marshland, dotted with big sharp rocks, tufts of wild beach grass, and scrubby gorse. I was afraid of the leeches, and willed my feet to touch the ground only fleetingly. Still, my canvas shoes were wet through, and my feet were cold and squelchy. I stumbled on, trying to catch up with Jin-ho, who at last turned around and waved.

Winded, I slowed down. I could now see the two black dots of my cousins on the shoreline below. Jubilantly, I stretched my arms up to the vast blue sky like a seagull, and wheeled down the hill until I tripped and fell. The ground was damp, so I jumped up quickly, leaving a wet stain on my behind. Standing at the edge of a dune, I could smell the tang of the tides, salty seaweed, and clean, cold sands. I took off my tennis shoes and hung them over my shoulder by the laces, which made more damp spots on my pink cotton dress. Never wanting to see them again, I threw my dripping wet socks away into a bush.

Jin-ho was hopping up and down barefoot on the shore next to his two cousins. The boys were catching minnows. Jae-dal was twelve— two years older than Jin-ho—the eldest, and heir to the estate. Jae-dal was bossy and quite brave. He was the handsomest cousin I had: tall and square shouldered, with pink cheeks and thick, unruly black hair tucked behind his ears. He wanted to be a soldier.

"No, no. Not *there*, Jin-ho. Over there . . . Only the fat ones. Myungja! Come and help instead of standing there like a loon." I smiled shyly and joined them at the inlet. Jin-ho elbowed me affectionately, and I got down to the tricky business of trapping quicksilver minnows in my hands and dumping them into the tin pail.

Later, when the water in the pail was quite thick with flashing whitebait we climbed to the crest of a hill, and Jae-dal deftly made a small fire in a sand dune out of dried twigs and goldenrod stems. Clumsily, I wove together some green stems with my fingers to make a tiny grill net, over which we roasted the minnows. We apportioned the cooked fish according to rank; Jae-dal, the eldest, getting the most, and I the least, but I didn't mind because Jae-dal was so handsome. The roasted minnows were very smoky and juicy, and quite delicious: hot in our mouths in the cool air. The thin, darting orange flames and blue smoke of the fire was both comforting and exciting to us, making us feel even more hungry and alive.

Then my brother amused us with impressions of Aunt Chungsun bossing one of the farmers with a stick. Jae-dal laughed until he was bent over with a stomachache. Jae-sung, who was my brother's age, was very shy, and mostly watched, munching silently and huddling his thin shoulders. Then Jin-ho mimicked Uncle Yong-lae preening himself drunkenly in a new coat, until he fell on his back with his feet in the air. Jin-ho was wicked. We all laughed heartlessly, Jae-dal loudest of all. Jae-dal would make a good officer, I thought, observing his graceful swagger. We made our way slowly back up the hill to our grandparents' house, Jae-dal humming a song—out of tune—and rhythmically swinging high the empty pail, as if parading the king's colors.

The grown-ups were having tea and cakes on the veranda. The lowering sun through the unfurling leaves of the giant maple tree cast a dappled shade over the porch. Despite our little fish-roast we thronged round the bamboo table like hungry baby birds as our aunts and grandmother clucked and fussed over us and sent us indoors to wash our hands and faces. Jin-ho was scolded specially for having extravagant ash around his mouth.

"And where are your socks?" my grandmother demanded of me.

As I went to the kitchen for a towel, I overheard Grandfather Kang talking to Father in his study.

"Yes, perhaps it would be wise to move to Seoul. Your own father is not here to give you good advice, so this is mine, dear boy. Go and see what the opportunities are. You have many contacts there; it should be easier to find work in the city than here, now that the Japanese have got your father's farms. Go and see."

My father replied in a low voice, "But this will be impossible, sir. Yangyang is part of me. . . . It's all I have left of Mother and Father, you know. And the children love it, too, I think."

Grandfather nodded sympathetically. "I know. But now that your brother is so ill, you are right in saying that you have a responsibility to keep up the estate, and help his family, as well as your own. There simply aren't the opportunities here, my boy, unless you would work with the Japanese." Father was silent.

"Will you sell your farm then? You know I would buy it from you, but I am afraid it is quite beyond me now," said Grandfather Kang.

"Yes, I will have to sell up, sir. I have no choice in the matter."

My mouth was dry with anxiety, heart pumping. It could not be possible. Sell the farm? Leave Yangyang? Before I knew what I was doing, I ran into the empty nursery and sobbed and howled into a silk mat, hiding my head in its folds. I felt as if life itself, my very own breath, were being sucked painfully from my body.

I cried until I fell asleep. I was still asleep when we left for home in the evening. I can vaguely remember my father carrying me out to the car.

"It must have been all the sea air," said Grandmother, waggling my inert hand. I didn't answer or speak to anyone. Not even to Jin-ho. I refused to even open my eyes. My heart was too heavy. This, I remember, as my last day of childhood; by nightfall it was over.

CHAPTER SIX

Father Goes Away

That summer, my father went away to Manchuria. We did not know when he would return. Baby Uncle drove him to the railway station in Kangnung in the Packard. He looked jaunty sitting next to his brother, fedora set at an angle on his head, suitcase thrown carelessly in the back as if he were going off on a joyful expedition. Everything seemed all right. They both turned around and waved as the automobile accelerated, leaving us in a wake of dust.

But from my mother's strained face as she waved after him, I wondered if he might have been putting on a bit of a show. Financial opportunities in Korea were so scarce, said all the grown-ups, that, as father could speak fluent Chinese, he was obliged to go all the way to Harbin to investigate business possibilities.

The sale of our farm had never been mentioned aloud, and despite my efforts to glean more adult intelligence behind doors, I heard nothing further. Although I was relieved that there seemed to be no urgent danger of losing the farm, the first, heavy seed of fear had been planted in my heart, and nothing could remove it. Overhearing my father talking to Grandfather about the sale, I had felt grief for the first time. The soft, dreamy room of innocence had been stripped overnight. Nothing now felt quite the same. Sorrow had been a shocking, hard sensation.

While there was no further mention of leaving Yangyang, I kept Father's conversation secret from Jin-ho. He was more sensitive than I, and that summer had already begun defying my father more openly than before. I feared that this rumor would upset him violently.

Jin-ho had recently declared his intention of becoming an artist. When he ought to have been doing mathematics at Father's desk, instead he would be found on the floor painting wildly untidy ink landscapes on great sheets of cotton paper. My father had caught him once, and rebuked him with a coldness in his voice that I had not heard before. When Father had left the room I comforted Jin-ho, shyly touching his ink-stained hand. He looked both angry and afraid, and shook me away.

Father wanted Jin-ho to become the first professional in our family. Father himself had not been raised to such work, although he had been sent to agricultural college after his formal tutoring was complete, in case Uncle Yong-lae should need assistance with the running of the estates.

But the country was changing so fast under the harsh rule of the Japanese, that aristocrats now found themselves with neither a civic role, nor means of subsistence. How long would Uncle Yong-lae, in his present state of disrepair, be able to hold on against the clever laws of the Japanese bureaucracy? Would my father alone be able to break his fall?

Although Father had gone to Manchuria with a few contacts, he told my mother that he did not expect magic solutions. Jin-ho was to be his last hope. Jin-ho was to become a lawyer, or anything, really, so long as it guaranteed an income to support the family. But as father's hints had become more insistent, I could see Jin-ho's spirit straining the other way, as clearly as one could see the direction of water flowing in a stream. The stream was running away from us.

For a month we heard nothing from Father. The summer, as abundant with blossom, insects, and fruit as always, felt incomplete without him. In the evenings the crickets in the green-tumbled fields croaked like an assembly of broken-stringed violins, and I wanted to tell Father that they were the loudest they'd ever been, but for the first time I could remember, *Aboji* was not there. The violet and peach-clouded sunsets were as glorious as ever, but where I once felt happy and complete, basking in the exuberant midsummer light, now their beauty produced in me a strange sort of ache.

I don't remember much more about that summer. The same rituals were observed. Meals were taken, visits were made to relations nearby, cousins took us boating and fishing, and my admiration for handsome Jae-dal grew stronger; I became expert at weaving fiddly little minnow-nets out of goldenrod stems in order to please him. Myung-hi cried with her usual alacrity. Mother was often distracted when we asked her questions, and became cross when asked about Aunt Pusan, who had returned, shakily, to her baby son and her husband's custody in the South.

Uncle Yong-lae was now rarely seen about the estate. Mother said that his health was very bad, and that we must not disturb him by ringing our bicycle bells and stopping in for tea and cakes as we used to do. Baby Uncle had moved out, and was living in Seoul with distant relations. Yong-lae's wife sometimes came to see Mother in the afternoons with her smallest baby, who had colic, and they talked in hushed voices in the shade of the crab apple tree. She still looked very beautiful, and wore silk-satin in the daytime, but she had circles under her eyes, and I never dared talk to her.

Something strange was building up inside of me. My chest felt heavy. Perhaps it was Father's secret that I was wanting to forget. It separated me from everyone else, and when I heard the sound of rushing leaves in the dark, it was no longer soothing, but sounded like the stirring of trouble. I worried terribly about Jin-ho. It saddened me that he was increasingly far away from us, not wanting to play with my sister and me, or come to the village. He shut himself up in Father's study and came out only at mealtimes, or to go off hiking at Nagsan cliff by himself. It was as if he were trapped in a bubble of unhappiness, and though I could see him, I could not touch him or call out to him.

At last we heard from Father. A package arrived from Manchuria in July, and we were relieved and joyous. Even Jin-ho came into the garden to hear Mother read out Father's note to us. We sat in a solemn circle on cushions in the grass around Mother's long skirts. The note was short and unsatisfying. He was very busy, and did not yet know when he would be returning, but was sure that we were being helpful to Mother and obeying everything she said. P.S.: He also hoped we liked our presents.

Indeed, we did like our presents. There was an ornate gilt box of French chocolate liqueurs, confections which we had neither seen before nor tasted, silk, lace-edged handkerchiefs for Mother, three books of translated poetry for Jin-ho—Keats, Virgil, and Li Po. There was a blond German doll for Myung-hi (which frightened her) and two gramophone records—one of *Tosca* and one of *The Magic Flute*—although we did not have a gramophone. But best of all was my own present, a breathtakingly sumptuous blue velvet dress whose bodice was embroidered with seed pearls, in a design of leaves and roses. That these gifts were impractical did not in any way disappoint us; rather, it made me adore my father even more.

What Mother did not tell us about Father's letter to her was that Father had failed to secure a solution to our financial dilemmas.

Perhaps this accounted for his inspired selection of gifts to please us. It was not until many months later that we realized how desperate the family situation had been.

Although it wasn't spoken of, my father had fully taken over supporting my uncle Yong-lae and his family, as well as looking after the estate. But how much longer could Father afford to do so? The trust left to Yong-lae by my grandfather had already been used up. Much land had apparently already been sold to the Japanese governor-general, including a particularly large northern estate in Wonsan. Old servants had been forced to leave the big house. During my father's absence I had seen the families of serfs, tithed to our family for generations, leaving their farms. Thousands of Koreans were now emigrating. I had assumed that our families had been forced to evacuate by the Japanese for official purposes, not guessing that Yong-lae had dismissed them, or comprehending that our wealth and feudal ties could ever be at risk.

But in Manchuria, it transpired, my father's connections could do little more for him than provide opulent hospitality. Friends of my grandfather took him under their wing in Harbin; he saw impressive displays of dancing girls at the Metropole Hotel, and ate many dinners at the homes of distinguished burghers, but the promising leads he was given in zinc mining and transnational railway expansion schemes came to nothing.

My father was young and had led a sheltered life. Although his manners were admired by his hosts' wives, their husbands quickly detected that he knew nothing of mining or railways. In these politically unstable times Grandfather's friends felt they could not afford to take a risk on him themselves, and salvaged their consciences by recommending him to the appropriate officials, who also sensed that he offered nothing that could be of material value to them. The booming industrialization of Manchuria under the Japanese brought opportunities for the canny, experienced businessman, but for a *yangban* scholar in Chinese classics, it brought rather less. My father returned in August with more chocolates and straw sailor hats with blue ribbons.

When Father tucked me into bed the first night of his return, I looked hard into his face as he bent down to say good night. I tried to find in his eyes some new hint of what was to happen to us. He had said nothing of importance at supper; instead he entertained us with amusing descriptions of his fellow railway passengers, and of the strange food in Harbin.

Suspicious of his overly reassuring smiles, I held on to the sleeve of his serge suit for a moment as he tried to leave my room.

"What is it, Myung-ja? Shall I call your mother? Are you thirsty?"

My eyes were drinking him in, memorizing him. I had missed him so, and the whole of my happiness felt as if it depended on what he would do next. Would he sell the farm? All the things I had wanted to tell him over the summer now seemed irrelevant; the small, passing beauties of sunsets and flowers that I had longed for my father to elevate with his special recognition had, in his absence, faded in my heart, and created a vacuum which I could not explain to him. Moreover, I wanted him to say something to bring Jin-ho back to us, wanted him to forgive my brother, and restore our peace.

I could not speak. I felt I could not ask him anything important; I might jinx his efforts to salvage our future. By my silence I wanted him to know that I implicitly trusted him. Instead of speaking, I scrutinized every passing shade in his eyes for an extra hint of his mood and what it might mean for our family.

"What is it, my dear?" said my father, "I am very tired after my journey," he gently loosened his sleeve from my fierce grip.

I didn't know how to say what was worrying me. I didn't want to let him go while my throat was so tight with emotion. I wanted to trust him, but really, I could not. In the grown-up world anything could happen; my uncle could drink himself into oblivion; my beautiful, good Aunt Pusan could end up in a straitjacket; my father could go far away and leave us; our dear home could even be sold. Grown-ups could do these things.

Suddenly it was too much. "What will happen to us, Daddy?" I blurted.

He looked at me in tired surprise. "Why, what do you mean?"

"Are you going away again? Will we starve? Will we have to leave our farm?"

Father's masked expression softened.

"My dear! Have you been so worried? That is not as it should be. You must let your mother and me do the worrying."

His reply only worried me more.

"But . . ."

"But nothing, Myung-ja. Listen to me and obey me; this is your simple duty as a daughter."

A tear rolled down my cheek.

"We will be all right. There is nothing to fear. You are overtired, little one."

I so wanted to believe him that I nodded my head vigorously on the pillow, tears running down my neck.

"There is nothing to fear, silly."

Father smiled, but my blunt questions had chipped his assured facade, for he did not deny what I had said, and his earlier brusqueness betrayed him further.

There is nothing to fear. There is nothing to fear. I repeated his words to myself in the dark after he had left the room.

The sound of the wind rushing through the leaves echoed my disquiet. The rushing of trouble.

There is nothing to fear.

But the memory of Father's masked eyes contradicted his promise. Somehow this physical discrepancy carried more weight than his words. I did not believe him.

PART THREE

GRANDFATHER

CHAPTER SEVEN

Mansei

Seoul
1919

Bong-lae! BONG-LAE!" shrieked my little brother, reaching for my coat sleeve. "Don't leave me by myself, I'll get lost!" I was irritated, because he was right; I had temporarily lost track of him in the crush of demonstrators, and if I'd allowed anything to happen to him, my mother would surely kill me. As it was, I had promised her that I would absolutely *not* join in the *samil*—national independence—demonstration, but would be studying safely indoors with little Gong-lae, under the careful eyes of our elderly tutor.

But it would have been absurd for a hotheaded, patriotic young man to have kept such a promise on this historic day. It was March 1, 1919. The day when the whole of Korea was to rise up in peaceful protest against Japanese rule. Today, at two o'clock, the declaration of Korean independence would be read aloud simultaneously at various locations in the city, and all across Korea, addressed to the wider world. The signed declaration would be delivered to the Japanese governor-general that afternoon, and the independence leaders would turn themselves in for immediate arrest. Even thinking about it brought tears of passion to my eyes.

Strong feelings had been stewing amongst the people for some time. Two months ago our former emperor, King Kojong, had died under very peculiar circumstances. He had refused to sign a document for the Japanese to circulate at the Paris Peace Conference declaring that "The Korean people are perfectly happy, and are grateful to Japan for all the wonderful things that Japan has done for them."

Shortly afterward the King was dead; officially of apoplexy. He had been slim and in good health, and died after eating a bowl of rice. By coincidence, the young, healthy maid who had brought him the rice also died suddenly, at the same time. Only Japanese doctors and officials were allowed to examine the king's body. Suspicions were immediately raised, and the underground independence movement began to hatch protest plans with fervent purpose.

The Japanese bureaucrats could hardly oppose plans for national mourning, so secret societies in every city and village began to coordinate and assemble their delegates in Seoul around the official day of mourning on March 3. When the Japanese authorities began to suspect something odd about the huge influx of people to Seoul, the underground leaders changed the date of the protest to surprise the Japanese.

My fat college friend, Kwang-suk—also nineteen and from a *yangban* family—was active in the independence movement, and briefed me on everything. He said that exiled Korean revolutionaries in Shanghai, Siberia, Hawaii, Kando, and Japan were coming back for the rebellion.

Kwang-suk had told me that the *Independence News* was being printed in people's garden sheds, fishing boats, and even in tombs, and then being distributed across the country in huge hollow cakes baked by housewives, and in giant gourds sent to Seoul by farmers. Everyone was joining in. Janitors and coolies collaborated with editors, and students dressed as porters had even infiltrated the Japanese High Commission and managed to deliver onto the desk of Terauchi—the governor-general—two pristine copies of the *Independence News* every week. Terauchi was incensed. (How 20 million Koreans managed to keep their vigorous activities a total secret from the Japanese, I couldn't tell you.)

Everyone had been told of, and had agreed to, the pacifist terms of the demonstration pledge. Under no circumstances were violent actions to be undertaken, or even oaths to be spoken. It was of the first importance to demonstrate the Koreans' high, honorable, and fair behavior to the world, and to show that our only interest lay in freedom. Our only weapon would be to speak the word, *Mansei*: "May Korea live ten thousand years."

I held my brother's hand tightly. We were now moving in the direction of the park. We were being pushed along by the crowd, which was fantastically varied; old and young, rich and poor, scholars and ministers, tradesmen and women of every guild and caste, many wore dun mourning colors for the king. All had been instructed to use only their voices, to say only, "*Mansei.*"

Japanese mounted police began to appear in the distance. I was so full of excitement that I could say nothing to my brother. Both of us were absorbing through every pore the extraordinary emotion of the circumstances. Gong-lae's eyes were bright when he looked at me, his cheeks flushed. Ordinarily we were not encouraged to walk the streets of Seoul without a chaperone, but I had convinced our old tutor that we could not possibly miss this chance to pay our respects to the dead king, and he bowed his head in agreement—only on condition that I excuse him from joining us, due to his weak heart.

Finally we reached Pagoda Park, and stopped by a bandstand which was thronged by people. The atmosphere was extraordinarily charged, but calm. A strong feeling of family solidarity emanated from the crowd. With the Japanese nearby, such a feeling was an illicit luxury.

I was thrilled to the soles of my feet to be part of this moment, and on a practical note, pleased that I could see the speaker. Gong-lae, standing on a crate, had a good view, and we exchanged excited smiles.

Suddenly a tall, clean-shaven man climbed the parapet, and began to read a document forcefully in Korean; it was the Independence Declaration. A tense, hopeful silence fell upon the crowd. As he read the lengthy statement, its words washed over me like fresh water, rinsing away the lies and the hurtful justifications of the Japanese. Its message of justice, courage, and restraint reached the multitudes of parched faces, who drank in each utterance with unanimous relief, whether they could hear the exact words clearly or not.

Never had I read—much less heard—my inner feelings of anger and longing for freedom expressed aloud. Tears streamed down people's faces. Some of the faces around me were raised upward, straining to savor the precious ideas, some heads were bowed, shaking with emotion. People were holding on to one another for strength and support, some were on their knees in prayer.

"With this we declare our Korea an independent nation, and Koreans a free people. We announce her independence to the ten thousand nationalities of the world, and so reveal the Great Truth of the equality of man. . . . In making this declaration we have the authority of five thousand unbroken years of independent history, and the approval of a sincere and loyal people. . . . No power under the sky can thwart us. . . . It is our one urgent duty to achieve national independence.

"During the last decade we have tasted for the first time in our history the bitter sorrow of oppression by a foreign people, intoxicated by a doctrine of power and the philosophy of domination by conquest. We have been deprived even of the right to our subsistence! We have been oppressed in our intellectual and spiritual development. We have been degraded from the ancient glory of our origins; deprived of the priceless opportunity to move with the tide of world culture, therein to make our unique contribution. . . . We shall not

judge Japan's treachery—nor do we resent her falsehoods in claiming, through her scholars and politicians, the works of our ancestors
as her own, and in her lust for conquest, deliberately misreporting
our cultural roots to the West. We are too eager to seek out our own
faults . . . and have no time for blaming others. . . . Today it is our task
to reconstruct ourselves, not to destroy others. . . . The statesmen of
the Japanese are idolaters of militarism; contrary to the Universal Law
of Virtue. This wrong must be righted. Korea and Japan were joined
against the will of all Koreans; the result has been a deadly oppression
by force, prejudice, and misrepresentation. In such circumstances
these two nations, whose interests are directly opposed, can never live
in harmony. . . . Each day deepens their mutual resentment . . . hardened the longer it lasts, inducing the destruction of the nations of the
whole of the Far East. . . . The age of force and arms is gone . . . the
age of right and justice has come. . . . We are twenty million, and
the heart of each is like a square-edged sword. We do not hesitate, and
we do not fear. It is for us to regain the freedom that was ours. . . .
Today the spirit of human brotherhood and the common conscience
of man protect us. . . . Truth is advancing with us. . . . We go forward
in the light which lies ahead."

Then the man on the platform quietly read off the thirty-two sig-
natures of the Korean delegates who had drawn up the statement.

Then he raised his arms and cried, "*Mansei*: May Korea live ten
thousand years!" The echo of his voice carried down through the
silent assembly of people. Then, with a mighty pause the crowd
breathed as one body and unleashed an almost frightening sound,
thousands of tongues as one tongue, as if the sky had a voice and were
speaking: *"MANSEI! MANSEI!"* It rolled through the crowd, gain-
ing unbelievably in volume. *"MANSEI!"*

Then, a tremendous roar broke from people's throats, and they
reached into pockets and satchels, and started waving the outlawed
Korean flag, *Tae-guk.* Tearfully, they waved it. They waved it with

their whole bodies, as if their arms alone could not fully perform the task. Those who did not have flags waved their handkerchiefs, hats, scarves, anything they had.

"*MANSEI!*" rebounded the roar. Others climbed the parapet to make speeches, but could not be heard above the din.

Leaflets appeared throughout the crowd announcing that at this moment, all over Korea, the declaration had been read, and that we were joined together anew as a nation. The fliers stressed that at all costs our march through Seoul must be a peaceful one, whatever the provocation or violence meted out by the Japanese. I grabbed Gong-lae's hand and tried to worm our way back through the crowd to the city center, where we had been instructed to go next, to chant "*Mansei*" at the foreign embassies. I kept looking around for the police. I couldn't believe that they had kept their distance during this unprecedented, bold public display. Had they been ordered to stay back because of the link with the king's state funeral? Had they sensed the importance of the occasion? It was unbelievable; the Japanese police were hardly famous for sensitive restraint. . . .

Before I had entirely finished this thought, I heard the sound of men yelling in Japanese and the clattering of horses' hooves on the paving stones. My heart leapt in fear. Turning around, I saw a mounted policeman with an iron hook reaching into the crowd and yanking a young man off his feet by the neck. Where the hook had caught him in the back of his thin coat, blood ran.

"*Mansei!*" shouted the boy weakly—he looked about my age. I looked around and Gong-lae, still holding my hand, stared in terror.

"*MANSEI, MANSEI,*" I found myself shouting in support of everyone else. Suddenly the fire brigade appeared, and Japanese civilians, men and women, had come out of their houses wearing expressions of hatred and fear, brandishing household knives and broken glass.

A young Korean mother, wearing a white linen *han-bok*, was

clubbed over the head by a mounted policeman, and fell unconscious into the gutter. Drops of bright blood spattered over her white gown and onto the swaddling cloths of her tightly clutched baby. The same policeman lifted his weapon again, and clubbed her baby with a blow of even greater violence.

The cries of *"Mansei"* faded in the throats of those who had seen this act, and people ducked, clasping their heads from the random blows. An old farmer with missing teeth took the initiative, crowing *"MANSEI!"* with increased fervor.

"MANSEI! KOREA!" I screamed as loudly as my lungs would allow. My brother, nine years old, piped in too, screwing shut his eyes, and stumbling behind me, his fingernails cutting into my hand. The blue-uniformed policemen were seriously outnumbered by the crowd in places, and made up for it by "hooking" and shooting unarmed people whenever the opportunity presented itself. The pacifist nature of the march made no difference to the police.

A stocky Japanese baker lunged a samurai sword into the parade, and stabbed an old *yangban* man in a horsehair scholar's hat. The gentleman's shocked expression upset his Japanese assailant, who stabbed him again to produce the look of fear he was apparently waiting for: instead the gentleman raised his bleeding hand, and said evenly to the shopkeeper, *"Mansei!"* and stumbled on before collapsing in a cobbled alleyway.

Although I was seeing people being killed around me, and scores being wounded, we carried on our peaceful march with strangely redoubled determination, which lent us a thrilling sense of strength; for the integrity of the occasion assuaged the violence we were receiving. At last, we had an opportunity to show the Japanese—and the outside world—our contempt for their regime.

Bringing along my little brother had not been the wisest idea, however, and I did not allow myself to picture my mother and father's reaction to our being caught here in the middle of the march.

Although I knew that weapons would defeat the purpose, I secretly wished I had something, anything, to protect my brother with.

Just then, I saw a little boy of about five smiling and waving his Korean flag at a policeman. When he skipped back to rejoin the troop of schoolchildren, the policeman shot him in the back, and then bayonetted him with unnecessary vigor. Tears of anger welled up in my eyes, and I screamed *"MANSEI!!!"* at the nearest Japanese. Before I knew it, I felt cold iron around my neck, and then a sudden sharp piercing pain as the hook entered my skin. Blood began to stain my white linen shirt and coat, and I was amazed. My little brother started to cry.

We were both pushed into a line of what looked like thousands of arrested demonstrators heading for Chong-lo police station. Some still shouted *"Mansei!"* but I was too shocked and confused by what was happening to keep up my revolutionary fervor. My neck hurt. I worried about catching an infection from the dirty hook. The mounted policeman escorting us occasionally swung his hook through the line of prisoners to punish stragglers, and to wound anyone who annoyed him.

Finally we reached the police station, and my brother and I were placed in a cramped, windowless cell with about seventeen others, many of whom were more badly wounded than I was. One boy had had his nose cut off, and although he was losing copious amounts of blood, the guard refused him a doctor. I felt as if I might be sick. We were told that it was forbidden to talk or to sit down. I smiled to reassure my brother, but I was afraid, and far out of my depth; it shames me to admit that I wanted my mother.

As soon as the guard had turned his back I heard whispers that all of the city jails were overflowing, and that thousands of women had also been arrested and killed. It was hot and damp in the cell, and it stank. I negotiated a spot in the corner with a kind, plump journalist, behind whom we hid from the guard so that we could sit down. I could remember nothing much until about two o'clock in the morning, when a warder woke us.

"No sitting!" He kicked us both with his heavy boots, and after handcuffing us, escorted Gong-lae and me into the examination room. He and another Japanese guard kicked us in the back and legs all along the corridor, and one of them kicked Gong-lae in the stomach after he had fallen down.

The two guards delivered their final kicks in the presence of a bored Japanese prison boss and a Korean translator. My back and sides were aching, and I could barely breathe. My little brother was bent over with pain. When I went to help him, they kicked him harder to show me not to interfere, and hauled him to his feet by his pigtail.

I swallowed my fury and revulsion and pretended to speak only Korean, telling the examiner that we were a farmer's sons from the country. I made up names and invented a village after the surname of my brother's nurse. If they knew that we were *yangban* children or, worse still, even distantly connected to the royal family, our family would be targeted and persecuted. I kept my replies as stupid and as brief as possible.

"Why did you shout *'Mansei'*?" said the examiner, smoking a cigar.

"Because everyone else was shouting it."

"Do you know what it means?"

"I think it is a cheer of good health to the king."

"LIAR!" He slapped my face. "YOU KNOW PRECISELY WHAT IT MEANS!"

"I am sorry. But no," I said, rubbing my cheek.

"HOW DARE YOU? Are you a Japanese citizen?"

"I am a Korean boy, and so is my brother."

"IDIOT! That means you are Japanese. Why don't you speak Japanese? This is now your language."

"We do not go to school, we work on the land."

"Backward yokels, eh? YOUR CLOTHES ARE NOT PEAS-
ANT CLOTHES!"

"They are hand-me-downs from the *yangban* master's boys."

And so on. The nondescript examiner squinted at us through his
cigar smoke, like the sheriff in the cowboy novel that I had just borrowed from Kwang-suk. As the questioning continued I did not fear
him so much. He just shouted a lot, like any bully. Just when I thought
we would be released—on account of our being so young and hope-
less—the Japanese man gave us a phony smile, and invited us to wait
in the next room for our punishment.

I was taken aback. We had broken no law. Surely they would not
punish my brother any more; he was only a child. And what more
could they do with me? Beatings, a night in prison, forbidden to speak
or sit was not enough? Blood still seeped from my neck wound; but I
kept my mouth shut.

In a tiny, brightly lit cement-block cell, one of the guards who
kicked us and the Japanese examiner himself each grasped a four-
edged club—sort of like a big table leg—then, with a shout, they both
started to beat me with these sharp-sided clubs, one on my front, and
the other on my back. I have felt nothing remotely as agonizing before
or since. I passed out almost immediately. Seeing that I was so easily
defeated, the officials dealt my brother only six blows.

When I awoke, I was back in the prison cell. I didn't know the
time. I could barely move for bruising. Also, my stomach was cramped
with hunger, and my mouth was caked dry. I had neither eaten nor
drunk anything since breakfast the previous day. I looked around for
my brother, and to my huge relief, he was crumpled up, asleep in the
near corner. When the guard saw that I was conscious again, he took
me back into the examination room for more questioning.

"Please, sir, may I have some water?"

"NO! NOT UNTIL YOU TELL THE TRUTH," he shouted.

"But I have told the truth, sir, and my brother and I have had nothing to eat or drink for a whole day and night!"

"SHUT UP!"

The examiner puffed inexpertly on a fresh cigar, and asked me more questions about my family and friends, and about where I was staying in Seoul—the same questions they had asked the day before. I was surprised that they had not believed me. I lied again, as consistently as I could. At the end of an hour, they picked up the four-edged clubs. My whole body was too tired to feel fear, but with a strange sort of detachment, I knew that I couldn't take any more. Without pride, I begged them not to beat me again.

The Japanese examiner smiled, answering with an almighty wallop to my shins that knocked me down. I banged my chin on the concrete floor, landing on my bruised hip bone. My shins felt like they had been shattered into splinters. Even though I was lying prostrate, they rained blows onto my exposed side. I tried weakly to protect myself, and had to be carried back to the cell. There, at last, my brother and I were given water, but I could barely swallow, and even standing still, my ribs ached and I had shooting hot pains to my back and shins, and skinned, bleeding abrasions where the blows had met bone.

I can remember little of what happened next. There were hours of waiting, and again I could not tell if it was day or night in that windowless cell. Suddenly, I thought about home. My mother and father must have been furious with my tutor, and furious with me for endangering my little brother's life. I was so weak and hungry that tears of self-pity welled up in my eyes.

The cell became even more crowded than before. The stench of sweat and urine became stronger. There were constant comings and goings, sounds of clanking iron, and guards shouting orders—only exhaustion guaranteed sleep. Finally each prisoner was given a small handful of kidney beans and half a cup of water. I had never felt hunger like this before. From then on, we were given a handful of beans three times a day. To our humiliation, there were no lavatories. We were left to defecate in our cell. The stench was such that I breathed through my mouth.

I was grateful and impressed with my brother for being so grown up. He was subdued, but understood the danger, and was unlikely to betray us. When they questioned him, he continued to play dumb, and cried loudly whenever they kicked him. They were strict about the "no talking" rule (beatings if you were caught), so we communicated only when it was absolutely safe.

A fourth day and night went by with a nightmarish repetition of the questioning and clubbing, and bean torture. The portly journalist who was looking out for us disappeared for a whole day, and I thought he had been released until they brought his body back into the cell on a stretcher. I examined him, afraid that he was dead, but while his face was ashen, his broad chest was rising and falling very slowly. Then I saw that his hands were covered in blood, and his blackened, ringed thumbs were practically severed in half, still seeping blood.

I had never heard of this torture before: hanging someone from the ceiling by the thumbs using metal wire, but found it horribly ingenious. Sickened, I was afraid he might get gangrene if not treated. Later when the guard returned to give us our ration of water and beans, the journalist still did not move when the guard kicked him, and he was enraged by the inconvenience of having to remove him.

A couple of hours later, the journalist was returned to the cell on a stretcher, unconscious, his thumbs crudely bandaged. They rolled him off, like a loaf of bread from an oven tray, and relocked the cell door. He slept for many hours. Later, when he had regained his strength, he told one of the older men, a university professor, that the examiner had burned his genitals with his lit cigar.

The mind boggled at such treatment. Before this independence march, I had little direct experience of the Japanese. My father, Lord

Min, had raised us to believe the best of all people, and told us to think of the Japanese government as misguided, rather than evil. He had told me that there were educated Japanese, decent individuals who regretted the unjust and dishonorable actions of their government. He showed me a letter published in the newspaper *Nichi Nichi Shimbun* from colonial proconsul Inoue, denouncing his countrymen's behavior in Korea:

> All the Japanese are overbearing and rude in their dealings with the Koreans . . . the Japanese are not only overbearing, but violent in their attitude toward the Koreans. When there is the slightest misunderstanding, they do not hesitate to employ their fists. Indeed, it is not uncommon for them to pitch Koreans into the river, or to cut them down with swords. . . . If merchants commit these acts of violence, the conduct of those who are not merchants may well be imagined. Under such circumstances it would be a wonder if the Koreans developed much friendship with the Japanese . . . for this state of things, the Japanese themselves are responsible.

Father smiled at the newspaper. "You see?"

Lord Min had always said that whatever should befall us, we must not lump people together and detest them as a whole—that this would make us as prejudiced as those who would oppress us.

But now, in prison, I struggled to accept his words. Prison officials, I realized, were hardly going to be the most enlightened citizens. But before my eyes flashed the sight of two grown Japanese men kicking my collapsed nine-year-old brother in the stomach, and I could feel nothing but lowly hatred.

My underground activities had so far been confined to safe, civilized meetings of well-brought-up students who gathered once a week in one of our barns to discuss the philosophical and ethical implications of the Japanese occupation, and to draft possible practical solutions. We spoke of honor, of freedom, of the ideal of fraternity among Oriental peoples, and of the danger posed to this Oriental brotherhood by greed and Western industrial development. But there was a unanimous sentiment among us that the Japanese, through history, had shown themselves to be fundamentally unsound. Quite apart from being unable to tell the truth about their own history and ancestry, their bellicosity and puffed-up self-regard made them a joke among the educated and uneducated alike, and gave Orientals a bad name abroad.

In this shadowy barn, we drank cups of fine tea from a carved brass tray served by a faithful old family retainer, and flattered ourselves that we knew best. The world need only consult us, and we would graciously set them straight about political and cultural matters in the Far East. None of us had been abroad yet ourselves, but this did not diminish our sense of innate authority. We were idealistic and ambitious, dedicated to serving Korea in some tangible way when we came of age.

I was roused from my thoughts by the elbow of the indefatigable journalist with the bandaged thumbs.

"One of the new detainees says that at midnight tonight, the revolutionaries are going to ring the Liberty Bell to signal the start of a renewed independence drive; pacifist again. From midnight, shops and schools will close, and workers are going on strike."

Hearing this news, I was half excited by the prospect—proud to have been in a tiny way part of the effort, and half dreading it—for cowardly reasons. A renewed independence initiative, however peaceable, would give the Japanese further license to maltreat those of us already imprisoned.

Luckily, a couple of hours later, after another questioning-and-beating session, the examiner appeared to tire of our stubborn stories, and ordered us to be released—on condition that we return to our masters at once, and sign an agreement banning us from Seoul and any further political acts.

With time only to wave a frantic good-bye to our brave journalist friend, my brother and I found ourselves unceremoniously dumped back out on Chong-lo Avenue, black and blue, filthy, and stinking of ordure. My eyes straining with the shock of daylight, I was never so ecstatic to see this bustling, wide street again.

After being restored immediately by coach and horses to our father's estate in Yangyang by our conscience-stricken tutor, and undergoing a gentle, but strict dressing-down from father and a lengthy examination from the family doctor, I met with my underground independence colleagues as soon as I could.

Apart from clearly advertised cuts and bruises, I was found to have three broken ribs, a fractured shinbone, and the infected gash on my neck needed six stitches. I could not walk without wooden splints and crutches. My brother was instantly put to bed with some sort of stomach virus, cut legs, and cracked ribs, and attended to hourly by my weeping mother and older sisters, who dismissed the nurse, and dabbed the cuts and bruises on his face and body themselves with cold cloths of bound ice.

Our elder brother, Yong-lae, who was not interested in politics, was roused from his habitual ennui by the brutality our adventure, and even appeared to be somewhat envious of the attention being lavished upon us.

When I began to tell Father of our time in prison, at first the expression on his face was one of shock, but then he went white cold with rage, and left the room midway through my description to compose himself. My mother urged me to finish, her jaws clenched tight. She tried to get me to stay in bed for a few days longer, but I was eager to get back to the barn and discover from my friends what was happening in the rest of the country.

To my embarrassment, my friends, especially Kwang-suk, greeted me as a hero, only a few of them having been in Seoul for the demonstration. Those who'd been there had fled from the police. I assured them that my actions had been more those of an unlucky bystander rather than of a revolutionary hero, and to my slight disappointment, they accepted this explanation without argument.

Since my release, we heard through the *Independence News* that indeed hundreds of thousands of protesters had been arrested and tortured, there were twenty thousand wounded, and seventeen thousand killed outright. The numbers were astonishing. When I heard the report that many had died in prison, I wept, almost with shame, that I had survived.

Despite the alarming response from the Japanese, Koreans were continuing to follow the directives of the independence leaders. Students were still chanting, "*Mansei*: Live ten thousand years, Korea," and continued their pacifist strikes in the hope of attracting the attentions of the Western powers now assembled at the Versailles Peace Conference.

Money was being gathered all over the country to send to Syngman Rhee's Korean government-in-exile in Shanghai. My father had sent a large contribution, and had added his name to a petition of ex-nobles to the Japanese government, demanding an immediate restoration of our monarchy in recognition of independence from Japan. It was risky to sign one's name on so explicit a document, but Father knew the moment had come to make the appeal.

A few days later, Kwang-suk came back in a state of shock from a trip to the Suwon district. He had gone on an information-gathering mission for the local independence leader, upon hearing rumors that the Japanese had begun to massacre Koreans all over the country.

He had gone secretly to Chai-am-li, by a back road, to avoid the police, who were blockading the area to frustrate investigations. It was a small village in a peaceful valley, of no strategic importance. Kwang-suk arrived, disguised as a laborer. When he approached by the back road, he said there was a strange silence around the village. He could hear no cattle, or carts, or children crying.

As he came over the brow of the hill he saw that it had been decimated by fire. Only a few half-burned hovels survived, and cattle had been slaughtered. He found widows sitting in front of their gaping black doorways rocking back and forth, unable to speak to him. Their possessions had been turned to rubble and ashes; only stone kimchi jars remained.

One of the older girls finally spoke to him; Japanese soldiers had come and forced all of the men of the village into the wooden church for a compulsory public order meeting. Once all the men were inside, the soldiers stuck their rifles through all of the paper-screened windows and began shooting, while an officer set fire to the grass roof. Those who tried to flee by the door were shot. The handful of women who tried to enter the church to save their husbands were bayoneted to death, and the church was burned to its foundations. There were no survivors.

Kwang-suk went on to Su-chon, and with a sickened heart found that an identical plan had been carried out in the church there; same slaughter of all the male inhabitants; same burned-out homes; widows and orphans in a state of deep shock. He himself left the scene unable to speak. The word *Mansei* now made him gag.

We listened in disbelief in the safety of our barn. Nothing could express the emotions I felt. So extreme were the acts that Kwang-suk described that I could not at first engage with what had been done. That a pacifist movement should provoke such a reaction shocked everyone. The brutal catalog of Japanese reprisals was published the following week in the *Independence News*. Next it was reported that women had been stripped, beaten, raped, and sexually tortured in prisons. The prison deaths and rural killings went on.

As I rested from my experience in jail, and as my bruises and cuts began to heal, I felt more and more unwell inside. I could not bear to hear any more news of violence. I did not want to go to the meetings in the barn. I was suddenly exhausted, beyond any physical cause. All I wanted to do was to sleep, and to sleep still more.

Many years passed. Despite the sacrifices of life, the enormous drives of organized effort, and the petitions and appeals to august international councils, the world did not respond.

Eventually I married. My children were born. My honored father and mother died, and when the maid closed the mansion's shutters on the day of their funeral, an era passed that was never to return.

World War II broke out.

Still Korea stood in chains.

PART FOUR

MOTHER

CHAPTER EIGHT

School Days

Seoul

March 1944

I looked in the mirror, smoothed the bosom of my starched blouse so that it sat unrucked beneath the navy blue jacket of my school uniform, adjusted the elastic of one of my plaits, and straightened my badge. With an affectionate glance at my reflection, I turned to leave the bedroom, grabbing my felt hat, white gloves and satchel from the floor.

The noise of morning traffic filled the street outside our house. Taxis and buses sounded their horns and you could hear the streetcar clanging in the distance. Myung-hi was waiting for me by the front door in her uniform, which was identical to mine, only her buttoned jacket strained over her chubby stomach. My mother was in the kitchen calling to us not to be late for school.

"And did you see Jin-ho leaving the house? If you see him later, please tell him I want him home for supper. No nonsense." I agreed, and Myung-hi and I took our tin lunch boxes from her, warm with freshly cooked food, and placed mine carefully in my satchel. Myung-hi put her small gloved hand in mine, and together we left the house, the fresh March wind making me shiver a little.

It was only a short walk to school. For nearly eight years Myung-hi and I had been attending a Catholic girls' school in downtown Seoul. It was now run from the Japanese mainland and Korean teachers were required to undergo their training in Tokyo. A hysterical Nipponese nationalism had become a commonplace feature of our lives—World War II had been going on for five years.

Upon Father's return from Manchuria in August of 1936, our entire Yangyang estate was sold to the Japanese governor-general. Uncle Yong-lae and his family were refused permission by the Japanese to stay on in one of the cottages, as they had requested. Father had been obliged to buy them a small house in Sokcho, some miles away. Yong-lae had become a chronic drunk, and was too ill to travel far. Our sorrow was so profound that, eight years after the liquidation of the estate, we did not speak aloud of the loss of the land, or of the sad condition of my uncle.

Our family, too, had been forced to leave Yangyang, and Seoul was the only promising destination. Baby Uncle and a cousin at City Hall had helped us to find the house in Myong-dong, which was very central, and after a time, I came to accept and even relish our new life there.

Our one-story, wooden-gabled house was small, but comfortable, furnished with as many of our family's unsold Yangyang possessions as Mother had been able to squeeze inside to remind us of home in Kangwondo, but there was no denying that it was poky and undistinguished compared with what we had been used to. Myung-hi and I shared a room, and the small garden courtyard at the rear of the house was a travesty of the abundant green that I had been able to see from my old bedroom window.

To remind myself of Grandfather Kang's gardens, I planted a small row of tiger lilies in a corner of the cramped *jang* terrace. Apart from my lilies—which weren't doing too well—I had no particular fondness for our new home. It was a daily reminder of our changed fortunes, but I was old enough to begin to grasp the seriousness of everyone's privations under the Japanese, and felt lucky to be settled comfortably.

At first, the shock of losing our family seat and leaving Yangyang had been so overwhelming that I noticed little about our new surroundings; I was grateful for the bustle and distraction of being in such a lively place as Seoul. As the capital city, there were naturally great numbers of sophisticated people there in 1936, but I was unprepared for the exotic and cosmopolitan mix of White Russians, Manchurians, Chinese, Americans, and Europeans to be found there staffing the embassies, teaching and attending the universities, working in communications and the arts. And of course, a large Japanese population lived there as well — in all the best houses, we couldn't help noticing.

But in the following year, the mood of the city became frightening. The Sino-Japanese War had broken out, and in December 1937, the Japanese sacked Nanking. With the Nanking massacre, there was a sudden, aggressive show of military intention in the streets. Although Korea had been under Japanese military dictatorship for decades with a constant police presence, I had been sheltered in the country, and to me, this heavy-handed display of force was novel and terrifying.

No one was certain how many civilians had been killed in Nanking, but there were rumors first of tens of thousands of dead, and then came news of the killings of hundreds of thousands of unarmed Chinese civilians. My father heard foreign reports on his contraband shortwave radio. Members of the Korean independence movement exiled in China sent news of dismaying tortures inflicted on civilians by Japanese soldiers. Father's colleagues in the underground resistance movement discussed little else at that time.

Although Father himself had been tortured many years before by the Japanese, he refused to tell us children about it, so it was not until the rape of Nanking that I first heard of their cruelty.

As I said, following the siege, there were armed soldiers everywhere in Seoul and full military parades with tanks. Loudspeakers blasted out the deafening and incoherent sound of war bulletins screamed out in Japanese. The shouting broadcasters annoyed me—with the loud volume of the *tannoy*, there was no need: it was doubly aggressive. My brother Jin-ho watched the parades condescendingly, finding the crude display amusing, but I wasn't so sure. There was a thuglike menace about the steel-helmeted Japanese soldiers with their huge samurai swords, and I didn't like passing them on the street, even when accompanied by my mother. That winter the normally friendly people in our neighborhood became quiet and suspicious, literally looking twice over their shoulders at passersby. The kind Japanese woman across the street, married to a Korean, had stopped coming out of her house altogether.

However, over the last few years, the military tension in Seoul had diminished somewhat. The Japanese were so busy fighting battles abroad that Korea, already long subdued, received less strident attention from their armed forces.

Last year, I had overheard Father joyously telling Baby Uncle about the Cairo Declaration, which had been broadcast on shortwave: The United States, Britain, and China had jointly proclaimed that ". . . in due course, Korea shall become free and independent." Although it was frustrating to have to continue to wait for freedom, with this publicly aired declaration Father said it was the first real signal that there might be an end to the war, and with it, Japanese rule. To hear that *the outside world* wanted to curb the Japanese gave Father crucial new hope. . . . I was too young to have strategic hopes.

What I understood about the war was basic. For six years, young Korean men of all backgrounds had been drafted and forced to die for the Japanese flag. My brother had avoided the draft only through well-timed bouts of illness. Two and a half million Koreans were conscripted into forced labor for the Japanese at home, and nearly a million had been sent abroad to work.

Something called the Volunteer Labor Corps also had been set up, rounding up schoolgirls as young as thirteen to work for the war effort in Japan and China with the promise of "study in Japan." This was later revealed to be forced sexual slavery for the Japanese troops that took place in special hidden camps established for that purpose. Girls were ordered—with the threat of death—to submit to sexual relations with long queues of hostile Japanese soldiers, who often maimed their breasts and genitalia with bayonets and knives. Girls' enlistment was heavier in the countryside, where people were poorer and more gullible, and progressive education was harder to come by.

For the past six months, Father had been living undercover in Kangwon-do, having had to flee Seoul in the middle of the night to escape being captured and taken to Japan into forced labor. A friend in government tipped him off about the household searches, and he had missed the raid on our house by two nights. Father slipped away to the country quietly, and the subsequent police search seemed a strangely routine event during such warped times. We were all just thankful to have avoided more serious troubles. After a bit of string-pulling, Father was now ensconced in a job at a local coal mine, with forged papers certifying that he had held the position for several years. We had heard nothing from him now for months. It was dangerous to write letters, as mail was censored.

Korea had grown even poorer during the war. The Japanese immigrants in Korea were given the best jobs at higher wages than those paid to better educated Koreans, who were now forced to take whatever menial jobs they could. All of our natural and manufactured resources went directly into the Japanese war effort. Food, minerals, fuel, trees—even our metal chamber pots were collected and given to the Japanese army. Although my mother had pleaded with the soldiers, they confiscated my grandfather Min's silvertopped cane, his gift from the king, to melt down for munitions. It was one of my father's most treasured keepsakes. Sickened, we agreed not to tell him it had been turned into enemy bullets.

Since Father's absence, we now kept the wireless on pretty constantly; Mother for news of international events, and we children for the music. When Father was home he had a habit of switching it off automatically when he entered a room, so much did the blatant propaganda irritate him. Newspaper articles and wireless features were, of course, loaded with pro-Japanese opinion—which I took to be general opinion.

Being a rather dreamy and coddled teenager, I didn't really know what the war meant or why anyone was fighting. My mother and father would never speak to us of such grown-up matters as war. Apart from the disagreeable curiosity of food rationing, I would even say that the backdrop of a world war was positively exciting, now that the surly, depressing troops had left the city. As time went on, the dangling threat of Father's imprisonment and the reports of people being killed no longer felt real to me.

While Father was away, my mother had converted to Catholicism, urged on by her devout sister, Aunt Chosan. This did not seem terribly significant at the time, as Catholic missions had become accepted even by conservative members of society as being respectable and even quite tenable. I sensed that my mother, separated from her family in Yangyang, needed something extraordinary from which to draw strength now that she had to run the household singlehanded. I did not understand the deeper mysteries of her conversion, but saw that she missed Father very much, and Jin-ho was becoming thoroughly unmanageable. While waiting for Jin-ho to return late at night, the rosary beads in her pale hand were a visible sign of comfort during the hours she endured alone.

Myung-hi and I arrived at school at eight o'clock sharp. We separated, and lined up for our attendance check before entering the ivy-covered building. We attended Sook Myung College, an exclusive Catholic girls' school. Although my father was against our attending it at first—he was a staunch Taoist, and quite a reactionary—he was eventually convinced by Mother's arguments for the high academic reputation of the school and for its modern facilities. There were rumored to be seven hundred *yangban* applicants for one hundred places, so our winning places there pleased Father well.

My school was a world in itself: an imposing, redbrick Victorian folly set in green parkland, containing its own elementary and high schools, cathedral, convent, monastery, presbyteries, gardeners' and caretakers' houses, and even its own hospital. King Kojong had been a benefactor, and had personally approved the school's European design. Once a year we received a royal visit on Founder's Day— nowadays minor princes and princesses came to the school. To us, the royal visit was mainly an occasion for mass haircuts and uniform- ironing. For the staff it caused a far greater excitement, exalting their morale as well as exercising their rarely used roll of red carpet, giving the gravel a good raking, festooning the front steps with gay flowers, and giving floors and shoes alike a glassy shine.

Within the school's long, echoing corridors we filed two-abreast in strict formation, but whenever teachers were not looking, my friends and I broke into gleeful, skidding runs on the polished floors, and held impromptu sliding competitions at the end of the queue. A pleasant smell of cheap hand soap permeated the halls and classrooms.

Before the nine o'clock bell rang, I crowded around the potbellied stove in my classroom along with the others to snatch a place to keep my tin lunch box warm. Then we performed frenetic physical exercises in the inner courtyard, ending with dreaded cold showers in scratchy black wool tank suits. This was followed by an almost equally unpopular fifteen-minute meditation period, during which we were obliged to sit cross-legged on a hard wooden floor without moving. The discomfort of this position always made one of my legs fall asleep, and produced in me a most unspiritual state of aggravation. After this daily test of limb and temper, the school band played the Japanese national anthem, and Miss Chang then led us in compulsory school prayer, in which we all had to pray for Japan to win the war.

We were kept extremely busy. Besides our academic classes, we went to Mass and choir practice, there was Bible study, and domestic science in ruffled white aprons. There was also a punishing round of well-drilled volleyball games and gymnastics sessions, supplemented by jump rope and hopscotch, and marbles tournaments in the playground. The sound of our zealous gym instructor's blasting whistle still reverberates in my ears.

With the war on, our school staged precision air-raid drills and militaristic mini-parades, for which we sported special blue serge uniforms with nasty bloomers, and carried first-aid kits containing tourniquets and exciting-looking tubes of antiseptic first-aid cream. To get us properly into a war mood, we even spent the odd afternoon digging a decorative trench behind the school.

Frankly, I loved the air-raid drills. Sitting in the underground bunker behind the kitchens was a welcome diversion from our more boring classes. Sometimes I sneaked out to go to the bakery across from Myong-dong Cathedral where I would buy hot, soft white rolls dusted with brown sugar and cinnamon. The bakery, Ton Katzu Ya, was a dusty, empty place run by a grumpy Japanese couple who never smiled or said hello, even though I was a regular, risking punishment for the sake of their mouthwatering rolls.

Although a good student, I was lazy. I suffered particular ennui in Japanese composition class. The plain and po-faced Miss Takagawa, with her thin face, steel-rimmed spectacles, and bowl-shaped haircut, made us keep a daily diary in Japanese. To amuse myself, fill up space, and tease Miss Takagawa, I included quotes from my favorite books—ponderous choice phrases from Balzac, Gide, and Tolstoy, which I grafted onto my juvenile observations about friends and family. To my amazement, it took her two weeks to catch on, but unfortunately for me, she did.

At the beginning of Monday's lesson, she called me up to the blackboard in front of the class. There she surprised me by saying nothing, but wheeled around and gave me a hard slap on the cheek. Pupils were often hit by the Japanese teachers.

"You are a liar and a cheat! You set a bad example to the other girls! You must swear never to lie again!" The blow to the side of my face stung badly, and I was shocked by the severity of her reaction. I had just been fooling around, not taking the exercise seriously. It was hardly a case of *lying*, I itched to point out once I had recovered from the blow, but for once kept quiet.

"Repeat after me: 'I swear never to lie and cheat Miss Takagawa again,'" she said, her face distorted with a rage bordering on hatred. I looked helplessly around the class; some of my schoolfriends looked horrified, while others giggled unkindly behind their cupped hands. Anger boiled in me as I repeated aloud Miss Takagawa's little baby punishment phrase. From then onward I nursed a stubborn resentment against Japanese composition class. Although I had to keep that stupid diary every day, I subtly avenged myself by filling it with elementary joke-drivel that slipped past the literal-minded Miss Takagawa.

I also hated calligraphy class. I was no good at it. My teachers told me I was impatient and sloppy, and this was true. I tended to cram a week's worth of calligraphy homework into one night so that I could get on with reading eyeball-popping Edgar Allan Poe stories—or *Edogawa Rampo*—as my Japanese teacher called him.

I loved my English class. It was taught by the intense little Mr. Itami, who, according to rumor, had had his two front teeth extracted so that he could better pronounce the dreaded *th* sound that most Orientals were incapable of mastering, but he was kind and enthusiastic, and I liked him very much.

But why was it that all compulsory classes were dull? During history class, which consisted of the wide-bottomed teacher, Miss Kendo, scrabbling Japanese war dates importantly onto the blackboard for the class's duration, several of us used to read novels under our desks. Another was "Japanese Tea Ceremony." At first we were quite amused at this strange requirement—anything non-academic had immediate and obvious attractions—but repeating over and over the dinky movements and slow ritualistic gestures demonstrated, my friends and I began to find it too silly to enjoy.

It was in a class like Japanese Tea Ceremony that the vast difference between Korean and Japanese national character revealed itself and, for me, seemed to undermine their cultural assimilation goals. Even the simple contrast in our respective approaches to food bore this out. To me, Japanese cuisine was bland and overly dainty, while Korean food was robust, complex, and mouthwateringly spicy. The occasional bit of raw fish and rice was delicious, but the poverty of it—its deliberate minimalism and the limited culinary enterprise involved—was monotonous and peasantlike to Koreans raised on a more varied cuisine, involving piquant, labor-intensive marinades and hot sauces.

This alone convinced me that I would never be the Japanese citizen they were trying to mold me into. I felt the same resistance to their art and manners. Although it was impossible not to admire the pretti-

ness of the works of Hiroshige and Utamuro and the skill of many of
their ceramicists, in my inexpert opinion it was all too decorative, and
did not move me deeply. As for manners, while I respected their formality, their extra-polite behavior struck me as rather phony. Still, that
is a digression. All in all, I was grateful that the Japanese Tea
Ceremony involved no homework.

Despite an unoriginal antipathy to homework, I managed to be
something of a star in my class: popular; quite bossy, with messengers
and slaves, though I rarely carried out threats or stayed cross for long.
I won prizes for languages and music, and even sang solos for the
school choir that were broadcast on the wireless. I was terribly proud
of that, and so, predictably, was my entire family. Sensing that I was
musical, Baby Uncle brought me back a violin from his last trip to
Harbin, never guessing the effect it might have on my life. The violin
slid along my arm and cheek as if it had always been there, a natural
extension of my own limb. My mother found me a violin teacher at
once.

Despite living in a police state, I have to say that I was enjoying
my little life. None of us questioned it deeply that classes were held in
Japanese, or that speaking Korean in school was forbidden and carried
a fine. After all, the teaching of Korean language and history had long
been banned by the government. All of our essays obviously had to
be written in Japanese, and we had to converse in Japanese around
teachers. During volleyball games I used to shout in Korean, but having had to ask my mother twice for the fine money, I quickly learned
to be excited publicly in Japanese. Not easy, as the languages are
emphatically different.

We were even given Japanese names in school. I hated mine:
Michiko Takayama. Thank goodness none of my friends ever tried to
call me that. I was extremely proud of the ancient Min name. To my
prejudiced ear, Japanese names lacked gravitas and languor, their
mincing, staccato rhythms were derisory: Kinky, Junky, Junko

Anyway, you couldn't change people's *names*. It simply wasn't possible.

Westerners might not comprehend our outward compliance, but we were trained from birth to uphold as a virtue the Confucian law of obedience. We learned to say *hai*, yes, to everything in Japanese, but to feel *anio*, no, in Korean, in our hearts.

By now I had grown to love Seoul. I was sure that it was the most beautiful and thrilling city in the world. And at fourteen, everything felt new and fun. I loved walking through the ancient city gates—North, South, East, and West—and passing by the important-looking railway station, content not to go anywhere myself, but knowing that adventure could begin here at any moment with the purchase of a ticket.

Short of pocket money, friends and I entertained ourselves simply, swinging our satchels on meandering walks in Piwon, the royal gardens of Changduk Palace; nearly eighty acres of lush woodland. We also met up in the melancholy summer pavilions of Kyongbok Palace, where minor members of our royal family still lived, and gazed at the shuttered windows across the lotus pond. The inner circle, including the prince regent, had been taken to Japan under armed guard, where they were living "in exile."

Garden visits also served a nutritional purpose. During summer storms, my friend Kum-ji and I went on naughty outings to the botanical gardens, where it was fine to admire the dripping peonies in solitude, the park guards having fled to their barracks. Entire orchards lay unwatched. With one eye on the footpath, we calculatedly gorged ourselves on as many peaches, plums, apricots, and nectarines as we could, and then I filled my roomy raincoat pockets to bulging point with wet, precious cherries to take home to Myung-hi and Jin-ho.

Most weekdays after school I walked Myung-hi home, and then skipped off down Chong-lo Avenue to buy a bowl of watery soup and rice crackers with my meager allowance. We were on rations during the war, of course. Despite the boiled potato and fish-oil jelly supplement we got at school, I was always hungry by the end of the day. After soup and crackers I went to the public library downtown, where I passed much of my spare time. As this was where I did my homework, I was allowed to stay as long as I liked. Waving at various classmates, I installed myself at one of the long communal tables, and tried always to find a seat near one of the small French windows, where the light was better. The library was bliss; freedom from prying grown-ups keeping tabs, or asking one to perform tiresome errands.

After the library, my friends and I often stopped off at the Cinema Foto Shop, where we would buy photographs of favorite movie stars to keep in our school satchels for spot perusals. So far I had collected Ronald Colman, Jean Gabin, Fernandel, Robert Taylor, Gary Cooper, Vivien Leigh, Laurence Olivier, and Takamine. Jean Gabin was Baby Uncle's favorite actor, so although his charms were rather too subtle for my appreciation, I cultivated an interest in him anyway, hoping that some of Baby Uncle's sophistication might rub off on me.

Occasionally, Baby Uncle took me and a friend to the cinema, which was a fantastic treat. Although we were usually confined to watching sunny Deanna Durbin and Shirley Temple films to preserve our innocence, we sometimes convinced him to take us to a gloomy French film, which was the height of pleasure.

Being fledgling teenagers, we were obsessed by our looks, deprived of glamour by the military chastity of our Japanese uniforms. It seemed perfectly natural that my chief concern, in the midst of our country's brutal subjugation, should be whether or not I should exchange my plaits for a permanent wave. And, of course, there was much ginger experimentation with my mother's smuggled lipstick in the school lavatories.

However, as World War II continued, one's vanity was checked by the school's increased drive to aid the war effort. We spent entire afternoons sequestered in the gymnasium wearing lumpy serge parade uniforms, sewing quilts for the Japanese army and chipping mica into little flakes for paint. I didn't really know how the war was going, nor did I care very much. I was too busy to think.

In addition to the free child labor the Japanese were getting from our expensive fee-paying school, the administrators even had the temerity to post a notice on the bulletin board requesting that students leave their families and join the Volunteer Labor Corps abroad. As I said before, no one then knew that this organization was the front for the so-called Comfort Women. My friends and I thought that being asked to leave home at our age was going very far indeed. We were not the simpletons such notices took us for. Maybe we even had a sixth sense that there was something funny about it. Not one girl in our school signed up.

My friends and I exploited our status as schoolchildren as much as we could, and appreciated the freedom it gave us from the onerous wartime responsibilities we saw adults having to perform. For once I felt lucky to be female, and not to have to think about killing people, among other unfeasibly grim tasks.

After the wrench of leaving Yangyang and the sorrows of our family's dispersal, I did not like to recall the past, and indeed I refused to remember it. At bedtime, I tried with all my might to forget the lush green canopies that had sheltered me, and to prefer the noise of traffic to the sound of wind roaring through leaves. I set my mind toward work and play with great determination and practicality. I kept out of trouble. After all, I now had the violin! This, I told myself, was more than enough for me.

But if my life at that time was jolly and hopeful, I am sad to say that my brother Jin-ho was acting out an altogether darker fate.

As Father had feared, Jin-ho turned out to be a rather talented painter, and was not conforming at all with Father's wish that he should become the family's first professional and our financial savior. The Mins had produced many artists and poets through the centuries, some good, some bad, but Father felt that this was neither the time nor place for being an artist: there was a war on, and his own drubbing experience in Manchuria had told him that to cling to traditional *yangban* attitudes and pursuits was to be doomed in the brash new future.

I had not seen Jin-ho that morning to tell him to come home early, as I'd promised *Omma*. I guessed that he was skipping school again. He was supposedly studying economics at Hanyang University, but mostly he went to the pictures, or to the museum, and often he visited a barmaid's lodgings, where he kept an easel and went to paint. I know about that only because I once followed him there.

Although I knew he was hanging around with a raffish crowd, I was still shocked and hurt to find this evidence of a secret, rather seedy adult life, away from us. When I saw Jin-ho again after following him, I was uncomfortably suspicious of everything he did and said. Although he behaved no differently at home, he now felt like a stranger to me, a double agent.

Father's sudden removal to the provinces was a godsend for Jin-ho, who had become the focus of all of Father's discontent. Jin-ho had grown up to be very handsome; fair, tall, and thin, with expressive black eyes, childish long lashes, slender hands and wrists, and shiny, floppy hair. He was terribly romantic looking; even as his sister, I could see that. Jin-ho was also funny, witty, and hugely intelligent. To me, he was just right.

Yet, according to Father, Jin-ho looked like "a complete pansy." He was undisciplined in his schoolwork, and showed signs of unabashed artyness in his dress and speech. Convinced that Jin-ho was too skinny, Father bought him a punching bag, and made him lift weights every day. In addition, Jinho was required to get up at five-thirty each morning to begin these grueling exercises. As part of his "spiritual training," Jin-ho was made to follow the exercises with marathon early-morning runs, ending in cold showers—for extra mental toughness.

When Jin-ho showed no obvious signs of filling out, Father hired a fitness instructor to teach him to box. All of this, Jin-ho loathed. At first he went along with it to keep Father from harping on about his weakness, but being constitutionally languid and mentally quick, he soon grew bored and resentful. Despite all of Father's efforts to turn him into "more of a man," Jin-ho remained as skinny as ever.

The only real change was that Jin-ho became angrier. He had already run away to the country twice, and had been picked up hitch-hiking by the police and kept in prison overnight. He was lucky to have escaped national service detention as a result. For this public act of filial disobedience, Father horse-whipped Jin-ho in the courtyard.

I remember it so well because this violence was new and shocking in our household. I felt sick hearing the terrible low, vibrating snap of the whip, and Jin-ho's pitiful, stifled cries. My mother's imploded grief was almost equally distressing to witness. What was happening to us? It felt unreal, nightmarish. It also struck me so forcibly because I thought it would be the only time the beating would ever happen.

But I was wrong. Jin-ho skipped school. Jin-ho missed an exam. Jin-ho stole money from Mother. Jin-ho had joined an outlawed Youth Independence Movement. Jin-ho ran away again. And there were savage beatings for these failings.

"But, *Omma*, I'm *bored*, I tell you," Jin-ho had complained to Mother in his unprepossessing way.

"For shame. Education does not exist for your entertainment, you know that," Mother answered curtly, looking up from writing a letter. Unlike Father, she had to force herself to adopt a harsh tone with her son.

"But there's no point, Mother. I don't want to be a Japanese civil servant, I want to be an artist. I still want to be. Despite everything."

My mother sighed. "You *know* how your father feels about that. Why go over old ground? Why keep fighting against him? You will never convince him, Jin-ho. Don't be so foolish. I refuse to speak of it with you again. You must recognize your duty to your family, and that is all there is to say on the matter. I would like to sympathize with you more, but you are only creating your own troubles."

"Mother. You don't even *try* to understand. You don't respect my gift, I have a duty to that gift as well as to my family," said Jin-ho, lowering his eyes. Mother was stung by this frank remark, and could say nothing, torn between her absent husband and her only son.

Jin-ho's continuing defiance had obviously been bitter for my father. Not only was his son disobedient, but during the past year Jin-ho had returned home drunk enough times for Father to worry, and to remind him of his brother's early demise. My mother had told Father he was being oversensitive, but *Aboji* was frightened of the same destruction overtaking his own son. Ambitious for Jin-ho, and his family pride still inflamed by the lost estate, Father was determined to prevent further disgrace. Father would never admit to being afraid, but we knew that his helplessness had made him overanxious.

As it was, Father had been sending money to Uncle Yong-lae's family for years and bailing out Baby Uncle, who, as the youngest son, was not really expected to contribute to the family purse. Although with his excellent court education Father might have obtained a high-ranking job working for the Japanese, his pride had not allowed him to contemplate it. Our rich neighbors in Seoul worked for the Japanese trading in munitions. But knowing this, Father had never spoken to them or even once discussed them, neither during nor after the war. To him, they were traitors; they simply did not exist.

Wartime opportunities were scarce, and mostly mired in the black market. Before fleeing Seoul for a time Father had tried being a dried cuttlefish broker, a distributor of wedding cakes, and a broadcaster, but to be honest, he was not terribly good at business, nor did he enjoy the confinement of an office. His mind was discursive and philosophical rather than tightly focused. Although he began his ventures with genuine goodwill, it did not take long for disenchantment to arrive as the unlikeliness of his endeavors began to sink in. Although Father had long ago cut off his pigtail and removed his tall hat, he was still a *yangban* lord, and could not so easily change.

While we were naturally worried that the Japanese authorities might discover Father's hiding place (he would be sent to prison), we were grateful that he was temporarily spared the worry of employment conundrums, and relieved that he had escaped the fate of forced labor in Japan. This we all knew, would have destroyed him.

According to Baby Uncle, who had managed to visit him at the coal mine, Father was happier than he'd seen him for some time—perhaps he had merely said this to assuage Mother's worries. Baby Uncle said Father was "highly comfortable" staying with the family of an old friend, the boss of the coal mine who knew the Min clan. He would not allow Father to do anything but the lightest administrative work. Apparently, Father was spending most of his days in his office reading novels, and gazing out at his beloved Kangwon Mountains.

Father's absence also temporarily relaxed the strife between himself and Jin-ho. My brother was now eighteen, and rarely around the house. He was also seldom at university despite the beatings his truancy had cost him. In common with some teenage boys, Jin-ho only seemed to appear at mealtimes, seasoning our dinner conversation with sparing, vinegary remarks.

Tonight, as we sat around the table, with our rice, kimchi, and dried fish rations, Jin-ho's presence was softer than it had been for some time. He was quite vague when Myung-hi asked him if he would help her with her art assignment. My mother and I glanced at each other over across the table. Jin-ho barely ate anything.

"Do eat something, *yubo*," said Mother, using an old term of endearment.

"What? . . . I'm not hungry. I'm peaceful."

I scrutinized his movements to see if he was drunk, but that did not seem to be the case. Then I looked into his eyes, and they looked strange, the pupils dilated. As the meal progressed, Jin-ho relaxed his body until it slumped against the wall, and as we were taking tea, his head began to nod.

My mother prodded him. "This is too much, *yubo*. Sit up straight. If you're tired, please go to bed at once. Are you feeling all right? There's no reason not to go to bed if you're ill," she said worriedly. "I won't have this sort of behavior at the table. You may leave the room now."

I was rigid with curiosity; perhaps he had taken some drug. I remembered seeing an odd-looking glass pipe at the window of the barmaid's rooms. But I could hardly believe he would be so wicked. Myung-hi, suspecting nothing, placidly munched her rice cake. Mother would certainly never have guessed that he might be smoking opium. To her, Jin-ho was still an eight-year-old boy. I felt stricken at the seriousness of such a possibility. No one I knew even discussed opium-taking; it was taboo in our circle, a great sin.

Jin-ho did not reply. His head hung at a strange angle. "Jin-ho,

I'm speaking to you. Here. Have some tea, you must go to bed at once," urged Mother, placing a celadon cup into his clammy hands. Jin-ho's eyes rolled sideways to look into hers, and after a few moments, he dropped the cup, spilling tea over the linen tablecloth. Myung-hi jumped up in surprise, and Mother and I dragged Jin-ho— who was heavier than he looked—off to his room.

"He must have some sort of virus. Perhaps it's influenza," Mother whispered to me behind his drooping head. "I will give him some ginseng and honey. At least it wasn't rudeness," she said, as if bad manners were the ultimate shame. I said nothing, and left Mother to undress him. Having seen the stubborn, broad maternal faith in her eyes, I dared not contradict her. She believed that nursery remedies could still fix him, and there was a part of me which wanted to believe that they could heal him, too. But deep down, I knew that something terrible was wrong. A black stain was slowly spreading over his soul. I felt that nothing could help him.

That night, lying in bed, I was anxious and distressed. Myung-hi slept on in ignorance. Despite Father's brutal treatment of him over the years, I could not excuse Jin-ho. We had loved him tenderly, my mother, sister, and I—and he returned it with this apparent scorn. I was angry with him, unable to understand how he could desert us, abandon us now, when Father was away, and he had the chance, at last, to make things right, to show his true strength.

I thought back to when we were small children in Yangyang. I had lived for his jokes and his inadvertent kindnesses. Jin-ho had always been selfish, but I forgave him, because he did not mean to be so. I protected and loved him anyway. Lately, protecting him had been my only link with him. On his side, he could give nothing. It was an agony to lose my limited sway with him.

Despite being angry, my fondness for him was so strong that it hurt. But there was nowhere to put it now; Jin-ho could not receive it. My love seeped out of him like milk from a cracked bowl. Although he slept in the room next door, for months it had seemed as if his room were empty. I wept as if he were dead.

CHAPTER NINE

A Radio Broadcast

Seoul
15 August 1945

On this particular morning I awoke to the sound of a horsefly droning near my ear. As the buzzing noise grew louder, it turned out to be the engine of an airplane. During the past few days, there had been more air raids than usual. That morning, the closeness of the plane made me feel uneasy in my bed. Nine days earlier Hiroshima had been bombed, and Nagasaki had been attacked just a few days later.

Half-asleep, I noticed from the heat of the sun that it must have been rather late. Being the summer holidays, it didn't much matter what time one got up. The weather had been unusually hot for weeks, and I felt a bit groggy. I moved my face out of the warm, blinding path of a sunbeam, and allowed my nerves to recover, lingering under the protective coverlet, limbs rediscovering in the indented mattress the delicious position that had yielded the night's most satisfying repose.

Just as I was slipping back into a dream, Myung-hi pattered into the room and stood over me. I opened an eye and saw her gap-tooth and pigtail-tips bobbing above me.

"When are you getting up? I want you to take me swimming. *Please!*"

I groaned and flipped over.

"Daddy says I can only go to the swimming hole if you take me."

"It's too early to go swimming. Leave me alone."

"Oh, *please*. Besides, it's not early at all. I've been up for *hours*. *Omma* says you should be up anyway."

"Yes, yes . . . We'll see. Now go away, and give me a bit of peace."

"If I go away, will you *promise* to take me swimming?"

"I'll think about it."

Out of the corner of my eye, I could see that Myung-hi looked disappointed, but recovered enough to skip out of the room. The exertion of being cross had thoroughly woken me, and I could not relocate the elusive, seductive island of sleep so recently enjoyed. I considered the option of staying angry at Myung-hi for the rest of the day just to punish her, but in this hot weather, maintaining the pique would be more costly than it was worth. I threw off the light silk coverlet, and rose from my bed, stretching lazily.

I looked into the courtyard and saw my father sitting on the step in his shirtsleeves, reading his newspaper with intense concentration. The sight of him gladdened and lifted me. I was not yet used to seeing him around the house again; it still felt like a prolonged special occasion for him to be with us after nearly a year in hiding. After the Allies' demand for Japan's surrender last month, Father had decided to risk moving back to Seoul. I waved at him from my window.

"Ah! Lazybones!" Father called out, not looking up from the newspaper.

"*Aboji!* How hot is it?"

"Hot . . . Look at your lilies. They're dying."

"Don't say that! I'll come and water them."

Father nodded, distracted, and went on reading his paper.

"The emperor is going to speak on the wireless today," he announced, jumping up and going inside. I put on a cotton shift and slippers, and went into the empty kitchen for some cold barley tea and melon. Myung-hi sat in the shade of the back step, talking to her rag doll. Mother had gone to Mass, and Jin-ho was off somewhere. As usual, no one knew where he was.

I heard Father's shortwave radio crackling and whistling through the thin wall of the kitchen. Then the doorbell rang, and I opened the door to Baby Uncle, who looked cool and spry in a pale seersucker suit and Panama hat. He was carrying a couple of books under his arm. I peeked at the spines, they were novels by Tanisaki and Ishigawa. His passion for Japanese literature eclipsed his political sentiments. Of all the Min brothers, Gong-lae had the most intellectual flair, making daring, flashy connections between the exalted and the mundane, and spouting impressive foreign literary quotations just at the right moment in an argument. However, Baby Uncle was undisciplined with it, and Father was far from impressed. Uncle pinched my cheek.

"How's my great musician, then? Still finding time to practice despite breaking all those hearts?" His smile was broad and easy.

"You're the one who breaks hearts, Uncle."

Baby Uncle bowed at the compliment, and swept past me to Father's study.

"Bring me some cold cider, would you, niece?"

I went down to the dark cellar, and struggled to fill a pitcher from the vast two-gallon jug which nestled among the melting ice blocks and wood shavings. I climbed the stairs carefully to avoid spilling the sloshing liquid, then brought a tray into Father's study, and handed glasses of cider to Father and Baby Uncle, who were hovering by the wireless, enveloped in a veil of Uncle's pungent pipe smoke. I tucked myself into a corner of the room and pretended to read a book in order to be allowed to listen to them talking.

"What do you think of Russia declaring war on Japan?" Baby Uncle asked Father.

"The more the better. They'll have to surrender now."

"But what about the huge Communist Russian army marching into Korea as if it owned the place?"

"Well, there are thousands of expatriate Koreans fighting against the Japanese in that army. Let's hope the Russian presence is just temporary. To accept the surrender of Japanese troops, like they said."

"You really think they'll surrender, then?"

Father narrowed his eyes. "Eventually, yes. But what then? It will be dangerous for us; there are vultures waiting to pick our corpse."

"Who are the vultures, Daddy?"

"Americans, Russians, Chinese . . . It seems they all want a slice of us. But don't go repeating what we say here. I mean that quite seriously, *yubo*."

I agreed eagerly, and then went to water my lilies, which I had forgotten to do earlier. Their yellowing stems were parched and wilted, and I felt slightly guilty as the soil at their feet drained the water instantaneously. The stuffy cloister of the courtyard was too hot for human beings as well as plants. Not entirely welcome in Father's study, I went out onto the front steps to get some air and see if I could spot *Omoni* returning home from the cathedral. Father and Baby Uncle were absorbed in their discussion, which they broke off abruptly now and then to observe some point which was being made on the radio. Myung-hi followed me out of doors, but sensitive to the strange mood of the moment, did not ask me again to take her swimming, and, even more unusually, said nothing at all as she stood by my side.

All of Seoul lay silent. The only sounds were the odd barking dog and the isolated clang of a distant streetcar. The street was empty and ghostly; many were fighting on the front lines, working in factories, or had been shipped abroad to uncertain destinies in Japan, China, and

Manchuria. Baby Uncle had just been recruited as a translator in a munitions factory in Harbin, and would soon be leaving us.

The August sun burned like molten liquid over the front step and the baking street, and the facades of all the houses were bleached out by a close white haze. The smell of sewage and tides wafted in on a faint breeze from Chunghak-dong Bridge. I could not see our mother approaching, so I went to my room to practice the violin, and Myung-hi returned quiescently to her doll.

Soon I heard the front door slamming, and knew that it was Jin-ho arriving, rather than my mother, who did not slam doors. I felt intense relief to hear his footsteps in the hall. One could never be certain when he would turn up, and with Father back, he tended to stay away more than before. I poked my head around my bedroom door, welcomed him with a specially bright smile. My brother waved laconically in my direction as he headed for the kitchen. Jin-ho cut a rather stark figure these days. He had grown even thinner, and was now a member of an underground nationalist military youth organization whose chief trademark, as far as I could see, was a brutal crewcut. I thought Father might have been pleased by his butch change of image, but quite the reverse: Father was convinced that Jin-ho was falling under the spell of the group's Communists—an end worse than Art.

Mother soon returned, and sat in the dining room to catch her breath. Perspiring lightly, she fanned herself slowly with a paper fan, ivory rosary beads deposited in a swirl on the table, and high heels kicked off. I brought her a cool glass of cider.

"Quick, all of you: come at once!" shouted Baby Uncle.

My mother, sister, brother, and I looked at each other quizzically and obeyed him. We stood in a circle around the wooden RKO radio where Father and my uncle were seated, transfixed.

The static was atrocious, but we could just make out the announcer, speaking in Japanese on the national radio station—the most somber tones imaginable—that it was precisely twelve o'clock. Accompanying background music was funerary. At this moment, the announcer—unbelievably—instructed the nation to stand, wherever we were, whatever we were doing, as we were about to hear news of the gravest import. We were already standing. Then the Japanese national anthem was played. We all looked at each other blankly. Who had died? I wondered.

Then there was a lengthy, charged silence that froze me to my mother's side, and seemed to hold us all in tense expectation. A weird voice came on the air: an old man's voice, high and strangulated, speaking in such an antique formal manner that I could barely understand him. Of course, it was Emperor Hirohito. We all looked aghast at each other. The emperor had never before addressed the public. His voice was shaking badly, and although I could not understand the individual words he was using, I got the drift of his extraordinary speech all the same: it was an announcement of Japan's total surrender. Korea was to be liberated.

My blood tingled at the solemnity of the moment. With my mouth hanging open, I looked at my mother and father, both shocked, unable to speak. Then gradually from the street came the odd sound of front doors slamming, footsteps running on the pavement, and muffled whoops of exhilaration. Someone started hooting a car horn. Myung-hi and I squeezed each other's hands tight. Jin-ho impulsively lifted my mother off her feet. My father, overcome by the awesome news, walked into the hallway and sat down, apart from us. Averting his head, Father wept silently, shoulders shaking.

Later, when the acute shock had ebbed away, and we were all sitting in the relative cool of the shaded courtyard, Father became animated, his speech rambling.

"I can't believe it. I can't believe it has come so soon. It has come! We have waited and waited. . . . Our whole lives, we have lived under this sentence. . . ." He spoke as if he had been awakened from a deep sleep and was surrounded by strangers. He looked at my mother as if she were the only one who understood him. Baby Uncle nodded at his brother's comment, and lit his pipe contemplatively. "I can't quite take it in, either. The war is over, too, thank God," he said, smoke curling from the corner of his mouth—not that the war had greatly curtailed his pleasure-seeking, as my father was fond of pointing out.

"I shall still go to Harbin if the government needs me, mind you. Besides, we shall need the money." So far, Baby Uncle had managed to avoid forced labor and the draft through imaginative applications of his charm.

"Shouldn't we be celebrating or something?" asked Jin-ho, looking at Mother expectantly.

"I *am* celebrating," Father said evenly.

"I know what you mean, darling, maybe I can scrape up some extra rice tonight," Mother smiled. Jin-ho looked disappointed, and stalked off awkwardly to his room, frustrated in his hopes for an excuse to drink. I was sorry to see him go away, despite his tetchiness, but glad that he had not left the house altogether. Although he was still drinking quite a lot, I had not seen any glaring evidence of further opium-taking. His visits to the barmaid's lodgings continued, but he had become far more discreet about his exploits since Father's return.

Father relaxed as soon as Jin-ho left, and became more animated, chattering to Uncle about the possibility of getting back our land and maybe even the Yangyang estate. My pulse raced. Could that really be possible? Questions started to enter our thoughts: What *would* happen to all the property that the Japanese had confiscated? What about all the antique treasures that they had looted and shipped back to the mainland? Would the Japanese leave at once? Would the monarchy be restored, or would we have a democracy? Would Koreans now earn the high wages that the Japanese had received for the work taken from us? What about the schools? Would we now be taught Korean subjects at last?

Of course we would, scoffed my father, slapping my uncle on the back. I could not remember seeing him so boldly cheerful. What was so different about him? His voice sounded louder, but perhaps it was just that he was actually smiling, after what felt like years and years.

As for me, I felt confused. Although I wished to feel as confident as my father, I did not. Something in me did not dare to feel free. The haughty attitude of my Japanese teachers and the politicians, the bullying hateful treatment I had glimpsed in their police and soldiers, and all the stories I had grown up with, made me feel deeply on guard, despite an outer carelessness. It seemed impossible that the Japanese had been vanquished. I feared that it was somehow an elaborate ruse, and they might return like a fourheaded monster when least expected. The physical destruction and political humiliation caused by Hiroshima and Nagasaki had seemed like cinema to me. I read that the suffering of Japanese civilians had been grave, but I could not pretend that it greatly concerned me. I prayed for their souls at Mass, but I prayed with my head, and not my heart.

However, their surrender must have been real. The mighty emperor himself had been wheeled out to break the news with a fanfare. The failure of the Japanese had been trumpeted on the radios of millions of people throughout the world. Had this not been assurance enough?

I might eventually accept the change, but now, and for the whole of my lifetime, the Japanese had been our jailers. I could not imagine what freedom would feel like. Despite being surrounded by my family, a subtle sense of fear stayed with me; whatever would replace it had not yet arrived.

That night we held no outward celebrations. Although it had been a day of unfathomable importance, supper was another uninspiring round of watery soup, steamed dried fish, rice, and kimchi. Our rations had been running low for some time, and having used up our supply of flour, eggs, and sugar early in the week, Mother could not bake a cake as she hoped she might, or even make some tempura.

Baby Uncle, however, had fetched from his rooms half a bottle of *soju*, and filled our little glasses to the brim for a silent toast to freedom, and the end of Japanese rule. As we raised our trembling glasses, the occasion felt distinctly surreal, and I could not look anyone in the eye. We bowed our heads. The occasion was too momentous to be addressed with a glib physical gesture. The *soju* burned a blazing path down my throat, and Jin-ho smiled.

After supper, Uncle Gong-lae amused us by singing pop songs he'd heard on the radio, and made extravagant smoke rings with his pipe. He opened his chest as he'd been taught by his music tutor, and belted out a soulful rendition of "Shanghai" before delivering a mesmerizing falsetto version of "Bong Sun Wha," batting his eyelashes as he sang. He disliked serious opera, but had a fine tenor voice, and was a natural actor, which was lucky, as he had to invent most of the lyrics as he went along; hilariously repetitious and banal. He looked immaculate in his seersucker suit, like a film star—Myung-hi and I clapped delightedly at the end of his recital, and even Jin-ho allowed himself to whistle. Father and Mother sat back, chairs pushed away, flushed with laughter.

When I went to bed that night, I realized that everything had changed since I had last been beneath the covers. The house was the same, the same members of my family inhabited the bedrooms, the streets were intact, Seoul was the same city it had been this morning, the same horsefly even circled the ceiling sounding like an airplane, but at noon that day a miracle had taken place.

In the invisible, abstract, and perplexing realm of adult conscience, a cataclysmic landslide had occurred. Japan's surrender would produce a chain of a thousand million changes whose material effects would be far beyond my reckoning and wisdom. Yet as I went to sleep, I felt comforted by my ignorance of the future. I loved my family—painful as it could be to be a member of it at times—and as long as my country was allowed to regain its dignity, I felt a childish sense of trust in what would happen to Korea.

Over the next few days the impact of Japan's surrender became more tenable. There were spontaneous parades and marches through the center of Seoul. People sang "Arirang" and waved the Korean flag. It was the first time I had ever seen a Korean flag. The freedom to wave the *Tae-gŭkki* was so new, people did so with great spirit: some with grave deliberation, others with indignation, some with gaiety. The dancing white flags with their brightly colored emblems made my spirits dance, too. But my sister and I watched from a distance; we were not allowed to join the crowds in case things should get too wild.

There were few Japanese faces on the streets. The houses of Japanese high officials and merchants were left empty. Office buildings were deserted. No one had seen the exodus; they had fled in the middle of the night. The suddenness of our release from the Japanese was surreal.

We stayed close to the radio during those early days after the war's end. Long-suppressed Korean songs returned to the airwaves. When I first heard "Arirang," sung full-throated to the accompaniment of the *kayakum* and the *changgo*, I was moved, unexpectedly, to tears.

The radio announcers—who now spoke to us in Korean—warned everyone to stay at home, especially at night. There was a curfew, and the remaining Japanese officials and military police feared violent reprisals from celebrating Korean citizens.

But a broadcast was made that diminished our joy, and caused confusion across the country. The announcement stated that Korea had been divided into two halves to facilitate the withdrawal of the Japanese. Northern provinces had been placed under the jurisdiction of Russia (whose Soviet army of occupation was already crossing the Yalu River) and the southern region under the protection of the United States. The 38th Parallel had been chosen by Colonel Dean Rusk so that Seoul would fall under the control of the Americans, who would soon be arriving to accept the surrendering Japanese troops.

Father was concerned that this decision had been taken without Korea's consent. Further, it was such an arbitrary division. What would happen to our relations in the north of the country? They were not Communists. Would they be allowed to leave? My mother and uncle convinced Father that the situation was temporary, and that he should not worry.

The weeks went by swiftly. Myung-hi and I went occasionally to the swimming hole just outside the South Gate and played and read in the courtyard. We also went to the markets, which still offered little food, but now stocked enticing goods abandoned by the Japanese upon fleeing Seoul; I was ecstatic about a few gramophone records I had found there; concert recordings of Jascha Heifetz and Yehudi Menuhin, in pristine condition. What bliss! When I saw my friends, we gossiped about the future and exchanged rumors about what would happen at school in the autumn.

With the departure of the Japanese, it was as if Father's life were beginning again. He had become full of almost electric energy, and I was impressed that his presence was required at so many political meetings across Seoul. An interim government was in the process of being set up, and the capital was full of returning political exiles— Nationalists, Royalists, Democrats, Communists—all jockeying for preeminence. Father joined the Korean Democratic Party, the KDP, along with many of his conservative friends. U.S. troops would be arriving shortly to occupy the South and to oversee the instatement of a provisional government.

We rarely saw Jin-ho. The less we saw of him, the more my mother seemed to go to church. She also made frequent visits to the sick, but she seemed happier since Father was happier. Both of my parents looked younger and were more cheerful than I could remember for many years. We were still poor, and many things were unsettled, but the freedom of Korea was hugely exciting, and we were swept up in the changes without complaints. Even the dreaded monsoon rains that came that summer seemed to be part of a cleansing, generous force that would transform and renew us, softening the hard bitterness of half a century's subjugation.

CHAPTER TEN

Namsan Park

Seoul

Autumn 1945

Over the last couple of weeks American B-29s had been dropping leaflets over Seoul announcing their imminent landing and occupation of "The South." The silvery planes flew lazily, some even somersaulting acrobatically in the air above our heads, the twisting white ropes of their jetstreams melting into the hazy blue skies. This delighted me. I found the planes beautiful, and was touched that these anonymous pilots were communicating with us from such a great distance, like messengers from God, bringing glad tidings. My father now no longer joined us in the air-raid shelter during drills but simply stood in the courtyard with a hand on his hip, and listened to the pilots' course in silence, as if waiting for something more impressive to happen.

Then, three weeks after Emperor Hirohito's broadcast, the Americans landed at Inchon, and marched into Seoul. I remember that day very clearly. It was a hot September morning, and it was the first day in my life I had ever seen a black person, or men in shorts with hairy legs. The wide main boulevard, Chong-lo, was suddenly bristling with columns of sweaty, sunburned soldiers in helmets and fatigues, carrying backpacks and bayonets. Men dragged heavy artillery, and tanks rolled by them. Officers in jeeps accelerated past, leaving behind a haze of drifting dust. To me, it was like watching a parade of friendly science fiction aliens.

I was hugely excited. *Everyone* was excited, and we rushed into the streets to catch a glimpse of these exotic hulks who had come to liberate us from the Japanese. Unlike the remaining Japanese soldiers who beat people up and arrested them—mean in defeat—the Americans were open-handed, and generous-looking. Corny as it sounds, they were heroes to us, saviors who had won the war. Although we had heard announcements that they would come, the reality of their arrival and its significance was overwhelming. They, on the other hand, looked puzzled at their joyous reception. Our grateful tears and rapture were curious, even embarrassing to them. The soldiers had no idea what liberation from the Japanese meant to us. They were just here doing a job, most of them tired, disoriented, and impatient to return home.

The radio had been issuing more broadcasts telling everyone to stay at home. We did not hear until several days later that there had been trouble from the very moment of arrival of the 24th Corps at Inchon. Several hundred Koreans had waited on the docks waving flags and bearing gifts of flower bouquets to welcome the troops. As the Americans disembarked from their ship and the Korean delegation moved to greet General Hodge, the Japanese police opened fire and killed five of the Koreans instantly, wounding nine others. Among the slain were Labour Union leader Kwon Pyong-gun and peacekeeping activist Yi Sok-ku.

Having driven back the Koreans, the Japanese formed a delegation of their own and moved in to play host to the Americans themselves. General Hodge later congratulated the policemen who shot the civilians. Hodge was quoted in the newspapers as saying, "Koreans are cats of the same breed as the Japanese." We could not believe such crassness, nor could we understand him revealing his intention to treat Koreans, the people whom he was liberating, with greater disrespect than the enemy. The Americans' collusion with the Japanese was neither forgiven nor forgotten.

I read later that Hodge had been placed in charge of South Korea solely because he was based in Okinawa, and could be shipped out in the quickest possible time. Hodge was a combat soldier whose staff contained no Korean experts, State Department advisers, or civil affairs teams—his deputy was a West Point graduate chosen for his excellence as a football player. Japanese police and officials ingratiated themselves with Hodge's command, buying extravagant gifts and disporting themselves in a more docile manner than the more fiery and chaotic Koreans. Despite Hangul having been redesignated the official language of Korea, the country's political matters were still being conducted in Japanese. Hodge rebuffed the newly formed Korean interim government, and decreed that the Japanese should govern the Koreans until such time as a United States military government could be formed. However, when the State Department heard of his blazing gaffe, they ordered him to drop the policy at once.

My father and his colleagues in the Korean Democratic Party were forced to move fast to gain recognition. In October, the U.S. command held an official welcoming ceremony for Dr. Syngman Rhee, returning from exile, while the Soviet command held a similar event for Kim Il Sung, a young revolutionary Korean captain in the Soviet army, both famous nationalists on the hard right and hard left. They became leading figures almost at once. Rhee, in his seventies, who had devoted his life to fighting for Korean independence at home and abroad, was a virulent anti-Communist and an obstinate politician, notoriously irritating to Western powers. Father was not convinced that the abrasive Rhee was the right leader for Korea. About Kim Il Sung, we knew nothing.

Father was rarely at home now. Infighting factions, rivalry, and farcical language barriers between Korean and U.S. officials were creating chaos in the struggle to establish a new government. With Dr. Rhee unable to agree to a coalition agenda, the U.S. command started to negotiate terms with Father's party, the KDP, one of whose founding members, Cho Byong-ok, was a great friend of Father's from his days in the underground independence movement, and had urged him to join up.

With Father's attention safely turned to more momentous matters, Jin-ho started to stray again, exploring with impunity the seamier streets of Seoul. His English being fairly good, he managed to attach himself to some American GIs, and in exchange for telling them bits of local information, the GIs gave Jin-ho cigarettes and liquor, and introduced him to the red-light district near the East Gate. He rode around in jeeps, and came home drunk. My mother couldn't control him.

I had seen Jin-ho's reckless side many times before, but there had always been an essential refinement about him, an intelligence and wit that made you forgive him more quickly than he deserved. But swept up in his military adventures, he developed an odd coarseness and arrogance that I did not respect. He no longer seemed as interested in his painting, for which he had once sacrificed the family peace. Eventually Jin-ho became a live-in employee of the 8th Army. My mother worried about the rough influence of the soldiers on my impressionable brother—and with reason—but Jin-ho was elated. The liberation of the country in itself had lifted him, but the novelty of the occupying forces, their jargon, their strange food and manners, and their attractive hero power fascinated him. He was proud that they had singled him out, and felt he was being treated as an equal. When he came home Jin-ho would mimic the drawling accents and simian swagger of the men with such accuracy that mother even laughed through her disapproval. Not for the first time, Father's absence was a blessing. Jin-ho's exploits would have disgusted him.

Back at school, things had changed appreciably for the better. For a start, we were allowed to speak Korean. It took no time to adjust. It felt like wearing your shoes on the right feet at last. We now had new Korean teachers, and were taught proper Korean subjects for the first time in all of my years of schooling. There was a far more informal, easygoing air in the corridors and the gymnasium. No more Japanese national anthem, no compulsory tea ceremony, or fish-oil jelly. There was more laughter, and there was an air of freedom in the classroom so fresh and delicious my spirits were lifted like helium.

It wasn't until months after the Japanese left that I knew what freedom was. For the first time, my friends and I had the sense that we could be anything that we wanted to be. Certainly we were busier than ever before: English, French, and German lessons, cooking classes, the poetry club, chamber music group; my friends and I even learned how to dance the tango and foxtrot from a rather greasy middle-aged instructor from Shanghai. At night, when I lay in bed and tried to recall all the events of the day, I fell asleep about halfway through the litany. After a childhood spent in a comfortable sort of gray tunnel, my world suddenly became bright and wide, and was spinning faster and faster, a blur of new shapes and colors like a fairground ride. It was as much as I could do simply to be present at its joyous revelations.

One day in January my father came home from the headquarters of the KDP with a special gleam in his eye, and asked Mother to come into his study. She rose from her writing table with a questioning look and followed him. Myung-hi and I were practicing a traditional song for the school New Year's Concert, and paused to see if we could hear what Father was saying, but his voice was too low. Mother and Father talked for an unbearably long time, during which Mother stopped, cruelly made tea, and went back into Father's study to resume discussion. We were forced to keep singing, although the song was far less interesting than it had been before.

At last Father and Mother emerged, but said nothing. It wasn't until suppertime, when Jin-ho was present, that Father decided to make his announcement.

"Well. You all may be interested to know that we will be moving house next week."

We all sat up straight in our chairs.

"Where will we go, Father?" I demanded.

"To Waesung Terrace, in Namsan Park."

"But that is one of the best addresses in Seoul," I said.

"Yes, well. The truth is, I've been appointed press secretary to the home minister, Dr. Cho. It is a cabinet post, and an official residence comes with the job," he said, matter-of-factly. Mother looked extremely proud of Father, and served him more rice wine. Jin-ho held out his beaker, and Mother frowned, pouring him out some barley tea instead.

"Wonderful! Many, many congratulations, *Aboji*," I said, bowing my head.

"*Ne,*" echoed Myung-hi, dipping her head, "Wonderful, *Aboji*," she said, clapping her hands. Jin-ho nodded grumpily.

"You are to move back in with us, son, now that school is beginning again. There will be plenty of room now for you to arrange yourself comfortably, and I will be engaging a tutor for all of you children. I may have been neglecting you recently, and with my job becoming more demanding, it is our wish that you should be more carefully supervised," my father said, placing his chopsticks on their rest with an authoritative click.

Jin-ho looked contrary and apprehensive, but said nothing. I thought it a good idea that he should move back home. His moodiness and careless manner made me uneasy, and although Father could be too hard on him, indeed, violent with him, my brother still needed the stability of our family, and we were incomplete without him. Although Jin-ho could be irksome, as well as a dreadful worry, I missed his ironic presence, his sharpness, and turns of surprising tenderness which could instantly reawaken my affection for him. Also, the entertaining cast of friends which an elder brother brought home was an undeniable boon. I nudged his knee under the table, and smiled encouragingly at him. Although his eyes were downcast, he blushed slightly, and I considered the matter settled. He would be making the exciting move with us, and I felt that with our fantastically improved lot, the future could not help but hold hopeful things. My only regret about moving was that I would have to leave behind my bed of wretched tiger lilies.

The new house lay at the foot of Namsan Park, a vast, secluded wood. Our long drive was flanked by a winding avenue of maple trees. This closeness to green parkland was an undreamed-of luxury in Seoul at the time. After the evacuation of the Japanese, greedy and corrupt city planners and developers took advantage of the political chaos to build ugly new housing and commercial districts in former public parks. Serene swards, ancient flower gardens, and limpid reflecting pools were bulldozed. The influx of returning exiles and refugees fleeing the Communist regime in the North caused a severe housing shortage. No one seemed to have the power to prevent, or the will to demolish, the illegal, newly built monstrosities. Everywhere but here, and near the royal palaces, Seoul was awash with dust, dirt, mud, cheap concrete, glass, and steel, as construction swept through the city like cholera. We were grateful for our emphatic exemption.

The black iron gates to our mansion were set in a bower of azaleas, and the young chauffeur stopped the black limousine to get out and swing them open and clang them shut again before bringing the car to a final halt upon the gravel. A pair of mature cherry trees framed the daunting stone steps leading to the mansion's front door.

The plump, uniformed housekeeper opened the door for my mother and me, and we left our wraps in the vestibule, ordering tea to be brought into the drawing room, where there was a lit fire. I sat on a slippery, leather-upholstered antique sofa, and we chatted idly, warming our hands by the crackling flames in the grandiose fireplace.

Until recently, the rambling villa had been the residence of an exalted Japanese official evacuated by the American troops. The gardens were overgrown and neglected. It was a curious mixture of Western and Eastern styles. The reception rooms were full of rather pompous, carved, dark Victorian furniture, ornate gilt mirrors, chandeliers and fusty German etchings which my mother disliked. She replaced some of the worst offenders with our few remaining family pictures and more valuable antique chests of rosewood with inlaid mother-of-pearl, which better suited the predominantly Oriental architecture, with its horizontal sliding screens, wood doors, and paneling. However, the first thing Mother did was to have the woven Japanese tatami floor mats removed, and install Korean *ondol* floor heating in all of the bedrooms, which helped to ease the chill caused by the plate glass windows throughout the house.

Two loud gunshots coming from the back garden informed us that Father was at home. It was his habit on weekends to relax by indulging in target practice on the birds in the persimmon tree outside his study. At first my mother was horrified by this eccentricity, but Father argued that as he no longer had time to go pheasant hunting with his brothers in the country, he would take advantage of what sport could be had on his own property, using the pistol he kept in the safe. To avoid shooting members of the family, staff, and guests, Father suggested that anyone entering the garden must first strike the brass gong by the garden door as a warning when he was at home. This system caused some alarm, and on Saturdays, when there were many people in the house, the constant sounding of the gong could become farcical.

As we sipped ginseng tea, the doorbell rang, and the housekeeper announced a nervous, round-faced young man in a shabby suit, who requested to speak to Father. My mother and I bowed, and the young man was shown in to the study, while *Aboji* was fetched from target practice with a gong by our new maid, Son-young, whom we had engaged from the old Yangyang estate, along with the chauffeur, cook, gardener, and housekeeper. It was usual for Father to receive visitors at home, for the fraught political scene continued to hold a great deal of intrigue involving men in shabby suits, but it was slightly out of the ordinary for him to entertain a visitor on such a long interview on a Saturday, particularly without prior appointment, however neither Mother nor I commented upon it as we finished our tea.

At supper that evening Father made an announcement, the customary time for important family discussions.

"Do you all remember the young gentleman who called on me today? Well, I am pleased to tell you that he is to be your new tutor. Min Young-ju will be moving in with us on Monday. Furthermore, he is your second cousin, one of the clan from Sokcho, so I expect you to treat him with the respect and affection due to someone of his position."

We were silent, and Father continued with visible difficulty. "I will tell you this once, but I expect—and insist—that you not repeat this to anyone, nor will you mention the subject in Young-ju's presence. Very well. Min Young-ju—*sunsaeng-nim* (teacher)—as you will respectfully call him, has recently been orphaned, and the nature of it is such that you must know of it lest you say something inadvertently to upset him." Myung-hi's eyes bulged with curiosity, and even Jin-ho was looking at Father with rapt attention. Mother's expression was pained, and she looked down at her bowl.

"I regret that there is no agreeable way to express this. During the Japanese occupation Young-ju's father was mayor of a small village near the North. While the townspeople were poor and persecuted by the Japanese authorities, Young-ju's parents grew rich. In fact, whenever Young-ju's father came to Seoul he never visited us, but stayed in fancy hotels, so I hardly knew him of late. The long and the short of it is that when the Japanese left Sokcho, the villagers seized Young-ju's mother and father in the middle of the night and lynched them for being Japanese puppets."

A silence fell over the table. We were shocked both by the tale itself, and by my parents' speaking to us in such a frank and adult manner, particularly in front of Myung-hi. Mother then spoke: "Young-ju has no brothers and sisters, so it is our duty as his most senior relations to protect and comfort him. This has happened only recently, so I ask you to be most considerate to him, and avoid subjects that might cause him pain. It is also very important not to mention to anyone that Young-ju is our cousin, because an execution squad may be looking for him."

Myung-hi's mouth hung open. I wondered if she could even understand what pain was, in her world of dolls and sweet buns. Jin-ho too looked as if this story had switched on a light in some unused attic of compassion within him. Whatever worries we children might have had now looked petty, our characters mercifully untested. The news of this young man's violent misfortune refrigerated our blood.

Young-ju nodded politely as he passed me the soy sauce at the breakfast table. I bowed my head in return. Our tutor had been with us now for three months, and during that time our table manners had improved markedly. Our noisy, rambunctious, and brusque ways were converted into a miraculous new tactfulness which amazed my parents, and impressed even us.

Young-ju was fastidious in both his mental discipline and his personal hygiene. His short-back-and-sides hair, with central parting, was cut in such a precise line that I marveled at its symmetry each time he turned his head, and his fingernails were meticulously tended, unlike mine. His favorite philosophers were the Germans—Kant, Nietzsche, Heidegger, and Hegel—and he spoke their language fluently. He was also extremely sharp in mathematics and physics, and had won a scholarship place at Seoul National University for the following year. It came as no surprise when I entered *sunsaeng*'s room on an errand to find it clutterless, his books lined up alphabetically at forty-five-degree angles according to subject.

Sunsaeng was only nineteen, but his positive effect on us children was immediate and fairly considerable. Until his arrival I had been content to be girlishly conceited and quite chaotic in my approach to higher learning, but our cousin's unstinting way of curbing my blurting speech and forcing me to clarify questions and statements were medicinally bracing. Naturally, I worried that Jin-ho would resist all efforts at judicious correction, but to our surprise, he was apparently moved by the plight of our dependent tutor, and managed to humor him with a dilatory cooperation in academic matters, despite being older than *sunsaeng*. *Sunsaeng-nim* combined useful intelligence with modesty, whether or not one warmed to his rigid manners. Of course Jin ho could not resist ruffling his hair insolently on the staircase, and was given to making public declarations, well within earshot of our tutor, that *sunsaeng* needed a woman.

Our cousin was very composed and self-sufficient, and this worried my mother. His formality prevented us from treating him in our customary rough-and-tumble way, and because we never dared speak of his calamity, he must have felt dreadfully isolated. He did not smile much, and in repose his features looked sad. In contrast to his youth fully soft face, his downturned eyes were sharp and haunted. He took many solitary walks, and only occasionally accompanied us to concerts, lectures, and the cinema, preferring to study in his room. That he would be morose and traumatized after what had befallen him seemed natural.

Finally, Father asked him about life in the North, and our cousin was relieved to talk about it. He said that the occupying Communist Russian soldiers treated Koreans appallingly, stopping pedestrians on the roads with their bayonets in broad daylight, and stripping them of their watches, pocketknives, and jewelry before letting them pass. Furthermore, they were unbelievably filthy, uniforms and bodies alike, and stank. I think my cousin objected as much to the unsanitary crudeness of the soldiers as to their alien ideology.

"The North has become a nation of snoopers. The abolition of private property brings out the vindictiveness in everyone. The authorities are systematically eliminating all opposition, and showing no mercy," he said, swallowing hard. "After what happened to my parents some of our clan have fled to other towns, but only those who are rich dare to come South. Seoul is now not an easy place to find work, we are told."

Father listened in silence.

"If you know members of the Min clan who are in need, I want you to tell them to write to me, and I will see what I can do. Obviously we cannot help everyone, but there is space enough here for relations in serious distress," he said. My mother nodded in agreement.

My cousin bowed his head. "I will do that," he said.

And so it came to pass that during this postwar period our household was full of Min relations who came to stay with us as they sought work. With Father's new position, we were able to eat well for the first time in many years. My mother bore the brunt of the strain on the household as Father tended to absent himself on missions of "state importance," but she did not complain, and seemed actually to flower under the demands of looking after people. We had a strict routine: Mass three times a week, lessons with our tutor every day after school, and whatever evening activities could be squeezed in, plus violin practice for me. Looking back, it was an extremely happy time. Jin-ho even made a concerted pretense of being a dutiful son. But one event came to pass that left a terrible hole, a crater in the ground under my feet.

One day at breakfast we had a letter from my grandmother Kang. The postmark indicated that there had been a long delay in our receiving the letter, and my mother's ivory letter opener slit the envelope in one eager stroke.

She paled as she read the letter, and hurried to her room, covering her mouth with her hand. Father followed her, and we could hear whispers and suppressed sobs through the French doors of the library.

After an unbearable delay, Father emerged to tell Jin-ho and me that our beloved and beautiful Aunt Pusan had killed herself with cyanide. She discovered that her husband had been keeping a mistress and two children in a neighboring village. She had died at her dressing table, with a photograph of her son in her lap.

My father was stony-faced as he related this. It must have cost him a great deal not to give way to the emotion he felt, for he too adored my mother's sister, and had objected strenuously when she had married her husband, "the peacock," claiming that he could not forgive her for marrying someone so unworthy of her. He had refused to attend her wedding, and was subsequently hard on her whenever they had crossed paths. Her vulnerability had always been harshly dealt with by her family. I never forgot the time at Grandfather Kang's, when she had been put into a straitjacket, and kept isolated from us. Although she was the Kang's favorite daughter, after her marriage, Pusan-daek's depression had been viewed as caprice, despite her being twice as intelligent as her peers. It was perhaps because of her patent strengths that her family expected more of her. My mother, who had been extremely close to her younger sister, was too grief-stricken to emerge from the library.

Father cleared his throat and passed me a piece of paper. My throat tightened as I recognized my Aunt Pusan's bold hand, and a wave of despair forced me to sit down.

> My dear Myung-ja,
>
> Please forgive my cowardice, and try to ignore the dishonor that I bring upon the family. Know that you are my dearest little niece, and that I have always hoped the best for you. You are my special pearl. Please be kind to my son. There are no words I can use to hide behind or excuse what I have done to betray him, and to disappoint my family.
>
> Your loving aunt Pusan
>
> P.S. Please have my high-heeled shoes.

Tears slipped down my cheeks. I was astonished that she remembered me at all at such a time, much less remembered my silly penchant for wearing her shoes. I pictured them lined up in her silent closet, not believing that she would never dance in them again and turn heads on the street as she walked by with her strong, alluring gait. Literally, I would never be able to fill the shoes she left, and would not want to wear them.

When they arrived months later in a brown parcel from Yangyang, I unwrapped the package in my room. I made a circle out of the pretty, but ordinary pumps, and then sat in the middle, surrounded by them, moved by their sad durability. I sat there for some time, thinking of my aunt, and cried a little.

Because she had killed herself, no funeral was held in her memory.

CHAPTER ELEVEN

Fire on the Cliff

Seoul

Spring 1948

During those postwar months, it was like watching events from the window of a pitching train, new scenery barreling by almost too quickly to be identified, much less apprehended. Yet I never regretted the speed of the train and what serene vistas might be missed as a result, but was exhilarated with the sense that we were headed for an entirely novel and important destination.

With my father's new cabinet post, elegant parties and starchy government receptions were often held at our house, the preparations for which inevitably caused flurries among the forgetful household staff, and occupied my mother with more trivial matters than she might have chosen for herself. Having been raised for such responsibilities, however, she managed being a political hostess along with her work for the local women's committee and church charities, teaching a cookery course, looking after children and visiting relations, and generally holding the family together.

Despite having a housekeeper and cook, Mother did much of the shopping and food preparation herself to ensure that the quality was up to scratch, knowing better than her staff where to find the best wild mushrooms, *kosari* (bracken stems), and freshest seafood. She also still insisted that Sikmo prepared fresh soy sauce and soy paste, bean curd, and, of course, kimchi. Nothing came in cans or bottles that my mother felt was worth eating. The biannual kimchi-making in itself was a monumental effort taking days—and truckloads of Korean cabbage and radish, great quantities of scarlet chili, anchovy, garlic and sea salt for curing the mixture, and straw matting to cover the urns, which were then buried in the garden to be preserved. However, for large parties, Chinese caterers—then very recherché—were hired to provide colorful and extravagant feasts.

To my initial despair, we children were excluded from all parties, great and small. But quite soon I decided I did not mind being absent as I watched from my bedroom window the funereal parade of long black sedans and limousines pulling up the drive, and saw the rather self-important-looking politicians and local dignitaries tugging their dinner jacket lapels and nervously adjusting their cuff links on the doorstep. Few wives were present, and those who were seemed disappointingly staid and ordinary. Perhaps it was unfair, but I still compared all women to the brilliance of Aunt Pusan.

One night there was a splendid reception for the British ambassador, which I did regret having to experience by peeping around doorways and bannisters. I had never seen satin evening gowns that showed off the bosoms and hips of their owners before—except in Hollywood movies—and those had been in black and white. The brilliant jewel colors swathing the swollen female contours of these fleshy pink women were a mesmerizing sight. Korean women's traditional evening dress was sumptuous, but always extremely modest, indeed nunlike by comparison, and those who wore Western frocks made conservative choices.

From the top of the main stairwell Myung-hi and I were further rewarded by the sight of American and British army officers milling

about in the exotic plumage of dress uniform, mixing rather awkwardly with their Korean counterparts, gratefully occupying themselves with the careful study and discussion of alien canapés they had
just plucked from a tray. I could tell from my mother's lively expression as she emerged from the kitchen that she had witnessed a heated
exchange between Sikmo, our temperamental cook, and the Chinese
caterers. With a courteous smile to a prematurely drunken, red-faced
stranger, she nudged Father discreetly, and wove back into the party.

Father, oblivious to hints, was engrossed in conversation for
much of the evening with an intense, dark-eyed young Englishman,
the British vice-consul, whom I thought very handsome and who was
familiar to me because he had come to our school to give a special
guest lecture to our English Society—which I had barely understood
due to his Oxford accent. It was George Blake, chief of British intelligence in Seoul, subsequently imprisoned by the North Koreans, and
unmasked as a Soviet spy.

Yet that spring evening there was no outward sense of the explo-
sive political turmoil that was fermenting in the country. Many factions were fighting for ascendancy, but only two had power behind
them: the U.S.-backed conservative nationalists like my father, who
argued for a modern democracy and self-determination, and the
Communists, whose anti-Japanese rhetoric and hostility to the landlord class aligned them with the foreign revolutionary influences of
Russia and China, who sought to redevelop Korea by occidentalizing
it. Corruption and intrigue escalated despite the presence of the occupying American forces, and there had recently been a violent guerilla
uprising on Cheju-do island.

In Namsan Park, however, a small orchestra was playing in the
garden, and several Western couples were awkwardly dancing the
foxtrot on the uneven terrace flagstones. After supper the women
adjourned to the small drawing room, and the men enjoyed a show of

dancing *kisaeng* girls, courtesans, in the marquee. This, I know, because Myung-hi, Jin-ho, and I were sitting most uncomfortably in a treetop watching their performance. It was the first time I had seen *kisaeng* girls in action, and I could never forget the intoxicating, glowing display of the exquisitely painted courtesans in the warm, dim light of the festive paper lanterns, and the slow, hypnotic rhythms of the dancers. Their little bodies echoed the waves of twangy music, and cast giant, undulating shadows onto the white canvas marquee, stark against the leafy black night.

Although the show was quite innocent, the taint of sensual temptation represented by the paid dancers was considered too strong for ladies and children to be exposed to, and so we were forbidden to watch. In the outlawed caste system, which still resonated in Korean society, entertainers were considered, along with pig butchers, to belong to the lowest social class—quite the reverse of entertainers' status in the West, where they were quite worshiped!

After the guests had left and my parents and the staff had gone to bed, leaving much of the clearing up until the next day, Jin-ho, Myung-hi, and I sneaked downstairs to hold a party of our own. Myung-hi, despite her junior status, was allowed to join us on sufferance, due to her barnaclelike tenacity. We lit the candelabra, and gorged ourselves on trays of leftover Chinese delicacies, experimenting, as with a chemistry set—using our stomachs as receptacles— with the many different enticing bottles of liquors and liqueurs that stood on the sideboard in a fabulous array of glass colors and shapes, winking in the rich candlelight.

In the darkened ballroom the rim of my martini glass shone in a golden circle, and soon blurred into a double halo, whereupon I surrendered to the divan with a winter melon pastry. Myung-hi approached me with a half-eaten tray of cold fried octopus rings and glistening blobs of seacucumber, and I tipsily accepted a couple of each, placing them as neatly as possible on the linen napkin on my knee, where a flock of assorted canapés perched in a holding position for immediate consumption. Much of the food was unidentifiable, but truly delicious, I thought, chewing uncritically.

Jin-ho had found an unopened flagon of champagne, a drink I had only ever read of before in French novels where ladies' reputations were compromised. He lay sprawled on a sofa resting the bottle on his stomach between swigs, concentrating morosely and quite exclusively on finishing its contents by himself. I stared at him disapprovingly, feeling that French novelists would frown on Jin-ho's greedy and uncouth consumption of their national drink. I noticed too that Jin-ho confined himself to eating only from a tray of shrimp croquettes: Myung-hi and I, who were trying everything in sight, found this self-discipline puzzling and remarkable.

"You'll be sick if you carry on," said Jin-ho rousing himself to a loud admonition from his singleminded supine debauch. Myung-hi and I shrugged and continued sipping brandy, plum wine, and absinthe, and eating cake, raw clams, and abalone. Hours later, Myung-hi and I were indeed violently and excessively sick and confined to bed until the next evening, but thankfully no one said a word, not even Jin-ho. In that precarious state it felt as if a single unkind remark could unleash new floods of uncontrollable nausea.

Although no one scolded us for that tremendous raid on the kitchen and liquor supply, Father did have occasion to berate Jin-ho for subsequent solo strikes on the wine cellar, which Jin-ho did not bother to conceal, but rather highlighted by leaving empty bottles lying spent on the floor. He had also taken to stealing sums of money from Mother's chest, and surpassed himself by getting beaten up by a gang of hoods in the red-light district for some tawdry misdemeanor, and being brought home early one morning by the police. As our closest neighbor was the chief of police, Father was more sensitive and out-raged than usual about Jin-ho's flagrant defiance. A brutal thrashing followed, but the situation was now—and had sadly always been—beyond such measures. With an official public position to maintain, Father's abhorrence of a family scandal had escalated, and my mother's attempts to soothe Jin-ho with gentleness caused unspoken conflict in the household. I think we were only able to contain it because the house was so enormous. I felt sorrier and sorrier for our cousin, whose troubled head and heart needed no further burdening.

As time and familiarity softened the sharp edges of our new life, our tutor's hidden unhappiness began to emerge in relief. On several nights when I was returning from some errand in the guest wing, low, stifled moans could be heard in the corridor outside our cousin's bed-room. The noise stopped me, and I considered going in to him, but knew that it would be improper to do so, and that he would be morti-fied to have been overheard by anyone. Telling Jin-ho did not seem a suitable option. But a few nights later, when I heard him again, I told Mother, hoping something could be done to help.

There was quite a daunting distance between my cousin and the rest of us that went beyond the respect and deference that we, as his juniors, were expected to show him. This was partly to do with the violent tragedy which had orphaned him. It was as if the catastrophe, impacted, still radiated from him and threw us all back. But the gap may also have been due to the broad contrast in our characters, mak-ing it difficult to understand him, and to know how to cross the wide moat of his reserve. I admired his cool rigor and disciplined ways, but we, as a family, were heated and chaotic, and despite our tutor's best attempts to reform us, we were quite intent on remaining so.

I could not begin to imagine the mixture of bereavement, rage, shock, and fear that *sunsaeng-nim* must have felt on discovering his parents' murders at the hands of a mob. I could only compare it to something like an earthquake killing one's family, enforcing changes for which one could never be prepared. Not knowing what to do or say, I withdrew, and mostly played the violin in my room. As a kindness, I tried not to play anything too sad, but knowing that the instrument made a rather plangent sound whatever the music, I stuck to practicing works in a major key whenever possible.

Fortunately for our cousin, Uncle Gong-lae returned from Manchuria to stay with us while he searched for a suitable house in Seoul for him and his new bride to move into. Somehow no one was terribly surprised that Baby Uncle had secretly married the daughter of the munitions factory owner for whose firm he worked as a translator, having dropped out of agricultural college in boredom. Of course, we were brimming with curiosity and excitement at the news, but to our frustration he had left his new bride with her family in the North while he looked for a house in the capital.

Baby Uncle was much the same, still smoking that smelly briarwood pipe, but he did seem older and more mysterious with his new adventures. He had taken to wearing dark glasses and a trenchcoat, which gave him a cool intellectual air as he went about his affairs—rather like the French existentialists I'd seen on newsreels. *Sunsaengnim* was instantly attracted to Uncle's bookishness, and to everyone's pleasure, the two got on very well together.

At breakfast on the morning of his arrival he produced a photograph of his wedding from a large envelope. We all crowded around him and peered at the black-and-white portrait, silenced by the fierce gravity of their faces, which glowed like moonflowers against the gloom and dark leaves of the festoons that hung around the doorway of the temple. Knowing Baby Uncle's penchant for all things foreign and modish, we were not too astonished that Baby Uncle and his rich wife had chosen a Western wedding ceremony instead of a traditional Korean one, but this was still quite avant-garde, even for Baby Uncle. He wore a tailcoat and rather clumsily hemmed striped trousers—one couldn't be too particular about tailors in Manchuria—while she,

Kyong-sil-*daek* was swathed elegantly in white satin and tulle. I pored over her impassive face for clues to her character, but found little to go on. She was handsome rather than pretty, with no hint of coquetry about her. Father mumbled something vaguely disparaging about her family being in trade, but Baby Uncle took little notice, thinking, half-rightly, that his elder brother, as head of the family, was miffed at not having been consulted prior to the wedding.

Conversely, my mother looked at the puritanical face of my uncle's wife and seemed instantly to understand my uncle's choice of bride and to admire his judgment.

"For you, she is just right," said Mother, smiling at Baby Uncle. My brother, sister, and I looked at the photograph again with renewed effort, and although I knew precisely nothing about love and marriage, I flattered myself that on second glance there did seem to be some interior logic in the pairing of my handsome uncle with this unsmiling pea hen of a woman. Mother was always right, and Time revealed Uncle's wife to have been modest and strong, influential in curbing his more foolish tendencies.

Baby Uncle's wife's family, called Cho, was from Hankyung Province in the North, although their munitions factory was in Dairen, in Manchuria. Her elder brother was a famous lawyer who went on to become an even more well known Communist leader. Although Baby Uncle only ever talked about his fantastic fishing trips in Dairen, I gathered that he left the North out of discomfort at the ardent Communist sympathies of his wife's brother, who wished him to join the party. I could not prevent myself from giggling trying to imagine Baby Uncle as a Communist, or indeed, as any kind of a political creature.

Father and Uncle adjourned to the library one day and had a man-to-man meeting about family matters that involved many trays of tea and buns and much pipe-smoke. At the end of it, two main matters were resolved. One: our tutor would be sent on a spiritual retreat to a mountaintop monastery, and two: Jin-ho would be found a suitable live-in "chaperone" or bodyguard to safeguard his passage through daily life. We were all pleased by the swiftness and compassion of these resolutions, and for a time, with Baby Uncle's buoyant presence, there was a new and authentic harmony at our dinner table.

Before our tutor's departure to the monks, Uncle Gong-lae spent a lot of time talking to him quietly in the library, and together they stayed up late in the kitchen drinking *soju*. Our cousin never normally drank alcohol, but under the relaxing warmth of Uncle's interest in him, *sunsaeng-nim* let go just a little. One night as I went up to bed I heard them talking, and *sunsaeng*'s voice was breaking with emotion as he spoke, emitting painful squeaks and gasps of choked breath. But now I was relieved rather than worried by the sound. And in the very short time before his departure to the monastery our tutor's brow had cleared and lightened to a remarkable degree—so much so that I even risked playing Beethoven in the following days. Although no one said anything aloud then, Baby Uncle told us years later that our tutor had already once attempted suicide under our roof. His arrival had been a vital turning point in our cousin's life, and was an intervention for which we were all extremely grateful.

Our tutor was to have gone away only for two months, but in the autumn, he did not return. Instead he went to live with another, reputedly less melodramatic, family. I might have missed more intensely his vulnerable moon face and funny stringencies had we been left alone as before, for I felt sincere affection for him, but with Baby Uncle's coinciding visit, the vacuum left by *sunsaeng* was not merely filled, but quite overflowed with new incident. Where the afflicted *sunsaeng-nim*

paced the house in a decorous silence, his presence felt through his assiduous modesty and consistent abstentions of one kind and another, Baby Uncle could not have provided a greater contrast.

Baby Uncle sang incredibly loudly in the bath, as well as in the garden, caterwauling pop songs with jokily exaggerated vibrato. It was his habit to toot the automobile-horn twice in farewell when he drove off, and to toot twice again upon his return. He practiced archery in the courtyard, cursing with relish, and in quieter moments was no less noticeable, playing marathon games of *baduk*, Korean chess, with my father, leaving behind a souvenir fog of pipe smoke wherever he went. You would find him on the sofa reading Baudelaire in Japanese, crunching an apple with gusto. He had also taken to writing poetry himself, and much to my father's merriment, one of Uncle's obscurely intellectual verses about plum-blossom had been published in an agricultural quarterly. So relieved was Father that his youngest brother had not gone astray as Uncle Yong-lae and Jin-ho had done, that he was much more lenient about Baby Uncle's dilettantism than he would have been otherwise. Although Uncle would be earning something as a translator at one of the foreign press bureaux—thanks to Father—it would hardly be enough to support a family in style. The rest he would probably recoup with his usual gambling, at which he was both gifted and well practiced, and the family would turn a blind eye to it.

News filtered back from Sokcho that Uncle Yong-lae was still drinking destructively, but had taken up the study of law, and was being given a chance to work part time in the firm of one of his wife's relations. Meanwhile, our household had acquired a bizarre new addition in the form of Jin-ho's bodyguard, called Peking, who slept in Jin-ho's dressing room, and accompanied him to and from university every day—to ensure his protection from various enemies he had accumulated with his shady exploits as much as to enforce his attendance at university. Peking had a shaved head, strange, penciled-in eyebrows, and a very thick neck. I found him frightening, but realized belatedly that this was the point of Peking, and decided that he did his job quite well. I never did discover why he was called Peking.

The summer of 1948 was a landmark summer. The United Nations had been appointed arbiters of Korea's future with the objective of returning the country to Koreans after democratic elections in the South. The North refused to cooperate with the UN. Leftist parties boycotted the elections, and so the right won a majority in the new constitutional assembly. The transition was fraught: prior to the elections ten thousand suspected Communists were arrested, and around six hundred were killed in the South. The North was suspected of staging political unrest in the South through terrorism, strikes, and waves of arson—anything to discredit the regime—but on August 15, the Republic of Korea was officially founded, with Syngman Rhee inaugurated as our first president. It was a fairly stirring moment when the American flag was lowered over the Capitol Building and the *Tae-gŭkki* raised in its place, but far more momentous for me was a smaller event. I fell in love with an English teacher at my school.

It was a crush, really. I was terribly childish for my age, but immaturity did not prevent me from feeling those first pangs of infatuation with cruel intensity. Whenever I glimpsed a cup and saucer, or heard the word *coffee* spoken on the radio or passed a café anywhere, I felt a deep rush of joy, and when the liaison was over, inevitably, those same things made me cry. Secretly, we would meet most afternoons in a coffee shop on Chong-lo Avenue. Although it was a very hot summer, we sat with steaming cups of untouched *kopi* before us, and talked with great animation about nothing. His name was Eui-hwon, and he had beautiful shiny hair and wore distinguished horn-rimmed spectacles. That he was a student teacher, without fortune or connections, made

our friendship controversial, and Father quickly gave me an ultima-
tum. I could either study hard and Father would pay for my education,
or I could go off with Eui-hwon and be cut off from my family forever.

There were many tears, both public and private, but by September
I had forsaken him. He asked to be transferred to another school, and
we never saw each other again. This disavowal might have seemed
weak on my part, but the thought of being renounced by my family
was more than I could have borne. Without Eui-hwon—and his
horn-rimmed glasses—my life, surprisingly, still felt full of promising possibilities, and the violin grudgingly resumed its central place.
Romance was a luscious, tempting bon-bon, but it did not prove vital
in the greater nutritional picture. Family was my thrice-daily bowl of
rice upon which I depended for life.

By December, if you used my father's moods as a barometer, the
country was experiencing mounting pressures from within and without. He came home late in the evenings exhausted and somewhat frac-
tious from the strain of rows within the government, and power
challenges from other nationalist parties. He also faced the bewildering complexities of responding to the machinations of the Russians,
Chinese, and Americans.

That month the USSR had reportedly withdrawn its troops from
North Korea and left a Korean Communist government in its place—
although they had not allowed the UN access to monitor the handover.
The Democratic People's Party (DPP), under Soviet-trained Kim Il
Sung, was widely regarded as a Stalinist puppet regime. They claimed
jurisdiction over the whole of Korea, and took the threatening and
unexpected step of militarizing their side of the 38th Parallel with

tanks and guns, starting a provocative cold war against the South. Violent guerrilla uprisings in Yosu and on Cheju-do in the autumn had taken thousands of lives.

Although Father relished working at the center of policy making after a lifetime of being marginalized by Japanese rule, he was constitutionally averse to compromise and to the oily little insincerities of office-politics, phenomena he blamed for creating the dark circles under his eyes. He saw himself as a man of honor and principle, not of consensus. Perhaps others saw him as being a bit brittle and supercilious, but this had been the manner of his upbringing. We forgave his ill temper at home, and stayed out of his way, hoping that government matters would soon become smoother. To the ignorance of our entire family, Father had been investing his capital in a gold mine, hoping that the mine would make him rich, and so allow him to quit his post altogether.

But nothing, it transpired, went smoothly during that epoch. One afternoon Mother received a telegram from our grandmother Kang. It reported that our cousin Jae-dal was dead. Without warning, he had gone to Nagsan cliff, poured petrol over his body, and had immolated himself in protest at the Communists' takeover of the family's northern estates.

No tears came as I thought of him, although I felt ill and melancholy for many weeks. I did not condemn his decision to die rather than see the Communists revoke his birthright. It may have been a rash act, unnecessary even, but it was Jae-dal's proud way, and he was not a fool. Unlike Father's family, the Kangs had remained in the North in the hope and belief that Communism would be rejected by sensible people like themselves. The Kangs were too traditional, their roots too deep in their land, ever to leave it. How could Grandfather Kang abandon his cherished gardens and orchards? Although I understood Jae-dal's grief, I felt shaken by the impetuous violence of his act, picturing him alone and in agony on that cliff, a place so much the symbol of our childhood happiness. Nagsan cliff would now be utterly changed for me. In my memory, the comforting campfires he'd laid would be eclipsed by this hideous conflagration, the soil now sad and branded with death.

After the shock had passed, I imagined him over and over in my mind; his dark, twisted torso writhing in a shower of flame. From far away he must have looked like an inanimate torch, a farmer's pyre. But instead it was dear Jae-dal, my tin-soldier, his young life alight, crying out above the crackling flame, his soul seeping from his wasted skin in a trail of terrible smoke.

Before sleeping, I pictured him alive on that last day, walking to the cliff's edge, where that vast, racing black ocean would have stretched lonely before him. *Come back*, I called to him in my thoughts.

No longer would I follow behind him as he strode ahead through the tall grass leaving behind an easy path for me. No longer would he wave back to me from the sands below like one who had mastered the tides, the wind whipping a lock of vivid hair across his pink cheek. No longer would I weave my small nets for him.

I could not return to Nagsan beach again.

In the spring of 1949 the American occupation troops withdrew from Korea, despite continued skirmishes along the 38th Parallel, and despite our country's entreaty for protection until South Korean armed forces were fully trained.

At the general elections in May of 1950, President Rhee's party won only a quarter of the two hundred seats in the National Assembly, and Kim Il Sung was massing his Northern troops in heavy numbers along the 38th Parallel. Amidst this national tension Father had lost his fortune in the gold mine, and although we remained in residence at Namsan Park, we had become paupers overnight, and bailiffs had come to confiscate our valuable possessions. The family was in shock, and Father, who had been away in Kangwon-do trying to rectify his disastrous financial affairs, was in danger of losing his place in the cabinet.

CHAPTER TWELVE

Ninety Thousand Troops

Seoul

25 June 1950

This particular Sunday night I slept very badly. Although it was a cool summer evening, the bedclothes were damp when I awoke. My dreams were nightmarish visions of burning machinery and thundering noise that prevented me from hearing what my father was trying to tell me. I awoke several times at the sound of explosions that seemed to be coming closer.

Father had only just returned from Kangwon-do, and was not current with government developments. There had been a marked increase in military exercises during the past week, and strafing from low-flying airplanes was not a terribly unusual noise to hear outside the window. When I peered out of the window at Namsan Park, the horizon lit up with gun flash, and the firing seemed to be increasing in frequency.

I calmed myself with Father's assurance to Baby Uncle that Taiwan was the more likely focus of a Communist *coup* than South Korea, with Chiang Kai-shek ripe to be ousted. Besides, the newspapers and teachers at school all had been saying that if the North were to attack, the South would certainly win by lunchtime the same day. Exhausted, and wanting badly to believe this, I succumbed to a shallow sleep.

The next day, Monday, the twenty-sixth of June, I went to school as usual. There was a news blackout, which was rather odd, but I thought nothing of it. I was excited and keen to get to school to see my friends, and discover what was going on. The sky was overcast that morning, and I can remember waving good-bye to Jin-ho at the corner, as I normally did.

Father had recently dismissed Peking, Jin-ho's strange, eyebrow-penciled thug of a bodyguard, whose presence drew too much attention, and Jin-ho was far happier without him. At eight o'clock the streets looked the same as usual, but it was odd that there were only a few people on the streetcar, and they looked distinctly jumpy.

We passed the South Gate, and as we turned the corner, my pulse began to race. As the trolley neared the railroad station; even from a distance one could see that something sinister was happening. As we got closer, there was a chilling, portentous sight: orderly lines of long, black, sleek government motorcars—like our father's—stood empty and abandoned before the station entrance. Crowds of anxious-looking Westerners swarmed round the ticket entrance, clearly bent on fleeing Seoul, struggling with trunks and suitcases, while untidy piles of boxes and crates stood scattered over the pavement in front of the waiting area. Koreans, too, were pushing with their families to get through to the ticket office inside, belongings hanging from every limb. An army jeep drove past at frighteningly high speed, nearly overturning a pony cart, and just missing a confused old couple trying to cross the street.

At the entrance to a nearby bank, a huge crowd stood outside its locked doors, stunned, while some businessmen banged desperately on the door to no avail, shouting for the manager. I could not imagine why anyone should do this, or why a bank would be closed on a weekday morning. My heart began to pound harder. For the rest of the trolley ride, my mind swam with questions and I peered down every alley we passed, watching hurrying people on the streets for clues to what was happening.

At school, a small knot of animated girls stood at the entrance to our home classroom, their black-haired heads clustered together, whispering. My friends In-sook and Soon-ja waved me over to their group. Just then our headmaster, Mr. Choi, called for our attention.

"Attention, students! Attention. Today there will be no classes. In fact, there will be no school until further notice," he said calmly. "The explosions you are hearing are not military exercises. The North Koreans are coming. You must go home at once and await instructions from the radio. A state of emergency has been declared. War has started. I am sorry, but I can tell you nothing more. You must hurry home."

Some girls surrounded the headmaster, shouting questions, but my friends and I, frightened and stunned, clung to each other's arms and tripped down the steps of the school. Despite the buildup of military exercises it had not occurred to us that the risk of attack had been so great. We stumbled out into the street, feeling lost.

And so, with a puzzling anticlimax, were we informed of the outbreak of the savage Korean War; a war unannounced until the second day, taking an entire nation and its leaders by surprise. It was a humiliating shambles. The military could not believe the attack. It was an early, near-fatal blow to our wobbly-legged democracy, and one from which it would take nearly four decades to recover.

"Our family is leaving Seoul tonight," In-sook told us. "My father says it's not safe to stay under the Communists."

"Myung-ja, your father must know what is happening. What has he told you?" Soon-ja asked me.

"He has been away," I said, "I don't think he knows anything, or

I doubt that we would still be here. Anyway, he never talks about government affairs in front of me, that's for certain." The girls were silent. Tearfully, we said farewell to In-sook and embraced her with a sense of urgency. Soonja vowed to visit me as soon as she could, running as she waved good-bye. She lived on the other side of Seoul. Hurriedly, I made my way to the trolley shelter, and after an excruciatingly long delay, caught the next streetcar home.

Now there was open panic in the streets, and I began to feel more frightened still. Seoul was suddenly seething with people, bumping into each other, writhing like a mass of startled worms, squirming away in every direction. Poor families, carrying saucepans and rolled-up bedding as well as their babies, jostled through the crowd looking lost and alarmed. Seeing the glazed, pathetic expression on a grandfather's face, tears welled up in my eyes. I prayed to God to let me reach home safely to find my family still there.

As we passed the U.S. embassy there was an extraordinary scene; pandemonium had broken out, and billowing clouds of gray smoke surrounded the building as a small group of American workers were hurriedly burning huge piles of documents, flames jumping from the pages as the charred sheets dropped onto the embassy steps. Hundreds of desperate Koreans and large numbers of Europeans were shouting and besieging them for information and help, some waving bankrolls in their harried faces. The frantic civil servants grimly carried on burning their files. As the trolley turned a corner I saw a Korean woman, shouting someone's name, collapse weeping on the embassy steps as her appeals were ignored.

I felt slightly faint. All of the tram passengers stood at the windows transfixed by the chaotic spectacle on the streets. After what felt like years, we reached my stop, and I literally sprinted down the long graveled drive, heels flying, and flung open the heavy gates, for once not bothering to close them behind me.

The front door was ajar, and I swallowed tearfully on hearing the sound of voices coming from beyond the vestibule. *They were still here*. Inside, my father was on the telephone in his study with his back to me, and my mother was hovering by the radio in the kitchen with Myung-hi and Sikmo by her side. The voice of President Rhee came on the air:

Stay calm. Do not attempt to move. I repeat: Do not attempt to leave Seoul. Stay where you are. You will be safe if you stay in your homes. Stand by your radio for the latest war bulletins. This is a state of emergency. For your own safety, stay in your homes. I repeat: Do not attempt to move.

The president's voice was shaky, and not in the least bit reassuring.

My mother was very calm, telling Sikmo to serve lunch as usual, and to take an inventory of our food stores afterward. Sikmo, all plump, with reddened cheeks and round, chapped elbows, wiped away a tear and busied herself by putting on the rice, exhaling loudly, and talking to herself with nervous inanity. Myung-hi and I did not know what to do with ourselves, or what to say to each other. We must have helped to set the table, but there was not enough to do in the kitchen to distract us from our fears. At lunch Father looked very strained, and said that Kim Il Sung had launched a surprise attack on Onjin early yesterday morning, and ninety thousand troops of the North Korean People's Army had crossed the 38th Parallel by dawn.

"The North says that we struck first, but that is a lie. The Russians may not have directly ordered the invasion, but they gave Kim Il Sung their approval and their tanks, weapons, and planes. Worse, the Communist Chinese are also heavily behind the North Koreans, apparently training their guerilla troops," said Father, swooping with his chopsticks for the bowl of kimchi. "It was very clever: our troops were still away on weekend leave, and could not respond to the attack," he said with some amusement.

"I can tell you this: they've traced the timing of the invasion directly to the double-crossing spy, Kim Souyim, who was living with her American-colonel lover, in his house, and all the time sending precise intelligence information to her Communist boyfriend, Lee, in the North. She told them exactly when the American occupation troops would be leaving Seoul, and when the South would be most vulnerable," Father told Mother.

"*This* you will not be reading about in the history books, I can promise you; the Americans will be too humiliated to let it be known that a *colonel*—married, at that—excuse me, children . . . was responsible for such an outrageous security breach. Of course they executed the spy Kim yesterday. Firing squad," said Father. We absorbed the amazing story in silence. We had been reading in the papers about the trial of the traitor, Kim Souyim. I had no idea that her treason was at such a high level, and that she had made the Americans look so foolish. I was surprised that Father revealed it in front of my sister and me. He was clearly shocked by it as well.

"But what are *we* going to do, *Aboji*?" I asked Father.

"We will stay here for tonight until the situation is clearer." He sounded very confident, and finished his lunch with gusto. Sitting around the table, we were in a strange suspended state. We had no clue of what was to happen to us; we were numbed by the swiftness of events. The news of war was surreal; nothing had happened that we could see, or touch, or smell. The invaders were still far off, and our lives for now were unaffected by the news. Namsan Park, our house, and the streets beyond were intact; the hands of the clock continued to revolve at the same slow speed; but a creeping, quickening fear had transfigured my inner world.

I can remember little about the rest of the second day of the

Korean War, but one thing loomed more terrible than anything else. Jin-ho never returned home.

On the radio the next morning we heard the president repeating his order for citizens to remain in Seoul. When Father telephoned his government colleagues there was no reply. They had left Seoul during the night. Father said that President Rhee's radio announcement was prerecorded, and guessed that he had fled south to escape the advancing Communists.

"*Aboji*, why should he pretend to be in Seoul and tell everyone to stay here if he's not in Seoul himself?" I asked.

"Because he doesn't want the Communists to think he is a coward, and to hand them the capital city. Think of the chaos," he said, walking out to the motorcar. Father and I had decided to venture out into the city to see if anything had changed overnight.

Jin-ho had still not returned, and we were badly shaken. Mother, of course, was particularly upset, and asked Father to look for him around the university. Father said he would, but told her not to worry, that Jin-ho was old enough to look out for himself. She shook her head, disconsolate.

"Perhaps he is with a girlfriend, perhaps he is with friends. Either way, we can do little if anything about it. It's typical of him to make us worry; *so* unreliable," said Father, edgy with frustration. *Aboji* climbed into the driver's seat, and put the vehicle into gear with rusty movements. Our chauffeur had fled during the night. As we drove through the gates of the mansion we saw immediately that the chauffeur had not been alone in his decision.

If yesterday's streets had been full of people, milling confused and directionless in the city center, today there was a positive stampede of citizens leaving Seoul, but this time in only one direction.

south. Alleys and boulevards were jammed with carts, wheelbarrows, trucks, buses, cars, taxis, bicycles, jeeps, all honking and revving, overwhelmed by the masses of shouting pedestrians choking the roads. I had no idea that Seoul could hold so many people. We were literally unable to pass, and it took us an hour to get through to the side street where we were forced to abandon the automobile. I was hot and tired, but my adrenaline was surging madly, electrified by what was happening. I checked every face I could to see if Jin-ho was among them, alarmed by the blind fear mirrored in people's eyes.

Father gripped my hand, and pulled me through the crowd to the steps of a court building, shouldering our way to the top step, where we had an overview of the mob. Millions of people were heading toward the Han River like sheep toward the edge of a cliff. Many were screaming.

"What is happening?" Father asked the old man next to him.

"They say the Communists will be here by sunset. Everyone is heading south. Look at them panic! They can't all get across the bridge; the ferries are overcrowding. Two of them sank about an hour ago, and hundreds of people drowned last night. Trying to get across on overloaded dinghies. Some tried to swim over, and drowned halfway," said the man.

"What will you do?" I asked him, trying to suppress a feeling of hysteria.

"I am too old to go running anywhere. I will stay here. My son is smart. He has found a sewage pipe big enough for us to hide in comfortably. I am not afraid of these bullies."

We wished him luck, and with great difficulty walked back home against the current of desperate people, screaming and weeping, many dazed and in shock. Father said we must leave the motorcar, in case any Communist sympathizers saw us.

Overwhelmed, I stopped searching for Jin-ho's face. It was too unlikely that I should find him among the hordes of escapees, who knocked and bumped into us so much that my body felt bruised. The heaving scene was infernal, nightmarish. I felt breathless and claustrophobic, irrationally incensed at the chaos around me. I gripped my father's hand with all my might and pressed forward.

"You cannot bring your violin, and that's final," said Father. Taken aback, I could say nothing at first. My mother, busy packing some jewels into a small silk purse, gave him a long look.

"The first thing that will give you away as *yangban* is carrying an expensive musical instrument in a crisis," he said, putting a small bowl over his head and purposefully cutting his hair around its perimeter into a quite convincing peasant hairstyle.

"*Aboji*, I beg of you! Please understand," I cried, "I don't have a choice! I *have* to have my violin. I will hide it! I will hide it in a paper bag, covering it with something. I promise no one will search me," I said with a ferocity that startled my parents. Mother caught Father's eye and nodded with all of her authority. I grasped her hand, repressing tears of anxiety.

It was evening. To my alarm, Father had decided that we should remain in Seoul and face the worst. We had no alternative. We had no relatives in the South with whom we could stay, and we were bankrupt. Father's plan was to assume a new identity. If the Communists found Father, a *yangban* lord, and member of the enemy government, they would execute him, and probably the rest of us as well.

Father arranged for us to take refuge in a small house across town owned by a family friend who was fleeing to Taegu with his family. In this modest house we would pretend to be refugee farmers from the North, and stay there, for a while anyway, as long as our identities were not discovered. At least we would have shelter, he argued. The only hitch in the plan was Jin-ho's continued absence.

If my brother were still alive and in Seoul, how would he find us once we had left? Father thought that Jin-ho might contact Baby Uncle, and Baby Uncle—who was in Manchuria—would work it out. This was too roundabout for Mother's liking. What if he needed us quickly? Was there no one in Seoul we could entrust with our whereabouts? Father finally agreed to leave, along with some other decoy documents, a scrap of paper in the safe with our friend's name written on it, and hope that Jin-ho, who had stolen cash from the safe before, would return in need, remember the combination, and discover the name. My mother was distraught by the flimsy nature of the plan, but could think of no alternative. There was no time.

The radio announced that our army—the Republic of Korea Army—had been ordered to retreat in the face of the hugely successful Communist drive south. The ROK generals and American observers had underestimated the massive scale of the invasion. It was later revealed that only one-third of the undertrained ROK Army had been deployed against Kim Il Sung's crack Communist commandos, and over a third of our weaponry was immobilized, needing repairs. We had light weapons and artillery, but no tanks or antitank weapons, no combat aircraft, and only a few small navy ships, having been earlier denied weapons and equipment by the U.S. Defense Department, determined to minimize its involvement in Korea. But as a direct result of this shortsighted policy, Truman was forced to commit the U.S. Air Force and Navy on only the second day of the war. Now, despite Washington's commitment, ROK generals, privates, and colonels alike were reduced to joining the straggling refugees retreating south of the Han River, both in jeeps and on foot.

Luckily we had no time to think about what was happening. Myung-hi had gone very quiet, but was busy helping Mother sort out papers, and planning our disguise for the escape downtown. Sikmo had left us that afternoon to find her family on the east coast, despite Father's advice that she head south or stay with us. I was more upset than I'd thought to see her go. When I realized that I might not actually see her again, I clung to her hot, plump hand. At that moment her hand held everything familiar—all the dull comfort and precious loyalty that I had taken for granted throughout my life. For a moment, she held my small hand between her own great paws in a warm bun of affection before turning away, both of us averting our eyes awkwardly to avoid tears.

Sikmo left behind an enormous dinner, using up as much as she could of the unexpected surplus of fresh food that we could not take with us. Father took no wine that evening to keep his head clear for any emergency. We ate silently, and with grim gratitude, not knowing what future meals we might be able to count on. My sister and I went to bed at the usual time, and I remember reading a short story by Kipling before turning out the light. The distant sound of pounding artillery and mortar fire filled the darkness beyond the house. Despite this unnerving serenade, on our last night in the mansion in Namsan Park, I managed somehow to sleep. I dreamed no dreams.

By the next morning, Wednesday, Seoul had fallen. Just three days after their attack, the North Korean Communists were already inside the capital. I did not look back at the house as I shut the big iron gates behind me and my family for the last time. We walked fast toward the center of Seoul, the low flying aircraft overhead making us all nervous. Apart from a small pouch of jewels and a paper bag stuffed with cabbages (to hide my violin) we left everything behind, and walked the streets disguised as poor country peasants; without luggage. Father had a half-grown beard as well as his new bumpkin haircut, Mother wore an old-fashioned white cotton *han-bok*, and my sister and I sported pigtails, too-small pinafores, and scuffed lace-up school shoes. We looked quite convincing.

The palpable tension in the capital was mounting. The seething crowds had vanished, leaving only the destitute and the elderly wandering the eerie pavements. Some half-crazed civilians wearing red armbands were running through the streets urging the dazed onlookers to cheer the arriving Communists; "Our saviors!" they proclaimed, waving their arms. People glanced away from the zealots, confused. Then, from behind us, came a low, unimaginably dreadful sound: that of marching boots. And suddenly, they were there in our midst: the advance troops of the North Korean People's Army. I caught a glimpse of olive green uniform and camouflage foliage stuck in a soldier's helmet, and my heart stopped. My mother and father sagged before me involuntarily, and we halted where we stood, not breathing and not looking back, and allowed the silent column of enemy soldiers to march by us. It was a surreal moment.

We tried to look happy as we walked along, as if relieved to have reached Seoul after a long journey from the North. Luckily no one was paying the least attention to us, such was the confusion in the streets. There were knots of frightened people, then acres of deserted pavement, with all buildings shut and locked, and blinds drawn in people's homes. At one window I could see motionless fingers holding down the bottom of a paper blind. Then as we neared the Han River Bridge, the mood and tempo of the scene shifted. Suddenly, scores of panic-struck ROK Army soldiers and disoriented civilians started running and screaming, dropping their possessions in the middle of the road. We tried to trace the source of the panic, but couldn't see what was happening.

I was so scared, my mind emptied completely. Adrenaline kept my feet flying over the asphalt like a cat being chased by a dog. One could hear a crescendo of running footsteps, the sudden zooming of a motorcar engine, and the sickening, invasive din of low-flying aircraft. Sweating, we soon reached the new house, a nondescript building in the middle of a row: the street dead quiet. Exhaling with relief,

Father produced a latchkey and quickly opened the front door, glancing at the neighboring houses. As soon as we were inside—I think Myung-hi was the last to enter and was just removing her shoes—there was an almighty, thunderous, shattering explosion. The sound made my lungs shake.

It was the Han River Bridge. President Rhee's retreating army had bombed it, and we were now trapped in Seoul with the enemy.

CHAPTER THIRTEEN

In Hiding

The next day I awoke in a strange bed, disoriented, and feeling small. The bed mat was a normal size, but I was dwarfed by the monumental unreality of waking up in a war zone. The unwelcome events of yesterday came teeming back into my head, scenes too overwhelming to oppose. My thoughts were scrambled with surprise, my heart uneasy. The silence in the streets was unearthly. I remembered that the Han River Bridge had been blown up. I couldn't believe that we had been abandoned by our president, and virtually left to die by the fleeing army.

The sight of Myung-hi, still asleep nearby, was comforting in this singular situation. It was doubly strange waking up in a stranger's home, with its own specific smells and unfamiliar objects. We had taken over the house of a police captain whose father had worked on Lord Min's estate in Yangyang. I was grateful for the decent shelter that the policeman's house offered, but it was extremely odd all the same.

Yet strangeness quickly became the norm. We were fortunate that they had left behind most of their possessions, food, clothes, linen, books, furniture. The house looked intact, reminding me of the children's story "Goldilocks and the Three Bears" that we had read in English class, where it looked as if someone would be returning at any moment. I felt slightly guilty trying on the clean dress and undergarments I found in the cupboard of the daughter's room. Luckily, she had quite good clothes, and being only a little bit taller than me, the garment fitted well enough, and her wardrobe would do for Myung-hi, too.

Looking at my sister, my mind returned inexorably to the fact that Jin-ho was still missing, but I could not bear to dwell on it; the thought of what might have happened to him was too upsetting. I reminded myself that we were lucky to have escaped any harm ourselves. I chose to believe that Jin-ho was still alive.

Walking down the corridor to the kitchen, I found my father checking and double-locking all the doors and windows, and pulling tight the blinds and curtains so that it looked as if the house were empty. We had tea and rice for breakfast out of strange bowls and cups, and Father told us that henceforth our name would be Kim. He had already burned all of our identity papers and photographs. Mother and I would look around the storeroom later to see exactly what food remained, and make plans to ration our supplies. We all looked at each other with the same set expression, as if to say that this would make a pleasant enough hiding place—or prison—in which to see off the invaders.

There was a shed in the garden which Father told us had a bomb shelter beneath it, and the houses on either side of us stood deserted. This was encouraging. Father forbade us to approach the windows or leave the house in case the Communists should be watching. Naturally Father banned violin playing, but I was grateful merely to have the instrument near me.

According to the radio, which Father played very low in the basement, China had immediately lodged a protest against the United

States' "armed aggression" in South Korea, and the United Nations was considering intervening in the war, North Korea having violated a UN charter. Father was hugely relieved at this, and said that he felt sure we would be rescued in a matter of weeks or even days. Although I was utterly ignorant about politics, I could read my father well, and his spirits seemed artificially high. Despite his confident manner, I knew he was frightened for his life, and for what would happen to us should the Communists find him.

This first day in captivity had been so unique that it passed very quickly. Yet as we grew accustomed to our situation, Time became warped with the repetitive routine of our days, and distended with the heavy sense of waiting itself. During the following months we became inured to the sound of nocturnal gunfire. We came to sleep a different kind of sleep.

Once they had captured Seoul, Kim Il Sung's army temporarily halted its southward advance to regroup. Father was mystified by the continuing success of the Communists. He and his government colleagues had condescendingly dismissed the North Koreans as "a bunch of old-fashioned peasants using cast-off Russian weapons," thinking they would never dare to launch a serious attack on their own brother nation, the mighty American-backed Republic of Korea. But how misguided they had been.

For a couple of weeks it had been extremely quiet in our part of the city, near Chang Chung Park. So far, we had not stirred from the shuttered house, and no one had yet tried to enter. However, mounting curiosity and dwindling food supplies prompted Father to send me out into the streets of Seoul on a mission. I was to discover where stores were open or closed, to note the position of soldiers, observe the stationing of unusual numbers of tanks, and see what sort of overall condition the city was in. I was especially excited, as Father was allowing me to go via Soon-ja's house, so I could see if she was still in Seoul. I gained Father's permission by reminding him that Soon-ja's brother had worked at the American embassy, and might have reliable inside access to the latest news.

Father was unable to undertake the mission himself as his presence would draw more attention, and it would be fatal were he stopped. He spent all of his days alone in his bedroom playing *baduk* and practicing calligraphy, so that if anyone came he could hop easily into bed, pretending to be an invalid. As I was now the eldest child, the duty fell to me. Anyway, I was thrilled to have something important to do, and longed to get out of the house, despite the possibility of danger. The policeman's family had a meager library, which I had already exhausted, and I hoped to be able to borrow some books from Soon-ja, should I find her still in Seoul.

I made myself as unbecoming as possible, disguising myself as younger than I really was with no makeup, hair in pigtails, wearing an untucked boy's shirt, ill-fitting cotton skirt, droopy ankle socks, and flat rubber shoes. Father unbolted the front door for me; I peered out, blinking into the sun, and scanned the deserted pavement. *Aboji* nodded encouragingly, whereupon I skipped off down the dusty street.

Although it was a hot day, it was heaven simply to feel the air moving against my face, to feel freedom again after the long confinement. The quiet scene before me was reassuring, and my lingering fear shrank to pocketsize. Seoul was a ghost town, its streets eerily empty. I felt quite conspicuous against this backdrop, but kept sneakily to back alleys and side streets, moving fast to avoid seeing any soldiers or familiar faces. Soon-ja's house was near Seoul National University, and although it would take me about an hour to get there, I was relishing the adventure.

On my way, I saw a few nervous old people walking the streets, and some destitute-looking mothers with babies. There were one or two vegetable stalls open, which I thought was a good sign. No physical damage seemed to have been done to the city at all along my route. You couldn't even tell that there was a war on. But just as I was thinking this, an open truck rounded the corner, packed with swaying, armed North Korean soldiers. My heart thumped in surprise, and I cast down my eyes to avoid engaging their attention. More convoy trucks passed. I walked on as fast as I could, and was not stopped.

When I arrived safely at the gates of Soon-ja's house, I was relieved and surprised to find her inside with her family. She was overjoyed to see me, but I noticed that she checked her emotions slightly on her mother's entrance.

"Where are you staying? What have you been doing?" demanded Soon-ja, as her mother handed me an enticing plate of watermelon and a glass of cold cider, which I consumed lustily. I remembered Father's warning not to reveal where we were living.

"Father got separated from us in the exodus, so Mother and I are staying in a friend's house near the old antiques market," I lied. She looked at me with slight suspicion.

"You must tell me exactly where, so I can come and visit you."

"I'm afraid we can have no visitors at the moment, my mother is very ill." It was partly true. With still no news from Jin-ho, my mother had been increasingly unwell, and had started having migraine headaches.

It was almost like old times, chatting with round-faced, gap-toothed Soon-ja, and eating melon in the baking courtyard.

"School has been turned into a political reeducation center, you know," she said, spitting a black seed into a white saucer. "I went along to see what they had to say. It was incredibly interesting, you know. There are some girls from our class there."

The girls Soon-ja mentioned were known Communists, although their parents were not.

I thought of you. Someone mentioned getting you involved,

being such a leader and all. But you have to watch out what you say now; you have to show willingness to renounce the old ways. Aristocrats like your father are being shot now, as enemies of the working people."

Chilled, I smiled and changed the subject. Could I borrow some books? She agreed readily. Her parents were cultivated people with a prodigious library. To my delight, I found a collection of O. Henry short stories, Goethe's *Sorrows of Young Werther*, and a novel by Maupassant. Reading escapist Western novels had become my only pleasure.

Our talk finally got around to the war, and she confirmed that the UN forces would be coming any day now to intervene in the fighting. She said, with pride, that the North Koreans were on the brink of taking the whole of the South. I was flabbergasted by their quick progress.

"The North Koreans have massacred South Koreans in Taejon and Chonju. There are thousands and thousands of people in concentration camps. Political prisoners. Can you imagine? South Koreans are even being tortured and massacred by South Koreans on nothing more than suspicion of being 'unreliable,' " said Soon-ja, speaking with a new, and very adult, sang-froid.

I was confused, and decided to cut short my stay; as I left, she handed me a newspaper, "Have a look at this," she urged, smiling. It was the *Red Star*. I flushed, and as soon as I was out of sight, I threw the newspaper into a trash can. It was as if she were not at all the same person. I felt betrayed and scared. I could not see her again. She knew my father's position very well, and I believed that she would report us.

The summer days were long and passed extremely slowly. I lay on my back, inert on the bed, and watched the trajectory of a fat, sluggish fly

as it chugged through the thick, still air, making an annoying amount
of noise in the shuttered room. Myung-hi and I spent a lot of time napping, swatting flies, and reposing in the small, sunny courtyard, where
Father now allowed us to venture. We also spent hours grooming ourselves with great care, although we never left the house.

I was cross because of an argument I'd had with my mother earlier about reading English books. She said I was risking their lives. If
anyone found them, she claimed we would be accused of being
American collaborators or spies. I told her not to upset herself, that
she was exaggerating, but she disagreed and forced me to hide my
books and dictionary beneath a board in the bomb shelter. I made a
great fuss about it and lost my temper. It was too much. As it was,
everything had to be hushed: the radio, voices, doors opening and
closing. I was more than fed up. Back in my room, I looked longingly
at the unplayed Edith Piaf records propped up uselessly against the
wall.

I found myself yearning to leave Seoul. It had become an awful,
stinking city, a purgatory where we awaited death or deliverance. I
longed to be in a green paradise, far away from this hot, dusty gray
war zone, this cramped, mean house, and even away from my family.
I wanted to play my violin loudly. I thirsted for challenges and thrilling
stimulation. Maybe I would go as far away as America. And why not?
Before the war I had applied for a scholarship to study music in New
York. I did not expect to win it, but now I was rather hoping I would.

We were all feeling the strain of being in hiding. Further, everyone's health was suffering. Father, who had aged terribly from the
mental tension, looked worst of all, but gradually we had all become
emaciated. We ate hardly any fruit or vegetables, took little exercise
apart from dull household chores and some dispirited calisthenics, and
had had no contact with friends or relatives.

Mother managed the household well, as always. Although she
obviously missed the convenience of maids and Sikmo, she got the

best out of Myung-hi and me, and the three of us took turns washing clothes, cleaning and preparing the food in as normal a way as possible. I believe she missed going to Mass far more than any material luxury, and she continued to pray regularly for Jin-ho.

With little else to do, our lives revolved around meals and sleeping. We ate the same meager dish repeatedly; a cloudy broth of potato and barley enlivened with occasional shreds of dried shrimp, a sliver of summer squash or turnip green, a pinch of kimchi and a teaspoon of rice. Although I had mouthwatering fantasies about gorging on *kalbi*, strawberries, and sweet red-bean cakes, the ritual of eating, as well as the food itself, was comforting: I sipped the weak broth, trying to be grateful that I was not among those starving to death on the roads south.

Unlike me, Myung-hi was good-natured and docile, her temperament more like my mother's, whereas mine resembled Father's. Being the youngest and least likely to be raped or tortured, she had inherited the task of running vital errands. Although she found it extremely boring and didn't understand much of what was said, she rarely complained about having to attend the Communist rallies on our family's behalf. She was an ideal representative. Having a naturally trusting and somewhat bovine facial expression, none of the Communist officials thought her bright enough to be useful, or ever questioned her at these potentially hazardous meetings.

Recent Communist radio broadcasts had been urging all "traitors" to give themselves up to The People's Court, where they would receive mild sentences and the clemency of reintegration into society, whereas all traitors found hiding would be executed in house-to-house searches. My father did not trust the North Koreans, and gambled to remain where he was. Nevertheless, these broadcasts did not encourage sound sleep, and Father would start at the slightest noise, whatever he was doing.

The moan of the air-raid siren interrupted my thoughts, but I did not move in any hurry. I peeked out at the hazy blue sky through the closed slats of the bamboo blind, and it looked the same as it did every day. Blue and hazy and boring.

Just then, there was a violent, cracking banging on the front door, like a heavy object hitting the wood. Instantly I slipped into the corridor, where my mother and Myung-hi had already gathered, cowering. We held our breath for a moment without moving. The sharp, loud banging started again and went on violently for what felt like a long time before Mother nodded to us, and opened the door.

Four North Korean soldiers in khaki uniforms with machine guns burst inside.

"EVERYONE OUTSIDE!" shouted the tall officer, pointing with his gun.

"NO SHOES!"

We obeyed automatically, and shuffled out into the courtyard. I prayed for Father. Already I pictured him being led away in handcuffs, or even being shot against the wall.

"My husband is in the bedroom; he is an invalid, terminally ill. Please spare him," pleaded my mother. "We are northerners, poor refugees here." We gripped each other's sweating hands. The courtyard gravel poked painfully into the soles of my feet.

"NO TALKING."

I thought of my English books, and inwardly thanked Mother for making me hide them. The soldiers did not appear to be very interested in questioning us. One of them kicked open the sitting-room door, and started tipping over furniture, hand and foot. He went straight for the desk, and opened the lid by smashing it with the butt of his gun. A sewing basket fell to the floor, and everything spilled out, including Mother's silk jewelry purse, which held our last precious items, a gold watch of Grandfather's, a few jewels, a gold fountain pen, wedding cups, and jade rings she had concealed from the bailiffs.

When the commanding officer was not looking, the soldier stuffed all of my mother's treasures into his trouser pockets. The soldier guarding us grabbed the chain around Mother's neck.

"What's this?" he squinted, knowing full well what it was.

"It's a crucifix," Mother replied.

"Foreign rubbish. For poor northerners you people sure have lots of expensive things."

"They aren't our things," said Mother, anxiously straining to hear Father's interrogation at the hands of the officer.

"I am very sick, sir," we heard Father say.

"YOU PATHETIC OLD MAN. Why have you come south?"

"We were starving on our farm, and we had no relatives to turn to."

"And why should we treat you well here?"

"Because we want to be good Communists."

"SHUT UP," shouted the officer. There came a loud crash, like the sound of furniture being kicked over.

"Please leave us alone. My wife and daughters cannot cause any harm. I beg your kindness, sir."

"Shut up, you old fool. SHUT UP AND LET ME PASS," shouted the officer, apparently throwing my father to the floor. I was sickened by the sound of the thud.

"Your husband is very educated-sounding for a farmer. I don't think he is a farmer. Do you?" insisted the soldier, yanking and breaking her chain, and pocketing the cross. He grabbed her left hand and pointed to her wedding ring. She looked up, frozen with disbelief and dread, but pulled it off and gave it to him without hesitation. She understood that it might be a trade for my father's life. The soldier said something to his officer, and they carried on ransacking the house room by room, crashing, banging, and shattering things as they went along. They seemed to stay forever. After filling their pockets and backpacks, they left, leering. Their visit appeared not to have been an official search, but a pretext for looting. After they left, Mother fled to Father, who was bruised but otherwise uninjured. Myung-hi and I collapsed onto our beds, too shaken to speak.

The following three months we spent in silent confinement, growing thinner, and listening tensely for noises. I kept my English books permanently in the bomb shelter.

One day in September my father burst into the kitchen.

"The radio says that General MacArthur and the UN forces have landed at Inchon, and are on their way to Seoul."

My first feeling was shock at how emaciated and gray my father looked standing there in the doorway, needing to support himself with a cane, but the pang of sadness passed, superseded by cautious pleasure at the news.

Free again? Strange adrenaline surged through my numbness. I felt wobbly, disbelieving, like a death row prisoner being taunted with clemency. My mind raced drunkenly from one thought to the next, visions of food glowing before me: fresh steaming, aromatic noodles glistening in sesame oil, plump shrimp and bright chili sauce, crackling roast pork and slithery black mushrooms, ripe strawberries, glasses of milky *kamju*. I thought of playing my violin, my opera records, seeing old friends, even going back to school would be fantastic fun, a privilege, even. I was quite delirious.

In our confinement, my family had lost hope of the war's end. From the Communist radio reports over the previous two months we learned that the Korean People's Army had succeeded in taking an astonishing ninety percent of the South, despite the arrival of U.S. combat troops, the 8th Army, First Cavalry and 25th Infantry Divisions, 24th Division, 2nd U.S. Infantry Division, and 1st U.S. Marine Brigade. UN troops had repelled two Communist attacks along the Naktong perimeter line, but the Communist offensive threatened Taeju. The latest arrival was the British 27th Brigade. Although I was bored by the mechanics of war, later I learned that there were serious equipment and ammunition shortages. American soldiers were inadequately trained and led, and demoralized. They could summon up no grand outrage at Korean Communists, as they could at the Pearl Harbor–exploding Japanese. Would MacArthur's daring offensive be too little too late?

Within days, you could tell that something big was about to happen. Far from my fantasy of a rescue team of handsome, garlanded soldiers arriving at our front door to lead us, smiling, to safety—and restore our former wealth—I heard the hostile and unwelcome sound of nervous artillery shelling and the shuddering zooming of low-flying American aircraft as they swooped to mark their targets. Although UN forces had succeeded in recapturing Kimpo airport, I was terrified. The blind machines of war could not discern a South Korean from a Communist.

By late September there was a mighty battle for Seoul. Without warning, we were suddenly being bombarded. There were tremendous explosions at close intervals, but one was not exactly listening for patterns in the raids. We had spent all day in the dark bomb shelter in the garden. My nerves were worn away, hot and raw with exhaustion. Now it was evening. I sat on my books, which offered little comfort now. There was nothing to do but listen to the aural pageant of our city's destruction; I winced and cowered at the cacophony; treble notes of shattering glass, tenor blasts of ripping walls, vibrating bass of exploding concrete and masonry. I could hear the rushing, tearing edge of flame and the belated, mournful whine of sirens filling the desolate night air.

Why were they trying to kill us? Why liberate us at all? I thought to myself with bitterness. The smell of ash and smoke permeated the shelter. I looked at the faces of my mother, father, and sister for comfort and reassurance, to stop the rising gorge of panic that gripped me at the closer blasts.

Every emotion flickered through me as we sat there: obvious ones like self-pity, terror, anxiety, anger, helplessness, as well as more unexpected visitations of boredom, impatience, and excitement. Was this shack to be my grave? Would we all die at once? What would I do if I were the only survivor? Were there funerals during a war? Who paid for them all? I was hungry, as always. When would we eat again?

I looked at my mother's face, and was taken aback. Anguish weighed down the corners of her eyes and mouth, and I could almost see pain emanating from her, like heat waves off the hood of a motorcar. I knew she was thinking about Jin-ho. Lately she had had terrible nightmares about him, and seeing her suffering face, my own buried worry for Jin-ho emerged through the woolly trivia in my head. As the bombs fell I held my mother's hand and prayed an odd sort of prayer with an intensity I'd not summoned before.

A vision of Great-grandfather's temple on Mount Sorak filled my whole being; I imagined my entire family there with Jin-ho, Aunt Pusan, and Cousin Jae-dal, alive again, safe, healed, and restored. I imagined one thousand chestnut trees, with mighty trunks, encircling and protecting us from danger. The wind rushed through the leaves, making a powerful hushing sound, a sound of peace, that drowned out the bombs.

Tears filled my closed eyes. I might die before ever being able to see this temple. Jin-ho might already be dead. Would the chestnut trees remain after the war? Would the temple survive after we were gone?

Exhausted, I slept a little. Toward dawn, when the close, heavy bombing had nearly ceased, we ducked back into the house and had a skimpy supper of cold rice. Father asked my sister and me to scout the streets nearby to see if there was any better shelter to go on to. But once out in the street we knew immediately that it was too dangerous to move. The streetlamps were shot out, and there were huge, shocking, ragged black cavities where a few neighboring houses had been. I could hear shrapnel and bullets flying everywhere with hot speed. The sounds were so close, I could hear the metal whistling. Blood pounding hard, I leaned back against a wall, my nerves keyed tight with vigilance. I pushed Myung-hi back inside, and ducked back to the corner of the house, where I stood trembling, and watched what could be seen in the crepuscular gloom.

As I observed the direction of the shelling, it soon became clear that our street was caught in the cross fire between North Korean troops and the Marines. I could see no soldiers on either side, but heard and saw where the bullets had strafed the sides of houses, leaving clusters of deep pockmarks. Although I had stood there for only five minutes, it was, for me, the longest five minutes of the war. It was by far the most intensive fighting I had heard or seen, and I was more terrorized than I thought it possible to be. Every breath came with vivid consciousness that I was breathing, and all I thought of was surviving through to the next breath. Then I saw a straggly group of older women running out from a doorway, fleeing desperately toward the park, some of them falling. An old man followed them, was shot in the leg, and collapsed onto the cobblestones. Another old man, bearded, ran past screaming in terrible agony, hit by napalm. A pathetic little boy in rags ran after him, arms outstretched. Some bedraggled people, all civilians, were scurrying past on their hands and knees. Their humiliation was awful to see. Then the shelling came closer than before, and I was driven back into the house shaking and breathless.

My parents were huddled in the cold kitchen, talking, ignorant of the violence just outside. With the arrival of liberating UN forces, Father said he was sure that the Communists would be driven back by this massive air attack, and even ventured that the war might be won as a result of this battle for Seoul. He told us to be comforted. I turned away and went silently to my room. Terrorized by the scenes I had just witnessed, I could not feel soothed. Ordinarily, the thought of being released from the Communists might have lifted me, but just now I could not share in my father's optimism. I felt destroyed. We were all so exhausted, that despite our hunger pains, we managed to sleep through the last air-raid sirens.

I awoke at around eight o'clock to a great commotion outside in the streets. There was an exceptionally loud noise of footsteps running in front of our house. Before the bombardment it had been sepulchrally quiet. Now the grinding of heavy machinery, and the revving of motor engines filled the vacuum. My sister and I dressed hurriedly, and went to the front window, where we raised the blind a few inches. My mother, already dressed, brought us a tray of tea, which we drank swiftly, peering outside. Father joined us, and we saw huge numbers of civilians massed on both sides of the street, some cheering and waving Korean flags. Where had they all come from? UN tanks rolled down a main street in the distance.

With Father's permission, *Omma*, my sister, and I slipped out into the street to join the crowd waving at the the columns of soldiers. There were thousands of them marching, bearing weapons and ammunition, and occasionally turned to acknowledge the spontaneous applause that broke out from bystanders, most of whom looked bedraggled, dazed, and delirious. Myung-hi and I held hands, waving with our free arms. I could not quite believe their presence. I was confused to hear sharp exchanges of gunfire in the distance, the UN takeover apparently not quite complete.

We returned indoors to Father, and told him what we'd seen and heard. His face creased into a rare smile. "How quick they've been in coming! It's like a second liberation!" he said. The mood in the house lightened palpably, and we allowed ourselves to relax as we sat around the kitchen. This was a novel luxury. But as we sat there, the thought of Jin-ho formed in the silence, and loomed over us all, staining the bright atmosphere with sadness. I could not bear to see my mother's pain and to pretend any longer.

"It's Jin-ho, isn't it. You're afraid that he is dead, *Omoni*."

Omma looked up, aghast, and then her face softened, and she dropped her head, nodding, her small shoulders almost imperceptibly shaking.

"I know. I am scared, too. But what can we do?"

I put my arms around her.

Later that day, Father, exalted by the prospect of peace, decided to break his official state of hiding. Wearing a low hat, and aided by a walking stick, he took Myung-hi and me outdoors to get a better view of our neighborhood and to see, unlikely though it was, if any emergency food provisions were to be found. Because of Father's particularly weak condition, we had to walk very slowly and gently—a pace quite difficult to maintain with the occasional exchange of gunfire at our backs. The Marines and resisting North Korean troops were apparently still fighting in parts of the city. To be safe, we stuck to the main street.

The sun beamed down in dull shafts through the undispersed dust from collapsed buildings and smouldering fires, masking the scene with false cheer. No sooner had we reached the corner joining the main boulevard than Father ordered us to go home, trying to shield our eyes with his hands. Everywhere you looked, there were charred bodies. Women, children, old people, soldiers of both sides, lay curled on the ground in eerie stillness, blackened, and disfigured. To my left a trench was brimming with corpses, and near my right foot I saw something that looked like a burned log, but looking closer, discovered it was a leg. I felt sick from the putrid smell around me, a stench that I cannot describe.

I suppose it must have looked like a street in any war, in any city, but this was my own city, and I had never seen a battle scene before. It was otherworldly, apocalyptic. Telephone poles stood skewed sideways. The public buildings were unrecognizable ghosts of themselves. Those still standing had gaping, glassless windows, black smoke stains streaming beneath their openings like dark circles beneath the eyes of a blind man. But the majority of houses and shops were at least half-bombed, some with one wall remaining, and a bookshelf or stove still preserved, a quaint reminder of normality. But mostly you couldn't even tell where the buildings had been. Instead of a block of houses, there was an acre of rubble: wing-tipped roof tiles, corrugated iron, wiring, chunks of plaster, splintered beams, broken glass, a children's toy, branchless trees, a human limb, excrement, and ashes.

The East Gate was still standing, and seeing the spire of the Catholic cathedral visible in the distance, tears filled my eyes. I thanked God, for not a single pane of glass in our house had been cracked, nor had our walls been touched by any bullet. This seemed miraculous. Returning home with Myung-hi, I was sobered by our good fortune. Despite the vivid scenes of carnage we passed again walking home, I was not as afraid as before.

When we got home, we told mother everything we had seen, and somehow this helped to reduce the scale of my revulsion and horror. The devastation was also made more bearable by my ignorant belief that we were going to win the war at any moment, and that we would soon be free. How wrong we were!

There was practically nothing for dinner that night. We were now eating the very last of the rice, and were rationed a teaspoonful each with our watery barley soup. During the past weeks we had run out of greens and fruit, and did not know how much longer we could continue. We were all skeletally thin. Although my stomach continued to growl through the night, the terrible sights of the day conspired to deaden my appetite.

The next day there was a loud knock at the back gate. Father hurriedly got back into bed, and we tensed ourselves for another house search. Weakened by hunger, I was dizzy as I rose to my feet. We could not see anything at the window, so Myung-hi and I, steeling ourselves, accompanied Mother outside to the gate.

There, leaning against the doorway in the sun, stood Jin-ho, smiling and positively plump with good health. He wore army fatigues and his hair was cropped, a huge canvas haversack slung across his shoulder.

"*Annyong*! How are you doing?" he said casually, as if he had been away for the weekend. My mother nearly choked when she saw him. Wordlessly, she seized his hand and pulled him indoors. Father looked stealthily around the doorway and, seeing Jin-ho, gasped and had to steady himself. We surrounded him, touching his face and clothes, making sure he was real. Overwhelmed with astonishment, relief, and joy, our heads bowed, we melted into one body.

"You are alive. Alive," repeated my mother, her tears dropping onto his hand, which she held tightly and stroked, her head bowed, too moved to even look at him. Her shoulders were shaking. He smiled with indulgence, and we were all silent for some time.

"You are so skinny, all of you," he said.

When the shock was over, Mother made Jin-ho sit down, put a

cup of barley tea in his hand, and we all clamored to know what he had been doing and where he had been.

"First I have something for you," said Jin-ho, opening up his haversack; it was stuffed tight with food. Again, our eyes filled with tears, even Father's. It was one of the few times in my life I believed in God without reservation. To me it was proof that we were truly being looked after, with a tenderness and generosity far beyond my mean hopes. Out of the canvas bag came a big sack of rice, a bottle of soy sauce, some dried plums, dried fish, two heads of fresh cabbage, pickled turnip, tins of pink American meat called corned beef, American sweets called Tootsie Rolls, sugar, flour, six apples, and a bottle of *soju*. It was an impressive haul, and we clucked and fussed over Jin-ho until he could bear it no more.

"So tell us, TELL US!" demanded Myung-hi with high spirits, nibbling a slice of peeled apple to make it last as long as possible. "Where have you been?" Like thirsty sunflowers, our faces followed him around the room as he moved.

"Well, on the first day of the war I joined the Military Youth Corps from the university campus. We had to mobilize right away, and there was no time to go back and tell you. We left Seoul the day they blew up the bridge. I've been working as an interpreter for the U.S. Army ever since, traveling to different bases in the south," he said, squaring his shoulders and puffing his chest with mock pride. My mother shook her head in disbelief.

"We thought you were dead! Shame! You should have told someone!"

Jin-ho reminded her gently that he didn't know how to find us. In the end, he had been able to wire Baby Uncle, who eventually suggested the policeman's house.

"Baby Uncle's brother-in-law, the Communist lawyer, has done you a favor, Father. He has spread misinformation to the Communist

Intelligence Agency in Seoul saying that you had all fled to Pusan, which stopped them searching for you. You were on their list," said Jin-ho. We were silent as we considered this, grateful for so many blessings.

"Why are you so fat?" asked Myung-hi pinching his cheek. It was true; I had never seen him looking so chubby. Jin-ho pinched her in retaliation.

"Obviously, they feed me. They eat strange food. Quite good, though. Everything is big and bland and meaty. . . . Nothing cut into pieces; just huge hunks of plain-cooked meat and whole potatoes as big as grenades. The only spice they use is a giant bottle of sweet red sauce made from tomatoes," he said with excitement. "Anyway, sitting at a desk most of the time, I don't get much exercise," he said, manfully flexing his biceps. Father nodded.

"Have you been ill, *Aboji*?" Jin-ho asked Father. Father shook his head distractedly.

"We have been worried, son. Ill with worry. For you, and also, thinking that at any moment we might be discovered and killed." Jin-ho was silent. He looked at our faces quietly for the first time.

"I am sorry I have not been more of a help to you. Forgive me." Father got up unsteadily and walked away.

Although Seoul was a devastated bomb site and would probably remain so for many years, at least it was a liberated bomb site, and at last we could move and speak freely in the house and on the streets. Supper that night was a celebratory occasion. We had all calmed down a little by that time, profoundly relieved to have Jin-ho with us, as well as thankful to have real food, and a mouthful of warming, precious wine.

We had extra rice with our fiery turnip kimchi, and Mother

improvised some dumplings from the new flour and tin of corned beef that Jin-ho had brought. Although the dumpling dough lacked egg, she managed to stick the edges together with gluey cornstarch. Grilled, then dipped in soy sauce and chili, the dumplings were supremely and memorably delicious. Everything we ate made my mouth water, and I was afraid to let my appetite go, in case it should prove bottomless. As I listened to Father questioning Jin-ho, I sucked cautiously on a Tootsie Roll, enraptured by its novel flavor.

As Jin-ho spoke, Father looked at him with new respect. Indeed, my brother was more confident and grown up than before; his more moody, arrogant, and self-indulgent qualities were not on display at that moment, anyway. My mother looked at him with adoring, satisfied eyes. At last we were all together under this strange roof, bony, ragged, and flawed as we were.

"You'll never guess who joined the Volunteers with me," teased Jin-ho. We could not guess.

"Our funny old tutor, *sunsaeng-nim*. He has been working at the air base at Kimpo since day one of the war. We've gone out a few times. He's still the same as ever. Doing very well, too. Good with maps and statistics. Got him drunk one night with some Yank pals of mine, and had to carry him home," said Jin-ho wryly.

"Myung-ja, you should go along to the air force personnel office on Monday and see about a job; there is a clerical position going. You studied English. It would be fun," Jin-ho told me, "and good for her education, *Aboji*," he added to Father.

I looked at Father pleadingly. He studied my face in silence, and shrugged in weary skepticism.

"She should be very safe with her brother and cousin around," said Mother on my behalf. "What a good experience that would be for her, my dear." I smiled gratefully at *Omma*. My mother had repeatedly encouraged my sister and me to go further in our education and ambitions than she had been allowed to do, telling us that if we achieved more, perhaps we would be valued more, and be better treated by the world than women of her own generation and those of past generations. I lobbied Father gently for the rest of the evening. At last he gave in, and on Monday morning, face scrubbed, and dressed conservatively in a white blouse and straight navy skirt, I accompanied my brother to Kimpo Air Base in a jeep.

Air Base

I spent the following months of the war living in the barracks at Kimpo Air Base working as a secretary to a Captain Rick Lang. Although I warned him that first day that my English was poor, and that I had never even worked before, Captain Lang just unfurled a broad, toothy, easygoing grin, and said I would be perfect for the job. He was the first Yank I'd ever met, and I thought he was wonderful.

The sudden change in my circumstances was surreal. From cowering in a bomb shelter to striding the tarmac of a U.S. air base was a poignant, almost corny contrast. Being interviewed by Captain Lang, a cheerful, blond, blue-eyed Californian hulk, replete with peaked cap and dashing midnight blue air force uniform, I felt—temporarily, at least—like the heroine of a Hollywood war melodrama. God had again answered my prayers for deliverance. Not only was I paid a good wage, which I dutifully sent home, but a new world opened up to me then, an exotic Western world, on my own soil. And not least, I was fed, too.

And how was I fed? Worried about how scrawny I'd become in

hiding, the captain and a few of the staff concentrated on fattening me up. Their success was rapid. With touching pride, the cook, Moe, a barrel-chested Iowan with hairy forearms, fed me fried slabs of curious stuff called Spam, big plates of streaky bacon, sausage and eggs, veal cutlets with ketchup, mashed potatoes with gravy and butter, and cherry pie with canned whipped cream. My gastronomic horizons were widening so abruptly and radically that my taste buds were in a pleasant state of continuous crisis. Moe also loaded me down with boxes of Saltine crackers, Oreos, Fig Newtons, and sugar-sprinkled doughnuts, cans of string beans and condensed milk, jars of dried coffee, and packs of Hershey bars. The soldiers gave me Hershey bars at every opportunity. The abundance was staggering, and not a little embarrassing.

I brought back most of the rations to my mother on weekend leave. She was delighted to have a steady source of staples coming in, even if she found some of the flavors and textures rather bizarre. She learned how to make delicious dumplings from the otherwise inedible Spam, and used to doctor the canned string beans with chili, sesame oil, and garlic to make quite a passable *namul* dish. Father pretended he wasn't keen on the dried coffee, but I noticed that he'd taken to drinking it sometimes when no one was looking. Myung-hi's favorite food item was the doughnut, whose sugar granules adhered to her nose, like a cat with cream on its whiskers. That this largesse should stem indirectly from Jin-ho, whom we had ceased to believe was even alive, made the modest upturn in our fortunes even sweeter.

At the air base, I didn't really have much to do, but in the beginning the whole experience was fantastic fun. To say that I was privileged, even for a short time, to have enjoyed such a soft experience of the war would be understating things.

Kimpo itself was a rudimentary airstrip encircled by lights, plunked in the middle of rice paddies, with hangars and sheds, and four F-86 Saber jets on the runway on permanent standby. A squadron

of Australian Meteor planes also was based there, with a nurses' compound close by. The atmosphere was lively, industrious, and on the
whole the tone quite educated, in front of women, at least. There were
about forty people working at the weather station from all over the
United States: cartographers, meteorologists, GIs, Korean clerks,
interpreters like Jin-ho—of whom I saw little—and miscellaneous
menial workers. My very proper and pretty roommate, Miss Moon,
was a dentist, and her sole purpose at Kimpo was to clean and attend
to any emergency that might befall the men's teeth.

Captain Lang was in charge of the supply section for the weather
station. In a small, canvas-walled office, sporting a navy blue uniform,
I sat at a gray metal desk, under a bare lightbulb, slowly typing request
forms for clothing, stationery, or rations. I also did a bit of filing,
which made more strenuous demands on my English comprehension
skills. I scraped by with the aid of my well-thumbed dictionary and
the apparently boundless good humor of the captain. At first I was a
bit in awe of this big pink foreigner with white eyelashes and freckles.
He was more foreign than any other I had met, both in mind and in
body, but he was not authoritarian and formal in the way that a Korean
man would have been in his position. He even told me to call him Rick,
but I called him Captain Lang. He told me I was stubborn! Miss Moon
and I giggled behind cupped hands at his familiarity. He was so relaxed
that at first I wondered if something might be slightly wrong with
him, mentally. We spent a lot of time sitting around his office eating
Fig Newtons (his favorites) and drinking milk, and my boss cracked
jokes that I strained to understand. The wireless was always turned on
and the services station remorselessly played the song "Goodnight
Irene," to our rapid regret. I showed him the location of the classical
music station on the dial, but no one there, himself included, was keen
to listen to a Korean station, superior though it was, when they could
hear the star-spangled voice of home on the airwaves in the form of
the Mormon Tabernacle Choir.

Captain Lang told me all about his wife, Candace, and their three children in Fresno. Of course, I was shown snapshots of them; pink and blond, like Captain Lang, with fat cheeks, sitting on a bright green lawn. By the intimate, watery gleam in his eye when he looked at the photo, you could see how badly he missed them.

The slightly balding, manly station commander, Major Hollis, was quite keen on me, actually *all* of the American staff were outrageously flirtatious by Korean standards, but despite being nineteen, I was still my father's daughter, bent on safeguarding my innocence. No hanky-panky of any kind was conducted either by me or by Miss Moon, who was also from a good family. When Jin-ho was at the base, he kept a playful eye on me, but there was no need as I was wonderfully well treated, so much so that a couple of envious Korean mechanics spread rumors that Miss Moon and I were whores. (At the time it was said that UN troops were frustrated at the lack of prostitutes in Korea after the surplus they'd enjoyed in Japan, and did not comprehend the importance of chastity in our society.) Miss Moon and I had spacious quarters to ourselves in a Quonset hut, and a houseboy to serve us, who was about six years old. The GIs dubbed him Shorty, and he was everyone's pet. He was a war orphan, and had lost an eye in the bombing of Seoul. He wore a black eyepatch, which gave him a piratical, comic-book air. He often asked me to play Korean folk songs on the violin, which I rarely had the time to touch, and he would gaze at me with a practical sort of yearning as I played, like a thirsty dog watching its master at the sink. It was upsetting to see. I didn't like the thought of giving Shorty hopes of easy affection that I couldn't continue to fulfill. Shorty's spirits were always exaggeratedly high, and both Miss Moon and I worried about him. He waited on us as if his life depended on it, and I felt sad that this was really the case.

In early October, South Korean and U.S. troops crossed the 38th Parallel and began pushing north toward China. The North Koreans were retreating, and General MacArthur was confident of sending his men home by Thanksgiving. By mid-October Pyongyang fell and was occupied by UN troops. Kim Il Sung and his generals fled north into the mountains, possibly into Manchuria. Meanwhile MacArthur and his men were still marching north toward the Yalu River, ignoring reports that China would not tolerate any threat to its borders. To the horror of watching world governments, China entered the war, sending in its first troops on October 25, a savage attack supported by tanks and air power, crippling a large flank of the 8th Army. In early November, MacArthur ordered a genocidal air war, bombing and napalming every factory, village, and city possible in North Korean territory. Five hundred fifty tons of incendiary bombs were dropped on Sinuiju alone, one of many towns emphatically removed from the map. From the Yalu River south to enemy lines, the country was a burning, blasted desert. To the ignorance of the West, the Chinese had by now committed somewhere between two to four hundred thousand troops, and were planning a major attack at the end of November. Meanwhile, the Russians were secretly flying planes and capturing POWs on the Chinese border. MacArthur, to the dismay of Britain particularly, wanted to drop between thirty and fifty atomic bombs along the Manchurian border, claiming that Russia would not react. That this tiny civil conflict should be escalating into a nuclear war was amazing and more than alarming to us.

But at Kimpo Air Base, I was far removed from battle and from the atrocities endured by my countrymen and by the soldiers. To compound their hardship, in 1950, winter had come early to Korea. Icy winds from Siberia blasted across the frozen plains, tearing through the sandy valleys and whipping the bare-headed mountains. Winter was always piercingly cold in Korea, but in these tin huts, without Korean *ondol* heating, one felt it more than usual, especially in one's feet. Freezing as it was indoors, I did not care to imagine what it must have been like to function *outdoors*. Miss Moon and I were fortunate to have a small potbellied stove in our hut, to which we were glued fast like magnets.

Being young and self-interested, I did not give much thought to strategic developments in the war, but drifted along, day to day, sure that grown-up deeds on the front line would never touch me. However, when I learned of the bombing siege of North Korea I was breathless at hearing of the excessive force of the American air attacks. I felt sick, suddenly thinking of Baby Uncle and his wife. Where were they? Alive? And poor Uncle Yong-lae in Sokcho. Could anyone survive the mechanized, time-delayed onslaughts of mortar shells and flaming napalm? I thought of members of Mother's family, my grandparents and Cousin Jae-sung, who had remained behind under the Communists. Were they alive? What of our old, greengated mansion in Kangwon-do? Were our former estates in Kaesong now blasted tracts of frozen mud? I comforted myself with the thought that at least Aunt Pusan and Jae-dal were already dead, and I did not have to suffer losing them again. But what of our temple? I could not allow myself to think on it. Until that point the jaunty radio announcements, crisp bulletins, and cocky American military banter seemed like part of an exciting, upbeat game to me, masking the destruction taking place, the extreme suffering and brutality being endured by frostbitten homeless civilians, orphans, soldiers, the wounded, and POWs alike.

Yet the abutment of suffering and banal normality went on with a reassuring sort of callousness. "Goodnight Irene" continued to play on the wireless, jets tore down the runway, jeeps came and went, supplies were requisitioned, new maps and reports were discussed and drawn up, divisions were radioed, plates of mashed potatoes and meatballs were served up. GIs played poker and smoked Lucky Strikes around the stove in the canteen, and no one spoke of death. Shorty sat curled at Miss Moon's feet by our stove as she combed his raven-feather black hair, while I read my self-imposed ration of two pages of *Wuthering Heights* per night with my mittens on, and slept soundly most of the time. I always said a short prayer for my family, adding a plea for the protection of the temple.

But this stable state of affairs soon changed. Just before Thanksgiving, General MacArthur sent a message to the troops that the war was almost won, and that with a final push, they would be home by Christmas. On the following night, the Chinese launched a surprise attack. There ensued a terrible slaughter, and within a week, the Chinese drove back the humiliated UN forces over eighty miles, the 10th Corps fighting its way back south through six Chinese divisions, the sky thick and rumbling with American planes attacking the enemy with napalm, rockets, and bombs.

Later, MacArthur blamed poor military intelligence for this appalling misjudgment of Chinese intentions, and claimed that had he received permission to bomb China, his troops would have been protected. The fact was, despite the superior air power and weaponry of UN and U.S. troops, the Chinese and the North Korean guerrilla soldiers possessed greater mental and physical resilience, and their blistering, terrifying surprise tactics more than atoned for their lack of equipment. The violently cold conditions helped no one's spirits. The effect of the wind alone was instantaneously devastating. We heard that soldiers' noses and fingers literally dropped off at a touch. Two thirds of Chinese casualties were from horrendous frostbite, with only a third from combat. The morale and discipline of the UN troops had reached a new low. It was said that American and British troops despised Koreans for our brutal treatment of one another, and had lost interest in defending the South, with some American infantry refusing to fight altogether.

Meanwhile, during that winter of 1950–51, the Chinese deluded themselves that glorious victory was near, and that they would reunify Korea under Communist rule, with China invited to a seat at the UN for its pains. Truman was still refusing to rule out use of the A-bomb. The foreign press spoke of World War III as a feasible reality.

That December, beginning with the Chinese retaking of Pyongyang, U.S. and UN troops began a humiliating retreat south, withdrawing from Wonsan and evacuating Hungnam. Truman declared a state of national emergency. For us, at the air base, life changed. Now there was a nervy, charged sense of purpose about our tasks, with more work to be done than usual, often to the accompaniment of air-raid sirens. A Chinese plane had taken to dropping mortar shells over Kimpo at night. The Yanks at the base called him "Bedcheck Charlie." Although the pilot had terrible aim, the distant explosions made Shorty whimper, and Miss Moon and I cringed involuntarily in our bunks.

We heard, with mounting apprehension, that China had rejected UN calls for a cease-fire. On Christmas Day the Communists recrossed the 38th Parallel, and we barely had time to think. On New Year's Day, the Communist offensive began in earnest. But, to my ignorance, a new fighting spirit had apparently entered the U.S. troops. With the accidental death of General Walker and General Ridgway's appointment to his command, Ridgway had brought about astonishing changes in the 8th Army. However, for the people of Korea, now fleeing in great numbers in arctic temperatures from both the Communists and from the bombing, a perilous new nightmare had begun. The refugees had nowhere to go to, many were sick and starving, and had been separated from their families. Three hundred thousand refugees were said to have journeyed south through the snow from Pyongyang alone.

On the afternoon of January 4, 1951, I found myself in a jeep with Miss Moon, Shorty, a senior meteorologist called Jim, and a driver, Phil, on the Kimpo road leading to the MSR (Main Supply Route) south to Taegu. There was a serious jeep shortage, and we were exceedingly lucky to have one at all. The entire base had been evacuated for the Chinese advance, and orderlies were dismantling the huts and preparing to destroy the landing strip. I had felt safe at Kimpo surrounded by officers and GIs, and although I was rather excited by the adventure, as I stepped into the flimsy-looking jeep, I felt an ominous sense of fear. Miss Moon and I were wrapped up in hooded parkas and army blankets for the journey, and were well provided with rations and emergency supplies. We had both been moved by Major Hollis's generosity, and found him to be thoroughly honorable, particularly in his kindness to Shorty, who sat sandwiched happily between Miss Moon, me, and Jim's toolbox. With difficulty, I pulled my hood-string tighter with mittened hands. By jeep, the speed limit being five mph, the trip might take many hours or even days. I took a deep breath, and as I looked up at the sky, snow flurries spiraled in luminous points against the gloomy clouds like tiny dead stars descending slowly to earth.

There had been no time to say good-bye to my parents and sister. Jin-ho had promised to go to them and convince them to stay in hiding, rather than to risk their lives on the frozen roads. Jin-ho would also go to Taegu, probably on the last train south. Our tutor had been in Pusan for some time already, acting as an interpreter. I had seen little of him, and missed his sensible presence in this confusion.

As we neared Seoul, the sight before us was breathtaking—epic and tragic. The city was in flames. Snowy, shark-toothed mountains ringed the burning buildings. Those buildings still standing were dark, without electricity; streets were corridors of livid flame, casting a blood orange glow against the black silhouette of wing-tipped rooftops. I could make out Bridge Street, the Town Hall, the Choson

Hotel, and Capitol Building in the fire; I prayed that the damage would be confined to the modern quarter of the city, and would not reach my family. At Capitol Corner I saw the pathetic white banner stretched between lampposts: WELCOME UN TROOPS WITH BOUNDLESS GRATITUDE!

Worse still than the destructive flames was the sight of the massive, silent, snaking file of refugees lining the supply route in their thousands. It was biblical in scale. I thought they were insane to take to the roads in these perilous conditions, many wearing just cotton and silk, and most of them shod in thin rubber slippers, carrying great bundles on their heads, burdened with heavy backpacks, bedrolls, and infants, but realized quickly that desperation and terror, not madness, drove them on.

Hundreds of thousands of souls were massed before us. Miss Moon and Jim and I looked at each another aghast. With five of us, our luggage, and crates of supplies there was no room for other passengers in the jeep. People clamored for help. *"SUWON! SUWON!"* shouted a fierce little girl in a yellow silk jacket, raising her arms to be lifted inside the jeep. I remonstrated that we couldn't take her, and felt deeply ashamed. *"SUWON! SUWON!"* I heard her scream to the next vehicle, more promisingly, a truckload of orphans, but they did not stop for her, either. Soon, beleaguered by an inexhaustible stream of pleading, earnest faces, we stopped responding altogether.

The road was atrocious, mud frozen fast into washboard ridges that shook our internal organs and teeth as the jeep traversed them, even at low speed. On top of this, the Siberian wind bit through our hoods and layers of blankets with pathetic ease. We tried to conserve heat by not speaking. My feet had gone numb over an hour ago, but as I saw the misery of the vulnerable and ill-dressed poor, babies and old people struggling imponderably slowly along the road, I was smitten by guilt at having both protection and transport.

The Main Supply Route was jammed with unwieldy vehicles,

tanks, jeeps, carts, convoy trucks, passenger cars, diplomatic Rolls-Royces, bicycles, and oxen in a gridlock of grinding gears, mooing, and hooting horns. Our driver asked a policeman what the holdup was.

"The Chinese are nine miles away, *that's* what! There are four hundred thousand troops coming! Keep quiet and let me do my job," snapped the officer, waving and blowing his whistle hysterically. Other policemen were bawling and pointing their rifles at refugees to move them out of the way in a desperate and futile attempt to keep order. I later heard that corrupt police were taking pretty lone girls off the refugee lines, those destitute and separated from their families, and selling them to brothel-keepers to service the UN soldiers, who were demanding more prostitutes.

As we passed the Han River, loudspeakers were blaring: DO NOT ATTEMPT TO CROSS THE RIVER. I REPEAT. GO BACK TO THE BANK. THERE IS NO ROOM ON THE ROADS. ALL PEOPLE CROSSING THE RIVER WILL BE TURNED BACK.

Despite the tannoy warning, scores of people were gingerly but gamely crossing the snow-dusted, olive green ice of the wide river with children and livestock, in an attempt to flee Seoul. Then I saw a young South Korean policeman shoot a couple of bullocks whose fall cracked the ice, and civilians started to scream in panic. When this still produced no obedience, troops on the bank fired pistols and mortared the ice to stop people from crossing the river. Snow and ice sprayed the air, and people twisted to avoid the bullets. I couldn't believe what I was seeing. Our driver said they were forced to turn people back now; these peasants could easily be infiltrating Chinese soldiers disguised as refugees. We were all silent in response.

The railroad station was a scene of havoc. There must have been five thousand people swarming around the one train to Taegu like crazed bees, and hundreds clinging to its sides and sitting stubbornly atop carriages. It was an embryonic disaster, the road jammed and the snow deep, people were now walking along the railroad tracks. Hundreds were later killed as they stuck blindly to the tracks. I thought of Jin-ho, who had been issued a place on the train, somewhere in the midst of it all, and groaned inwardly at the extraordinary scene he would be facing. Yet Jin-ho would be all right, I felt. He would land on his feet.

As the wind cut into my face like an icy knife, I thought of my parents again. It was not safe to stay in Seoul, but neither was it safe to leave. With the city's imminent fall, there would be a variety of shootings, hangings, beheadings, prison sentences, and ostracism in store for those found by the Communists. Would Father's nerves last the strain again? Would *Omma*'s health sustain another separation from her children? Could they be so lucky to escape detection a second time? I thought the odds were extremely unlikely. But at least they would be spared the indignity and peril of refugee hell. I couldn't picture them surviving this harshness.

As we bumped and juddered along slowly, we heard a tremendous explosion coming from Seoul. It made the jeep shake, and we jerked in our seats.

"There we go! That's the Han River Bridge," said Jim, with a tone as flat as his crew cut. It was the second time within seven months that our own fleeing troops had destroyed it. It was a shambles, I said under my breath, impatient at our slow pace, and appalled by the scale of the mayhem and destruction.

A few hours later we were still in a slow convoy of vehicles, with silent refugees trudging along both sides of the road, nowhere near Taegu. We had succumbed to taking on board a lone, pregnant woman and her little girl, who were now squeezed in next to us, having earlier collapsed in the road before us. She and her daughter both slept, while Shorty inspected them disapprovingly. The wind had increased, and inactivity had hugely lowered our resistance to the exposure. Misery was a mild word to describe the ache caused by the searing wind. Miss Moon and I took turns holding Shorty on our laps as a wind-breaker and lap-warmer, but our feet, faces, and hands were frighteningly paralyzed with cold. Verbally, we offered around bars of chocolate, but apart from Shorty, none of us could withstand even the momentary pain of exposing our mittened hands to the bitter, razor-sharp air. As the hours crawled by, it was so uncomfortable we had all sunk into a sort of frozen trance. In this state, at least the hellish sights we were seeing did not fully penetrate my heart.

In the twilight gloom I saw three peasant women with bundles on their backs running to the river and stamping holes in the ice. They bent over, shoving their bundles repeatedly into the black water and holding them there. I heard high, faint cries, and from the insane wail-ing that accompanied these strange actions I gathered that these women were drowning their babies, presumably to halt their suffer-ing.

The enormous, heavy skies grew blue-black, and the vast, sweep-ing plains surrounding the road stretched out slightly paler blue with their snowy blanketing. Faint, flickering campfires occasionally dot-ted the roadsides, creating a false cheer where huddled refugees had managed to light fires, and the fortunate were grimly cooking caul-drons of rice. Once in a while we saw a dead body lying abandoned in the road. The frozen ground was too hard to bury anyone. These anonymous bodies were eerie, inanimate as sacks of potatoes, unteth-ered to any identity, home, or possessions. The mysterious life force sapped from their veins, they lay there still as stopped clocks. As we drove on through the bitter, blue, wind-whipped night, I felt as if I were entering deeper and deeper into an unknown, icy oblivion.

I barely remember arriving in Suwon four hours later. My body was a stinging, numb, exhausted carcass, and I was only partially conscious. We gave some rations to the wind-burned, pregnant lady, who thanked us quietly and disappeared into a dim alley with her little, drooping daughter. What became of them, I didn't like to guess. The dark, narrow streets were crowded with army vehicles and hordes of drunken men. I recall a wooden building, raucous voices, and the smell of hot stew, dirty socks, and whiskey. Miss Moon and I were found beds in a back room of some air force battalion headquarters. It was a cramped hole of a place, and my feet never thawed out.

After another long, freezing journey the following day, we finally arrived in Taegu, on the Naktong River. There again, thousands of displaced souls were massed together at the railway station, awaiting something. Although it scarcely sounds possible, twenty or thirty thousand refugees had taken it over, and were squatting around campfires, some fatally near the tracks, while fresh snow gathered on their miserable possessions and coated their shoulders and hunched backs. The hundreds of people clinging to the top of the train carriages had been killed at the first tunnel when they were scraped off the train. Some of those who managed to cling successfully onto the sides of the carriages died of cold in the slipstream during the seven-hour journey, and had to be prized off the cars, rigid at Taegu. I did not find Jin-ho at the station, but stubbornly believed he had made it and would eventually turn up.

Like Suwon, Taegu was an awful, smelly, provincial backwater, only the air was, thankfully, warmer. Its chief feature was its railroad station and canal, spanned by a bridge where the local girls posed artfully, wearing their best clothes. Miss Moon and I were billeted at the air base, where we carried out the same sort of duties as at Kimpo, but conditions were much more squalid, and the atmosphere drearier.

After the scenes I had witnessed on the roads south, I felt different, altered by the extreme and widespread scale of the suffering. The ghostly, abandoned villages on the road to Taegu were desolate and tragic. Wrecked, burned-out hovels stood coated in hoarfrost, as if touched by the wand of a wintry curse. Ugly patches of purple and rust-colored ash stained the snow. Abandoned tanks and smashed vehicles lay on their sides, and telegraph poles listed at drunken angles.

Many Korean civilians, babies, girls, old men, suffered slow, excruciating deaths by napalm, and were left alone outside police stations, where they died on their feet. Being gangrenous, they were refused places in hospitals in case they should infect wounded soldiers. It was some weeks before the overburdened Civil Assistance Command set up civilian hospitals.

Each time I looked at Shorty I was reminded of the broken families I had seen, the pitiful poverty, and the senselessness of it all. The three months of the war that I had spent in hiding at the policeman's house had been a weird interlude. Although we might have been killed by the Communists at any time, my family had been fortunate to have experienced only psychological suffering and malnutrition. Those months had been a kind of disturbed, suspended sleep from which I was now waking violently. I had pretty well lost my sheltered innocence and, temporarily, at least, my optimism.

The Americans on the base were also dispirited and sour. I wondered at their outward indifference to the refugees, and regretted some of the men's complacency toward the decimation of the people and country they had come to protect. I overheard some of them expressing hatred for Korea. My heart burned with regret at their avowed loathing, and with embarrassment at their tactlessness for speaking so before Koreans who worked alongside them. I remained grateful, in an official sort of way, for the mortal sacrifices they were enduring on our behalf, remembering that they were only following orders from authorities based abroad, but the rosy, Hollywood picture of war that I had naïvely held was turning gray. Captain Lang and the other kind men I had come to know at Kimpo were reassigned elsewhere. Shorty was shot and killed by a sniper's bullet on an errand. After a month in the limbo of Taegu, we were flown unexpectedly to the hell of Pusan. The Communists were pushing the UN forces still farther south.

I cannot think of Pusan without remembering my dead aunt, and the nocturnal tenderness with which she had brushed my hair all those years ago in Yangyang. But there could be no greater contrast to my aunt's beauty than that provided by the squalid port of Pusan in 1951.

We arrived on a C-47 army plane. Flying over the low blue, frozen hills of Kyongsang Namdo, Pusan city sprawled low and flat until it could push no farther into the Sea of Japan. Pusan was the southernmost UN-occupied city in Korea, where the perimeter line stood. I had never visited it before, nor wished to, despite my aunt's former presence there. We Seoulites were rather sniffy about Pusan, a lowly port with neither artistic nor royal connections to lend it architectural and cultural distinction; Pusan was to Seoul what Marseilles was to Paris. It was a busy fishing and trading depot, which, at that time, stank of fish, tides, and sewage.

During the war, Pusan was seething with refugees and army personnel. Half a million citizens plus nearly half a million refugees were cramped and squeezed into every available corner of space. There were sweeping fears of an epidemic, and the UN Assistance Command toured the schools and civic buildings that had been turned into shelters, setting up DDT centers where people were sprayed like livestock against lice. As at Taegu, the UN had arranged rice rations for the starving.

At Pusan Air Base, where we were stationed, at last I encountered Jin-ho and our tutor, Young-ju, climbing out of a jeep. They told me at once that my parents and sister were safe, and were staying here in Pusan with relations I had never heard of. I was overjoyed. *Sunsaeng-nim*, round-faced as ever, was thriving. From the set of his thrown-back shoulders it was evident that he positively adored wearing a uniform, and was enjoying the stiff regulations and pomp of army life. He had been assigned as an élite interpreter to a U.S. Air Force commander in Pusan, and had even translated a meeting between him and General Ridgway on one occasion. He was kept busy most of the day and night.

Jin-ho, to my alarm, was far from well. Although he kept face to those who did not know him, his condition was transparent to me. From his glassy, dilated eyes, waxen skin, and markedly soporific manner, I suspected at once that he was taking opium again. Jin-ho had been dividing his time in the National Defense Corps between a U.S. infantry division and a unit of rather wild Australian pilots, running messages between various camp headquarters, telegraphing, translating supply demands, and haphazardly communicating with ROK army officials. According to Jin-ho and *sunsaeng-nim*, the NDC was a corrupt and shambolic organization, barely able to feed and shelter its volunteers. Jin-ho was sleeping at a barracks near the fetid harbor, and *sunsaeng* told me he was trying to watch over him, although his demanding job prevented much involvement.

To my dismay, Miss Moon and I were separated into different compounds, and suddenly I was sharing a freezing shack with fifteen strange women, and very uncomfortable and basic it was, too. I never touched my violin. Just seeing the instrument now reminded me painfully of Shorty, who had gleaned so much pleasure from the silly tunes I had played for him. Despite my careful attempts to remain aloof from the child's affections, I had grown very attached to him. His death haunted me.

Soon I learned from Jin-ho that a former school friend, Chae-young, was living with her parents in a big house with servants on the outskirts of Pusan, and with barely any wrangling I found myself invited to stay with her for as long as I was stationed in Pusan, and I accepted this generous invitation with alacrity. Fresh linen, proper

Korean food, and civilized family life—in that order—began to transform my flagging morale. It seems I would have made a useless Communist.

Every day I rode Chae-Young's bicycle to the air base through the frozen, foul streets of Pusan, a hard, hilly journey which took me an hour. There I performed unexciting secretarial tasks for the air force weather station, and visited my parents once a week at their digs nearby. They were justly in good spirits.

On the eve of the second fall of Seoul, our loyal police captain—host, called up to duty in the capital, miraculously reappeared to evacuate my parents, getting them permits for the last train south. Their release from being in hiding was a substantial relief to them, and they were now enjoying the novelty of being in a wholly different city, among old friends, even if the epic upheaval had exhausted them in their already weakened state. It saddened me that they had both aged so markedly through the strain of their ordeal, and their current laughter could not reverse the deep lines of worry on their faces, which had held a longer tenancy. They had seen little of Jin-ho, and as they were ignorant of his chronic trouble, I decided to keep it from them.

At last we got a letter from Aunt Chungsun, giving us spartan news of our family in the North; Baby Uncle and his wife were safe in Manchuria, Yong-lae had survived the Communist takeover by changing his name. My grandparents Kang were alive, along with Aunt Chosan, and skinny Cousin Jae-sung had been imprisoned for subversive activities, and had not been heard from for eight months. Although the news was not uniformly good, my eyes filled with tears as I replaced the letter in its envelope, grateful to have finally received some small, but richly nourishing communication from our beloved Yangyang. Its memory was nearly obscured by the smoke of war and the distance of years. Despite the passing of time, I still flinched at the thought of Jae-dal's death on Nagsan cliff, where the embers of his suicide still burned for me. Placing the envelope in my pocket, I touched the paper tenderly. It was a frail relic of happier, simpler times, when I could still look up innocently from the basket of my father's bicycle and see the winged green gates of our farm rising up to greet me.

Meanwhile, the retreating U.S. Army carried on bombing Korean cities, decimating Seoul, Inchon, and Wonsan. Korea was being subjected to the heaviest and most continuous bombing ever recorded in history. The attacking Chinese came to a halt just south of Suwon. Whole villages in the South were depleted of their male population as the ROK army started a massive drive for volunteers to restock its troops and renew its fight against the Communists. The situation was grave. Ten divisions' worth of equipment had also been lost by the retreating South Korean army. To compound matters, there was much Communist guerrilla warfare in UN-occupied areas, with an estimated thirty-five thousand wildcat guerrillas, many of them women, carrying out sieges in isolated areas. There were also horrific mass executions of suspected Communists in the South in police-run prison camps, which disgusted and appalled the UN forces. One Western journalist wrote that he had seen Belsen, and that Pusan's concentration camp was worse.

On January 24, the Chinese staged an attack. The following day, General Ridgway launched a counteroffensive, repulsing two divisions of Chinese troops, largely unopposed. Ridgway's army suddenly began to fight back with new determination and toughness: by March 15, UN forces had retaken Seoul, now bombed and mortared beyond recognition, having changed hands four times within nine months. One week later, UN troops crossed the 38th Parallel. Wonsan had sustained 861 straight days under siege; the longest continuous bombardment of any city in military history. With these brute tactics, Ridgway had decisively turned the tables on the Chinese and remotivated his disheartened men.

By April, the word on the base was that UN forces had pulled together, their spirits higher, with greater goodwill to each other and to their cause. This was felt at Pusan, and I was grateful for the lightened atmosphere. In the second week of April, the unthinkable happened: General MacArthur was fired by President Truman. *Sunsaeng-nim* had to explain to me that MacArthur and Washington clashed over military tactics concerning China, and that Truman could no longer control MacArthur. However, following the initial shock and apprehension wrought by the news, people at the base seemed happy that General Ridgway had been made supreme commander. He was extremely well liked and respected as a combat soldier, even if he lacked MacArthur's film-star charisma.

Reading a history book about this war years later, I was shaken by MacArthur's testimony to Congress upon his return. This, the book points out, was General MacArthur's response only a quarter of the way through the war:

> The war in Korea has almost destroyed that nation. . . . I have seen as much blood and disaster as any living man . . . and it just curdled my stomach. The last time I was there, after I looked at that wreckage and those thousands of women and children . . . I vomited. If you go on indefinitely, you are perpetuating a slaughter such as I have never heard of in the history of mankind.

CHAPTER FIFTEEN

Farewell

Summer, 1951

I stood on the airstrip at Pusan surrounded by my family, with a small trunk and violin case by my side. It was a humid July afternoon, the sun was strong and hot on the crudely laid tarmac, and I remember the exact tint of the blue sky, and that there was a huge cloud that looked like a white zeppelin passing overhead. I can remember precisely because it was the afternoon I left Korea.

Two weeks earlier I had received a letter at the air base from Columbia University informing me that I had been accepted as an undergraduate music student, and had been granted a full scholarship. After the initial jubilation, I had felt every possible emotion over the news, and never just one at a time; the feelings were always a combination of difficult opposites. The war was only half over, and I felt torn at leaving my family at such a moment. However, armistice talks had begun at Kaesong, and so there appeared to be some hope of a resolution. In the end my mother and father made it clear that there was only one possible answer to the university's offer, and even said that they were quite proud of me.

On hearing of my good fortune, Major Hollis and some of the men at the air base clubbed together and bought me a ticket on a cargo plane to Yokohama, and a room there overnight in a five-star hotel. From Yokohama I would catch the boat to San Francisco, and travel on to New York. Their bold generosity stunned me, and moved me far more than I could express to them then.

That day in July I had no notion of leaving forever. It was as if I were only going away on holiday. The farewells took place swiftly, and I have since played them back over and over again in my head, slowing down each encounter, frame by frame, freezing each moment until it is sapped of life.

I felt no sadness as I looked into Miss Moon's eyes. "I don't know why," she said, her voice shaking slightly, "but I feel as if I will never see you again." She held on to my hand tightly before letting me go.

I had already said good-bye to Father, who was away meeting with friends about starting up a new Monarchist Party. He had grown nostalgic for the old days and the old "graceful" values, stricken and angered by the indignities that Korea was suffering at foreign hands. *Aboji*'s thoughts had been very far away from all of us these past months. He had vaguely registered the expected aristocratic prejudice against my becoming a musician and having a performing artist in the family, but had come around to Mother's insistence that times were changing, and that I had to study *something*. Father treated my departure, as I did, as a mere interlude, and showed no overweening emotion. As I embraced him shyly on the steps of our cousin's house, he patted my back with absentmindedness, the edge of his spectacle frames gouging into my cheek, leaving a painful red mark.

My tutor, in his ironed uniform, stood awkwardly on the perimeter of my group of friends, and squeezed my hand at the last moment. "Good luck, and study hard," he added, as I knew he would. Jin-ho, looking peaky and ill, picked me up and spun me around with some difficulty, so much fatter had I grown on a diet of mashed potatoes and Spam. I looked at him with my usual indulgent disapproval, not knowing that I was never to see him again.

Myung-hi was next to say good-bye. Now as tall as me, her broad, placid, smiling face was on a level with mine, her smooth forehead undisturbed by serious thoughts or regrets. Lastly, I turned to my mother, who stood quietly behind me. She looked cool and elegant in a sky blue voile dress and low pumps. I saw threads of gray in her chignon, and as I looked into her eyes, they filled with tears. Her mouth opened, but she said nothing.

Now the plane's engine was roaring loudly, and nothing could be heard anyway. The wind snapped our cotton dresses against our legs and tore at our carefully permed hair. *Omma* held me tight, holding my head like a baby's. I did not want to feel pain, and was surprised to feel it, even for an instant.

Then I walked up the gangway, and waved to the dear circle of friends and family below, feeling quite myself again, excited and buoyant. It felt like the beginning of a brilliant adventure, like something that happened only in the movies. An air force sergeant helped me arrange myself comfortably near a window over the churning wing propeller. The few other passengers on board were all middle-aged U.S. Air Force officials. I buckled my safety strap, and secured my violin case into the next seat.

I saw the group waving to me from the ground, and caught sight of my mother, crying, and leaning against Jin-ho. I realized I had never seen her cry before. My eyes smarted, overwhelmed by love for her but, summoning a protective hardness, I refused to weep. After months of fear, upheaval, and trauma, I longed so to enjoy this adventure, to soar above the mean, shabby, war-crippled villages that littered my country. I wanted to *live*, to be young and careless again. With a little loosening of focus, I succeeded. At the window I waved gaily as the plane taxied down the bumpy airstrip, twisting backward in my seat, waving wider and bigger the smaller my grieving mother grew.

The next afternoon, I stood at the railing of the ship, and looked out at the Pacific Ocean stretching boundlessly wide before me, glittering with gold sunlight and kelp black currents. It was beautiful, and lonely. Although the skies were clear, the seas were rough. The ship's sharp hull plowing through the swelling waves made a loud, deep, rushing sound that matched perfectly the strong feeling in my heart. Cold, damp spray chilled my bare legs.

I did not look around then at the few passengers on deck, nor look back at the hazy coastline of Yokohama and Japan, and the whole of the Far East. I only looked forward, my eyes filled with vague, persimmon-tinted clouds and the massive dome of the celadon-pale summer sky. The scale of my voyage only then sank in to me, and I felt a sudden pang of fear, mixed with chagrin, guilt, and bursting hope. Somehow, I could sense that the dark horizon of the East had receded behind me, and was no longer visible. The powerful rushing sound of the engine and the waves vibrated through my body, and I was sick over the railing.

I could not look back.

PART FIVE

DAUGHTER

CHAPTER SIXTEEN

Kimpo Revisited

Korea
1987

Sitting at the window of the plane, I felt totally sick to my stomach. Nine hours into the flight, I still had food poisoning from my stay in London. After meeting my former art tutor, I'd been to see a football match with my old friend, Duncan. Was it the beefburger I'd eaten at Highbury? The thought of it revolted me, and I quickly looked out of the window to distract myself from the memory of the gristle-studded, fatally greasy burger. I pitied the old French couple sitting next to me whom I had to climb over with embarrassing frequency to reach the WC. Punctilious and tight-lipped at the start of the flight, by now they practically groaned with disbelief when I stood up yet again, muttering to each other in French, though I had offered to switch places.

Earlier, in the departure lounge at Heathrow I'd felt childishly excited seeing the Disneyland-blue Korean Air jumbo jet sitting pregnantly on the runway. Not feeling too horrible then, I sipped a ginger ale to settle my stomach, and glanced around at my fellow travelers, mostly Koreans, some generic Eurobusinessmen, and a tour group of corn fed American Mormons in synthetic leisure wear sporting laminated name tags. Already, the world's parameters were shifting in a weird direction.

This perception increased as we flew over Alaska to refuel. Its virgin territory presented an almost lunar landscape, a *tabula rasa*. As we descended, swirling, nordic star-shaped patterns of navy blue conifers and whitest snow covered the earth. Baked blue with cold, fresh snow lay like ash in volcanic-looking crevices and gullies, pale blue mountains were stacked out against the sky, creamy gold where the sun struck their secret faces. In my heightened, slightly delirious state, it felt as if this pristine frontier were a St. John the Baptist of landscapes, prefiguring the more important one, still to come. Such airy musings were soon punctured by more urgent imperatives; I jumped up again to go to the lavatory, vaulting over the sleeping French couple with gymnastic difficulty and mounting mortification.

Eventually I managed to sleep a bit, but the combination of nausea and excitement discouraged repose. The mere smell of beef gravy on the food trolley provoked a digestive mutiny in my entrails. Glassy-eyed but intensely curious, I watched the Korean stewardesses, as they bent and reached, wondering if they could provide an advance notion of the Koreanness that would greet me in a higher dosage upon landing. But besides having Oriental faces, they bent and reached identically to all other stewardesses I'd seen.

Eighteen hours after leaving England, the announcement was made for passengers to: *"Prease fasten your seatbewts fo randing. Komapsumnida!"*

I sat up, rubbed my eyes, and looked down through the thick glass window at the dim, night-covered cityscape, swirling into view in heaving waves of light. Evidently not built on a grid, the streets were crazy swirling patterns of multicolored spangles, the concentration of lights polyphonic and emotional. One could make out mountains as areas of curving, solid darkness, uprising. I felt a thrill, not quite believing that we were actually in Korea, about to land, about to see my uncle. Although excited, I was pretty apprehensive, and feeling extremely weak and ill. In coming here, I was facing my shadow; the giant Eastern specter I had been avoiding all of my life. The slim phrase book in my coat pocket was a risible foil for such a confrontation.

I vaguely remembered my mother mentioning Kimpo as an air base where she had spent part of the war, but, looking around, I doubted it could be the same place. This was a vast, spanking-new international complex. In the shiny arrivals hall a Korean man in a suit waved to me. It was my uncle Hong-do, whom I did not immediately recognize. Identically attired businessmen thronged the airport entrance in all manner of animated poses. That everyone here was Korean should not have been a surprise, but somehow the reality was quite different from my projections. The sudden density of Korean nationality about the airport created a slight chemical change in me. Or so it seemed. Just what sort of change it was, it was too soon to tell. In airport officials and travelers alike, a distinct air of calmness prevailed, with undertones of charged industriousness.

"You made it!" he said, taking my suitcase and planting a kiss on my cheek. "You look terrible. Was the flight bad?"

I explained my food poisoning episode, and he nodded.

"OK, we'll stop at a pharmacy and get you some medicine. Then we will eat something, and I'll take you back to your cousins', where you're going to be staying."

Hong-do looked extremely well, cheerful, a bit fatter, wearing elegant, expensive clothes. The March air outside was cold and sweet. I inhaled deeply, and stretched my arms before climbing into the back of the gleaming black Hyundai sedan in the parking lot. All of the cars in the crowded parking lot were brand-new Hyundais and Daewoos. Uncle got into the front with the chauffeur, a thin man in a dark suit with lank hair and smart white gloves.

We pulled into the thick traffic on the motorway leading back into Seoul in a cacophony of honking and irritable revving. Headlight and taillight glare bounced off the windscreen. We stopped short, unable to penetrate the wall of ferocious traffic, and the chauffeur smacked the horn in frustration.

"I'm sorry I can't put you up myself, but we're moving house, and my wife and children are away visiting relatives. I'm staying with my mother-in-law. But our cousins, the Parks, are old friends as well as relations, and they speak perfect English. He is a television producer at KBS and his wife is an editor at an English newspaper. They will be good hosts."

"Fine," I said. "Sounds good." A wave of scary nausea rose from my roiling stomach, and I clutched the door handle. The danger passed. It was about eight o'clock in the evening, and my eyelids were growing heavier and heavier. When I woke up, we were in the parking lot of a huge concrete high-rise building on the edge of the capital. Uncle had already gotten the medicine and had eaten supper alone while I had slept. I apologized for my condition.

"Don't worry, don't worry. You will get better soon. Come and meet my cousin and his wife. And their two daughters."

The driver carried my suitcase to the entrance of the high-rise. I looked up and around. The tall building was surrounded by other identical buildings with parking lots. You knew where you were because there was an enormous number, at least forty feet high, painted on the side of every building, as if designed so that airline pilots could orient themselves at fifteen thousand feet. These

Orwellian numbers lent the apartment buildings a military, barrack-like air. Inside, the uniformed guard nodded to my uncle, who stood rocking on his heels in the marble lobby, whistling. He glanced at his watch as the steel elevator rumbled down the long shaft and arrived. Then he punched the number eighteen, and up we sped, smiling at each other, wan under the fluorescent lights.

Hong-do buzzed, and the door opened. A small, slender woman in glasses and a red mohair sweater smiled and bowed slightly. *"Annyong hashimnigga,"* she said. In the far corner of the large apartment an elderly woman with a short perm sat on the floor in slippers watching Michael Jackson on television; this was *halmoni*, the maid-nanny. She rose and bowed. Two little girls wrapped themselves around their mother's waist and legs, staring at me with wide, friendly eyes.

"Please come in, come in," said Mrs. Park in a soft voice, taking my satchel. A tall, square-shouldered man in a tie and pullover—extremely handsome—came up behind her and nodded formally.

"Anna, this is our cousin, Park Kwang-wook," said Hong-do. Kwangwook also smiled and welcomed me in flawless English. The little girls sidled up to me shyly, tilting their heads to one side, eyeballs swiveling to take in every angle of the pale stranger.

My illness was explained, and with little fuss, I was put to bed in the spare room. *Halmoni* gave me a plastic bottle of pink liquid, making vehement downward-flushing gestures with both arms.

"I'll pick you up in the morning, and we will go visit your aunt Myung-hi," said my uncle, waving and shaking hands with Kwang-wook.

Dully noticing my pleasant surroundings and the warmth of the company into which I had been welcomed, I melted into bed, almost delirious with fatigue, and fell asleep at once.

I awoke the next morning to the sound of Schumann being played vigorously on a piano in the next room. I was a bit disoriented, but feeling much better. It was only seven o'clock by my watch. The Schumann broke off abruptly, replaced with a battery of accomplished scales and arpeggios. I wondered who the player could be. The room was lined with many books in a variety of languages. I opened the curtain and looked out of the plate glass window with great curiosity. Before me stretched my first daylight view of Korea.

The March sky was broad and hazy, gray-blue and mist-strewn, the modern concrete balconied apartment buildings and parking lots of the previous night were now revealed in their full brute glory, unrelieved by the gaily colored vertical trim decorating the tenements' edges. Here and there stood a young, newly planted tree, isolated and vulnerable amid the acres of asphalt. Beyond the apartment complexes lay vacant building lots, brown scrubby plains adjoining bare woodland, ringed by omnipresent blue mountains. Seoul's boundaries were evidently stretching farther and farther into the countryside. I was somewhat disappointed with my initial impression. From here, I could see no traditional wing-tipped tiled rooftops, no ancient palaces or parks, no crowds exuding a tang of Koreanness, only the odd speck approaching its specklike car. It was a new residential development, comfortable and contemporary by any standards, but apart from the ersatz blue plastic wing tiles adorning the entrance canopies, I could have been in Los Angeles, Bonn, or Buenos Aires.

Letting the curtain fall, I dressed quickly and passed through the apartment. I was startled to see that the pianist was the six-year-old daughter, Misook, attacking the keyboard with Horovitz-like assurance. I entered the kitchen, where Mrs. Park was breakfasting on rice, fish, and red-hot kimchi. Mr. Park had already left for the office.

"Good morning," Mrs. Park said, bowing her head. *Halmoni* moved briskly at the stove. I was offered coffee, toast, and cheese, which I accepted, and was puzzled when Mrs. Park pushed a can of

sweet corn across the tablecloth. She looked at me with shy expectation.

"Thank you . . . *komapsumnida*," I said, not knowing what to do
next.

"I know Americans like corn. Would you like to have it now with
your coffee?"

"Er, maybe not just yet, thank you. But thank you for your
thoughtful gift. You are very kind."

We talked a little about practical arrangements; she was easygoing, polite, and approachable. Her two-year-old daughter, Son-
young, with her half-moon eyes, round, pink squashy cheeks, and
fluffy black hair, made a feast of little baby noises and flirted with her
chopstick.

The loud sound of a man chanting over a loudspeaker filled the
apartment.

"What's that?"

"It's an announcement saying a man is here to sell pots and pans."

I nodded in surprise.

Halmoni joined the din by vacuuming the apartment, but stopped
in her tracks before the television, enraptured, as tearful newlywed
quiz-show contestants disgorged their love letters into a red heart-
shaped microphone. The doorbell rang, and my uncle entered, smiling, stretching his arms in a relaxed fashion. He was wearing another
sharp suit.

"Are you ready?"

By now I was, and said good-bye to Mrs. Park and the children:
"*Annyong-i kyeseyo!*" I managed to remember. They all stood at the
door, a many-armed squid waving me down the corridor. As I waved
back at the children I had the strange feeling that I had known them
for a very long time.

Outdoors it was cold, and the morning light was extraordinary;
electric-bright but diffuse; it was like gazing at a pearlized lightbulb.

Glancing at the blue, shark-toothed mountains on the horizon, I got a sensation of exhilarating altitude and exposure. The landscape was indescribably *different* It looked exactly like those stylized Oriental prints, only now I realized that the trees and mountains weren't stylized at all, but quite accurate.

In the car my uncle spoke energetically, filling me in on key events affecting the country. The Olympics were about to be held in Seoul, as well as presidential and local elections. There was great optimism in the city; much business being conducted, many new buildings going up to accommodate Olympic events and visitors. The country was putting on its best new clothes for the world audience, but was having to sew them as they went along.

As we drove down a four-lane road—most streets had no names, my uncle said, because their Japanese names were abandoned and not replaced—one could see that frantic construction was happening everywhere: hotels, sports complexes, office buildings, and above all, bridges. The wide banks of the Han River were strewn with cranes and diggers, iron girders stood up to their calves in the waters of the Han, a third of the way across its wide expanse at various junctures along its great body. Uncle said they were even building and planting flower beds and trees at night to meet the construction deadlines.

At red lights one could see the ubiquitous election placards; headshots of sober assemblymen were plastered horizontally across concrete walls like rows of stamps, a series of six identical images of DJP candidates alternated with a replying series of opposition candidates. Against vivid-colored backgrounds, unsmiling leftists in suits contrasted with beaming right-wing candidates in suits.

"There's a power struggle going on now between President Roh and cabinet members from ex-President Chun's era. Chun was the last military leader. Corrupt as hell. A tyrant. Roh is the first civilian president we've had in decades. The opposition candidates, the two Kims—Kim Dae-jung and Kim Young-sam—say that Roh is a puppet of the old military regime, but I think Roh is genuine in his pro-democracy reforms. He is just cautious."

"What reforms?" I asked.

"Lots of things. The press is already much freer than it was. Legislation has been passed to improve conditions and wages for workers. What else? The age limit for travel has been lowered to thirty from forty-five."

"There was a ban on travel?"

"Yes, foreign travel. You could only go away on business before. To strengthen the economy. Plowing tourist money back into the domestic sector. I hear it's still hard to get a passport unless you're rich, with connections, but that will soon be relaxed. All the protectionist markets are being opened up now that redevelopment is nearly complete," said Hong-do, smoking a Marlboro with the window cracked open.

"You have no idea what's been accomplished here since the war. We had to start again from nothing. Seoul was a bomb crater," said Hong-do.

Looking at the city now, it was difficult to imagine what it must have been like in my mother's day. Would she recognize any of it? The hastily erected buildings from the sixties and seventies looked temporary, prematurely obsolete, like aging multi-story parking garages. Bright spanking new skyscrapers soared above with empty-headed ambition. The blank reflective windows mirroring the clouds held no memories. Mongrel one- and two-story shop fronts from the late fifties with old-fashioned wooden shutters, lurid neon plastic signs in Hangul, and striped barber poles were liberally mixed into the ad hoc architectural mosaic. Not being able to read the Korean signs, I could only guess what sort of shops they were. Here and there stood a graceful traditional villa with timbered cornices, marooned among brash commercial neighbors like a lady in an eighteenth-century wig and gown standing next to a shoulder-padded businesswoman with a bob-

One would never guess that Seoul had once been an elegant, green capital, filled with beautiful old monuments. Invading Japanese arsonists and the bombing of the Korean War had eradicated most of Seoul's testimonial layers of history and archaeology. I felt slightly miffed imagining that tourists must mistake Seoul for a newly minted city, aping the commercial development of the rest of the world.

As we approached the center of the city, Seoul's concrete arms began to wrap tighter and tighter around the cars, compressing and slowing the traffic. The road was heavily congested with new cars (all Korean-made), trucks, and military jeeps. Aggressive taxis pointlessly passed slower cars, straddling two lanes—one of oncoming traffic— for the best advantage. Other vehicles did not appear to mind the taxis' kamikaze opportunism, preserving their energy for more original out-rages.

"How many people live here?" I asked.

"Around ten million. Nearly tripled in size since the war. The government's thinking of moving the capital farther south, to Taejon. Too great a concentration of people in Seoul, and too close to the DMZ."

"What's the DMZ?"

"The Demilitarized Zone; the border with North Korea."

"Is it dangerous being close to the border?"

"Well, they say it is. There have been rumors of tunneling and hydroelectric power-dam sabotage. Odd kidnappings and border killings. Different from your mother's day, when she visited my grandfather's estates there, the ones overlapping the 38th Parallel. Now, we South Koreans can't even go there. My generation has never *seen* the North. Northerners have never seen the South. Only in pho-tographs. We can't even send a letter to our relations there. There is no radio or television contact. It's worse than the Berlin Wall."

Swarms of pedestrians now paused at the traffic lights and surged down the sidewalks. Women carried babies on their backs in a sort of wrap tied around their waists, forming one unit. Everyone seemed to be in a tremendous hurry. Most people were running, not walking. There were few Caucasian faces in this part of town. This reversal of racial dominance felt quite pleasant. After the spiky, fuck-you atmosphere of New York, this homogenous unanimity was restful to the senses. The sense of brotherliness also felt hermetically sealed, from the inside out. I was definitely outside its perimeter, in no-man's-land.

"By the way, I'm going to have to go back into the office tomorrow, so I've found you a young companion, a student, to be your interpreter, to show you around. I would take you myself, but it's a busy time for me now," said Hong-do, leafing through his leather business diary.

Next we drove through a tree-lined residential area and the driver pulled over in front of a two-story stone villa behind a high wall.

"Where are we?"

"This is Sung-dong," said Hong-do, hoisting himself from the car, "your aunt's house." He twisted his cigarette butt into the asphalt with his shoe. "It used to be your grandparents' house before they died. I grew up here," said Hong-do, yawning and stretching his arms. Through a swinging gate, we entered a large courtyard where a short, stubby-legged yellow dog with a fan-tail was tied up to a bare cherry tree, barking fiercely. It was a new breed to me, indigenous to Korea: a *chindo-kae*. Hong-do gave a lazy knock, and the heavy front door swung open. A tall middle-aged woman with cropped, wavy hair let out a cry, bowed, then seized my hand, squeezing it hard, and smiled at me with a slightly sad expression, all the while exclaiming volubly to my uncle in Korean.

"*Annyong hashimnigga,*" I mustered. At this modest greeting she looked at me as if I were little less than a genius.

"Ah! *Ne, ne!*" she said, her eyes filling with tears, and she embraced me suddenly. Then she led us into the darkened house, and Hong-do and I slipped off our shoes. The floor was strangely warm and cushioned underfoot like a vast electric blanket. We sat down on thin mats on the floor, which was deliciously warm to the touch. It made one want to stay sitting at all costs, even sprawl on one's stomach.

"It's *ondol* heating, the Korean way," said Hong-do, seeing me test the floor with my palm.

My aunt Myung-hi was in the kitchen preparing tea.

"She says you look like our mother when she was a girl," said Hongdo.

Tears filled my eyes, as if someone had bumped a painful bruise I didn't know I had.

Sitting here on a silk mat on the floor of my mother's sister's house, shoeless and speechless, I felt as if I were in a profoundly foreign land, but at the same time there was a faint echo of familiarity about everything. It was all new, yet everything fitted perfectly, as if its imprint might already exist in my consciousness.

Aunt Myung-hi—she told me to call her *Imo*—brought in a tray of ginseng tea and slices of swirly sesame cake. "This is *kkae-gangjong*," she said. She passed me a dainty ceramic cup with both hands. I accepted it with two hands and bowed, as Hong-do had done. A pine kernel floated on the clear russet surface of the tea. I sipped at the bittersweet liquid and ate the honeyed cake. *Imo* and I studied each other. She had my mother's nose and mouth, but her face was rounder and her expression more passive. Her eyes had a haunted, downturned look, making her look somewhat older than she was. We asked each other various questions through Hong-do. She spoke English from her schooldays, but was unconfident now. Aunt Myung-hi had spent most of her life nursing my grandparents when they had become ill, a sacrifice not uncommon in Korea. She had married late ("a cheerful man of no consequence," my mother had said), and borne no children.

I looked around the room. It was more overtly Oriental than the

Parks' apartment. Old scrolls with calligraphy hung from the walls along with etched brass platters. A carved, antique ivory statue of a Buddhist priest stood in a niche with a miniature bonsai. There was no sofa or visible television, no coffee table or armchairs, just low wooden dining tables, antique chests, and silk mats. It was understated and elegant.

She and Uncle Hong-do talked more, filling me in on the conversation now and then.

"We want to take you to the cemetery outside Seoul where our family tomb is. Would you like to go?"

"Yes, of course," I said. Although I was eager to go, I felt a sense of foreboding at the gravity of the suggestion, keen to start off my visit on a possibly lighter note. As if sensing this, my uncle said, ". . . Of course, we will take you to galleries and palaces, and go to the markets and shops in Myongdong. . . . I've got other surprises planned, too. But we would like to take you to Moran cemetery before you leave, to pay your respects to your grandparents."

I agreed. My thoughts then turned to the names of the relations written down on the piece of paper that my mother had given me.

"I forgot to ask you before, but what about seeing Uncle Jin-ho, and my mother's old tutor? And Baby Uncle? Where is he now?" I said.

My aunt and uncle both started slightly and looked at each other.

"Tutor is abroad at a medical conference. Min Young-ju is a big honcho now, an internationally renowned surgeon and hospital administrator. I'll try to find out when he's coming back to Seoul."

"And the others?" I asked.

There was a long pause.

"I'm sorry to tell you this, but our brother Jin-ho is dead," said Hongdo.

"He spent most of his life in a sanatorium. After your mother left, my father had him locked up, sectioned. . . . Didn't she tell you? He was a drug addict. He became mentally ill after the war. He went downhill very rapidly. It was a tragedy for our mother . . . your grandmother. She was against his incarceration, but Father insisted that it was for Jin-ho's own good. It made her sick. Really ill. She never recovered from it . . . never."

Aunt Myung-hi's face grew sadder, and she nodded her head, rocking back and forth as she sat there. The news was too awful to sink in at once.

"And Baby Uncle?"

"Same thing, sort of. Gong-lae died last year of a heart attack. I'm sorry . . . I know he would have wanted to take you around Seoul and told you all of the family stories—like he told your mother. He was a real *bon viveur*. A real character. Your mother was a favorite niece. Gave her her first violin. Everyone said they were very close."

"Oh," I said, not knowing what to say. "I am very sorry. . . . It sounds glib, but I really did want to meet them very much." I could not yet grasp the notion that it would not be possible to meet them. Ever.

"Is Yong-lae dead, too, the drunken poet-uncle?" I asked.

"Yes, he died ten years ago. He was buried by his wife's family in Sokcho."

It was like arriving at an important rendezvous only to find that the venue itself had burned down.

"I see . . ."

"Yes, it's true. But listen. Let's not dwell on the past. We will entertain you well . . . you'll see. Now we had better be getting back. I have a business meeting downtown later. I will drop you off at the Parks' on my way," said Uncle, rising from the floor. My aunt followed us into the courtyard, and made a playful kicking gesture at the barking dog.

"The dog is an imbecile," she said in fluent, slightly accented

English, frowning at the wagging, absurdly fanged animal. My aunt held my hand very tight in both of her hands and gazed at my face without speaking. Her eyes were at once very frank, and also veiled with sad experience. Her face was eloquent. I felt I understood her, without speaking. My aunt, or *Imo*, as I was meant to call her, said something to Hong-do in Korean, and waved us into the waiting car.

"You will see her again at the weekend," said Uncle. Our driver folded up his newspaper, hurriedly drew on his white gloves, and turned the key in the ignition. He revved the engine loudly, and with a gratuitous honk at a turning car, we ground off into the hurly-burly of rush-hour traffic.

The sun was setting over the Han River, and Seoul, cradled in the lap of the blue zigzagging mountains, looked transformed. The panoramic postcard skies were illuminated with wildly romantic purple and rose-colored clouds. Stacked lights of the low buildings on both sides of the river glittered densely. The wide Han itself was a curving liquid plain of winking diamond light, the moving edges of its fast currents catching the oblique rays of the lowering sun, and the half-built bridges stood in dramatic silhouette against the sunset.

There was still a military feel to the city with its outsized numbered buildings and convoys of jeeps preparing for their annual joint military exercises, but Seoul seemed to relax and become more gregarious at night. Tinny red, green, and blue neon signs lit up everywhere, competing for attention. Huge neon crucifixes appeared along the road, helpfully signaling local churches for sinners in the night map. Glowing red-white-and-blue barber poles twisted on every corner.

"What are these barber poles everywhere?"

"Barbershops. Not the same as in the U.S., though. You can get the best shave and massage there, and they give you a manicure and pedicure at the same time. A three-way massage. Very relaxing. Havens, where men can go. There's nothing like them in the West or in Japan. It's very civilized. Not . . . lewd."

"Can women go in, too?"

"No. Only for men. That's life here, I guess. Men get away with murder," Hong-do laughed.

As we drove along, I felt stimulated, and at the same time peaceful. Looking affectionately at Hong-do in the semi-dark, I wondered what I had ever found difficult or odd about him. He was utterly friendly, direct, and uncomplicated. It surprised me to think that maybe I had been the complicated one. Obviously, we were on Hong-do's home soil now, which might affect things. He was clearly happy and at ease here. In Korea, our family name drew respect, and this was important to him. Perhaps, back in the West, his pride had been wounded more badly than we knew. But since that awkward time Hong-do had grown up, as I trusted I had also done. I couldn't quite work out the reason for the change between us, but welcomed it.

Although the sad news of the deaths of my uncle and great-uncles had rocked me earlier, I felt quite numb about it now, resigned. Catching a certain angle of my uncle's face, I got a sense of déjà vu. I remembered being in the back of Hong-do's car in Manhattan, gunning up West End Avenue. I remembered that feeling of safety as I sat back on the cushioned seat, with the automatic locks depressed. Although a mundane episode, it had induced a precious feeling in me: a fleeting sensation of solidity. Perhaps it had even been the first time I had experienced an extended family protection, slight and inadvertent as it was.

An idea came to me. "Hong-do, would you take me to the mansion in Namsan Park where my mother lived before the war? The one with the iron gates and the garden where Grandfather shot birds from the trees? I would really like to see it. Have you been there?"

My uncle was silent.

"Do you know which one I'm talking about, or have I got it wrong?" I pressed him.

Finally Hong-do spoke. "It's not there anymore. It's a parking lot now."

"What?"

"Yup. Shame, isn't it?"

"Well, can we go anyway? I'd like to see the general area."

"I don't know," he said doubtfully. "I think it would make you sad. It's just a parking lot like any other parking lot, in a beautiful place, high above the city. They built a big luxury hotel next to it."

"Oh," I said, disappointed. "What about the other house in Seoul, the small one where they hid during the war?"

"The policeman's house? Also a parking lot! We might pass through the district sometime, but there's not much to see. The whole character of the place has changed. The low houses and courtyards are replaced with chain-link fence and ugly warehouses."

Suddenly it felt as if I had missed too much to catch up. The central pieces of the puzzle had been lost. What I was seeing now of Seoul was an untrue simulacrum of what had existed before, distorted, changed, substituted. These ugly buildings of the present were meaningless to me. My uncles and great uncles were dead, my mother's childhood homes were parking lots. I sat quiet, taking in the sad absurdity of it, overwhelmed by useless anger and grief over things which could not be undone.

Exotic new urban scenery flooded past the window, clamoring for observation. I tried to release my stung and bitter feelings. Although still deflated about the loss of the past, it was too early on in my visit for bitterness. There were many unknown things and places still to be discovered. I still had an aunt and an uncle, and the Parks. Hong-do's voice, low and subdued, broke the silence.

"What do you think? Should we go to Mount Sorak and find Greatgrandfather's temple?"

I was taken aback. It was as if he'd read my feelings.

"I'd like nothing more."

"Let's go at the end of your stay, then. I've got deals to tie up here first, and then we'll take a trip. We can drive up to Yangyang, to the old estate, and then head into the Sorak Mountains. We'll have to hike up to the temple. First I'll have to find out where it is from someone. . . . I don't know of anyone in our family who has been there. Still, we'll worry about that later. OK?"

I spent the remainder of the ride in an excited silence, drinking in the challenging new scenery with renewed eagerness. Still jetlagged, thoughts flipped quickly but lightly through my mind. When we reached the gargantuan apartment building in Myong-il-dong, it now looked, if not exactly homey, distinctly more welcoming than it had when we had left it that morning.

Mrs. Park and *Halmoni* were sitting placidly on floormats watching the news while Son-young clambered over them as if they were human jungle gyms. The spangling sound of a news jingle filled the living room. To my surprise, the broadcast was in English.

"*AFKN*: In Touch With *Your* World," gushed an unctuous, car salesman-like American announcer. "The American Forces Korean Network brings you CNN News! Training unit updates, news from Osan Air Base! The *latest* sports results, and *American* programs!"

Mrs. Park looked up and smiled. She had a very warm and ready smile. She asked me about my day, and smiled again. Son-young pitched herself over her mother's back and fell with a thump to the floor, laughing. Mi-sook, hair in neat pigtails, interrupted her homework to peep around the door at me with a serious expression.

The sound of a stern male voice on a loudspeaker blasted and crackled through the apartment. I asked what it was.

"It's an announcement for tenants who want their laundry done."

"Isn't the loudspeaker a little intrusive?"

"No, we're used to it. It is mainly there for military drills and emergencies, should there be an attack from the North."

"A bit like Big Brother, isn't it?"

Mrs. Park paused for a moment.

"I don't see it that way, really. It's a safety measure. Anyway, we are raised to put the well-being of the group before . . . individual convenience. But it cuts both ways, I guess," she laughed.

Halmoni, unimpressed with CNN news, rose from her mat and shuffled into the kitchen in her pink quilted slippers to prepare supper. Obvious as observations went, Koreans made much use of the floor; kneeling, squatting, lolling, and sleeping on mats were the norm, not to mention using it as a heating conduit. Traditionally, one also ate at low tables on the floor, although the Parks had a Western-style high table and chairs in the kitchen, and used beds and sofas, too. But despite these concessions to vertical living there was a residual sense of elected simplicity and horizontal earthiness in household arrangements. Children were shown much physical affection, passed from lap to lap like living treasure, and although manners were far more formal than in the West, there was no Western sense of "personal space"; I had felt that walking down the street earlier. Being close together was not to be avoided. People brushed and knocked against each other without complaint or excuse, like the benign bumping of close family members.

Son-young was, at this moment, lying curled in my lap, gazing into my eyes like a purring cat as I stroked her fluffy hair. "*Ajuma*," she murmured to me; Auntie. Her spontaneous use of this Korean nickname combined with her adorable gaze won me over completely.

Mr. Park walked in through the door, and the little girls descended on him hungrily. His tired face broke into a grin, and as he hung up his coat they danced up and down, tugging on his trouser legs, before the elder, Misook, solemnly carried his briefcase into his study, as was clearly her regular routine.

The children had already eaten, and were being read to by *Halmoni* when we sat down at the kitchen table for a simple supper. We had clear soup, dressed spinach, bean sprouts, and shredded carrot *namul* dishes, two kinds of kimchi, rice, and *bulgoki*, and for dessert, delicious crunchy juicy pears that I'd never tasted before. As I bit into one, my mother's slightly irritating habit of buying hard, unripe pears suddenly made sense to me; she had probably been trying to reproduce the crisp texture of Korean pears, and I felt sad that I had complained.

The Parks told me casually of their jobs, how the liberalization of press censorship under President Roh was going slowly, but mostly getting better.

"We're a conservative country," said Mr. Park. "We want democracy, but Korean-style democracy. We don't want to imitate European and American culture; we want to retain our Confucian ways, Korean ways. Our ideal is the Choson dynasty, our age of enlightenment," he explained, "when the arts and sciences flourished under King Sejong the Great. So much of our culture has been wiped out by war and invasion that we have become tenacious about our heritage.

"Right now, we must accept American troops until our stability is more concrete. With U.S. troops we get all this"—he waved at the television—"the sitcoms, and the American pizza chains, and pop music, and fashions, which is not *all* bad, but we do not want the American way of life; the cult of the individual, the broken families, high crime and drug abuse, the uneducated masses. This is alien to us. We believe in the old ways of respect and selflessness. Having the best washing machine is not so important to us."

"But what about the role of women? You work outside the home, Mrs. Park, isn't that contradictory to the Confucian way, where women stay home and must obey men?"

Mrs. Park cocked her head to one side. "Yes, but we pick what we like best about Western culture, and leave out that which does not suit us. That is an unfair advantage, perhaps."

Mrs. Park worked at the *Korea Times*, an English-speaking newspaper something like the *International Herald Tribune*. She edited features, and was one of the highest-ranking editors at the paper. She was terribly gentle in manner; I could not picture her telling bullying male reporters what to do, and told her so. She smiled her habitual smile, and said, "I speak softly, but carry a big stick."

My cousin Kwang-wook—I was still surprised that he was a relative—nodded over his ginseng tea. He too was very understated, not the brash, self-important sort of television producer of my acquaintance in New York. At KBS, the national broadcasting company, he produced international arts programs. With the Olympics coming up next year, he was busy with new series on modern Korean music and dance.

"We will take you to a concert, if you are curious," offered my cousin.

"Why do the students riot so much?" I asked, before going to bed.

"Well . . . It is an embarrassment to the government; it is their way of demanding change. They do not trust the corrupt politicians," said Mr. Park with some indulgence.

"They are idealistic; not like the generations before them, brought up to compromise and suffer. . . . They don't see the North as a real danger—they just think it is American imperialism. But it's not as simple as that," he said.

"Korea's endless struggle against foreign domination has become . . . the crucible of modern Korea," explained Mrs. Park.

"Struggling against an outside enemy has become our whole identity," added her husband. "Our generation and our parents' generation were unshockable; used to corruption and compromise. We were brought up to obey authority, and bury ourselves in hard work. Drink and dance—Koreans are good at that. Quick to anger and quick to forget. Sing out the pain, express the *han* that we carry as Koreans, and work like crazy to build the future," said Mr. Park.

"The students don't believe in this?"

"They are confused. They do not understand the sacrifices made for them. They think it's always been this easy. They think that if American troops pulled out, all our problems would be solved. We would be reunified with the North into one happy family, 'free at last' from foreign oppression . . . never mind the political-economic conundrum of communism versus capitalism that reunification would bring. Also, the students want contradictory things: they have demonstrations in support of traditional Korean farming methods, but spend their money on American fast food and T-shirts with English slogans printed on them, and some poor girls have double-eyelid operations to look more Western," said Mrs. Park.

"Western students don't bother much with idealism these days, with or without double eyelids," I said, belatedly. We finished our tea in silence.

"Ah," said Mrs. Park, suddenly looking tired, "I must go to bed, I'm afraid. Please excuse me. Good night."

There had been a lot to absorb that day, and I was exhausted too, now that bed had been mentioned. Tomorrow would be a big day. I would be going downtown for the first time, unchaperoned, to meet my interpreter, Miss Cho. I went to sleep with a slightly better understanding and sympathy for Korea's struggle for identity. It was a conflict of values I shared. Hearing them speak of the insensitivity of the Americans, and the Parks' gentle denunciation of their presence in Korea, I felt somewhat uncomfortable, yet did not feel American like the Midwestern Mormons on the plane or like the homesick soldiers with their CNN basketball games. I felt no need to defend the West's strengths: its spirit of tolerance, its polymorphism, its artistic creativity, its enterprise, and its occasional gallantry, qualities which extended somewhat beyond fine washing machines, but which were disappearing fast.

Thoughts swimming in unmanageable, too-deep waters, I drifted off toward the near shore of sleep.

I woke up late, surprised to have slept through Mi-sook's morning piano practice. My hosts had left already for their offices. Entering the kitchen for breakfast, I was a bit startled to see *Halmoni* entertaining a friend in the sitting room. Or rather, *Halmoni* was in the kitchen cooking, while her elephantine friend with a frizzy perm lolled on the sofa watching television, and gorging herself on a punnet of strawberries with her white-stockinged feet kicked up in the air. Her charge—a wobbly-legged girl in diapers—wandered around the apartments, occasionally receiving a screaming volley of abuse from her supine guardian. *Halmoni*'s forceful buddy, engrossed in her quiz show, did not even look up as I passed behind the sofa.

Halmoni looked tired. I learned that this was partly because she went to Mass every morning at four-thirty. Her eyeglasses steamed up from the stove, she smiled, bowing, singing a hymn with quavering vibrato as she prepared her own breakfast and mine. As I ate my white-man's repast of cheese and toast at the table, *Halmoni*, wiry and spry, stood in the pantry gobbling with fantastic swiftness a bowl of garlicky, chili-red fish and *kimchi*, which cast a heavy pong over the kitchen. We communicated entirely through a combination of grunts and pointing.

I slipped out into the street, armed with my phrase book, and the address of the Regency Hotel, downtown. The "street" was actually an anonymous four-lane highway filled with honking juggernauts and speeding cars. I remembered my uncle's instructions, and stood self-consciously on the curb, not merely hoisting an index finger, but waving like a survivor on a sinking ship, shouting *"T'aek-shi!"*

Passing taxis slowed down a bit, drivers glancing mistrustfully at me through their cracked windows, and drove coldly past. Most of them appeared to be full of people. I was clearly doing something wrong. Finally, one old driver took pity on me and coached me on my technique: *"Odi!* Where? You must say. Where!" he barked, with some amusement. I told him where I wanted to go, and he shook his head and drove off with a screech.

I shouted my destination at the crack of the next taxi driver's window. To my surprise, the very mean-looking driver braked to a halt, and I got in, despite the fact that there were already two other male passengers occupying the cab, fore and aft. I smiled at them with excessive gratitude, not realizing that multiple fares were the norm, and pretended to be relaxed as we jerked and weaved through the traffic. The driver's belligerent manner contrasted starkly with his genteel white gloves. He had a red, thick neck, and sat against one of those seat-covers with wooden back-massaging beads all over it, but the beads did not seem to be soothing him much. The men in the cab were businessmen of indeterminate age, and ignored me out of embarrassment. Although it was only noon, someone in the cab had been drinking heavily; the chap in front, I hoped, and not the driver, whose angry red face leered at me contemptuously in the rearview mirror. I prayed we would soon be there, hoping he had understood the address I'd given him, half fearing that he would eject me from the cab at some industrial complex hours beyond Seoul, with me able to say in Korean only, "Hello," "Good-bye," and "Please bring me an apple."

To my relief, the driver found his way eventually to the Regency Hotel, dropping me off first. I gave him a wad of thousand *won* notes, and entered the spacious, gleaming reception area, where I was to look for a young woman wearing a wide red hair band, Miss Cho. The Regency was one of the premier luxury hotels in Seoul. It also happened to be owned by Hong-do's mother-in-law, along with a petroleum processing plant, shipbuilding company, construction business, fiber-optic manufacturing base, tennis racquet factory, sport-shoe factory, and bicycle business. Hong-do's mother-in-law, a widow, was the owner of a *chaebol*, one of the controversial multinational conglomerates responsible for Korea's postwar wealth.

The Regency Hotel was busy beyond belief, chauffeured black cars and limousines disgorging at every eyelash-blink foreign businessmen and bourgeois ladies in lavish traditional silk *han-boks* who used it as a meeting place. Cleaning staff dressed like organ-grinder monkeys in ubiquitous white gloves and bellhop hats, polished the marble floors beneath guests' feet with mammoth fluffy dust mops. The automatic glass doors slid open and shut hysterically. I sat at a small tea table reading a stiff menu in four different languages and watched, fascinated, the unfolding spectacle of Korean hotel commerce, with everyone moving and talking at double speed.

At last a young woman with a wide red knit headband appeared and looked about with a quizzical air. I stood and introduced myself. She had a very broad, open face, a few adolescent spots, made-up eyes, lush lips, and wore bright dangly earrings that suggested a degree of extroversion. I didn't take notice of her clothes but, looking around the lobby, realized that I was distinctly underdressed for the posh surroundings, and my raincoat—an old boyfriend's hand-me-down— looked positively shabby next to the new Burberry macs and elegant wraps displayed by our neighbors.

"Shall we go somewhere else? It's so expensive here," said Miss Cho baldly. Miss Cho smiled a winning smile and batted her eyelashes. She told me that she was a political science student at Seoul National University, and wanted to be a professor of media studies.

I treated her to a lavishly doilied tea and bun, and we chatted for some time, the luxurious atmosphere not stiff, but unexpectedly jolly. I mentioned that I had been surprised not to find more traditional architecture in the capital, and she suggested that we go at once to Kyongbok Palace, the old royal palace where, as I was often reminded, my grandfather's distant relative Queen Min and her court had lived before her assassination. I agreed, and soon we were off again in a taxi, driven by another white-gloved maniac with a wooden-beaded back-massaging seat cover.

Downtown Seoul was a festival of clashing opposites. We passed along seethingly crowded, dark, narrow market streets through to blindingly bright, wide, modern boulevards offering views of futuristic Yoido, the business district. Here, from broad antiseptic piazzas, monolithic office towers soared like mammoth glass sculptures on plinths, alien and unlovable. Through a few more traffic lights, we found ourselves deposited at the gates to the palace compound.

At Kyongbok Palace we encountered yet another country, antique and deserted, in the core of the rebuilt city. Faded oxblood pavilions, temples, and pagodas with soaring winged eaves, carved and intricately painted in ravishing hues, stood in serene groupings throughout the neglected formal grounds, which stretched for miles. Lopsided, rocky mountains rose up dramatically behind the palace rooftops, where no skyscrapers were visible. A grand, empty summer banqueting house stood at the edge of a huge reflecting pond covered with overgrown lotus leaves, now surrounded by a heavy chain. Where there had once been grass and gravel underfoot, now there was bare, dusty earth. Courtyards led into smaller enclosures, which led into the symmetrical wings and main chambers of the palace itself.

Elaborate gateways of massive proportions, carved stone walls, and steps separated the king and queen's pavilions. Miss Cho and I removed our sweaters in the hot sun. I leaned languidly against a balustrade and admired the deserted, slightly melancholy view.

"Most of it has been rebuilt quite recently, you know," said Miss Cho, "burned down by a Japanese mob at the end of the last century." On closer inspection, newer-looking masonry and paint could be seen amid the older architecture.

"I'll show you something," said Miss Cho, unself-consciously taking my hand and leading me to a distant structure. To my initial surprise, she did not let go and we stood side by side, holding hands. Although a bit embarrassed, I accepted the custom, finding her friend-liness charming. The grounds here felt even more spooky than in pre-vious spots; a disturbing atmosphere enveloped the place. We stood before a modest garden pavilion, with murals painted inside. Drawing closer, one could see that the paintings were commemorative rather than decorative in nature. They depicted the gruesome, bloody mur-der of the queen by the Japanese, and their burning of her live body in the garden. As the scene reasserted the unbelievable facts, I felt a recurrent sense of anger. Standing at the actual spot where the mur-der occurred was doubly powerful. There was only a typed sentence on a strip of paper in Korean and minimalist English to explain the mural's significance. I wondered what foreign tourists would under-stand from it.

"Why is there not more information?" I asked.

"I think there will be soon. The whole place will be smartened up for the Olympics, of course. But until now there has not been much need to explain. Every Korean schoolchild knows the significance of this place," Miss Cho smiled. "Maybe we don't care enough what out-siders think."

We walked slowly back to the main compound, and climbed the steps to the understated Throne Chamber. The scale and refinement of the palace were as impressive as any European castle I had seen, but there was no sense of audacious, egoistic opulence or glamorous artificiality about it. More subdued, the architecture suggested a grand, deliberate quietude.

I took a photograph of Miss Cho posed against a tall green-and-scarlet pagoda. Ironically, the only other visitors to the palace that afternoon were a tour bus of Japanese. Two Japanese women were having their photograph taken by the Japanese tour photographer, and had hired Korean national dress from the ticket seller for the picture: bright silk *han-boks* and replicas of royal crowns, so that tourists could take home a souvenir of themselves as Korean princesses. The two Japanese ladies beamed at the camera. Although they appeared to be ignorant of the symbolism, I was struck by their insensitivity in not realizing it. I took a photograph of them being photographed and walked away.

Outside the palace gates there was a streetcart vendor, selling something steaming hot. It smelled delicious. A businessman stopped and bought a little paper cone of whatever was being sold, and walked away popping things into his mouth. Leaning over to see the contents of the vendor's pan, I saw that they looked like nuts.

"What is it?" I asked Miss Cho.

"Roasted silkworms," she said.

I declined the opportunity to try them, but was pleased by the offer. I no longer felt as if I could be in Bonn or Buenos Aires.

It was now very warm, and we walked to a nearby park, where people were sitting on the grass. Miss Cho curled her legs demurely underneath her, while I stretched out on my back looking up at the hazy blue sky. I asked Miss Cho about her university course, and she answered quite monosyllabically.

"Ahem," Miss Cho said. I said nothing, absorbing the rays of the milky, spring sun with contentment. Then she coughed an artificial little cough. I opened an eye and looked at her. There was something in her expression that made me sit up. "What is it?" I asked.

"It is silly, I know, but in Korea you mustn't lie on the grass."

"Really?" I looked about with curiosity. I saw plenty of people lying on the grass.

"Yes," said Miss Cho, "but they are men. If a woman lies down on the grass it is considered . . . lewd. Everyone will think that you are a loose woman."

I was shocked. "But that's rather tough, don't you think? There's nothing sexual about *relaxing*," I argued.

"But there *is* something"—she lowered her voice as she uttered the word—"*sexual* . . . about lying down, a kind of . . . how do you say, *surrender*," she said quietly. I saw her point, sort of, feeling sobered by such decorum, and humbled by my ignorance of Korean customs.

"That's nothing," confided Miss Cho, eager to preempt any further gender infractions I might be liable to commit. "Women are not even supposed to show our teeth when we smile. *Very* unfeminine! You must hide your teeth behind your hand when you smile," she said, cupping her hand before her mouth to demonstrate the best teeth-hiding technique. Miss Cho admitted that the custom was old-fashioned, but she thought it was funny that I was scandalized by it.

"Laughing *and* showing your teeth is *very* vulgar!" she said. At this, I laughed aloud, unguardedly showing all my teeth. At this, Miss Cho laughed, and then we both laughed, molars bared, rocking back and forth until our stomachs ached. Businessmen and students looked over at us with alarmed interest.

We talked some more, and eventually got up from the damp grass, delicately brushing our backsides. Deciding that I had had enough sightseeing, we parted for the day. I had enjoyed Miss Cho's company very much. Again, I had the uncanny sense of knowing her already, a sensation I had experienced with the Parks and with Aunt Myung-hi.

Perhaps it was an emerging, and alien, feeling of fraternity. She flagged down a taxi for me (with no problem whatever) and stood at a bus shelter waving as the taxi screeched off.

The next day was Friday. It was another sunny, hazy day. My stomach had now fully recovered from the food poisoning, but my surrounding anatomy felt exhausted. I rested at the apartment for most of the morning, reading and playing with the squashy youngest daughter, Son-young. In the afternoon I went out to buy the little girls a present. I had not yet explored the neighborhood—daunted by the scale of the identical apartment buildings and afraid of not recognizing the Parks' building again—but decided the time had come to strike out into the concrete maze.

I held to the curb of the four-lane avenue like a stray bit of litter, buffeted by the wind and exhaust of the cars' slipstreams. I saw no shop signs along this traffic route, so, taking a careful look around to memorize the layout of the intersection and the orange-and-blue trim of the apartment building, struck off into a gap on the left, which seemed to lead into a slightly more residential complex of skyscrapers. An inability to read signs was a definite obstacle to the shopping process. I could make out the odd word if I stood in front of a sign for a ludicrously long time but, having a small Korean vocabulary, would not necessarily know their meanings having deciphered the characters, and to confound matters, some nouns and proper names shared the same spellings.

Finally, I found a crummy newsstand that also sold toys, and bought a little furry acrylic tiger—Hodori, the mascot of the Olympics—for Son-young, and a velvet hair ornament for Mi-sook. The plump, broad faced shop-proprietress stared at me as I browsed as though I had horns growing from my head. First I ignored her, and then tried to reassure her of my status as an earthling with a few normal smiles. Earlier, I had received a number of similar stares on the street. A gang of children had pointed and laughingly whispered to each other as I walked past, clearly unused to seeing Westerners on their rather remote turf.

"Olma imnigga?" [How much?] I had asked as I prepared to pay. She spat out a figure in a belligerent voice, and continued staring at me with an affronted, naked curiosity. I wondered if this was similar to what my mother experienced when she bought her coffee and newspapers in Starksboro. I left the shop with some relief, and retraced my steps back to the Parks' apartment complex on the opposite side of the road. It was getting dark. Crossing the cement tundra, I encountered a greengrocer's stall that was lit, rather romantically, by a ring of candles. The stall owner was a middle-aged man who rubbed his hands together and chattered to a teenage boy who looked like his son. They, too, stared as I studied the stall's contents. I saw a beautiful basket of dark red strawberries, which glistened invitingly in the candlelight.

"Olma imnigga?" I asked. The man barked something I could not understand.

"Ttalgi!" he said pointing to the strawberries. *"Ttalgi."*

"Ttalgi," I replied, not sure what he meant.

"Straw-berry!" said his son. *"Ttalgi!"*

"Yes. *Ne!* Strawberries," I said, understanding the deep mystery. I handed him some money and walked away, leaving the father and son laughing uproariously. I was quite pleased with my purchases and, despite being found to be such a hilarious person, proud to have completed the transactions and relocated my apartment building without getting lost. These were baby steps in a loomingly adult adventure.

❁

That evening the Parks, my uncle, and I went to a gala performance of traditional dance and music, as promised, at the grand Korean National Theater. We had dined out first at an elegant seafood restaurant, in a private paneled chamber where you sit shoeless on the floor at a low table, on specially designed back-supporting chairs. I was surprised to find floor sitting as comfortable as high-chair sitting.

Here, I had my first memorable taste of *hweh*, a classic raw fish dish. The fish was plucked straight from the tank, and arrived at the table flayed and filleted, headless but still wriggling on the plate in an alarming way. We plucked up the meltingly tender slivers with our metal chopsticks, dipped them in green horseradish paste and soy sauce, and then wrapped the fish in crisp, sweet lettuce leaves smeared with hot red salty chili sauce (*kochuchang*) or red bean sauce (*duenchang*), adding raw garlic slices and shredded green chilis for searing crunch. This was accompanied by clear, fragrant soup, quails' eggs, cockles, mussels, oysters, marinated octopus, kimchi and raw dressed shredded carrot, and rice.

It was the most mouthwateringly delicious meal I had ever eaten. In the clean, sweet, briny, sharp, hot, pungent tastes of this dish I had an odd sensation of being home. We drank little beakers of *soju*, the burning, sappy traditional liquor reminiscent of vodka. All of our faces grew red as we drank. As I looked at the flushed faces, I realized that this was the first time that I'd sat with a whole table of people whose faces also turned as red as mine when they drank alcohol. Although it was a tiny thing, this had never happened before, and was oddly comforting.

There was a specific atmosphere in the restaurant then that baffled me. I'd also felt it in the hotel the previous day. It was *Koreanness*, or at least an Orientalness. I felt it everywhere, but what was it? A calmness combined with bustle? Not exactly. It was something more subtle; a feeling of great energy, but without spiky neurosis; without the uneasy sexual striving and competition I felt in the streets of

Western cities. There was a quality of benign sisterliness in Korean women when they looked at you or went about their business that felt rather shocking. There was no hostile eyeballing—judging your looks, clothes, and status with men. There was a sense of warmth and tolerance. There was a *wholesomeness* about public places. Families went out together with their children. Businessmen drank together, and women met up separately. There were no visibly sexed-up single couples displaying their designer wardrobes, cars, and body tone. People were well dressed but modest. It felt extremely odd. At first, I wasn't sure I liked it. To one conditioned to such strife, the atmosphere lacked *edge*.

Later, in the modern concert hall of the National Theater, I took in the spectacle, again, with a weird sense of déjà vu: the swooping sleeves of the jewel-bright silk gowns, the rich thump of the painted drum, the nasal warblings of the stringed zither and hysteric trillings of the wooden flute, the exaggerated vibrato and stylized drone of the *pan sori* singer, the frenzied ritual of the monks' dance. I knew I hadn't seen these dances of the court of the Choson Dynasty before, or heard the folk opera, but for some reason, it did not *feel* as foreign as it looked and sounded. The music was especially foreign; Brahms was several galaxies away. Here there was no melody, no linear progression. Instead came swelling, arhythmic waves of sound, like legions of angry, tone-deaf, enormous-lunged bumblebees filling the auditorium, punctuated with unpredictable claps of drum thunder. The angry-bumblebee song swarmed on and on, and round and round without resolution. I thought I might not survive the experience of listening to it. There was nothing to hold on to. It was like lying in an insect-thick summer meadow that was tilting, and even turning upside-down.

The dancing was friendlier. The women's dancing was graceful, refined, and demure, not athletic, as in Western dance. There were no solos. All body parts were covered by long, stiff silk gowns. Feet moved as if on casters. Fans made kaleidoscopic patterns. The white-painted doll-like faces and black topknots were uniform, bold magenta and ravishing emerald silks. Finally, "*Arirang*" was sung; a traditional folk song described by the program as an unofficial national anthem. I knew I had never heard the song before, but the melody penetrated the pit of my stomach, and inexplicable tears ran down my face as the entirely Korean audience stood together and sang it, "*Arirang*," ringing around the hushed auditorium.

We drove back in a satisfied, tired silence, dropping Hong-do at his mother-in-law's in Bangbae-dong on the way home. I was curious to meet her, so Hong-do invited us inside for a drink.

The apartment was in a modern villa with iron bars over the small windows. The marble floors were very slippery and shiny, and all of the fittings and furniture appeared to be new. We sat on a leather-and-chrome sofa in a small reception room, and looked around silently as Uncle Hong-do poured out brandy in the study. There was a distinct hush in the apartment—of money and elderliness.

An old manservant in black pajamas shuffled through the Western-style dining room, switched out the lights, and continued on his way without acknowledging us. Hong-do brought through our glasses, and we sat sipping the liqueur, awaiting the appearance of the formidable Mrs Li. My uncle and the Parks spoke in rapid Korean to one another. Sitting there deaf to the conversation, I noticed a large framed color photograph of an aging lady in pearls and a business suit frowning down from the middle of an otherwise bare wall: Mrs. Li. Below this stood a chunky gilt magazine rack and a gold Kleenex-box holder proffering pink tissues. The main feature of the room was a black matt television set the size of a small car.

"My mother-in-law started a cement company with her late husband in the sixties. They built this conglomerate from nothing. They were dirt-poor. Now they are in—what is it called?—the Fortune 500, richest people in the world. Quite remarkable, really," said my uncle. Mr. and Mrs. Park looked at each other sidelong, with a muted sense of irony that I did not comprehend.

Just then a small gray-haired woman with a perm entered the room wearing a lilac angora sweater and navy blue slacks. Her feet were tiny, shod in calf pumps with metal bows on the toes. She nodded her head stiffly at the Parks and looked at me with no great interest. Hong-do introduced us in Korean, and she sat in a tufted armchair staring into the middle distance. Mrs. Li spoke no English. The Parks made quiet conversation. Hong-do spoke to Mrs. Li about me—I guessed, hearing my name and noting the slight change in direction of the gaze of his mother-in-law. Mrs. Li nodded. She sat back once again, and suppressed a slight yawn. She sat in fierce silence, declining refreshment, and then stood suddenly, bade us all good night, and clicked off stiffly down the marble corridor past a photograph of her children and grandchildren. I looked at Hong-do, and he avoided my eyes and the gaze of the Parks. We also stood, thanked Hong-do for the drink, and said good night, Hong-do waving us off down the quiet street.

In the car driving back, I mulled over the eventful evening, and felt a little hurt by the indifferent reception I had received from Mrs. Li, behavior quite unlike the warmth I had so far experienced.

"I don't believe she likes your family," said Mrs. Park, anticipating my thoughts. (Hong-do had told me that this quality of guessing moods was especially Korean; it was called *nunchi*.)

I asked Mrs. Park why Mrs. Li disliked us. Mrs. Park laughed. "They are nouveaux riches, and perhaps she has a chip on her shoulder about the old *yangban* families. From what I can tell, she is especially scornful because you are all poor now. They don't have time for anyone who is not rich. Talent, breeding means nothing to them."

I was grateful for this bit of enlightenment, and felt more than a little sorry for my uncle, understanding better why success in business was so important to him.

Recalling the day's events filled me with confusion. Sometimes I'd blended in with what was taking place around me, and at other times stood outside the experience, Korean and Western blood alternating in ascendancy, carrying on a lively but exhausting and argumentative dialogue. Being stared at by the schoolchildren and the shopkeepers, sitting in the grudging company of Mrs. Li, I had felt a consummate foreigner, deaf and dumb, perched outside. Yet eating *hweh* with my relations and listening to the traditional Korean songs at the concert, even hearing the alarming bumblebee symphony, I sensed with a strange authority that this was my food, my music; its heat and discordancies ran through my veins whether I liked it or not.

Yet despite these small surges of recognition, I felt Western here; more so than in the West, disappointed not to feel a more definitive clang of identification with Koreans. Although liking "them" hugely, and feeling an instinctive sympathy with them, there was either something impenetrable about Koreans, or something obtuse about me. Perhaps I was merely too impatient. Equally disappointing, none of my relations thought that I looked remotely Korean! ("Maybe a *little*," Miss Cho allowed, noting my crestfallen expression.)

A naïve part of me had expected to discover an instant identity, to be clasped to the country's bosom and greeted like a returning prodigal daughter. Instead I drew stares of indifference, incredulity, or sufferance. After all, I was an outsider. Being a half-caste had the same effect in the East as in the West. Your face was subliminally unsettling to both races. Eyes brushed over you as if you did not quite count, you were an aberration, a blip that would be smoothed over by the next manifestly white or colored face that came into view. You were a curious mutation of the gene pool. But there was nothing diluted about being alive in these colors; you were not fifty-fifty, but two hundred percent alive; not a half being, but a double being.

What *was* nationality? How influential was a set of genes? Going to sleep that night, I tried to relax, to stop taking my racial temperature. But I didn't want to miss anything. I had been asleep most of my life. It had taken an almost imperceptible miracle, in the shape of my uncle's visit years ago, to stir me toward the East. I sought clues to the mystery of this place with a thoroughly Western directness. I was learning, painfully, that there were things that could not be known by asking.

Lying down, gazing blindly into the dark, I was enervated by my mission. I remembered my scrap of paper with names of dead people written on it. This was the tiny keystone of the bridge I wanted to build. So far the bridge lay in a heap of broken stones, with neither a plan nor an engineer.

CHAPTER SEVENTEEN

Going South

A couple of weeks later, at seven forty-five A.M. precisely, I sat in a café at Seoul Station, waiting for Miss Cho to arrive. The easygoing chauffeur, whose name I could not remember, sat on his own at a discreet distance, drinking his coffee with slurps of gusto as we awaited my interpreter-friend. The grand, cavernous Victorian architecture of the station seemed, like much of colonial Seoul, to refer to some mournful past secret, inaccessible to transient strangers. My mother had mentioned Seoul Station in some of her reminiscences about the war. In recalling this, a faint trace of her girlhood presence accompanied me as I circled the echoing ticket hall.

Miss Cho and I were being sent south by my uncle, on a little railway tour of ancient towns and the countryside. He said that Seoul, like most capitals, was atypical of the atmosphere of the greater part of the country, and that a trip around rural Korea would illustrate his point much better than he could.

Miss Cho soon arrived, wearing her wide red hair band, blue plastic polka-dot earrings swinging, smiling and breathless, an overstuffed weekend bag weighing down one shoulder. She collapsed on the banquette next to me, blew her fringe out of her kohl-rimmed eyes, and, after dashing down a cup of *kopi*, consulted the train schedule. She seemed excited by the prospect of the trip, and I was grateful for both her company and her timetable-reading expertise. We dismissed the chauffeur with friendly bows back and forth, and made for the correct platform to Kyong-ju. From there we would be heading south to coastal Pusan and, on the return leg, I would join the Parks at their cottage in Yang-soo-ri.

On the train I looked out of the window, and had to admit that I had never seen a landscape like this before. Just fifteen minutes or so outside Seoul, the combustive, crowded, ruthlessly urban scenery had given way to wide purple plains, slate river valleys, and sparsely sprouting green rice paddies. The scale of the emptiness was monumental. The pale, hazy skies were epic, and the hulking gray mountains had an ancient, smooth quality that resisted characterization, but which if pushed, I could only weakly describe as being *very Eastern*. As we journeyed farther south, the gray skies turned misty blue. In the distance, layers of rocky peaks echoed each other, the horizon rising and dipping rapidly, like the nervous strokes of an electrocardiogram. At close range, the mountains were large and placid, like massive starving cattle, whose flanks were thinly furred with young spruces. Rocky ridges poked through the young timber like bony spines. Although "inscrutable" and "Oriental" formed a tired cliché, inscrutable was precisely the term for these ancient hills. Miss Cho, following the direction of my gaze, said that the planting of new timber represented "a filial yearning for the deceased." Although unsure of exactly what she meant, the poetic vagueness of her statement was satisfying.

The spare, elegant lines and cool hues of the landscape washed over me without the violence of beauty I had seen in the West. The colors were quiet shades of moleskin and mink, duck-egg blue and evergreen. I felt no urge at all to paint this scenery, for it already looked like a painting.

My imagination was not halted or speeded by memories attached to the land. Like the swarming sounds of the oboes of the Choson Dynasty court music, the formidable wall of countryside drifted puzzlingly past the window, utterly unique, offering nothing familiar to hold on to.

There was almost a feeling of vacuum in the valleys, a Buddhist minimalism about the effort made to inhabit this grandeur. On the next hillside a wing-tiled farmhouse stood beside a crooked cedar. Low storage barns and the occasional quarry or mill dotted the landscape, but no mammoth electricity pylons, sprawling factory estates, or shopping centers asserted the overriding industrial values of the late twentieth century. Not here, at least. These rice paddies and villages must have looked much the same as they had in the fifties, when my mother had fled south during the war. Yet elsewhere, Miss Cho assured me, development was increasing. Miss Cho was from Pusan, where one of my great aunts had lived. In Kyongsang Namdo, she said, there were more commerce and urbanization. Her father, an executive in a fish-packing company, drove through the thick of it every day.

"It is good that we are developing, but we must not ruin our country like other nations have done for a quick handful of money. We just want to show the world that we are not . . . lackeys—is that the word?—not lackeys of rich countries. Especially Japan. They are *too* smug," she said, wrinkling her nose. "And America. America is arrogant. In Korea, we can do the same things to get rich as they did. So what? Money is not everything, but Western countries really think so. I think we are more fortunate than they, maybe," said Miss Cho.

"In what way, fortunate?" I asked.

"Fortunate to know who we are. Over the centuries through invasions and wars, we have learned how to live without false material props and big . . . egos."

The word *ego* sounded bizarre coming from her mouth; an unexpected psycholinguistic burp. She continued. "If the West doesn't know who we are, so what? *We* know."

"But you just said you wanted to show the world you're not lackeys."

"Ah. That is different. I want to show the world we don't care, and that we don't need their approval, but we need their attention to do that," said Miss Cho, smiling. "That is why we students demonstrate."

"But the press pays no attention to the *reasons* behind your demonstrations, they only report the violence," I said, goading her a little. Miss Cho frowned. I had offended her. After a prompt apology, she forgave me.

On the sparsely occupied train, our companions consisted of several nuns and some salesmen reading spreadsheets. I mentioned that there were no foreign tourists.

"No, we don't get lots of tourists. . . . I think Korea is too different from what they're used to. Not like China. People are more comfortable with China and Japan because they know what stereotypes to expect. But it's a matter of public relations, too; we don't try to attract outsiders. We don't want to have to Westernize our country for tourists: if they come, it must be on our terms. Western countries don't Easternize their daily lives for a few tourists. Why should we?"

Courtesy of the super-express train, we soon arrived in Kyongju, in the southeastern province of Kyongsangbuk-do. Here, deep in the entrails of the country, everything felt subtly different. The sun, low in the sky, cast a diffuse light. The surface of the land was harder to read. The sky was bleached out and misty, the horizon blurred in the distance. The few bearings that I had previously enjoyed were gone.

Miss Cho and I took a crowded, beaten-looking shuttle bus into the town center. Someone stole my near-empty wallet. Like Seoul, Kyong-ju presented a similar jumble of the antique and the hurriedly modern, but its contrasts were still more extreme. "Kyong-ju," declared a sign in English, French, German, and Japanese at the tourist office, "is the cradle of Korean civilization." It had been the ancient capital of Korea during the Shilla Dynasty, in 57 B.C.

Miss Cho insisted that we go by tour bus for the best view of everything. The bus driver was typically hotheaded, honking with great satisfaction at everything that moved, the vehicle jerking and speeding at an alarming rate. The other tourists were a group of middle-aged Korean women from the country with ruddy cheeks and perms, wearing cardigans over their traditional han-boks. Being the only Westerner, I thought I might be allowed to blend in with the other Koreans, but the conservatively suited young female tour guide was neither to be fooled nor denied her opportunity to demonstrate her English skills, and at every stop, went through the entire litany of facts twice, for my sole benefit. We all died of boredom.

Miss Cho led me proudly through the grand and splendid temples of Sokkuram and Bulgoksa—the Parthenon and St. Peter's of the ancient Buddhist world, but again, so opposite in approach and execution as to be incomparable. ("You must stop comparing!" Miss Cho admonished.) We visited the oldest stone observatory in Asia, starkly beautiful. I saw every possible kind of image of Buddha; from heraldic, exquisitely painted wood-carved giants to crude sleeping gnomic stone totems, to rotund gold-leaf monsters. We saw the extraordinary proto-modernistic crown jewels in the nearby museum, and Royal Shilla Tombs. The royal tombs were haunting, monumental smooth mounds of turf, some encircled with low stone balustrades. It looked as if the earth itself were nine months pregnant. Yet in Kyongju, life was a tiny ant on the bloated carcass of the past. To me, it felt like a land of the dead. Being outside the town center, the monuments we visited were mostly deserted. During the eighth century, when it had been the Shilla capital, Kyong-ju had been *ten times* its present size.

I looked out of the bus window, unable to imagine what it had been like then, or even what it would be like to live there now. Who would one's friends be? Could one buy oil paints in Kyong-ju? A foreign newspaper? I snorted at the idea. Equally amusing was the thought of hippie Germans or American serial-lifestyle reincarnatees trying to reinvent themselves in this forbidding place, and imagining the expressions on the Koreans' faces as they arrived.

We went into a seedy little *bulgoki-jip* on the main street for a late lunch. Miss Cho and I were both tired. The waitress gave us insolent looks as we entered, grunted as she took Miss Cho's order for two bowls of *bi bim bab*, and muttered "*Yangnom*" (abusive slang for Westerner) for good measure as she retreated toward the kitchen inferno. The menu was printed completely in Hangul, with no romanization. It was a complete zero. I pointed to something at random.

"What's this?"

"Dried radish," said Miss Cho.

"What's that?"

"Snake wine."

"What's that?"

"Snake soup. *Paem tang*."

Although not averse to trying slimy things, I was not quite ready for snake soup. Despite the unfavorable atmosphere, the *bi bim bab* was delicious, a steaming mound of moist rice topped with smoky morsels of marinated grilled beef, pickled vegetables, sweet cucumber slices,

toasted sesame seeds, and red chili sauce, crowned with a glistening
fried egg. Again, the flavors satisfied me to the core, and made me feel
somehow welcome. We ate silently, and I looked out of the window
at the unfamiliar, puzzling scenery. Except for the atavistic recognition of the food I was eating, I felt that I was visiting a more foreign
place than I had ever been before.

Here in Kyongsangbuk-do was a startling Korea, unmediated by
the universality of city manners, technologies, roman script, and the
buffer of English-speaking relations. Despite Miss Cho's words about
tourism, I was surprised by its minimal concessions to the white man,
its absence of Coca-Cola and other bullying imports, its lack of chain
shops and VISA stickers, and above all the flinty truculence of its pop-
ulace. Granted, I had encountered only waitresses, pedestrians, bus
drives, market-stall holders, and a band of matrons, but I congratulated myself on absorbing their acerbity through the cement language
barrier. As the day wore on, my sureties had nearly vanished; I
enjoyed no leverage of understanding that which was not purely animal on the one hand or cerebrally encyclopaedia-based on the other.
It was not an unpleasant sensation.

Later, at the luxury Choson Hotel in which Uncle had booked us
for the night, things were rather different. It was set in the mountains
on a picturesque man-made lake, complete with a swan-shaped boat
resembling an oversized bath toy, room service, and televisions coming out of every orifice. Three coach loads of honeymooning couples
were responsible for the surreal proliferation of shy, identically blue-
suited young husbands and traditionally robed wives picking their
way through the coffee shop (liberally VISA-stickered) and land-
scaped rock gardens in their high heels. Restaurants serving Japanese,
American, and Italian food added to the impression of being in a kitsch
international theme park. Miss Cho loved it, and so did I.

Korea was so contradictory and utterly disparate, and so absorbing were the demands of such newness on my perceptions that I rarely thought of life back in New York. I couldn't imagine my friends here, and wasn't sure why this should be. Would they appreciate it? I feared they would not. It was too *particular* a place. I doubted whether any of them, apart from Laura, would understand what this journey meant to me. As it was, *I* barely knew what it meant to me. The realization made me feel quite alone, but it seemed to be a necessary kind of loneliness.

What would my father make of Korea? He might balk at some of the food, but the rest he would probably take to, as he had been attracted to my mother. When I thought of my mother, there was an odd displacement of time. I could not imagine her in the present; it was the teenage Myung-ja whom I thought of. Perhaps because she had never lived here as my mother.

In the bright coffee shop, I wrote a postcard to Laura—picturing a honeymooning couple waving from the swan boat—and kept one eye on the Korean music video playing on the monitor above the cashier. In it, a young man in a business suit was leaning against a tree by the ocean at sunset, crooning a love-song to the accompaniment of a synthesizer, his tie flapping romantically in the breeze. No postmodern sense of irony clouded the singer's brow: his expression was one of fervent rhapsody. Life was sweet and painful when you were a businessman in love standing against a tree in the sunset singing a love song.

The atmosphere in the hotel was extremely soothing. As I had noticed before, the absence of tension around me, the lack of attention-seeking, sexually competitive behavior, still felt odd. It was a big generalization, but it felt as if people were not hungry in the way that many Westerners were (self included). The Japanese also displayed this unseemly craving, the voracious *shopping-to-impress* energy, the rampant consumerism, the restless, copycat culture. Although the pace of Korean life was frantic and Koreans cared about the prestige that accomplishments could bring, contradictorily, I found Koreans themselves charmingly laid back and unmaterialistic. They genuinely seemed to care more about the greater Korean good than about their own. Perhaps it was this spirit of sacrifice and communality that created such a benign atmosphere. Although this harmony had been a bit baffling and bland to me at first, it was now rather a relief, like an alcoholic finding satisfaction in a really good cup of cocoa.

Miss Cho and I bade each other a cheerful good night from the snug confines of our twin beds, and to the reassuring rumbling sound of the hotel's enormous boiler I slept very soundly indeed.

The next day and night we spent in Pusan. Compared to Kyong-ju, Pusan was a throbbingly modern city, and for that reason, was somewhat less bewitching. The melancholy air of a vanished civilization hung powerfully over the plains of Kyong-ju, and this gave it a unique sense of ballast and authority. Its people had a distinctive look in their eyes: fiercely independent and proud. They were survivors, guardians of an obsolete culture which no longer served them, but around which they based their lives. The practical citizens of Pusan had a brighter, livelier cast to their eye. Like Seoulites, they lived for the future.

Pusan being Miss Cho's hometown, she perked up noticeably when we arrived at the station, and proved a vigorous proponent of its attributes. We stayed in a comfortable concrete hotel near the resort of Hyundae Beach, toured the famous fish market and beachfront, and that evening ate at a memorable restaurant on the strand with her shy, bespectacled, six-foot-three-inch accountant older brother who spoke no English.

Pusan was boiling over with activity and commerce. Everything was faster and hotter here: air, kimchi, tempers. Pusan was the second-largest city in Korea, and its traffic was thick and wild. Cars and trucks demonstrated a casual regard for traffic signals and stop signs, while buses—terrifying even by Korean standards—thundered by, screeching around corners, making lavish use of the horn. On the streets, irate-sounding merchants shouted at passersby for attention while they dodged taxis climbing the pavement. Miss Cho assured me that this Pusan fierceness was just an exterior protection: "On the inside they are soft," she claimed. I was skeptical. Yet her comment was soon borne out.

We caught a bus to the coast. The driver was playing pop music on a portable radio at full volume—a song that sounded like a woman in a disco being repeatedly hit over the head with a frying pan. The passengers seemed oblivious to the din. This diversion not being quite interesting enough for the driver, he amused himself by honking the horn. He had devised a whole language of horn-honking: he honked greetings to all fellow bus drivers and selected taxis, honked accident warnings, honked profanities, honked impatience, honked appreciation at passing female beauty, honked passengers who got off the bus too slowly, honked to let someone into the traffic ahead of him; he was a virtuoso.

Miss Cho and I stood pitching with the sudden jerks of the bus, shopping bags hanging from our arms. To my initial shock, the grouchy-looking old lady seated below us tugged our bags and wrestled them away from our grip. I was about to remonstrate when I saw that she was placing them protectively in her lap so that we would not be burdened. She nodded to us, her whole face creasing into a wide smile, as if we were doing her an enormous favor. Others on the bus also held the packages of strangers on their laps without exchanging a word. Later, while Miss Cho was phoning her brother, I asked a passing businessman where the nearest newsstand was. Not only did he tell me where it was, he seized my hand, clasping it tightly in his own, and frog-marched me there himself, standing outside on the pavement waving good-bye until I was safely inside.

The fish market docks, ringed by low, rugged mountains, were a riot of tangy smells, livid colors, and villainous textures. Small, pink-cheeked, black-haired boys in aprons emptied enormous woven wicker fish baskets from the sea, and unloaded the shining, flapping catch onto the pier. Squatting women in head scarves and bright rubber gloves sorted the silvery minnows, fish, octopus, eels, ray, and alarming-looking sea cucumber into plastic bowls and wooden slatted trays according to size, variety, and color, creating fresh displays of fantastic, rainbow-hued abundance. Shellfish of all kinds were heaped, shining, in infinitesimally graded sizes, from periwinkles to giant lobsters.

Indoors, in the pungent-smelling dry goods section, a woman was selling sixteen different varieties of kimchi—I counted. Her thin, bespectacled face was barely visible above the mounds of fiery shredded pickle piled high in their plastic tubs. We ate *hweh* for lunch at the market restaurant, my eyes filling with tears of pleasure as I slowly chewed the meltingly fresh raw flounder robed in its pungent chili sauce and lettuce crunch. We drank cold Korean OB beer, and our cheeks flushed red.

In the late afternoon, Miss Cho took me down to the celebrated rock formations on the coast, in the waters of the Korea Strait, where the East Sea met the the East China Sea. The waters were a deep teal blue, fading to pale jade near the shore, overlaid with a lace pattern of white-capped waves. Jutting rocks formed mysterious crumbling gateways against the sky. The sea at this southernmost tip of Korea felt different to me from any other. Again, ineffably *Eastern*. I admired the view, and yet felt a chill of detachment. There was something so remote about it. I felt like an astronaut looking out at a moon-scape through a cold fiberglass helmet. I felt a certain awe, a dull gratification at the view, but could not discern its place in the order of things.

A whitewashed lighthouse stood at the cliff's edge, where some daytrippers, mostly teenagers, and a few stiff-legged aunts and uncles picked their way carefully past us on the steep cliff walk. Miss Cho sat contemplatively on a nearby promontory. I stared out to sea, bemused, a wild wind ripping my hair at its roots. I remembered that my mother had had an aunt she called Aunt Pusan. Mother herself had been based in Pusan for a short time during the war. That's all I knew. Here at the tip of Korea, I waited for some revelation, some piece of the puzzle to slip into place.

No such enlightenment came.

We went to bed early that night. We were both tired from all the fresh air on our cliff hike, drained by the hectic vigor of activity we had seen in Pusan, and slightly drunk after our outing with Miss Cho's tall brother, who had taken us to a beach tent for a pre-prandial beer, and treated us to shots of *soju* to accompany our delicious bowls of sweat-inducingly hot *mae-un tang*.

The beach tent had been remarkable; inside its tiny, unprepossessing canvas walls was squeezed an entire nightclub with a blurry plastic window facing the sea, colored lights covered with fringed lampshades, a fully stocked bar festooned with candles and silk flowers, a microphone and speakers for the guitar-strumming singer, low stools, and a bored bartender watching a television that had been hooked up to an outside generator. Despite such comforts, you could hear and smell the sea. I had enjoyed this place immensely and Miss Cho and her brother were pleased that I was so pleased.

After dinner, we weaved slowly back to our hotel in the dark. The lights of Hyundae Beach were strung in a brilliant diamond curve along the the purple-streaked, inky black coastline. Car headlights occasionally flashed past, drivers giving a talkative honk as they rubbernecked by. My stomach was straining against the waistband of my jeans, and I yawned with teeth-bearing abandon in the hotel elevator, making Miss Cho giggle.

I performed my nightly ablutions in the fluorescent-lit bathroom cubicle, and examined my scrubbed face in the mirror, clean of makeup. I could have been imagining it, but I swore my face looked subtly different. Just as the day spent in Pusan had offered no similarity to any other day in my life—or to anywhere else I'd been—so my face appeared newly blank, mirroring the curious expansion I was beginning to feel in my fresh surroundings. I was even convinced that my eyes looked infinitesimally more Oriental. Miss Cho, standing behind me, said earnestly that she thought they did, too.

After lunch on Sunday I sat alone on a rock above the Parks' cottage in Yangsoo-ri, reflecting on my trip south. Miss Cho and I had parted, as agreed, in Seoul, and I had driven out to the country with the Parks on Saturday afternoon. The night before I had slept on a *yo*—floor mat—for the first time, and was awoken in the night by the cry of a loon. I had experienced more in the past few days than I could have possibly calculated or quantified. Certainly, the subtle sensations could not be contained in thought. Whatever was happening to me, it no longer felt as if I were wearing a space helmet.

The view from here was especially absorbing, and I entered into that. It was wild and scrubby, with the omnipresent steeply calligraphic mountains, soaring conifers punctuating the dipping horizon, and terraced rice paddies stepping up the hillside to my left. The neighboring farmer's small, exquisite wing-tipped barn stood to my right, spilling out golden straw. A pugnacious yellow dog, a chindo-

kae like Aunt Myung-hi's, occasionally barked at me from beneath its antique eaves. The enormous skies above were opalescent, strewn with gauzy, high-flung cloud. I shivered slightly. Here the damp winds and mists from the Great Yellow River of China met the headwinds of the southern branch of the Han River; it felt about ten degrees colder than it did in Seoul, and I had brought all the wrong clothes.

At the bottom of the hill, I saw Mr. Park in his red pullover, carrying Son-young on his shoulders toward his beehives, where their caretaker, a young farmer, was tending the honeycombs. This tiny village of seventeen families was yet another world within Korea. Although so close to the capital, it was intensely rural, and again different from the preceding surprises thrown my way. Along steep, crumbling, red clay tracks stood Yang-soo-ri, a slanting agglomeration of winged-roofed farms clinging tenaciously to the mountainsides, their modest, dilapidated appearance belying the prodigal character of their efforts.

According to Mr. Park, the farmers who worked this difficult terrain made their living growing rice and produce: turnip, cabbage, sweet potato, sesame, red beans, garlic, onion, dates, persimmons, pine nuts and chestnuts. There was no heavy farm machinery involved. Despite the picturesque fecundity of the land, there was a slight air of doom about the place. The Parks were worried that their caretaker, a surly-looking young man with a wispy beard, might soon be leaving Yang-soo-ri for the city. There were no young women left to marry. The young, girls particularly, had all but vacated the countryside seeking greater fortune and adventure in the cities, leaving the farmers wifeless, and as was happening all over the world, traditional farm life was disappearing with their migrations. I understood the caretaker's dejected expression as he cooked us a simple but delicious *bulgoki* lunch.

Before lunch Mrs. Park and I had washed the farm lettuce in the freezing cold water from the pump in the yard. Following Mrs. Park's example, I plunged each leaf separately in a bucket of clean water to remove every speck of grit, and laid each leaf on a platter for wrapping the tangy meat that was cooking on the grill. Two kinds of kimchi had been brought down in the car from Seoul, a mild radish variety, and a hot cabbage one. Rice was steaming away in a corner on a Bunsen burner, while dressed spinach and bean sprout *namul* stood ready in pewter bowls on the low, rough wooden table, bearing a heaping plate of freshly picked apples and pears, glistening with water droplets. The girls were delighted to be in the country and, hungry from their walk, were bouncing excitedly in their places at the table, snacking on shrimp-flavored chips and banging their chopsticks on their pudgy knees.

Attracted to the farm's rusticity, Mr. Park had bought the place for very little ten years before. The cottage was extremely humble, without electricity and indoor plumbing, but its sliding screen doors, books, comfortable floor mats, and bright cushions lent the place an intimate charm. It was cool inside, but the hot, intensely flavored food was instantly warming, and I remember that meal as one of the most delicious I have eaten in my life. As we ate, there was a tremendous, earsplitting explosion. To my surprise, the Parks and the little girls carried on eating without even looking up. I asked what this had been.

"Military exercises. The U.S.-ROK 'Team Spirit' exercises. We are used to it," said Mr. Park, reaching for some kimchi. "They are just testing a little bomb."

The caretaker cleared our plates clumsily, and we finished off our lunch with the crisp fruit and stimulating ginseng tea. After the meal, we went for a slow walk in the scrubby hills, which offered vistas of mellow, haunting beauty. All that could be heard were the rushing of a hidden stream, the sound of the wind through the pine needles, and the occasional sonic crack of fighter jets splitting the air.

On the way back to Seoul at dusk on Sunday the road was thick with returning traffic. Shiny new cars—all with identical boxes of tissues on the back shelf—filed along the scenic road that followed the curves of the wide Han River. The satin surface of the river reflected gold light—as golden as the burnished stomachs of the Buddhas in the Kyong-ju temples. The girls were asleep next to me, and the Parks and I were silently taking in the beauty of the mighty river, overhung with the drooping branches of venerable plane trees. In a field opposite, cows were lying down in the grass.

"They're overworked like the rest of us," said Mr. Park, staring somewhat enviously at the beasts.

"We came this weekend specially to show you Yang-soo-ri, but usually there's no time to come to the country," explained Mrs. Park. The Parks often worked ten-hour, six-day weeks with short or nonexistent holidays, which they assured me was typical, so great was the pressure for Koreans to achieve and to rebuild the country, not only for the Olympics, but to atone for the destruction of the past forty years.

"I'm even organizing things in my dreams," said Mrs. Park, "but you cannot drill water."

As if to underline the point, we passed a woman washing a pile of clothes in the river as the sun was setting. The urbanites in their cars passed by her without a glance. I turned around to see a farmer, carrying a load of burlap sacks, kicking the cows to their feet.

CHAPTER EIGHTEEN

Going North

It was gray and drizzling. I stood in a busy downtown street jostled by passersby with umbrellas, trying to hold a conversation with Aunt Myung-hi. We had just finished a quick but pleasant sushi lunch in Myong-dong, and I was about to catch a tour bus to the North Korean border. A large raindrop from someone's umbrella hit my nose.

"It won't be very pretty," she said, trying to convince me to take a scenic cruise with her down the Han River instead—when the sun was shining. My aunt was not at all curious about what the North was like, and thought I'd be bored by looking at a lot of soldiers and barbed wire. Yet even if she had wished to go to the Demilitarized Zone, she would not be allowed to do so. Being South Korean, *Imo* was forbidden to attend these tours, which were strictly for foreigners; spying and infiltration were taken extremely seriously by both governments. As it was, I had had to apply for military clearance to make the trip. But I insisted to her that I wanted to see North Korea.

"Even though you can't cross the border?" she asked, making sure I had no delusions about what the trip would entail.

"Even though we can't cross the border."

I was curious about seeing the DMZ itself, and out of sentiment, wished to travel as close as possible to our old lands in Kaesong, which Hong-do had shown me on the map. Aunt Myung-hi shrugged.

"It's all gone now," she said, looking into my eyes with a glazed stare. "It's no good going back," she asserted to no one in particular, reminding me strongly of my mother. She waved good-bye a little sadly from the pavement.

Through the blue-tinted window, Seoul sped past, stippled with droplets of rain. The gloom-bathed scenery was fairly unremarkable as we made our way to Panmunjom, the armistice village a mere thirty-five miles from Seoul. This was where UN troops and North Korean forces faced each other across a painted line.

Our guide was a bright Mr. Kim, in glasses and a blazer, who spoke in American-twanged English to our motley tour group. His tone was abnormally cheerful, in the manner of all tour guides, but the content of his speech was at odds with its presentation. Smiling, he listed a litany of North Korean assassination attempts on South Korean presidents and statesmen, airline bombings, propaganda warfare, U-boat sabotage, dam-flooding, secret tunnel-digging, kidnappings, and finally the brutal ax murders of U.S. soldiers in the Joint Security Area itself.

"For your own safety, no 'hippie clothing' is permitted. No pointing or waving is allowed. You will be photographed by the North Korean guards, and these photographs may be doctored and used for propaganda against us. When we arrive, you will each wear a blue armband identifying you as non-combatants."

I looked around involuntarily at the others on the bus, who looked rather tickled, as if being asked to wear fancy dress. Mr. Kim carried on his monologue as we sped quickly toward the DMZ.

"You will see," he said, pointing out of the window, "that there are eight concentric antitank walls surrounding the Demilitarized

Zone. Please do not take photographs of them. . . . That is not allowed. Thank you." We passed gigantic, clunky concrete gateposts painted in camouflage.

"Although you can't see them, behind those barbed-wire fences—the ones marked by skull-and-crossbones signposts—there are live minefields, and soon we will be coming up to the two checkpoints," said Mr. Kim.

Apart from these sinister martial indignities, the delicate blue-wash landscape looked the same as it had ten miles back, emphasizing the arbitrariness of the division. It had stopped raining, and the shadows of swift, brooding clouds darkened the plains. Within minutes Mr. Kim pointed out the landmark of Freedom Bridge—or, as it is also called, the Bridge of No Return. This somber national symbol was an unprepossessing black railway bridge, with moss growing on it, on the Imjin River.

"It is called Freedom Bridge, because after the signing of the armistice, thousands of prisoners were repatriated across this bridge from Communist camps. It is called Bridge of No Return, because if a South Korean ever crossed that bridge, he could never come back," said Mr. Kim cheerily. This was, he explained, the farthest point north to which South Koreans were permitted to travel.

"During the Korean War, ten million families were separated by the division of the country at the 38th Parallel. So separated relatives come here, to the Bridge of No Return, to burn incense and to offer prayers for the reunification of the country, and prayers for their relatives. This is as close as they can get to them. Millions of people come here because they don't know if their relatives are dead or alive. They pray for peace, so that one day they can hear from their loved ones," said Mr. Kim. "There was one occasion in September 1985, when some supervised relatives were permitted to meet in front of television cameras, but apart from that, no contact of any kind has been allowed since 1950."

As he spoke, a terrible lump formed in my throat that would not go away. Sudden, involuntary tears slid down my face. I turned toward the window to hide my distress. Some of our own relations still lived in the North: my mothers' aunts, Chosan and Chungsun, and her cousin Jae-sung, who was still imprisoned when she left Korea. Actually, we didn't know if they were alive or not. My mother's maternal grandparents, the Kangs, had been in the North when she left the country. Not knowing that war would divide Korea for nearly half a century, my grandmother had never said good-bye to her mother, and my mother had not said good-bye to her grandmother when she left for America. It was likely that my great-grandmother had died without seeing her daughter and granddaughter again. These deepest ties had been hacked off bluntly, mother from daughter, from generation to generation.

Seeing the Bridge of No Return, this unreal, charged situation became horribly concrete. The sadness and trauma caused by such a severing was unfathomable; a daily burden of having to live *not knowing* whether or not these closest relatives were alive or dead. As these thoughts crowded in on me, I felt leaden helplessness.

Had the country not been divided, I might have met them all, might have been able to bring my mother's news to them and theirs to her, perhaps helping to heal their wounds of separation, closing the broken circle on my mother's behalf. But instead, I sat on a sterile bus looking out across a minefield.

A strange pressure built up behind the lump in my throat, burning and pushing at my chest; a surge of grief so powerful that I knew it could not be mine alone, but an accumulated, collective grief. My mother's unclaimed loss lay within me, along with aunts', uncles' and grandparents' suffering, and the interwoven despair of myriad families similarly caught in this division.

I shifted in my seat, almost unable to breathe. I felt an overwhelming need to get off the bus, to breathe fresh air, deeply. Others on the bus looked out of the windows, or examined their maps and brochures, ever so slightly bored. Drawing little curiosity, I stepped off the bus for a few moments, telling Mr. Kim I felt sick. Sitting on the damp grass verge, head in hands, I forced back the inconvenient emotions with much effort, waiting for the lump in my throat to sub-side so that I could breathe. I knew that I must not begin to cry; knew that they were not the sort of tears you could stop. I was shocked at the intensity of feeling that had welled up from nowhere and ambushed me. The bracing, sweet wind was calming, and I got back on the bus, shaken, but thankful that no one had made a fuss.

On we drove. Next to the road ran a set of rusty railroad tracks. Mr. Kim said this had once been the main line to Pyongyang, and on through to Manchuria, Mongolia, and Beijing. Before the war, my grandfather had used these very tracks to reach Harbin. Now, of course, the disused tracks were choked with weeds, and farther on, blocked with sleepers, finally running dead into a pile of sand just south of the Imjin River. It was a sad, ghostly sight.

Just then we passed a truckload of UN soldiers carrying loaded M-16s, which reminded Mr. Kim to tell us that Korea was still in a state of war, and that the 1953 cease-fire was still in place. People on the bus clucked in surprise, and asked questions.

When we arrived at Camp Bonifas, Mr. Kim surrendered us into the safe hands of the laconic Private Kraft, a soldier from Alabama, who ushered us into a UN military building for our briefing: here we each had to sign an official declaration absolving the UN from any accountability should we be killed during our tour by a North Korean "act of hostility."

Wearing hard hats, we were shown into one of the 107 deep underground tunnels that the North Koreans had dug to invade Seoul. The North Koreans had painted the entrances black, to disguise them as Japanese coal mines, and they had remained undiscovered because of their depth. The tunnel we entered was wide enough to accommodate two men abreast, standing, and by army calculations, thousands of troops could have reached Seoul within two hours. Now they were stopped up with concrete. We were told of more petty wickednesses and acts of sabotage.

Private Kraft took us to an observation post, and pointed out the actual border, the Military Demarcation Line (MDL), dividing Korea on the 38th Parallel. It was a raised concrete cicatrice, running across the width of the land for 151 miles. To create a buffer zone, troops were withdrawn two kilometers from either side of the MDL. As we gazed out across the damp, barren plains, our thoughts were scrambled by a loud, tinny barrage of military music and shouted commands issuing from a loudspeaker on the North Korean side, a broadcast that was kept up day and night, either to bolster their soldiers' morale or to drive the enemy insane, or possibly both. North Korean sentries in black steel helmets shadowed us. Across the border, the private pointed out the two uninhabited propaganda villages, North and South, where citizens commuted to maintain the facade of normal villages. In unison, we stared blankly across at the unprepossessing huts. These places seemed to exist mostly for the purpose of displaying the grotesquely enormous national flags of both nations. The private said that the North Korean flag was actually bigger than the *Tae-gŭkki*.

"Their flag weighs six hunnerd pounds, and when we timed 'em hoisting it, turns out it takes 'em a half-ar to git the monster thang up and down," said Kraft, his southern accent getting stronger. "They go through several of these suckers every month, because they're so heavy, the dang things shred right up. Now let's go on through to the JSA, the Joint Security Area," said Private Kraft, straightening his camouflage cap, and leading on with his frightening-looking black-laced boots.

"You folks are lookin' at the most heavily armed border in the world," he said, pointing out the coils of barbed wire and trip lines, ground sensors, and the barracks where a crack team of combat sol-

diers were kept in a state of 110 percent readiness, attack weapons permanently loaded and cocked, able to engage in hand-to-hand combat
within ninety seconds.

The private led us to the circle straddling the MDL, where the village of Panmunjom had once stood, and which now hosted a group of
purpose-built viewing stands, barracks, and sky blue—painted huts,
bisected by a white stripe dividing the area North and South. A lone
North Korean guard in olive green stood motionless on the steps of
the North's headquarters, observing us with binoculars.

"Now here, they hold their MAC talks: the Military Armistice
Commission, that is, where—between you and me—both sides
spend a long time talkin' and not agreein' on one thang. There have
been four hunnerd and forty-two meetin's so far," said Kraft.

He showed us the small chamber where armistice talks were held,
and the long green baize table with microphones set up down the middle. A set of military police from both Koreas stood on guard duty,
staring straight ahead.

"On *that* side of the microphone, ladies and gentlemen, is North
Korea."

On the bus back to Seoul, I felt numb. The sadness I had suppressed earlier was frozen in my veins. Being on the tour with
Americans and Western businessmen had been an odd way to see the
border for the first time, the approach slightly cartoony. The tone
throughout had been jokey and amusing, wrapped in bright cellophane for easy consumption. I had felt vague discomfort when the private had referred to Koreans as "they," but had reflexively concealed
my half-Korean identity, not knowing if it was relevant or not. I'd felt
set apart from the strangers surrounding me, unable to imagine speaking to any of them, like a novice double agent, not knowing whom to
trust.

Looking over the barbed wire fence into North Korea I waited, as
I had in Pusan, for a flare of recognition to ignite in my consciousness.

But again, none came. Before my eyes there stretched only a mute, defeating expanse of mink brown fields and mauve mountains against a blue-clouded sky. No crowd of inborn memories was released by the air, the trees, the earth.

I could not imagine the voices of my grandparents, great aunts or cousins, or know what they would say to me, even if they had been alive. I could not picture Kaesong, where the old estates lay. As my aunt Myung-hi had said, that old life, those ancient, languid traditions, had gone, replaced by a corroded pride in the worship of "Dear Leader," of workers' cooperatives, and hydroelectric plants. Had it been a change for the better? The megalomaniacal Stalinism of Kim Il Sung had replaced one unbalanced system with another. Although the feudal aristocracy of my grandparents' day had exploited the poor, in North Korea, *everyone* was now poor—with the notable exception of Kim Il Sung and son—and forced to endure a chilling mental oppression as well. Although North Koreans presented their sacrifices to the state as unselfish acts performed under free will, it was transparent to everyone else that their chains were tighter and heavier than ever before.

On the drive back to Seoul I was sobered both by what I had seen and by what I'd been prevented from seeing. Members of our family lay hidden deep in the folds of Korea's military cloak, and could not be reached, the painted Military Demarcation Line providing harsh proof of a Korea torn in half, still occupied. The opposing worlds of capitalism and communism stood head to head at the 38th Parallel, inflexible and armed to the teeth. The extraordinary had been made ordinary by passing time, and only time itself could reverse the malediction.

CHAPTER NINETEEN

Filial Piety

One morning in early April, Uncle Hong-do, Aunt Myung-hi, and I drove off in Uncle's black sedan to visit my grandparents' tomb. The skies were purple and showery, with occasional dazzling shafts of sunlight lightening the fast-moving clouds. The dramatic weather made our journey more auspicious, and I was both excited and somewhat intimidated by the prospect of the solemn occasion.

Imo and I sat in the back, looking out of the windows in a contented silence. My aunt, wearing huge sunglasses and a worn but well-tailored coat, held on her lap a large bouquet of brilliant red, white, and yellow chrysanthemums and green laurel branches tied with a yellow bow, and wrapped in clear cellophane, which crackled festively when she moved.

From the passenger seat Uncle Hong-do handed me back a thick, heavy sheaf of Xeroxed papers, tied with a red silk ribbon. I grasped it and rested it on my knee.

"This is something you ought to see. It is the most recent section of our *chok-bo.*"

"What's that?"

"Our family genealogy. Every Korean family has one. Ours has four volumes."

I looked at the sheaf with interest, and some dread. The pages were filled with minute characters, organized into intricate columns and subcolumns in fine, spidery black ink, each character resembling a different, minuscule snowflake. I couldn't make out a single vowel or consonant.

"I can't read it, you know."

"That's because it's in imperial Chinese."

"Why?"

"It used to be the official language of the court, and it is still carried on in the writing of some important documents. My cousin Young-ju is now the head of the family, and he keeps the original book in a vault and adjusts the entries."

I was slightly relieved to find it indecipherable. About thirty pages deep into the document my aunt smiled and pointed out a little constellation of snowflakes with the red-lacquered fingernail of her pinkie.

"That is us! Jin-ho, Myung-ja, Myung-hi, and Hong-do. They did not get around to adding you yet," said Hong-do, twisting his head around to look at the page.

I gazed at the group of characters which jumped around as the car took small bumps and potholes, trying to distinguish aunts and uncles from the swarming print on the page, but as soon as I thought I could tell them apart, they blended back into the decorative pattern of a calligraphic snowstorm. Nonetheless, the heaviness of the book, its material substance and authority, the millennia represented in the tiny branching ciphers of names and dates, inscribed in the handwriting of the eldest Min, was remarkable in itself. More than a gift, it was a sort of talisman.

"Komapsumnida," I said to my uncle and aunt, nodding my head in thanks.

Soon we entered a town called Masok, in the mountains, still in Kyonggi-do. It was a quiet village on a dusty main street, with orange and blue election bunting hung from the lampposts. A coatless young girl in slippers carried a tray of steaming coffee cups down the street a few doors, and slipped inside a storefront.

Outside the town we took a turn at a wooden signpost where there stood a dense thicket of pine trees. "Here we are," said Hong-do. As we drove down a hilly, curving dirt track I was expecting a flat Western cemetery with large gates, mowed lawns and vertical grave-stones and monuments, but here, at Moran, nothing told me I was in a graveyard at all. For one thing, the cemetery, far from being flat and orderly, was a wild, flowing landscape of stepped mountains, full of umbrella pines. Only upon closer inspection did one see the gleam of low granite and marble altars, phallic markers, and geometric perime-ter bases containing the mounds of sculptured turf that topped Korean graves. Man adjusted to nature's existing contours rather than nature being razed to accommodate man. Even the tombs of kings were marked by a simple mound and tablet, as at the Shilla tombs in Kyong-ju, although royally enormous. Newer graves were distinguishable by the diminutive scale of the pines at the foot of the mounds. Here I understood Miss Cho's explanation of tree planting as "the filial yearning for the deceased."

We parked the car in an empty lot—it was a Wednesday—and, led by my uncle, we trooped across the face of a mountain that bore a scattering of pines and mounds. The sky had clouded over, and spat with rain now and then. My aunt carried the bouquet of flowers, blazing with fiery solar colors against the dun-colored, wintry grasses. My aunt and uncle were very silent as they walked along, their heads bowed in thought as they picked their way through the grass and stones in their city shoes.

Despite the peaceful beauty of the cemetery, I felt a muted sadness to be meeting my grandparents in this way. Their being dead was something of an impediment to a fulfilling relationship, and rather an anticlimax. However, as nothing could be done about this, I tried to summon up from memory as many stories as possible about them, so at least a one-way meeting could take place. In the car *Imo* and my uncle had told me, with sincere, almost tearful affection, how much my grandmother had been adored by the family. How strong and kind she was, how warm, how rare, and pure at heart.

When they spoke of Grandfather, their faces grew sad. They had feared him. At the end of his life, illness and many disappointments had embittered him. Above all, his unacknowledged guilt about Jin-ho's decline had worn holes in his heart and temper. Even at the end of his life, Hong-do said, grandfather had not been able to forgive others' weaknesses. His high standards were unscalable mountain peaks from which his children had fallen, breaking their bones. Jin-ho did not survive his fall. I learned that, despite my mother's success as a musician, this had not completely exonerated her in her father's eyes for marrying a foreigner and remaining in the West. Aunt Myung-hi had given her youth to looking after her ailing parents, who could not then afford a private nurse, only to be mocked by him for being dim and unambitious. Even so, my aunt's eyes filled with tears of pity for her father when Hong-do told me of it. Grandfather had been riddled with a cancer of criticism and pride; Hong-do, being a son conceived late in his father's life, was left to indulge himself, but still did not escape Grandfather's censure in marrying "beneath himself," to a girl without lineage. Yet my aunt and uncle told me that they loved him no less for the pain he had caused them. He was still the pillar of their lives, their respected patriarch, deserving filial piety. He had also been a man of his time.

None of us could have known of Grandfather's stinging self-reproach for failing in politics, for allowing his optimism to be broken over the wheel of Japanese oppression. His life had been a slow trajectory of loss: from being a *yangban* lord to a fugitive from the Japanese and then from the Communists; his loss of material fortune, his long public service blighted by the élitist conservatism of his views, at odds with the go-getting egalitarianism of the times. In Jin-ho's early death Grandfather saw the entire edifice of the Min family honor collapsing hard into the dust. For this he blamed himself. Despite Grandfather's courage in prison, in assuming heavy responsibilities from his drunken older brother, in trying to create a new democracy for his country, he felt it had never been enough, and he had taken to his grave this damning conviction of his failure.

I remembered my grandparents' elderly faces from photographs, dignified and worn. I could see my mother's features so clearly in theirs. I could see strength shining in their eyes, as well as telltale signs of hardship in their downturned mouths. As a child, I had felt an immediate warmth and recognition in gazing at these snapshots of two people who were technically strangers to me. And now, as an adult, I was walking toward them at last, their physical selves now invisible, their faults and attributes level, buried deep in the ground.

We halted in front of two large mounds with granite bases, set apart from the rest on the top of a windy brown hillside. Four healthy pines representing four children framed the tombs. Before the square tombs stood identical marble altars and two symmetrical stone urns. Aunt Myung-hi untied the ribbon of the bouquet, and divided the flowers in two, placing half in my grandmother's urn and half in my grand father's. Next to each tomb stood a black marble tablet, as tall as I. On one side was carved a single column of Chinese characters, and on the opposite side, a series of grouped characters, representing, so I was told, the names of all of their children and grandchildren, and parents and grandparents of both families.

"This is your mother," said Hong-do, pointing to a squiggle on my grandfather's grave tablet. "We must add your name to their gravestones someday."

I was silent, somewhat surprised to have been excluded. "Why is my name not there?" I couldn't help asking.

"I don't know. I forget . . . Maybe because you were a foreigner. But now you are not," he said, laughing. "Someday we will add it."

I looked at the earth where the bones of my grandparents were planted like seeds; I stood before them, a phantom hybrid. There was total silence in the graveyard, broken only by the occasional roar of wind through the pine boughs. My uncle and aunt performed a series of Buddhist prostrations before both of the graves, sweeping their arms and bodies to the ground three times in veneration, ending with their foreheads on the earth: filial reverence.

"Now you," said Hong-do. "Just do as we did."

"I'll try," I said, feeling a bit awkward, and proceeded to do an imitation of the prostrations. When I had finished, my aunt and uncle sat on the grass next to the gravestones and chatted in Korean, leaving me to do as I liked.

I too sat down on the grass before my grandmother's tomb, as if sitting before an empty hearth. Getting up for a better view of her tablet, I looked at it, almost willing a tangible warmth from the hard black stone. My fingertips traced the cold carved characters of my grandmother's name like a blind person touching braille, hoping for some comprehension, for some glint of her character to be transferred from its lifeless surface. A mild chill ran through my blood, echoing up to the top layers of my skin.

My earlier sense of irony and exclusion gave way. A lump came to my throat as I looked at the name that I couldn't read. But it didn't matter that I couldn't read it, because for once I knew what it meant. Here, before this grave, unlike anywhere else I had been in Korea, the landscape opened out to me, offering quiet revelations. I almost thought I could feel God's presence shifting behind the surface of place and time.

Seeing the black tombstone was like finding a lost negative, the matrix of my birth. I had begun here, among these indecipherable carved characters, part of the pattern of the living and the dead. I was not an unreal bubble, fragile and weightless, floating on the surface of life, hoping to be rewarded with deep and satisfying truths as I skimmed along, because I had an artist's ego, and felt deserving. I'd lacked a conviction of weight, of effect; was unable to sow or reap. In joyless conviviality, in scathing critiques of other artists, in misbegotten love, there was no room to be appalled by the blank sheet of my own life.

I ran my hand over the sere grass on my grandmother's grave. Perhaps it would be possible to start again. I might be able to paint. Not just produce selfish visual diarrhea, but try to create light, some needed illumination. If I could not create light, at least I could try and reflect it, rather than add to the darkness. Maybe it was possible to face a blank canvas and put something sincere on it. The idea of sincerity was faintly jarring, but it suddenly became clear that there was little point in painting from a mask. Maybe I could risk failing. If I was not a bubble, I would not break.

It was unlikely to be this simple, but it was a start. It was a flash of solidity. For the first time, I had seen the doorstep of home. If I could summon up this image and steer toward it now and then, I might not get so lost.

I thought of my mother, slightly sad to have come here without her. Perhaps one day we would be able to return together, without pain or arguments. For now, this was the best that I could do. Being here, thousands of miles away, was the closest I had ever been to her.

CHAPTER TWENTY

Yangyang

Uncle Hong-do drove along the highway chewing spearmint gum and noisily humming an Elvis song with showy vibrato. He honked at a bird on the road. It was early morning, and we were on our way to Yangyang. Hong-do's spirited driving created a buoyant mood in the car, but I was preoccupied with grating thoughts about the future. After nearly two months in Seoul, I had begun to make plans to return to the West, but was torn.

The Parks and I had become close, and wished me to stay on in Korea indefinitely. Mrs. Park had even offered me a job in the art department of her newspaper, and said she would help find me a flat. Intrigued as well as moved by her offer, I had gone to her offices to meet Mr. Choo, the president of the newspaper—obliging her by removing my shabby raincoat before entering his office. The interview had gone well enough, despite having only a sketchbook to show him, and Mrs. Park felt that with a little pinpoint lobbying, the job could be mine.

Miss Cho, too, urged me to stay in Korea. She had proudly taken me to her university campus, where the sting of tear gas hung in the air, and I'd met some of her friends in the Harmonious Guitar Circle, a music group she attended on Tuesdays and Thursdays. She tempted me with outings to gallery openings and films. She even offered— jokingly, I think—to take me to the National Kimchi Museum to swing the final vote. Although she was young and naïve in a way I had thought nearly obsolete, I had grown very fond of her and her endearing directness, and would find it a particular wrench to say good-bye to Miss Cho.

Not least, my uncle hoped I would stay. He had paid me the high compliment of introducing me to some of his key business colleagues, and even indulged my curiosity for seeing the inside of a room-salon—an all-male nightclub where beautiful hostesses lit men's cigarettes and placed ice cubes in their whiskey. A pancaked madam with blood-red talons had played a white baby grand in the foyer! I was captivated.

Hong-do did not, however, pressure me about moving to Seoul. He himself had experienced the profound upheavals the move would entail, and did not attempt to make light of them.

To stay or to go seemed a momentous decision, and I shrank from making it. Still wading in the shallows of Korean life, I couldn't hazard any pronouncements about what a future here might hold, and craved an impossible guarantee of happiness. Used to moving about, I was unfazed by decamping to Hell's Kitchen or Little Italy, or even trying Washington, Boston, or London. But a move to Korea was somehow off the terrestrial map, like moving to another planet. Quite why this should be so, I wasn't precisely sure.

The polar contrast between Korean and Western cultures was only a starting point. Staying in Korea would involve a renunciation of everything and everyone I knew. Telephone wire and written correspondence could not conquer the distances involved. With the crude exception of trade, I wondered if West and East could be connected at all. In choosing to stay, one's commitment to exile would need to be total, a form of taking the veil. In my mind, West and East were reduced to unfortunate stereotypes in which West was debased and hedonistic, and East was virtuous and unimaginative, a sort of cultural convent. Could one survive such a sudden deprivation of sin?

A mere two months before, my identity had been entirely Western; a 180-degree turnaround was surely inadvisable, impossible, and potentially fatal. Yet remembering my unexpectedly happy response to Korean ways, I was no longer certain if this was so. In coming here the racial split in me had widened rather than narrowed. One half wanted to stay, and the other wished to go. While the changes would be immense, the rewards of staying might exceed anything I had yet known. Arguments circled around my head, unresolvable.

Then a thought came that did not so much change the conflict, as deepen it. Korea was where the hurt in my life had been. Korea was where my mother, and her upsetting ways, had sprung into being. I did not reject Koreanness here, because it belonged here. But did *I* belong here, surrounded by millions of versions of my estranged mother? Coming here had been like removing shrapnel from a long-infected wound. The bullet was gone, but what would happen now? The wound was open. I dared not touch the skin surrounding it.

Uncle Hong-do honked at a cat on the side of the road and then, irresistibly, at a cow in the distance. There was no need, he had insisted, on my making a decision right away, and had suggested that we take this trip now to Yangyang and to the Mount Sorak temple. I was grateful for his relaxed approach, and had accepted wholeheartedly. Since he had first mentioned the plan, I'd looked forward to this time alone with him, glad that we had saved the best trip for last. So often had I pictured the temple amid the chestnut trees that I could scarcely believe that within a short time I would actually be able to walk right up to them and touch them. Part of me did not believe they were real. I had made sure to buy a new sketchbook and some fresh film for my camera, keen to record the great event.

It was another misty, sunny day. The Han River was a broad sheet of pale light. We were on the Yang P'yong Road, east of Seoul. The traffic here was thick with commuters and military convoys jamming the roads. We had already been stopped at a checkpoint for a random weapons search. Hong-do had optimistically brought his golf clubs and a dinner jacket, and the American sergeant who stopped us made rather insolent jokes about a dirty weekend. "She's my niece, you know," said Hong-do, affronted.

"Sure, Mac. That's what they all say," the sergeant said, lifting an eyebrow.

By lunchtime we had reached Kangwon Province. The traffic had thinned out considerably, and we had made good time, with Hong-do amusing himself by driving very fast and argïng about American imperialism at the same time.

"Japan and the U.S. do *not* want Korea to be reunified. They like us to be weak. That way we don't pose a threat. Are you kidding? You think Japan wants to lose its place at the top of the pan-Pacific heap?"

"That, I can see. But why should America want to keep Korea down? They fought for South Korea. Surely they would rather bring their troops home."

"Are you kidding? They fought *against* communism, not *for* Korea. Now they want to keep their regional influence: they get good trade and construction deals as a result of being here, and have a big military base in East Asia if anything big happens in China or the Soviet Union . . . there are thirty-seven thousand troops here. Don't be naïve!"

"I'll try not to be naïve," I said, not really in the mood for a serious discussion, and momentarily stirred to defend America against his accusations. But as he continued, I was moved by Uncle Hong-do's emotional tone. He wanted America out of the peninsula more passionately than any Korean I had spoken to. The American presence deeply offended his national pride.

"Like my father, I am a nationalist. He went to jail for his beliefs. Did you know that? He gave his life to politics, and got nothing back. In the past, politicians like him were either too undisciplined or tyrannical to create the stability needed for independence, but I think these guys we have now may have learned something from those past mistakes. It makes me sad that my father did not live to see the results of all that struggle.

"You can see that a unified Korea is dangerous to the status quo, can't you?" he asked, blowing smoke out of the window. "Left to our own devices, see what happens. With the war and Japanese oppression we've been frustrated. Unable to contribute to world development. We will go like a steam engine once left to get on with it."

He was probably right, but deep down I doubted that anything would change quickly or with as much impact as he hoped. I couldn't see the West relinquishing its sense of superiority over the East, for one thing. But for the moment I was too hungry to argue about it. "What about some lunch soon?" I asked. Hong-do said he knew a good place to stop in a few miles.

The cool, panoramic view was formidable. Blue mountains rose up around us like static tidal waves with icy peaks. The sun shone mildly on the lacy, scallop-edged rock faces, and left deep shadows in the valleys. Scarcely a tree survived the high altitude. We swayed around hairpin turns until we reached an A-frame roadside restaurant where a few cars were parked. Hong-do ordered for us both. Barley tea, seaweed soup, and a succulent dish of slippery wild mushrooms, *pyo-go*, with steaming, savory *kamja buchim*, potato pancakes with dipping sauce—a dish I'd not tasted before. The red-cheeked, glossy-pigtailed waitress was a specimen of robust good health, a convincing advertisement for a steady diet of mountain mushrooms.

We both ate with keen appetites, the food extremely fresh and delectable.

By late afternoon, we'd reached the outskirts of Yangyang. We had passed through more checkpoints, tricky conversational impasses, and breathtaking spring scenery. The delicate pink cherry blossom was out, glowing against the cobalt blue cliffs. Now the countryside was flattening out near the ocean shore, and the roads were quite empty. We passed a farm where rows of squid were hung up to dry on clotheslines like clean washing. The afternoon sun shone through the drying fish, semi-translucent and ginseng-colored. We slowed to pass through an antitank wall. We were closer to North Korea now.

"You know, I don't know where we're going," admitted my uncle. "I've never been here before."

"Wasn't there some relative you were going to ask directions of? My mother's old tutor?"

"*Sunsaeng-nim* is still abroad at the medical conference."

"How will we find the old place, then?"

"Ask at the hotel, I guess."

"That's OK. We'll find it. Can't be that many estates outside Yangyang," I said.

Yangyang looked much the same as many of the large towns we had passed along the way. It was far bigger and more built up than I'd imagined. There were many cars. Quite what would have made it seem like "our town," I wasn't sure. But it didn't feel familiar in any way. I opened the car window to catch a whiff of any clues to the past that might still be circulating in the air. Hong-do, too, was excited and hypervigilant, and together we strained to detect apparitions of former Min life. Nothing specific distinguished itself conveniently for our consumption, but I didn't mind. I was content to drive into the force field that had once been our ancestral home, and absorb its light, its shapes, its nuances. After all, there was nothing to be lost that hadn't already been lost, and only new sensations and future memories to gather. Merely spotting the road sign to Yangyang brought substantial satisfaction, its physicality reassuring. In gargantuan Seoul, seethingly crowded and overbuilt, the hope of picking up the faint signal of the past was remote, but here, in the countryside, there seemed more hope of discovering something consequential, whatever it might be.

Uncle had no trouble finding our hotel. There was a big sign announcing its existence on the coast road. The surrounding countryside was haunting and dramatic. Cliffs and tall pines pushed out from the mainland into a jade green sea. To the west, a gray mist gathered, darkening the horizon.

HOTEL NAGSAN BEACH **** read the sign outside a white concrete cube with plate-glass windows facing the ocean, and a smart parking lot with seven new cars neatly contained in its yellow-painted rectangles. We descended from the car, and went into reception, a chilly oblong marble space where a pretty girl at the desk wearing a name tag welcomed us, bowing her head. *"Annyong hashimnigga, "* she said, with a flirtatious glance at my uncle.

We had little luggage. Too little luggage. I shivered as the breeze from the sea penetrated my thin pullover with delayed effect. We were escorted down the corridor from the elevator by a young bellhop to adjacent rooms, 31 and 32. My room was clean and brutally modern. A bright yellow love seat was angled in the corner, and a small television counted for another item of furniture by the opposite wall. A tiny bathroom fought for existence by the door, and yielded a litter of miniature toiletries, from a coin-sized bar of soap to a tube of toothpaste the size of a nail. The shower cap, thankfully, was of normal dimensions. Through the nubbly yellow curtains there was a gratifying view of the sea. I felt excited being there. I picked up the box of matches in the ashtray and examined it; on the front of the box was printed a mini color photo of the hotel, with HOTEL NAGSAN BEACH printed in bold black letters. I put the box in my pocket, partly as a memento and partly as forensic evidence of the odd hotel's existence.

I knocked on Hong-do's door. His room was identical, only it had a blue love seat and blue curtain theme. He was lying on his bed, smoking and staring out of the window. "Shall we go for a walk on the beach?" I asked.

"*Anio*. I'm too tired now. Maybe tomorrow," he said. "I'll meet you downstairs in the restaurant seven o'clock," he said with a wave, "you go." I agreed, quite happy for a chance to explore on my own, and borrowed one of my uncle's acid green golf sweaters that didn't suit me at all. One of the liberating symptoms of being in Korea was a total, and probably unfortunate, lack of fashion consciousness.

The hotel was in an isolated spot, quite near to the fishing village of Sokcho. Apart from the hotel, the rocky shoreline was pristine and deserted, the sandy beach curving away into the misty distance, into an unknown horizon. It was windy, and the tide was coming in, the spume of the waves a frothy, brilliant white against the green-gray body of ocean, like an abundant foaming head on bitter beer.

I walked alone for about a mile down the beach. The damp sand was full of footprints, indicating a lively amount of activity, but curiously, not a single person was visible in either direction. There was nothing but a beach full of footprints. Where had the owners of the footprints gone to? I zigzagged along the beach, walking inside three different pairs of fresh tracks, none of which fitted my own, until I grew bored.

Eventually I came upon a crouched woman and a little boy playing at the shore's edge. The woman was wearing a red-checked head scarf and a baggy yellow cardigan, and she sat before two prodigious piles of wet black seaweed, rinsing lengths of the laver in a big plastic tub, and setting the clean strips on a blanket next to the unrinsed strips. She looked up at me without surprise and carried on working, her hard brown face tanned by the sun and wind, a long rake by her side, used to harvest the seaweed. Her little pinkfaced boy was catching minnows with a net and a pail. I watched him as he plunged his tiny hand into the bucket and tried in vain to trap a tiny fish in his fingers.

After passing the mother and son, not another soul appeared on the coastline. Along the next stretch of sand I saw an empty pavilion and a sentry box. As far as the eye could see, looped barbed wire fencing lined the beachfront. I walked up to the white sentry box and read a sign, printed in English and Korean.

WALKING ON THE BEACH AFTER SUNSET IS NOT PERMITTED. ARMED BORDER PATROLS WILL DEMAND THE PASSWORD.

NORTH KOREAN SPIES WILL BE SHOT. THANK YOU.

The sign's message produced its intended effect. I looked at the sky, a ravishing rose-lavender that complemented the green of the sea, and calculated how long it would be until sunset. The delicate, romantic hues of the landscape contradicted the harshness of the notice and the barbed wire, but conventionally, perhaps, I chose to believe the sign rather than risk being shot, and turned back toward the hotel. The headlights of a passing car on the shore road were already illuminated, so I quit the beach and made some haste along the edge of the road.

That evening after supper, my uncle and I sat opposite each other at a table in the semi-deserted hotel disco, eyeing with detached amusement a table of young vacationing workers, some singing raucously along with the performer onstage, while others slumped over their cocktails fast asleep, red and purple spotlights pulsing over their unconscious bodies. The spike-haired female singer, Ko-ko, had black-rimmed eyes, wore Corvette red lipstick, and a studded black leather jacket which enveloped her small, tidy frame. She did her best to look dangerously sexual as she sang a current Korean hit to an accompanying backing track, but looked suspiciously like a supermarket shelf stacker on her night off. My uncle thought her singing wasn't bad.

I nursed my glass of OB beer while Hong-do knocked back his third scotch. The echoey clanging percussion and unpredictable wailing crescendoes of Ko-ko made it quite difficult to communicate, but we hadn't much to say.

"What's she singing about?" I shouted.

"Cherry blossom lovers."

We were both a little downhearted. At dinner Hong-do told me that the present hotel staff and the new young chamber of commerce secretary in Yangyang had not heard of the Min estate. An old electrical engineer who came to repair my bedroom radiator was familiar with the family name, but could offer no tangible help, except to say that no large mansions survived in the area. The old noble houses would have been destroyed in the war either through arson or bombing, he said with some glee, and that such tracts of land would have been broken up and resold long ago.

My uncle and I had allowed ourselves to hope too much, we realized, talking over dinner. No one had mentioned to him the farm where my mother grew up, nor could he remember any details about its location, nor that of the mansion, the former family seat. Hong-do had always meant to go there, as he had intended to visit the temple, but had just never found the time.

Although I had known that the whole trip to Korea was a gamble, I couldn't prevent another strong wave of disappointment from washing over me. The absence of physical testimony of the family's past was unnerving. It wasn't exactly like searching for an old rabbit hutch on a back road. My great-grandfather had been the ruler of the province, with large private armies surrounding him. Could a fiefdom and its antecedents vanish utterly within a single generation? With Korea's extraordinary twentieth-century experience of annexation, class reforms, two wars, mass migrations, partitioning, and national rebuilding drives, apparently all it *could* do was disappear.

My uncle even looked a bit depressed.

"Listen, we'll drive around a bit tomorrow morning and see if we can find anything by accident, and then we'll head straight off for the Sorak Mountains. We are sure to be better rewarded there," he said, the ice cubes sliding toward his teeth as he drained his tumbler of scotch.

"I'm sorry that my parents are not here to take us where we want to go. Jin-ho would have remembered, too. That would have been better, I know. I am sorry it's turning out this way," he said.

"It's OK. I am enjoying it anyway," I said. As he looked around the disco at the wilting tourists under the strobe light, a purple spotlight flooded over him, followed by a red one. He smacked my shoulder, and shouted that he was off to bed. I waved with slightly counterfeit cheeriness, and surrendered to the exotic atmosphere of the disco, which would soon be closing. I felt comfortable sitting alone in the pulsating darkness. The few remaining people were too drunk and cocooned in their groups to be curious about me. Anyway, I had warmed to Ko-ko. She was a brave woman, undaunted by her natural disadvantages. With her raking red talons she clung passionately to the microphone, as if trying to convince it of her sincerity, pleading for amnesty from some obscure future punishment. At midnight the backing track stopped abruptly, and Ko-ko, divested of menace, gave a demure bow, head bobbing at the audience, by now just a few giggling girls and a couple of unconscious men. I slipped out of the chrome-trimmed nightclub, and made for my room.

Sitting on my bed, I felt restless. I was not tired, and so decided to take some air. Through my window a full moon hung in the sky, casting a cool milk blue light over the pounding, rushing ocean. Remembering the warning on the sign earlier, I dared not stray too far toward the beach, but instead stuck by the hotel, not planning to linger.

The night air was cold, fresh, and sweetly briny. Standing in the parking lot, I could see the glinting ocean through a hole in the foliage. Thin saplings with new leaves surrounded the asphalt at the far end. Despite being cold, I felt an urge to break through the flimsy curtain of undergrowth and find a quiet place to look out at the glimmering waves. My feet quit the hard pavement and sank into grass. I stuck my arms blindly through the screen of thin, whiplike branches and, once through, found myself practically on the edge of a cliff. I picked my way cautiously along the ledge, which was well lit by the moonlight. The ground was rocky and slightly squelchy in places, and water seeped in through the soles of my loafers. Then a clear and fantastic view opened out between the overgrown bullrushes.

I found a dry spot overlooking the sea and sat down, taking in everything: the wide, wide stretching ocean, the silvery patina of moonlight on its shifting skin, the strong smell of clean wet sand, the insensate crashing of the waves. Above the liquid horizon the arcing, cobalt sky was crowded with brilliant, close stars, and the dimension of time ceased for me, split by a lateral force of expansion.

I felt a strange thrill. Only yards from the ersatz hotel, with its sterile, mean, insistently contemporary trappings, lay an alternate, sweeping plane of experience. In moonlight, the landscape was relieved of its confusing excess detail, the strong character of the cliff emerged in subtler, almost liquid form—in light and sound. Night masked the bleak remoteness I had noticed earlier in the day. I shivered a bit recalling its extremity. The powerful bass crash of the sea rushed into the empty spaces in shadow, a sound too brutal to be soothing.

I wondered who had stood here before, and what they had felt as they looked out over the same horizon. There was something charged in the air. What had happened here? Had the boats leaving these shores not returned through the rough seas? Did the ghosts of spies and invaders haunt the cliff paths? Perhaps my own mother once stood in these tall grasses, gazing over the horizon of her unknown future. Perhaps it was chilling because nothing had ever happened, nothing had disturbed the lonely spell of the place. I turned suddenly at the sound of a cracking twig but could see or hear nothing further. Although a bit spooked, I stayed put. My hands were cold. I put them in my pockets and touched the edge of the box of Hotel Nagsan Beach matches in my trouser pocket.

I lit one of the matches and cupped it in my hands to warm them. The flame jumped and dwindled until it was just a glowing red droop-headed stick in my numb fingers. Then I lit another match, and let it burn out, enjoying the brief, vital flicker. But the meager light served only to make the darkness darker, and the coolness colder. With some misgiving I headed back to the hotel through the curtain of under-growth, casting a backward look at the spot where I had stood, and at the magnetic view that had held me there by some mysterious pull. I had the recurring sensation of circling around something I did not comprehend, and of not understanding exactly what I was searching for. Widening my eyes, I took a mental photograph of the view, hoping that later, by some sort of alchemy, it could be developed, and would yield information obscured by the immediacy of the present. As I looked back, I had a premonition that I would not return to Korea.

That night I dreamt of a terrible bonfire, and awoke sweating. In the dream, I saw a small, blackened face, like a dried apple core, in the middle of the white flames.

One Thousand Chestnut Trees

My uncle slammed the car door and ruffled his hair with his hands. He sat motionless for a moment and sighed before turning the key in the ignition. It was early morning. Neither of us had slept well. As we accelerated out of the drive, I swiveled around in my seat, looking back at the new concrete building in its idyllic perch above the sea.

"There's something funny about this place," I said, studying my souvenir box of hotel matches with the corroborating picture on the front. It hardly resembled the desolate gray shore behind us. In the photograph, the sky was sunny and blue, and the beach was covered with gaily striped umbrellas and bikini-clad tourists. Hong-do was glancing at the map on my knee as he drove along slowly.

"You think so? Pretty ordinary hotel to me. Kind of scenic, though," he said, still in first gear. "But, you know, I think this must be pretty close to where our grandparents, the Kangs, used to live. I remember my mother's descriptions of the cliffs between Sokcho and Yangyang, where they used to go fishing and swimming. It's a lot like this, in fact. There's not much separating Sokcho and Yangyang, as I figure we must be pretty close to their estate after all . . . what used to be the estate."

Well, that was something, I said brightly. I considered telling him about my nightmare, but decided against it. The face in the flames had probably been brought on by the exertions of Ko-ko, and the psychedelic disco lights.

As we pulled out onto the main road we brushed past a clump of overgrown tiger lilies among the weeds. This made me think of my mother. I noticed Hong-do's slightly disheveled appearance. "Did you take a walk this morning?" I asked.

"No. I figure I'll come back someday with someone who knows their way around. Besides, I wanted to get an early start for Mount Sorak."

"Doesn't Aunt Myung-hi know where the estates are?"

"No. She was a baby then. She doesn't remember anything," he said.

We headed along the coast road, which was lined with newly unfurled bracken and the occasional old pine tree. The grasses were deep and wild along the roadside. We absorbed the patterns of the countryside in silence. For miles and miles there was nothing but pastoral farmland and jutting rock formations.

"You know, the Kang side of the family used to own land all the way up across the 38th Parallel, same as the Mins. We had a young cousin who killed himself when the Communists took over their land."

"Really? I haven't heard that story. . . . Seems a bit extreme."

"Not really. Not if you're proud. It's a question of honor."

"Well, to a Westerner that's pretty extreme. Westerners kill *someone else* if their honor is bothering them. Anyway, honor doesn't really exist now. People just sue each other. Make money out of it all. It's the opposite of self-sacrifice."

"That's exactly why the West is decaying! People are morally lazy. Motivated by self-gratification. It's not like that here. . . . Sure, there is dishonesty and corruption, like anywhere. But duty and responsibility still mean something precious to us," he said.

"But who knows. Maybe you can't compare that sort of thing between cultures. I think my cousin's death was beautiful. . . . Try to imagine what it would be like to lose something your family has held in trust for centuries, what it would be like to lose something more precious than your individual life. . . ."

I thought for a moment. "I can't, really . . . but I know what you mean."

We drove along, silent again. My uncle looked down at my feet.

"Did you bring some heavier shoes?"

"No, 'fraid not," I said, noticing my heeled city loafers.

"Well, we'd better stop in the next village and see if we can find you some hiking boots. You can't climb mountains in those."

Uncle Hong-do was wearing some sneakers with elaborate molded soles.

"Yours aren't much better."

"No, but they'll see me through."

"How big are these mountains anyway?"

"I don't exactly know. Pretty big."

"These won't see me through?"

"No, they won't," he laughed. I didn't laugh. I was thinking about what he'd said about self-gratification and honor. He was right. Honor had virtually disappeared from modern life. Perhaps the Eugene Onegin, dueling sort of honor had been excessive, but maybe in excising the gentlemanly code altogether, the West this century had lost its sense of noble ideals, its higher soul. In removing a polyp, the lungs had been accidentally extracted, too. Honor interfered with self-indulgence and expediency, a tinny cheapness replacing its marble solidity. Instead of the oblique *longueurs* of *La Belle Dame sans Merci*, we had efficient genital-scorching satellite porn.

Perhaps, as my uncle said, rampant self-will was the enemy microbe responsible for the West's social ills. Maybe a late, harsh dose of Oriental Respect could redress its wasting condition.

I doubted it, somehow.

My thoughts returned to buying shoes.

We reached Mount Sorak around noon. We had been unable to find hiking boots in the next village, but discovered a dusty shop selling children's clothes where I bought some cheap tennis shoes in the largest size, and a thick sugar-pink acrylic sweater to insulate my increasingly inadequate trench coat. The sneakers pinched my toes, but without socks they might be all right. The lady shopkeeper had looked at me in disbelief when I bought the goods; whether she found me personally unbelievable or found it unbelievable that someone was actually buying her dusty wares, one couldn't be sure. She smiled ingratiatingly at my uncle, as did all the women entering my uncle's orbit, and gazed after us in continuing amazement as we returned to the car.

From Sokcho we drove inland and eastward. Bare hills the color of dusty plum swelled up around us, with dark evergreens running along the creases of their slopes. The hillsides were sparsely dotted with white toy churches and remote villages with blue wing-tiled roofs. We passed fish-curing farms that looked like wine vineyards from a distance, where complex systems of tied bamboo poles supported hundreds of thousands of whole salted cod, hanging in silvery bunches to dry in the wind.

"I don't know where we're going, you know," said Hong-do abruptly.

"I know. You said so earlier."

"But that was Yangyang. This is a little more . . . serious. I don't actually *know* of anyone who has been to Bong jong-am. I don't even know if anyone in our family has seen the temple. It's not exactly easy to find. Father must have come as a young man, but I didn't think to get instructions from him before he died."

Having failed to locate the Yangyang estates, I became a little anxious about repeating the experience with these somewhat higher stakes, but thought it best not to let on.

"Don't worry. You said that the monastery is quite well known, and if it's within the monastery, I'm sure we'll find it."

Mount Sorak and its surrounding range of mountains filled around 140 square miles of national park in the South, and stretched on into North Korea, where the chain became the Diamond Mountains. (*Sorak*, my uncle explained, meant "snow peak.") Our connection to this land went back some way. Before the Japanese had confiscated the landholdings in the early 1900s, it had been in the family for many centuries, before written records were kept. The hermitage of Bong jong-am, in whose grounds our temple stood, had been built by monks in 643 B.C. Now Mount Sorak was owned and protected by the South Korean government. Fortunately, the inaccessibility of the terrain had made development quite unfeasible, and the land was still mostly a wilderness. There were one or two ski resorts and a few hotels with hot springs around the state park, but here, more than anywhere else I'd been, the Korea of the Yi Dynasty was unchanged, and I was gladdened and relieved to see at last a landscape which remained intact, as it might have looked before the war.

As my hopes receded of finding traces of my mother's past, a vague but increasingly desperate wish emerged for *something* to have stayed the same. Unsettled by the scale of destruction and transformation that Korea had undergone, irrationally, I began to regret all changes, all upheavals.

Although I had no name for the feelings then, in the mute, gnomic landscape of Kangwon-do, I felt exhausted by being American, weathering a constant storm of revisionism and the accompanying babble of inflamed opinion, the abrasive worship of celebrity and riches, even the massive choice of junk foods in the supermarket was tiring—everything new, instant, improved—and largely inedible. America could not abide a lull or a vacuum. Even here, in the remote wilderness, one felt that it would soon come trampling in to reshape things in its own restless image, oblivious to the poetry of its emptiness.

As we drove along, I pretended to be intent on the passing countryside, but saw little, eyes glazed and unfocused. My discontent was more than displaced irritation with America or a rosy nostalgia for the past. I longed for something impossible: for a gentle unfolding of secrets; for a geological deceleration of time, for scars to be reversed, for my family to undie.

Mount Sorak stood before us like a bruised colossus. The vivid mountains we had seen elsewhere in our travels around Korea were insignificant compared with the forbidding snowcapped peaks and breathtakingly strange pinnacles that now soared up around the car. It was such a wild, forceful setting that I could not quite believe anyone had ever owned it. Seeing the vast extent of my great-grandfather's former dominions provoked simultaneous twinges of pride and guilt.

We parked outside a self-service canteen inside the park grounds. Although I'd donned my new pullover, the wind sliced through it like a laser. Yet even without the wind, the air was freezing. Hong-do turned up the collar of his jacket, and imparted a sidelong glance of suffering. "It's *May*, for God's sake," he said.

The immaculate wood-trimmed snack bar was empty but for a few napping elderly custodians in tidy white aprons propped up on a bench at the back of the room. Hong-do discovered from a waitress that there was another Buddhist monastery halfway up the mountain where one could take lunch, so we limited our refreshments to *kopi* and sweet biscuits. Hong-do crunched away, enjoying himself, and on second thought ordered a large plate of steaming red-bean buns.

There were no other hikers to be seen, which was not surprising, given the climate.

"Did you see the snow?" I asked.

"Yeah," said Hong-do. "We'd better get going. I don't know how long it's going to take to reach Bong jong-am, and we have to hike back down before it gets dark."

I was daunted, but boosted by an energizing sense of mission. Until this moment, seeing the temple had been a sentimental dream. I suppressed my excitement in case the experience should fall short of expectations, but felt confident that *any* outcome would be something to celebrate after traveling so far, and our being, as far as my uncle knew, the first contemporary Min family members to find our way here. It was our small North Pole, our Everest.

Outside the canteen we studied an enlarged map of the national park, which, being notated in Hangul, I left to my uncle to decipher.

"Hey! Here it is! Bong jong-am," he said, pointing. I craned over his shoulder at the green-and-brown-painted relief map, and squinted at a monstrous V-shaped mountain underneath Hong-do's index finger: "There. See?"

I nodded impatiently and shuddered as the wind penetrated my scalp.

"Let's see how far up we can drive," he said, glancing up at the chain of snow-covered peaks. We both got back inside the car, and I clenched and unclenched my fingers ineffectually, trying to warm them. As we wound slowly along the internal park road, the scenery grew more densely spectacular; alpine vistas of majestic proportions collapsed and unfolded around us like opera stage curtains as we drove through their center.

A few miles along the winding pass, the narrow paved road turned into a dirt track, muddy in some spots, and crumbling with erosion elsewhere. We saw another map and signpost from the car, and, having consulted the diagram to his satisfaction, Hong-do suggested that we abandon the car there and hike the rest of the way. We were, he insisted, very close to the lower monastery, Paekdam-sa.

Raiding our luggage, we put on as many layers as we could find. With misgiving, I took off my socks so they would not bind my toes, stuffed them in my pocket, and laced up my stiff, brand-new size-three tennis shoes—so white that they glowed in the daylight. Anticipating blisters, I was grateful to see a couple of Band-Aids in the bottom of my handbag, and transferred them to my trouser pocket. I slung the camera across my bulging pink-sweatered chest, checked for a sketch-book, and tied a bandanna around my neck, resigned to looking quite ridiculous. My uncle puffed a bit as he pulled a yellow golf sweater over his thick green rugby shirt and zipped his Windbreaker up to his chin. He checked his wallet, locked the car, and poked around the dead leaves with his foot for an appropriately lordly walking stick.

It was already one-thirty, and by my uncle's optimistic calculations we had a ten-mile hike before us. The ten miles out were what you could safely call "uphill." The sun was burning through the misty blue sky, and we hiked along at a fair pace, both of us slipping a bit on the dead leaves and slick stones. Protected from the wind, we grew hot within minutes, and began to shed our clownish layers, tying them round our waists. The woods were dappled with hazy light and cold pockets of shade, and smelled strongly of earth and decomposing leaves. An acid scent of spring floated in with the warm top layer of sunlight.

Apart from a rusting forestry jeep abandoned on the shoulder of the road below, we had not passed anyone. All that could be heard was the shuffle of our own progress through the spongy leaves, and the occasional slap of our soles on rock-face as we traversed the marked trail. Occasionally a strong wind rushed through the millions of still-bare tree limbs, making a powerful low and melancholy whistling sound that whipped hollowly up the face of the mountain. As I walked along, several paces behind Hong-do, I wondered about the thousand chestnut trees my great-grandfather had planted. Although it was probably too soon to start looking for them, I began to imagine them appearing in this stippled light. Planted at the turn of century, the trunks of the chestnuts would now be stout, probably screening the temple from sight. Their branches would reach high, stretching upward, dramatically, to capture the sunlight in the overgrown forest. I had no idea how much territory a thousand chestnut trees would cover. I pictured a hushed grove too wide to measure, with no scruffy weeds or saplings marring the ground. No other trees but chestnut trees would be visible. In summer, an impenetrable canopy of fanned leaves would shade the forest floor, roots carpeted by a vast expanse of velvety green moss.

My stomach started to grumble. "What do chestnut trees look like without their leaves?" I asked my uncle.

"Not sure," Hong-do said after a moment's reflection. "Hey, I see something," he shouted, craning around a pine tree. "There's a bridge up ahead." I caught up with him, and we both made our way toward a hanging bamboo bridge that spanned a wide, pebbly stream. A sonorous, clear bell could be heard clanging slowly through the tall pine trees, and I could make out the red trim of a pagoda beyond the bridge.

"This must be Paekdam-sa," said Hong-do.

"Thank God," I said. Along with the hollow gusts of wind, a sound of trickling water could now be heard, which developed into a dull roar when we reached the delicate bridge. I followed my uncle over the lightly swaying bamboo structure and was delighted to catch a waft of cooking on the breeze. Set against a picturesque waterfall of worn, curtained rock, the monastery was small and humble, a group of low white clay and red-timber structures with latticed screens and sliding doors. A fine powdering of pristine snow dusted the dark, swooping eaves and pebbled ground. In the central temple enclosure stood a monumental gold Buddha surrounded by flowers and smoking incense, before which three monks were prostrating themselves. A senior monk in dark blue robes and a heavy brown burlap coat approached my uncle, and bowed his shaved head. After a short conversation the monk showed us into the main temple to worship Buddha, and waited politely to lead us to a cell where we could have lunch.

Waiting for my uncle to finish bowing to the Buddha figure, I took off my shoes as was customary, my bare, reddened feet now exposed in the gelid air. I felt rather awkward when my turn came, feeling a Christian loyalty not to worship "any other gods," but not wishing any disrespect in the circumstances, prostrated out of politeness, and crossed myself out of habit.

The senior monk led us to a bare white cell with a low wooden table and two mats on the floor. He inclined his head to my uncle, and left us. My uncle and I sat cross-legged and silent, looking out through the open screen at the blue-and-white shark-toothed mountains and the twisted, thorny black trees in the distance. The shadows on the snow were blue. A solitary monk was meditating outside the temple entrance, seemingly unaffected by the cold. The sound of rushing water created a sense of dynamism beneath the profound peace and echoing stillness of the monastery.

"There are many hermitages in the mountaintops of Korea. Do you know why?" asked Hong-do, lighting a cigarette. I was silent. "Because the mountain symbolizes the Mountain of Vanity. Buddha overcame all vanities. The final, most testing stage of the monks' training requires them to ascend alone up the highest mountain."

"Bong jong-am is even higher than this, isn't it?" I asked with some apprehension.

"The monk said it was a long hike. Longer than I thought. He's not sure it can be done in a day," Hong-do said, looking away.

"We'd better eat quickly, then."

"Ah. Here it comes," said Hong-do, stubbing out his cigarette.

A young monk, about fourteen, with smooth pink cheeks, came in quietly with a steaming tray. From it he placed before us a suitably spartan lunch of two small bowls of steamed rice, a few shreds of pickled radish, a quartered potato with pickled sesame leaves, and warm kimchi. After our exertions in the sharp mountain air, this simple fare tasted exquisite. For dessert we were each offered an apple and bitter black tree-root tea, called *chikcha*. I could have eaten the whole meal again, and still found room for ice cream and cake. Uncle paid the young monk a modest sum, and, bowing, we bade farewell to Paekdam-sa temple and continued up the steep, crooked path.

The frozen ground was more slippery now, so the going was a bit slower. I had matching blisters on the backs of my heels, my ankles were a bit tired, and my feet were damp, but I was not doing too badly. Besides a bit of smoker's breathlessness, Hong-do said he was fine, and looked as if he were relishing the importance of the exercise, using his walking stick with a slight swagger. Our assault on Mount Sorak remained vigorous. As we reached higher up the mountains' flank I looked down at the rocky landscape below with a thrill. The sheer vertical peaks and crevasses were thinly furred with conifers and fuzzy gray beech trees. The shapes of the rock formations were fantastic: some were egg-shaped, others were needlelike promontories where hawks circled among the calligraphic pines. The pale light was different up here; it looked *old*.

The sound of rushing water filled the hollow valleys. As I looked down at my feet, I noticed something exceptional: we were following the bed of a stream, and as we climbed higher, the sap-clear stream had gradually changed into an astonishing emerald color. There was doubtless a scientific, indeed, a simple mineral explanation for this

transformation but it was amazing, even so. We stopped sponta-
neously by a rock pool to appreciate the depth and quality of the water
as it flowed into various inlets and channels, both of us silenced by its
eerie, enchanting beauty. Uncle Hong-do stepped down to another
pool and washed his hands and face in the water, then, closing his eyes,
he leaned back against a white rock to catch the sun on his dripping
face. I hopped from stone to stone, exploring the stream, and took
some photographs of it, never having seen water remotely this color,
so opulently jewel-like, and clear. I took off my shoes to dry and
warmed my clammy feet on a sun-baked rock, then lay on my side,
trailing a finger in the cold green pool.

Surveying the sun-dappled gorge from this incredible height, I
had a strange, disembodied feeling. I felt that I was in a separate universe, a parallel world, timeless and ancient, yet utterly virgin. In this
deserted, empty forest lay a grand, elegiac beauty, a primeval innocence. I felt profoundly happy on my rock, in this magical place—as
if idling on the edge of myth.

Just then my uncle called to me, suggesting that we hurry on along
the trail. It was getting late. I waved down at him, and laced up my torture shoes again with reluctance. I twisted slowly around the spot
where I stood, memorizing every detail so as not to forget it. The camera would be unable to capture the sweet balsam fairy smell, watery
music, and stippled emerald coolness of the gorge. As I lingered, the
moment was already becoming a memory, fading in my eyes even as
it existed in the present. With a bittersweet pang, I walked away from
the lulling place toward my waiting uncle, sensing that I would never
come here again.

I shivered a little. The sun's strength was waning.

"Come on. We'll never make it at this rate. I hope there's a shelter somewhere if we get stuck," said Hong-do, walking on ahead. It
was growing colder, without question. My blistered heels felt raw and
hot. I yelled to my uncle to stop for a second so that I could put on my

socks. This I did hurriedly, and it helped cushion my wounds a little, even if it cramped the toes. I scrambled to catch up with Hong-do, who had increased his pace.

Upward we hiked, for what seemed a punishingly long time. The cold wind buffeted our heads and withered our fingers. My legs were aching, and the terrain became more slippery still. We had been hiking now for a further four hours, and the sun was starting to set. I was numb from exertion, and could not think clearly. It would be impossible to give up now, so I trusted my uncle to see us through somehow. We would *have* to arrive soon, I thought; although we had not yet cleared the tree line, I was optimistic that we would make it to the temple by sunset. I could already picture the pagoda silhouetted against a fiery red sky, surrounded by a dense mass of bare black branches. The image spurred me on.

I was terribly thirsty and ate some snow, disoriented. The camera felt like a millstone around my neck. Several hundred yards away, a fork appeared in the trail by a large boulder, bearing a small sign saying something illegible. Hong-do, standing next to it, waved me closer.

"There's a base hut a mile on," he said, looking worn out. We trudged on, the news producing a slight increase of energy from some unknown reservoir within. My nose and ears grew numb. Low beams of weak sunlight angled through the sparse pines, and patches of snow began to glow blue rather than white in the oncoming dusk. The howling wind sounded lonelier up here.

At last, in the distance, a small brown wooden gatehouse appeared, an unlit, battered kerosene lamp hanging on the door. A painted yellow barrier, like a railroad-crossing lever, was closed across the trail of the path. My spirits surged at the sight of the gatehouse. We were very close now to Bong jong-am. I was sure of that.

As we approached the building, the silhouette of a head could be seen in the hut's window. Hong-do sighed loudly, patently relieved. I followed my uncle up to the window to converse with the gatekeeper. The man in the hut was in his thirties, and wore orange Mount Sorak National Park coveralls. He had very red cheeks and raggedly cut hair. He smiled in a desultory way, as if seeing people at dusk at an altitude of several thousand feet were nothing special. My uncle interrogated him with some urgency. The guard poked his newspaper and shrugged. Hong-do said something else. The man laughed and pulled out a detailed map, pointing at something with a big chapped red index finger. My uncle muttered something and craned his neck to see the spot where he was indicating. Hong-do went very quiet, and then made a joke, causing them both to laugh politely. Slightly more inclined now to help, the gatekeeper came out of his hut, took my uncle aside, pointing up the path, and gesticulated down it again, unleashing a volatile barrage of Hangul. I was brimming with curiosity and excited frustration. At this point my uncle indicated toward me, saying—and this I understood—that I had come all the way from America. The guard said something guttural, and turned back to his newspaper as if he had already wasted too much time explaining things to us. My uncle held up his hand in farewell, and turned his back on the gatekeeper. He walked toward me with a bowed head, and together we headed over to a sign bearing a red arrow.

"What?" I said.

"You're not going to believe this."

"*What!*"

"The trail to Bong jong-am is officially closed until the thirty-first of May. We can't go up."

"You are joking."

"I'm not joking."

"You're joking."

"I wish I were," he said.

A curdling, ominous silence fell between us.

"Did you tell him that we've come all the way specially? That it's the family temple?"

"Yes, I tried telling him that. But it's against the rules of the national park. It's not up to him, anyway. . . . But I'm afraid it's even worse than that."

"What?"

"We're nowhere near the place. It's an eight-hour hike from here, and he said we would need crampons, pitons, ropes, and down-filled clothes to make the journey. We would die of exposure if we tried to climb it as we are."

"You're kidding."

"No," he said quietly.

I was too tired to cry, but there was a painful, dry lump in my throat, and my heart was pounding in distress.

"God. What do we do now? We've come all this way. We can't just turn around, we *can't* . . ."

"We'll have to," he sighed. "And we'll have to hurry as well. The guard told me that there's a shortcut down the mountain. Apparently we came up by a ridiculously long, indirect route. If we get going, he said we wouldn't get back too long after dark. Luckily there are reflectors marking the path," Hong-do said, throwing away his hiking stick in disgust. "This is my fault. I should have found out all this before we set out. Made a couple of phone calls. This is really stupid. But I was sure it would be no big deal. What can I say . . . I'm sorry."

Nothing could be rectified. The disappointment was so stupefying that it did not really sink in. "Never mind," I said, tears welling up, "it doesn't matter." He gave a wan smile, and smacked my shoulder. With leaden feet, we started out back down the mountain under a darkening sky.

The trip back down Mount Sorak passed in a surreal, blue blur of defeat and trancelike exhaustion. My mind was empty as I stumbled and slipped on the uneven ground, falling down a few times in my haste, aching with cold and shock. I was aware only of the sound of Hong-do's feet beating out a slow, unsteady marching rhythm in the darkness ahead of me, and the hypnotic sight of red reflectors, zigzagging past my eyes. I cursed the mocking presence of the camera that weighed increasingly heavily on its strap around my neck. My Achilles tendons were lacerated where the hard edge of my shoes had chafed, but I felt no concern at the pain. The morning's jaunty purchase of the killer shoes seemed to have been centuries ago.

Eventually we arrived back at the car, quite dully amazed that it was still there, and that we had actually reached it. An orange streetlamp lit the deserted road ahead. All the park buildings were dark, and the parking lot was empty. My uncle opened the door wearily and slumped over the wheel, resting his head there. I slung my camera on the backseat and collapsed into the passenger's seat. No words were exchanged. Hong-do started the engine and got the heater going, and we sat there, stunned, side by side in the dark, staring at the fogged windshield.

Uncle Hong-do found a packet of broken biscuits in his overnight bag which we fell upon, and shared a revolting half-consumed bottle of stale *cho jung*, cider, which I found lying beneath the driver's seat. Hong-do announced quietly that he wanted to drive straight back to Seoul that night rather than stop at a hotel. It was only eight-thirty, and with no traffic we could be back in the city by bedtime. I aquiesced, not wanting to be reminded of our smarting failure in the morning in a sterile hotel dining room surrounded by efficient, well-equipped hikers. I thought he might be too exhausted to drive, but he assured me that he was OK, and accelerated decisively out of the gates of the national park toward the distant highway.

It was completely dark. There were no lights along the highway.

The engine roared dully, tires hissed on the tarmac. Houses, farms, factories, shops, hotels, restaurants, barbershops, cinemas, schools, hospitals, churches, military bases, cemeteries, docks, airports, and barbed wire were now invisible, the character and nationality of the landscape obscured. I could have been anywhere, on any highway, on any night, in any season of the year. The twin beams of the headlights illuminated a narrow aperture in the darkness directly ahead, revealing only a monotony of bleached verge grasses and the snaking stripe of the painted road lines winding insistently around curves, stretching on into motoring infinity. Occasionally an oasis of light loomed up in the form of a village or gas station, and vanished back into blackness.

I wondered what my uncle might have been thinking of as he stared through the windshield in exhaustion. Was he cross about our ill-fated mission, and the time he had lost away from the office? Was he saddened by the experience? Maybe he had already put it out of his mind. In my weakened state, I didn't quite know how to reach him with words. What had happened—or had failed to happen—was obviously regrettable. It was comical in a way. It might even have been quite hilarious had it happened to somebody else.

Sitting next to my uncle, I felt suddenly far away from him. He was sewn tightly into this landscape with many invisible threads, too closely stitched in to see it the way I did, upside down and sideways, like an astronaut in zero gravity. Nothing could cut him loose from it the way I was now, floating and twisting in the slipstream of this aborted mission. Cool, minute particles of detachment started gathering around me as I sat in the car. I felt empty, as if a part of me had already left, and had boarded the airplane back West. Perhaps it was too late to graft onto Korea. I was too formed, unable and unwilling to disintegrate, as one would need to, in order to begin a new life on the reverse side of the world I knew. I feared I might always be looking through a pane of glass, at a slight remove from whatever joys and tests lay in store. Or perhaps that was an excuse. A country of maddening extremes, Korea would not permit such detachment: fiery and cold, insular and gregarious, ancient and modern, urban and rural, frenetic and serene, ugly and beautiful, refined and earthy, spicy and bland, drunken and monastic, sentimental and harsh: its contradictions hit you in the solar plexus, permitting little reflection. Although I'd experienced tantalizing moments of familiarity, it was also the most alien place I had ever known.

The highway soon grew flatter and wider, and with it, my thoughts seemed to untwist. Earlier, on the mountain, the sensation of getting close to the secret temple had been a delusion. I had been fully, hungrily alive to the landscape around me, but the summit had never been attainable. My vision had been a mirage. What I had come to find was not one thousand chestnut trees. It seemed to have been something else, something intangible, that I had not sought.

Perhaps my only purpose had been to gather together the small, scattered fragments of my mother's blasted history, to witness them, broken as they were; to mourn them as they were, without attempting to make them whole again. That would have been far beyond my powers.

Along the overgrown and unrecognizable path to Mount Sorak an unexpected bond had been forged for the country I had once rejected. Unmeasured kindness had been shown me by unknown relations and strangers who owed me nothing. I had accomplished little; I'd visited my grandparents' graves, seen the sea at Nagsan cliff, lit a match in the dark, and had sat down by the side of a tour bus and wept for families like mine. It would have to be enough.

At the end of the path, it was not a temple that stood before me, it was my mother. My mother not as a careless young girl, but as she was now, with her difficult ways and her transcendent strength. Her slightly hard expression was chiseled by painful years, with deep recesses down which I could not penetrate.

Although I had not seen the thousand chestnut trees that day in May, I knew they were real and could not be destroyed. Years later, back in the West, I felt their leaves rushing through me, soothing me in times of distress, uplifting me in moments of peace. I knew then that they had always lived within me, but hadn't realized that they were there.

Uncle Hong-do sat beside me chewing gum noisily and humming at the wheel.

"We're nearly home," he said. His spirits had bounced back with typically Korean tenacity. I didn't know what had cheered him up. I still couldn't tell what he was thinking about. Remembering the night he'd left New York, with the cold threat of an indefinite parting and reproachful failure hanging in the air between us, it suddenly seemed a miracle that I should be here at all, and that we had even attempted what we had done, despite it having been a small fiasco. I glanced at his profile in the dark with affection, and looked back up at the road again.

The horizon before us brightened with a sulfurous urban glow. An airplane took off in the distance, its lights climbing upward. Although it had departed, those left behind could still feel its rumbling, disembodied vibrations. My uncle and I turned right at the next junction and joined a winking, swarming body of taillights and headlights that flowed into Seoul in an unintelligible language of motion.

ABOUT THE AUTHOR

Mira Stout was born in New York City. She attended Brown University, and has contributed to a number of publications, including *The New York Times Magazine*, *The Paris Review*, *Vanity Fair*, *The Spectator*, *The Times*, *The Independent*, *The Daily Telegraph*, *Vogue*, *GQ*, *Elle*, *Tatler*, and *The Financial Times*. She lives in London. *One Thousand Chestnut Trees* is her first book.

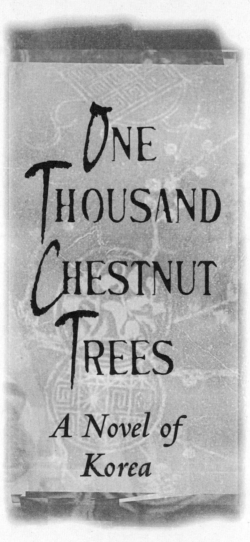

ONE THOUSAND CHESTNUT TREES

A Novel of Korea

by Mira Stout

Issues for Discussion

■ ■ ■

1. Uncle Hong-do's visit to Vermont has a lasting effect on Anna. Discuss the differences between Hong-do's personality soon after his arrival in America and years later when he is a businessman in Fort Lee. Did he seem more *American* as he embraced the American dream of success or did he seem simply more *capitalist*?

2. When Anna spends time with Hong-do in Korea, he is again a successful businessman. Are there differences between his personality as a businessman in Korea and as a businessman in America? If so, how does this relate to Anna? If we are all influenced by our cultural surroundings, as well as our cultural heritage, how might we use this knowledge to better our society?

3. Before Anna visits Korea, she feels little connection to her Korean heritage. In what way does this contribute to problems she has with her mother? Does her exploration of her ancestry help her to better understand her mother? Discuss what Anna's voyage reveals about her mother's character and how you think their relationship could change as a result.

4. Korea's history is a particularly violent one. Discuss the Confucian attitude of compassion toward Japanese aggressors. Given the repeated atrocities that Japan perpetrated against Korea over the centuries, what do you make of this pacifism? Do you find it frustrating? Or does the national refusal to violate deeply-held beliefs in the face of horrific suffering amount to a kind of victory over their aggressors?

5. Hong-do believes that America fought *against* Communism rather than *for* Korea during the war and that the continued American presence there keeps Korea divided and weak. What do you think? Hong-do is obviously a capitalist as well as a nationalist. If South Koreans are willing to risk having their country usurped by North Korean Communists, should American troops come home? Or is this attitude unfair given the fact that America and the United Nations had to "rescue" them before?

6. Despite Anna's disappointment at being unable to visit the family estate and the temple, she does experience moments of intense spiritual connection to Korea—a sense of mystical *déjà vu*. Have you ever visited the land of your ancestors and felt something similar?

7. Discuss the apparent differences between Korean and American culture. How do the two cultures perceive and value the concepts of family, duty, loyalty, and history?

8. Consider the plight of Aunt Pusan, who was all but ignored by her family during her depression. Contrast Pusan with other fictional and/or historical characters who have suffered from mental illness. How does her treatment compare with theirs? Do you think Stout uses Pusan to critique 1940s Korean culture?

9. In many ways, Anna's journey to Korea is also one of self-discovery. Learning about her mother's life helps her understand the difficulties they've had in communicating. Do you think that learning about her extended family's suffering and the history of Korea helps Anna to mature in other ways?

10. When visiting her grandmother's grave, Anna realizes that "maybe it was possible to face a blank canvas and put something sincere on it." Why do you think she finds the idea of sincerity jarring? How do you think her trip has helped her to understand the source of her artwork?